NO FURTHER

A GABRIEL WOLFE THRILLER

ANDY MASLEN

TYTON PRESS

For the real Sarah Hunt.

There the fire will consume you; the sword will cut you down — they will devour you like a swarm of locusts.
Book of Nahum, 3:15

A NEW JOB

How do you kill a man?

It's a simple enough question. And to a layperson – a school secretary, perhaps, or an accountant – it has a simple answer. Shoot him. Stab him. Push him off a building. Run him over with your lease-purchase Ford Focus that you optioned-up with the sports package including red racing stripes and leather upholstery. And, yes, these are all perfectly acceptable methods. But to a professional – a professional *killer*, that is – it merely leads to more questions.

Who is the man?

Where is the man?

How well protected is the man?

Do we mind leaving the man's body?

Do we mind if the man's friends or employers know who killed him?

Must we be silent when we kill the man or is a certain amount of noise permissible?

When these, and other, questions are answered to our satisfaction, then the process of choosing the method of killing can begin.

Gabriel Wolfe, professional assassin for Her Majesty's Government, was working his way through the questions. Sitting opposite him in the sparsely furnished office in MOD Rothford, a British Army base in Essex, was his boss at The Department, Don Webster. Gabriel had served under Don in the SAS when the older man had been known as Colonel Webster. Now he worked for a security agency, allied with, but not a part of, MI6, MI5, Military Intelligence and Special Branch. His brief as an operator for The Department was to eliminate those of Britain's enemies its sister agencies were unable, unwilling or unready to deal with. There might be questions of jurisdiction, international cooperation, secrecy, or simple logistics that created the operations The Department worked on. But whatever their genesis, he, and the other men and women who worked for Don, were kept busy.

"Who's the target?" he asked now, before taking a sip of the whisky Don had poured for him on his arrival. In his head he added the supplementary question, *Who am I supposed to be killing*? He chose to use that word, and not *eliminating*, *liquidating* or *neutralising* as some in the intelligence and security community, particularly the CIA, preferred to. If the order was legal, he'd follow it. That had been his creed in the Army, and it remained his creed now. If the order was to kill an enemy of the British state, fine. But let's call a spade a spade.

Don pushed a buff folder across the desk to Gabriel, who slid it closer, spun it round and opened it to find himself looking at a ten-by-eight glossy colour photo of a middle-aged man wearing steel-rimmed glasses that magnified closely-spaced dark eyes above a long, straight nose. He sported a neatly trimmed, greyish-white beard. He was frowning, and his lips were compressed into a thin line. He might have been a headmaster, worrying over his school's budget. Or a salesman, wondering if he'd make that month's target. Don spoke, clarifying the situation.

"Meet Abbas Darbandi. Mr Darbandi is a scientist. A nuclear scientist, to be exact. In fact, to be absolutely, one hundred percent, specific, Mr Darbandi is an Iranian nuclear scientist in charge of a project codenamed *Melkh*."

"Locust," Gabriel said. "What is it?"

Don explained. Project Locust was the design and manufacture of a tactical nuclear weapon, to be carried as a warhead on a medium-range ballistic missile.

"So if it's not a long-range missile, where's the target? I'm guessing Israel."

Don nodded. "That's what our friends in Vauxhall think. Obviously we want to prevent the Iranians developing that sort of strike capability, not least because we don't want a Middle East arms race developing. The Israelis know all about Darbandi's work, and so far they've been content to maintain a watching brief. But now they want action."

"Why haven't they just gone off and done it themselves? They're not exactly shy about that sort of thing."

"I've been in contact with my oppo in Jerusalem. Believe it or not, it's a manpower issue. They're overstretched and they've asked us for help."

"Where does Darbandi work?" Gabriel asked.

"Our Mr Darbandi works inside an Iranian nuclear research and development facility in Vareshabad. It's a small town – village, really – an hour's drive north of Tehran. It's been classified by the Americans as civilian, not military, but its sole purpose is developing a bomb. As to his personal security, how about seventy-five highly trained, heavily armed, battle-hardened and utterly ruthless members of Iran's Revolutionary Guard?"

The rest of Gabriel's questions Don answered with terse sentences carrying the maximum amount of information for the minimum amount of words.

No, we don't mind leaving the body. Yes, we do mind if Mr Darbandi's employers know who killed him. This is a highly secret, eyes-only classified mission from a deniable component of the British security apparatus. On balance, a silent approach is preferred.

Gabriel visualised a sturdy wooden bench laden with an assortment of weapons, both traditional and improvised. Our school secretary or accountant would in all likelihood recognise some of them. Either from TV or the movies, or their own homes.

A cricket bat.

A pair of pliers.

A hammer.

A dining fork.

A darning needle.

A corkscrew.

A meat skewer.

A cook's knife.

A bottle of bleach.

A lead-filled leather cosh.

A brass knuckleduster.

A piano-wire garotte.

A Böker tactical knife.

Other fighting knives, of the flick, double-edged and stiletto varieties.

A US Marine Corps tactical tomahawk.

A SIG Sauer P226 semi-automatic pistol.

A .44 Magnum Smith & Wesson Model 629 revolver.

A Mossberg 500 pump-action shotgun.

A Colt M16 assault rifle.

An Accuracy International AT-80 sniper rifle.

He rejected the firearms out of hand. Too noisy. Too hard to explain away if the shit hit the fan and he got caught. Shame.

The improvised weapons he also dismissed. Unnecessary.

That left the edged weapons.

Even in the age of drones, hyper-accurate sniper rifles and cyberwarfare, sometimes the only way to vanquish your enemy is up close and personal. When the ammunition runs out, you fix bayonets and get into it. If your enemy is closer than the length of a rifle barrel, you pull a knife.

"A blade," Gabriel said. "Silent, and we could put the blame on a local."

The older man nodded, letting his grey eyes close for a long moment. When he opened them again, he took a pull on his drink before speaking.

"Not much margin for error. You'd have to be standing next to him. Unless you threw it, of course."

"Yeah, well, I never ran away to the circus so I'd probably miss him. It was always Daisy or Smudge who won the competitions. Whenever they were short of beer money they'd always challenge me."

Daisy was Damon Cheaney, and Smudge was Mickey Smith, two members of Gabriel's patrol in the SAS. Both men were dead. Smudge at the hands of militia fighters in Mozambique, Daisy from an assassin's knife. More and more these days, Gabriel found that people close to him ended up dead. It made him wary of forming friendships, let alone intimate relationships.

"Fine. We'll hook you up with Sam Flack at some point. Remember her?"

Gabriel thought back to his first encounter with the MI6 quartermaster. That time, Don had tricked him into thinking Sam must be a man. He and Don had horsed around, making lame 007 jokes before she'd taken them to the firing range. There, they'd blasted away with an array of ammunition that culminated in depleted uranium 9mm rounds that punched through half-inch, military-grade, steel armour as if it were cardboard.

"How could I forget?" he said, examining an old scar on the back of his right hand. A piece of shrapnel? A knife? A garden tool? He worried that he couldn't remember.

Don smiled, grey eyes twinkling.

"Fool me once, eh? Now, let's talk about your team."

Gabriel looked up.

"What team? I thought this was a solo mission."

"Come on, Old Sport. This is Department business, not one of your little freelance jaunts. You'll need backup on the ground when you get to Tehran, not to mention an intelligence contact here in London. Or were you simply planning to waltz into Darbandi's place of work dressed in a DHL uniform asking for Iran's top nuclear scientist to sign for a parcel?"

Gabriel ran his fingers through his hair, which, he'd noticed with alarm, had become speckled with silver in the last few months.

"No, Boss. Sorry."

Don smiled.

"Don't be sorry. I think you'll find the company pleasant enough."

He reached over and pressed the intercom button on the hefty, slime-green phone on the corner of his desk. A tinny female voice buzzed from the speaker.

"Yes, Don?"

"Send her in, would you please, Pamela?"

Gabriel twisted round in his chair to see who this "her" was that Don had partnered with him. The door opened, and, as he took in the athletically-built young woman standing in the doorway, he smiled.

AIRSTRIKE

JULY 1999
PERSEPOLIS, IRAN

Squadron Leader Nick Avim had flown seventy-three combat missions as an Israeli Defence Forces pilot, some in hot wars, others as part of Israel's continuing peacetime battle against its enemies. This mission fell into the latter category. He checked his instruments. One hundred miles to the target. Well inside Iranian airspace now, he and the other members of his squadron were flying at 50,000 feet at Mach 2 – 1,535 mph. The official designation for the American-made F-16 he was flying was "Fighting Falcon." But the captain, like his fellow pilots in the IDF and the United States Air Force, called it the Viper.

The mission was simple, if risky. Mossad had received credible intelligence that a Hezbollah combat group were being trained by the Iranians in a deserted village outside the old city of Persepolis. Avim and his squadron were tasked with destroying the village and everyone in it. All were terrorists or terrorist trainers and, as such, legitimate targets.

The Vipers each carried a pair of AGM-65 Maverick air-to-ground missiles secured to hardpoints beneath their cropped-delta wings. Four Sidewinder air-to-air missiles apiece would cope with any threats from the Iranian air force. Keeping his radio communications to a minimum, Nick spoke for only the second time on the mission.

"Snakes – four minutes to run – confirm."

In turn the other five pilots acknowledged the order.

"Two."

"Three."

"Four."

"Five."

"Snake Six."

The six gleaming fighters dived from 50,000 to 5,000 feet, their wingtips leaving narrow threads of condensation behind them, the contrails white against the azure sky over Persepolis.

Avim could see the buildings of the village ahead in the distance, shimmering in the heat haze coming off the desert. He flicked the switch on the instrument panel to arm his Mavericks, confident that his squadron were doing the same.

With a minute to go – range 14 miles – he locked his targeting system onto two of the buildings and fired his Mavericks. He banked sharply to starboard and began a vertical climb, back to the jet's operational ceiling. Behind and below him, the rest of the squadron followed him in, arming, locking on and firing their own Mavericks. Between them, they launched 12 missiles – three-quarters of a ton of high-explosive anti-tank warheads – that streaked towards the terrorist training camp at over 700 mph. The missiles hit their targets 55 seconds later. Their shaped charges detonated with a series of shattering explosions, propelling jets of molten metal and superheated gases into the buildings and the cellars beneath them.

Avim and his squadron, three men and two women, turned for home.

Seventy-four, Nick thought.

* * *

Though credible, the Israelis' intelligence had been flawed. Badly. The people killed in the airstrike weren't terrorists or terrorist trainers. They were archaeologists. British, American, and Iranian. There was a single survivor. A thirteen-year-old boy. At the time of the attack, he had been riding a dirt bike a few miles to the west of the dig, looking for new birds to write down in his notebook. Ornithology was his passion. His brown-skinned hand gripped the pencil with a true convert's enthusiasm as he inscribed the genus, species and common name of each new bird he logged.

AN OLD FRIEND

MARCH 2018
MOD ROTHFORD, ESSEX, ENGLAND

The young woman who took the seat next to Gabriel was in her late twenties. Her dark, wavy, reddish-brown hair was loose around her jawline. Her large, grey-green eyes, rimmed with kohl, were twinkling with good humour as she turned to him.

"Hello again, Gabriel," she said with a smile. "How've you been keeping?"

"Hi, Eli. Not bad."

Don had travelled to Israel a few years earlier to headhunt Eli Schochat. Her background in the IDF and Mossad made her a perfect candidate. Since then she'd helped Gabriel defeat the vengeful daughter of a billionaire who'd been planning a military coup in Britain. Lizzie Maitland, long thought dead by the UK's security and intelligence services, had turned out to be alive and well, biding her time before striking back at Gabriel for ruining her chances of seizing power from her father after the coup. Since then

Eli and Gabriel had worked a couple of missions together, most recently in Cambodia, where Don had tasked them with taking out an ex-Khmer Rouge warlord.

"Nobody been trying to kill you since we last hung out together?"

"Actually, they have. Repeatedly. But," he spread his arms wide, "as you can see, they failed."

Her smile widened further.

"Good for you!"

Don interrupted their banter.

"When you two have finished chuckling over Gabriel's extraordinary ability to find trouble and then emerge unscathed, perhaps we could continue with this briefing?"

Eli straightened in her chair and pulled her hair behind her ears where she fastened it with an elastic band she took off her left wrist.

"Sorry, Boss. Won't happen again."

Don smiled.

"Yes, well, I'll believe that when I see it. Now, Eli, you've had some time to ponder this operation, what's your thinking on how best to get into Iran?"

Eli glanced sideways at Gabriel before returning her gaze to Don.

"There are a number of ways we could do it. I have contacts in Israeli security. The IDF as well as Mossad. We could fly into Tel Aviv or Jerusalem and then get a military transport to drop us near the Turkish-Iranian border and just walk in. Or we could go straight into Tehran on UK diplomatic passports. But I'm sure MOIS," – she pronounced it *moyce* – "monitor all our diplomats. That's the Ministry of Intelligence and Security, Gabriel." He nodded his thanks. "Two new faces would trigger increased scrutiny, which we could do without."

"And so?" Don prompted.

"And so I propose we hide in plain sight. It's the Tehran International Book Fair in May. We develop cover as publishers' sales representatives under the auspices of the British Council and infiltrate that way."

"MOIS people will be everywhere. It may be a book fair, but it's still in Iran. This won't be some lovey-dovey cultural exchange; they'll be scrutinising every stand, matching staff against visa lists, the works."

Eli smiled, and Gabriel realised how much he was enjoying being in her company again.

"I know, Boss. So we'll have to show our faces, talk literature with academics from the University of Tehran, give out business cards. We can manage that can't we?" she ended, turning in her chair to face Gabriel.

The movement stretched her grey T-shirt across her chest and Gabriel's gaze slid downwards for a second. He couldn't help himself. All of a sudden, he wanted Eli.

"Gabriel?" she asked again, her eyes appraising him, a shadow of an amused smile playing on her lips.

"Yes," he said, too loudly. "Yes," again, quieter this time, "I think we could manage to pretend to be cultural ambassadors for a day or two. How hard can it be?"

Don looked at his two operators, taking his time and breathing loudly through his nose. Finally, he spoke.

"You'll need support, both here and in Iran. Our friends in the Secret Intelligence Service have people in the embassy, but there's someone I'd like you both to meet in London. His name's Tim Frye. He's a good man and an expert on Iran and its nuclear ambitions. Here."

Don pushed a sheet of paper across the desk.

Gabriel turned it round to face him and began tapping the contact details into his phone. Eli did the same. When they'd finished, Don retrieved the sheet of paper and fed it into a crosscut shredder conveniently positioned beside his desk. He waited for it to finish and once the rough-edged whirr had stopped he spoke again.

"Eli's driving a pool car, but she can leave it here for now. No sense in your driving down to London in separate cars, is there?"

"No, Boss," Gabriel and Eli chorused, sounding like well-drilled soldiers, or perhaps just obedient children sitting in front of their stern, Victorian-style paterfamilias.

"You've some spare kit in the boot, Old Sport?"

"Weekend bag, Boss. Always got it with me. Better—"

"Safe than sorry, hmm, mm-hmm. Your favourite saying."

They said their goodbyes at the door to Don's office, the older man explaining he had "another bloody meeting to go to" before shaking their hands and returning to his desk. They made their way along the well-worn, blue-carpeted corridor and out onto the grassy area in front of the admin block that housed "Colonel" Webster and his ambiguous, "Admin Offices – Spec. Ops," as the metal sign screwed to the brickwork had it.

Gabriel knew there were still plenty of people in the UK who would be horrified to learn that their current government – and many preceding it – ran a covert assassination squad out of a boring-looking military base deep in the Essex countryside.

Plenty of politicians. Plenty of civil servants. Plenty of retired and not-so-retired generals who regarded anything short of outright warfighting to be not quite cricket. Yes, they could see the need for commandos, and they could just about tolerate Special Forces units.

But a squad of misfits deemed too unruly even for the SAS with its "rules are for other people" mentality? Special Branch rejects? Foreigners with useful weapons skills but lousy people skills? MI5 operators too ready with a trigger squeeze when a shutter press is all that's required? All trained, disciplined, briefed and if necessary psychiatrically "prepared" to kill without compunction, mercy or a second thought? No. This they could not swallow. Yet, somehow, this was how he was earning his living nowadays. Eli's voice punctured his inner dialogue.

"What the fuck's this?" she asked, jerking her chin at the grey Ford Mondeo he'd hired while he looked for a replacement for his beloved Maserati.

"It's a car. Why, don't they have them in Israel?"

"Cheeky fucker! You know what I mean. I thought you'd have

replaced the Maserati with something a bit better," she wrinkled her nose and pointed at the car as if it were a field latrine, "than this."

Gabriel shrugged. He unlocked the car and they climbed in, continuing the conversation as he trundled around the perimeter road towards the gates.

"I have been looking but I haven't found anything I like yet. At least this is anonymous." *Why do I feel the need to justify myself to you?*

Eli snorted.

"Anonymous? You can say that again. Why not go the whole hog and buy a grey chain-store suit while you're about it?"

Bested in the banter department, Gabriel kept his counsel as he rolled up to the gate. He buzzed down the window.

"Thanks for having us, Sergeant," he called, catching a waft of polleny spring air from the field across the road from the base.

The uniformed guard waved him on his way, and he eased the Ford over the one-way traffic treadles, listening to them clunk and clatter under his wheels. He turned left and, in an attempt to impress Eli, floored the throttle. The car did its best to respond, emitting a rough-edged roar as he hit the red line in the first three gears before easing off at a hundred, changing up into fifth and letting the car coast until it reached a more respectable eighty on the gently curving country road.

Without turning, Eli spoke.

"Was that for my benefit?"

He heard the gentle mockery in her voice. Liked her all the more for it.

"Did it work?"

"I suppose my pulse might have risen." A micro-pause. "A little."

"Then it was."

"So where are you living these days? I mean, now that your lovely little house in Salisbury got blown to bits?"

"I bought a new place. Plenty of room for guests."

He glanced sideways at Eli, who was staring to her left, apparently consumed by the English countryside rushing past.

"Oh, yes? Well I'm glad one of us has a nice place. I'm in a tiny rented flat in East London while they try to find me a decent place to live. I mean, have you *seen* house prices in London? Back home you could buy a *street* for what they want for a two-bedroomed flat."

"Yeah, it has got a bit crazy."

"Not for you, though, Mr Millionaire. With all your money, you must be—" Gabriel heard Eli catch her breath. "Oh, God, I'm so sorry," she said, laying a hand on his thigh for a second. "I know you only got it because she killed Master Zhao. I can't believe how tactless I am."

"It's fine," he said with a shrug.

It isn't.

"I'm dealing with it. Keeping busy helps."

It doesn't.

"He's still with me in here," he said, placing a hand over his heart.

I just wish he was still with me out here.

Gabriel pictured the face of the man who had raised him: Zhao Xi. Aged just five, Gabriel's younger brother Michael had drowned in Hong Kong's Victoria Harbour in an accident Gabriel still believed was his responsibility, if not his fault. Driven temporarily mad with grief, the nine-year-old Gabriel had woken from a two-week semi-trance with no memory of his brother. His parents had been unable to cope with his behaviour after that and had entrusted their remaining son to their friend.

Zhao Xi, or Master Zhao, as Gabriel had always called him, calmed the "Wolfe cub" down. He educated him in traditional academic subjects, including the languages for which the boy had a preternatural affinity. And he trained him in martial arts, both Chinese and Japanese. *Oh God, how I wish I'd arrived early enough to save you, Master. Five minutes would have been enough. I'd have recognised Beck and we could have fought her together. Now you're gone. And it's all because of me. Wherever I go, wherever I turn, Death follows me like a—*

"Gabriel, look out!"

CONCENTRATE ON THE ROAD AHEAD

Eli's yell snapped Gabriel back into the present moment. His speed had crept up to a hundred and twenty and the windscreen was filling rapidly with the squat rear-end of a little, red car whose name – Suzuki Wagon-R – and hatted driver he still had time to take in as he swerved round the cuboid vehicle on the wrong side of the road.

The driver of an oncoming car flashed his headlights in a frantic semaphore of dismay. Horn blaring – *interesting, his being able to hit the button and flash his lights, good driving skills* – the blue VW Golf veered over to the verge as far as the driver could manage, and Gabriel squeezed through the gap, elbows locked on the wheel, eyes wide open.

He pulled back over into the left-hand carriageway, heart racing, knees aching from the newly released adrenaline, watching the comically upright red car disappear in his rearview mirror.

Eli's mordant remark punctured the silence.

"I'd say our closing speed was just short of 300 kilometres per hour. Don would have been looking for a new team."

Gabriel ran a hand through his hair, scragging at his scalp.

"Sorry," he said, finally. "That's been happening a lot lately."

"What's been happening?"

"I just zone out. When I'm driving, mostly. Long motorway journeys are the worst. I get in at home and I get out at Rothford, or wherever, but I have no recollection of anything that happened on the way."

"Fuck me, Gabriel! I wish you'd told me that before I accepted the offer of a lift."

"I know. I'm sorry. Really."

Eli laughed

"Oh, please! Enough with the naughty puppy act. So you shat on the carpet? Big deal! You cleaned up after yourself, didn't you?"

Taken aback, once again, by Eli's forthright humour and quirky way with the English language, Gabriel smiled.

"So you don't want to take the wheel, then?"

"Nope. But if you're going to drive like that, at least get yourself some better wheels. Something that won't roll if you throw it round a bend at a hundred and fifty."

The rest of the journey to London passed without incident. Gabriel had driven as carefully and law abidingly as possible, earning the commendation "like a rabbi" from Eli. They arrived in Eli's road in Shoreditch at 5.30 p.m., having agreed that Gabriel would stay with Eli so they could travel to the meeting with Frye together. Both sides of the narrow-terraced street were jammed with parked cars, and Eli swore as Gabriel made a slow pass from one end of the street to the other.

"Shit! Fucking two-car families. Look at them all. Fucking Mercedes, Audis, BMWs and Porsches. You know, this used to be housing for ordinary, working-class people. Now look at it! Wall-to-wall German engineering and every one driven by some hipster idiot dressed like a lumberjack."

Gabriel laughed.

"Not a fan, then?"

"Of the Germans?"

"Of social mobility."

"Is that what you call it?" she said, as Gabriel turned left at the T-junction and started searching for a parking space a little further afield.

"Isn't it a good thing? People being able to afford better things?"

She folded her arms across her chest.

"Yes, if I can park outside my own house – sorry, flat. No, if I end up leaving my own car two fucking streets away."

Unable to keep the smile off his face, Gabriel couldn't resist teasing his suddenly irascible partner just a little more.

"And tell me, given her obvious distaste for my current set of wheels, what particular form of vehicle is the anti-social-mobility Miss Schochat driving these days?"

"A Mini," she said, flatly.

"A Mini?" Gabriel asked, injecting as much bogus surprise and astonishment into his voice as he could manage. "Now there's a car that simply screams working class. Does it have quotes from Lenin stencilled on the side? And they're owned by BMW. You do know that, right?"

"Oh, ha-ha, very funny. It's just, they're not the friendliest people round here, OK?"

"What do you mean?" Gabriel asked, frowning, as he scanned the sides of the street for a space into which to squeeze the car.

"It's nothing."

"No, go on. What did you mean?"

Eli sighed.

"I was invited round to a neighbourhood drinks party, and I mentioned that I was Israeli and that I'd served my country in the IDF. This fucking, bearded," she huffed out a breath of frustration, "*guy*, he just started in on me about Israel being an apartheid state."

"Okay. And how did that go down?"

"Oh, you know, fine. Although he did trip and fall into their goldfish pond later on that evening. I think he was drunk."

Gabriel smiled. He was thinking back to their trip to Kazakhstan to investigate a far-right politician who had a day job as managing director of an ammunition company. Timur Kamenko had ended up dead at Eli's hands, so an embarrassing soaking in a Shoreditch goldfish pond counted as getting off lightly for crossing the volatile Israeli.

With the car finally wedged in between an ageing Mercedes saloon and a Porsche 911, both the same approximate shade of metallic grey as Gabriel's Ford, Eli led Gabriel to her flat on the first and second floors of a Victorian terrace house not unlike the one owned by Melody Smith, Smudge's widow. Red bricks, with white-painted window ledges, sash window frames and eaves. A red-and-grey quarry-tiled path up to the canary-yellow front door. Terra-cotta window boxes filled with scarlet geraniums on all three ledges of the bay window.

Eli showed him around, waving her hand desultorily into each room like the world's worst estate agent, before pausing at a bedroom painted a vivid shade of pink Gabriel supposed would be called "cerise."

"That's my bedroom," she said, unnecessarily. "And before you ask, no I didn't choose the colour. The spare's at the end of the hall. You want a shower?"

For a second, Gabriel thought she meant together and wasn't sure how to respond, but then reality asserted itself as Eli continued speaking.

"There're fresh towels in the airing cupboard and you can use my shampoo or whatever."

Gabriel slid the slender chromed bolt home on the inside of the bathroom door and undressed. Then, leaning on the edges of the sink, he addressed himself *sotto voce* in the mirror, not wanting his murmured words to reach Eli.

"Are you picking up the signals, hmm? She did make a pass at you last time, remember? Yeah, I remember. But I pushed her away. Women don't like that kind of thing."

Then, faint as a breeze whispering through distant bamboo, he heard master Zhao's voice.

Wolfe Cub. Do not be too sure what women want. Listen to her. Not just what she says but the way she says it. How she moves. There are ways of communicating that do not require words; you learned that lesson well.

He frowned at himself, noticing the way the old silver scar on his cheekbone puckered slightly.

"Give me a good old-fashioned enemy combatant over a woman any day, Master," he said, and turned on the shower.

While Eli was taking her turn in the bathroom – "Make yourself at home," she ordered him before closing the door, though not, he noticed, sliding the bolt across as he had done – Gabriel made himself a gin and tonic, added two lime segments, and took it through to the sitting room. The bay window looked down onto parked cars. He grinned: Eli was right. The residents of Haberdasher Street, Shoreditch, were clearly doing well for themselves. Eli's Mini – painted a vivid metallic blue, its roof emblazoned with a Union flag – was bracketed by a pair of black Audis. The rest of the parking spaces were occupied by similarly luxurious cars, mostly German as she'd said, but dotted here and there with Swedes, Italians and, a brash interloper from across the pond, a fire engine–red Ford Mustang.

He'd read in an airline magazine about the new wave of entrepreneurial types turning this part of London into a version of Silicon Valley, albeit one with greyer light and more traffic jams. "Startups," that was the fashionable career choice nowadays. He'd lost interest halfway through the piece, when the journalist had admiringly referred to some 25-year-old CEO as an "app rockstar."

"Christ!" he said out loud, taking a pull on his drink. "You're getting old. You sound more and more like the old man."

Eli appeared in the doorway, towelling her hair. She had a second towel wrapped around her body, which, owing to luck or judgment, barely reached her thighs.

"Talking to yourself, Wolfe? You know, that's the first sign of madness."

"Yeah, and when they answer back, that's the second."

She came to sit next to him on the sofa. She smelled of lemon shampoo. A twist of her auburn hair had escaped from the towel at the nape of her neck. He was seized with a sudden urge to kiss her there, right on the knobbles of her spine. He rested a palm on the warm skin between her shoulder blades.

"Mm, that feels nice," she said. "Want to give me a back rub?"

She slid over his left leg and positioned herself between his knees. As Gabriel began massaging the muscles of her neck and shoulders, she arched her back and leant back against him.

"Mmm, that's perfect. Don't stop."

Under his probing fingers, Gabriel felt hard knots in her trapezius muscles. He dug in a little deeper, eliciting a groan of pain mixed with pleasure.

Eli dropped her head forward. Her hair towel unwrapped itself and tumbled to the floor between her feet. Gabriel looked at the other towel encircling her body, then he reached around to the front and tugged at the loose knot she'd tied between her breasts.

"Excuse me, Mr Wolfe!" Eli said, in an affronted tone that froze Gabriel's hand where it was. "What exactly do you think you're doing?"

Feeling a blush heating his cheeks, he withdrew his hand.

"I'm sorry. I just thought, you know, giving a girl – a pretty girl – a backrub, well, I thought maybe ...?"

Aware he was sounding lamer with every word, he dried up. Then Eli laughed. A loud, salty sound. She twisted round to face him, loosening the towel with the movement of her body so that it fell open.

"No. I'm the one who's sorry," she said, smiling. "I've been making a play for you since the day I met you and now you respond and I play the cock-teaser. She stood, so that the towel puddled at her feet, and held out her hand. "Come on. Take me to bed."

Gabriel stood, taking in her muscular figure, dark triangle of pubic hair and soft, dark-nippled breasts. He rested his free hand on her shoulder and looked deep into her eyes.

"You, Miss Eli Schochat, are trouble!"

"You have no idea," she replied.

In her pink-painted bedroom, Eli pushed Gabriel hard, so that he fell backwards onto the brass bed. With expert hands, she undressed him, dropping each garment to one side as she removed it. She straddled him, and he felt the heat of her as she sank down onto him. She stared at him, and he could see flecks of green glinting in the brown of her almond-shaped eyes. He reached for her arms but she took his wrists, firmly, and pushed them up and behind his head.

"Now you're mine, Wolfe," she said in a voice thickened with desire.

Imperceptibly, she began moving over him, forwards then back, rocking her pelvis a little more with each traverse. He tilted his own hips, falling into her rhythm. Her hair swung forwards and brushed his cheeks. The lemon scent he'd come to associate with Eli was mixed with a warmer, sensual smell that he realised was, simply, Eli herself.

Her movements were more urgent now and her lips had parted slightly.

"Now," she murmured.

Eli came first, arching her back and finally releasing Gabriel's wrists. He grabbed her hips and pulled her back and forth until he, too, reached his climax. She fell forwards, breasts squashed against his heaving chest, head pressed into the crook of his neck.

"Mmm," she said, into his left ear. "I've been waiting a long time for that."

"Was it worth the wait?" Gabriel asked, stroking her back.

"Every second."

She slid sideways and snuggled inside his arm, resting her head on the pillow beside his.

Gabriel looked at the clock on the bedside table. *Four-thirty in the morning? How the hell did that happen? We've been asleep for nearly twelve hours.*

He twisted his head to the right to look at his sleeping partner. Her red hair, free of its plait, was arrayed across his chest like exotic seaweed. She lifted her head and looked at him, smiling that gap-toothed smile of hers.

"Britta?"

"Who did you think? That Israeli slut you've been lusting after?"

Gabriel felt his heart bumping painfully in his chest and anger banking up in his brain.

"Don't call her that!"

"Why? She stole you from me."

"You left *me*, remember? You dumped me in Chiswick House."

Britta raised herself on her elbow and jabbed a finger into Gabriel's face.

"Your memory's going, Gabriel. You dumped me. Just like you dumped Michael in the harbour. If you're this confused, why don't you go and see that shrink of yours. *Hej?*"

Gabriel couldn't hold back any longer. He pushed Britta away from him. Hard. Started shouting. Felt her retaliatory blows raining down on his head and shoulders.

"Leave Michael out of it!"

"Hej? Hej?"

"Hey! Stop it!"

Gabriel jerked awake.

Eli had clamped her hand round his right forearm. He noticed his fingers were clenched into a fist.

"What happened?" he asked, wiping the sweat from his forehead with his free hand.

"You were hitting me in your sleep," Eli said, her forehead creased with concern. "And you were shouting. 'You left me,' you said."

She let go of his arm and gathered him into her own embrace. He let her pull him down and felt himself relaxing as she stroked the top of his head."

"I was dreaming about Britta," he said, after a pause.

"Well, duh! I figured that out for myself, thanks. How long since you two broke up?"

"About a year and a half. I'm sorry for hitting you."

Eli furrowed her brow.

"Yeah, well it wasn't quite the post-coital cuddle I was expecting. Are you sure you're over her? I don't mind talking about her, by the way, if you're wondering."

"I am. Over Britta, I mean. The way she put it, I could see it wasn't going to work. It was just a bad dream, that's all."

He looked at the bedside clock. Now it was giving a more likely readout: 7.00 p.m. They'd been asleep for a little under thirty minutes.

"Good," Eli said with a grin. "Now, let's do it again and then I'll take you out for something to eat. There's a great little Vietnamese place round the corner."

* * *

Over translucent *gỏi cuốn* – spring rolls stuffed with shredded cabbage, coriander and crab – and *nộm hoa chuối* – a noodle dish of lime, chilli and shredded vegetables – Gabriel and Eli got to know each other a little better. The bottle of chilled white burgundy helped.

"What about your parents?" Gabriel asked her after swallowing the second half of one of the fragrant seafood-and-greens *gỏi cuốn*. "Where are they? Israel?"

Eli nodded, speaking through a mouthful of noodles.

"Uh-huh. They live in Tel Aviv. Dad's a university professor and mum's an MP."

"Military Police or Member of Parliament?"

Eli apparently took the question at face value.

"She's a member of the Knesset. Trying to keep the hawks from declaring war on the Palestinians."

"What does she think of what you do? Or did, I mean. Working for Mossad?"

"She's a realist. She wants peace, like a lot of Israelis. But she knows we have to defend ourselves. If it's a case of stick and carrot,

I'm the stick, she's the carrot. How about you? Your parents still around?"

Gabriel sighed, not wanting to have to explain that he'd lost his father and mother on the same ill-fated day. Drained his glass and refilled it.

"They're both dead."

"I'm sorry. So how did they die?"

Gabriel scratched at his scalp then rubbed the back of his neck. *I'd rather have avoided this but it looks like I'll have to explain anyway.*

"They were on Dad's boat. He named it Lin, after my mum. He had a heart attack. Mum was asleep below. When she found his body, she drowned herself." *She was dead drunk, but you don't need to know that. Not now.*

"Shit! I'm sorry. You don't mind me asking?"

Gabriel smiled a rueful smile.

"It's a bit late if I did, isn't it?"

After this tense exchange, they lapsed into an uneasy silence, broken when the waitress stopped at their table to ask if they were enjoying their food.

"It's lovely, thanks," Eli said, with a wide smile. "Could we have another bottle of wine, please?"

BRIEFING

VAUXHALL, LONDON

Eli stood, arms wide, legs apart, smiling across at Gabriel in the bare security room. They had arrived at the Vauxhall headquarters of Britain's Secret Intelligence Service – more commonly known as MI6 – at 8.30 a.m., thirty minutes earlier. Squatting in front of Eli and running her palms up and down her legs was a slender black woman. Her plaited and beaded hair was tied back in a clicking hank to reveal a long, elegant neck. She stood, and moved on to Eli's torso: front, back, sides. Not rough, but not the gentle back-of-the-hands frisking airline passengers were increasingly getting used to. Gabriel watched the way the two women made and then broke eye contact as the security officer ran her hands over Eli's breasts. He caught Eli's eye. She seemed to be in pain. Her brow was furrowed and her lips were clamped into a thin pale line. His own search was no less thorough, and he winced as the burly officer in front of him sawed a blade-like hand up into the creases of his groin.

Nodding to each other once the body search was completed, the two security officers handed over visitor passes.

"Welcome to SIS, sir, madam," the female officer said with a smile that revealed a model's even, white teeth. "The lifts are through the door and on your left at the end of the corridor."

As they walked to the lifts Eli burst out laughing.

"What is it?" Gabriel asked, smiling in return.

"Oh, my God! I'm so ticklish! When she touched my tits I thought I'd wet myself!"

Gabriel laughed.

"Hardly the behaviour we expect in the Secret Intelligence Service," he said, affecting an upper-class accent that produced another howl from Eli.

"I know," she said, catching her breath. "They're so stiff here, don't you think?"

"It's stuffed with public schoolboys, that's why. And a few public schoolgirls, too, before you kick me."

"Yeah? I'm glad to see the Old Boy Network is still working well. In Israel, we recruit solely on talent and aptitude. You could be the prime minister's daughter and it wouldn't make any difference. If you can't shoot the balls off a mosquito at fifty metres, forget it!"

"So I'm guessing a lowly MP's daughter would have to do it at a hundred?"

Eli laughed, a warm, raspy sound that thrilled Gabriel.

Gabriel swiped his ID then tapped the touch screen to select the third floor.

The lift doors opened, and standing waiting for them was a slim, besuited man carrying a leather file case. Tim Frye, the Iran expert. He had to be late thirties, if Don's description of his experience was accurate. Yet he seemed younger. *Choir boy*, Gabriel thought. Frye had straight, dirty-blond hair going grey, divided with military precision by a parting that showed the white scalp beneath. His slate-blue eyes, open, trusting, peered out from beneath a high, almost domed forehead. Trained to notice such things, Gabriel picked up on a jagged, crescent-shaped scar on the back of his left hand.

Frye was all smiles as he shook hands, first with Eli, then Gabriel.

"Eli, Gabriel, welcome to the Iran desk. Well, its current occupant, at any rate."

"Thank you, Timothy," Eli said, returning his smile with interest. "Lead the way, please."

"Of course, and please call me Tim."

"OK, Tim," she said as he turned to walk down the corridor. Then she turned and winked at Gabriel. Mouthed, "Sweet!"

The Iran desk turned out to be a department of ten or so people, mostly men, though a few women were bending over screens or listening intently through headphones to audio feeds. One of the women wore a hijab in a striking, peacock-blue material that reminded Gabriel of his psychiatrist, Fariyah Crace. He'd grown to like her intensely during their infrequent sessions. He resolved to book himself an hour of her time before this latest mission got airborne.

"I've reserved a conference room," Tim said, interrupting Gabriel's train of thought. "Though we call it the goldfish bowl. You'll see why," he added with another self-deprecating smile.

As they walked through the Iran desk, a couple of heads lifted from their tasks to observe the newcomers. A hawk-nosed man with a beard and moustache of a deep black stared hard at Gabriel then returned to his keyboard.

The little room Tim led them to was a simple glass cube carved out from a corner of the open-plan space. A circular table and four chairs took up virtually all the space. One of the chairs was already taken. Its occupant stood as the other three entered the conference room. To Gabriel's practised eye, he appeared to be six two or three, and in his midthirties. Muscular beneath his immaculately tailored navy-blue suit and with a sharp-eyed gaze that suggested his default mode for looking at people was as opponents, or possibly enemies. At some point, his nose had been broken, though the surgeon had done a decent repair job, leaving only the faintest of scars and a bump that might pass for an accident of birth rather than a fight going sideways. Not a desk jockey, in other words.

"Hugh Bennett," he said by way of introduction. "I'm your liaison between the Service and our chap in the embassy in Tehran."

Gabriel and Eli had to ease past Tim to take a chair each before Tim could close the door and sit down.

He placed the leather file folder in front of him and interlaced his fingers on top of its richly grained surface. He looked first at Gabriel and then at Eli.

"How much do you know about Iran and its nuclear ambitions?"

Gabriel turned to Eli.

"She's the knowledgeable one. I just boot the door in and kill everyone inside."

Tim's eyes widened a fraction and a frown crinkled that oddly high forehead. The corners of Bennett's mouth lifted.

"He's joking," Eli said. "But it's true. Before I joined The Department, I worked for Mossad. We kept the Iranians under the highest levels of scrutiny. It is our government's stated aim to prevent Iran gaining a nuclear weapon. You know why, of course, Tim?"

Tim nodded his assent. Everyone in the global intelligence community, whichever side they worked for, knew that Iran was hellbent on Israel's destruction. Eli continued.

"We know they've been trying for years to acquire or develop a medium-range ballistic missile capable of carrying a nuclear payload. But as far as we're aware, they still haven't managed to build a functioning warhead. Five years ago, the Israeli Air Force conducted a number of strikes at their civilian installations in Bushehr and Arak."

"Not Vareshabad?"

She shook her head.

"At the time our intel said Vareshabad was a dummy. Mainly used for storing chemical weapons."

"Hmm." Tim scratched his head with the sharp end of a pencil someone had left lying on the otherwise pristine table. "I don't want to call Mossad or the IDF's intelligence into question, but as you now know, Vareshabad is very much involved. The hottest of all hot spots, you could say."

"Tell us about Darbandi," Gabriel said.

Tim nodded again and repeated the attack on his scalp with the pencil point. He did it so fiercely, Gabriel wondered that he didn't draw blood. The silvery skin of the scar on the back of his hand stretched and flexed as he worked at whatever was troubling him. Bennett, he noticed, kept his eyes lowered, and his mouth shut.

"Abbas Darbandi," Tim declaimed, in the manner of a university professor beginning a lecture. "Born 1966, Tehran. Studied engineering and physics at the Iran University of Science and Technology in Tehran, where he was awarded their equivalent of a starred double first. A brainy man, in other words. Was awarded a doctorate in nuclear physics from the National Research Nuclear University in Moscow, and also did three years' work in China at the Institute of Nuclear and New Energy Technology in Beijing. Returned to Tehran 1998. And here's why you two are here. He is within two or at most three months of completing a functioning nuclear warhead. Tactical, to be sure, and as dirty as all get out, but with a yield sufficient to flatten a medium-sized city. Like Jerusalem," he added, unnecessarily, in Gabriel's opinion.

"Would they do that?" Gabriel asked. "With Jerusalem being a holy city to Muslims as well as Jews and Christians."

"Opinions on the desk are, shall we say, divided. There are some of us who believe that no, the Iranians would not attack Jerusalem, for just the reason you advanced. It is home to about 280,000 Sunni Muslims and sacred to them, just as it is to Christians and Jews. That instead they would go for Tel Aviv, or Haifa. Weaken the Israeli state to the point that they could launch a conventional war to take the country."

"And the other opinion?" Eli prompted, frowning.

Gabriel knew how much it was costing her emotionally to maintain a cool, professional front, when the innocent-looking intelligence analyst in front of her was casually describing alternative scenarios for destroying her homeland as if they were chess strategies.

"And the other opinion is that there are radical elements within the Iranian military, especially the Revolutionary Guard Corps, who would be willing to sacrifice even a prize like Jerusalem. They would remind dissenters that Mecca and Medina are both more significant holy cities for Muslims."

"Where's your asset?" Eli asked. "We've tried for years to get someone highly placed within their nuclear programme. They have it locked down tighter than a rabbi's wine store."

"Would you believe it's a clerk at Vareshabad? One Karvan Sassani. A devout Muslim who, unfortunately for him, though the converse for us, was caught *in flagrante* with a hooker on a trip to Azerbaijan."

"Honey trap?"

Tim sighed and spread his hands.

"Our colleagues a couple of floors up excelled themselves. Now Sassani lives in fear of our giving him up to the MOIS torturers. That sort of thing makes a chap frightfully willing to be helpful."

"What do you have on Darbandi himself, Tim? As a man, I mean?" Gabriel asked. "Married, single, divorced? Gambler, secret dope-smoker?"

Tim smiled.

"If only he had vices we could exploit as easily as we did those of the hapless Mr Sassani. No, I'm afraid Darbandi is a simple, home-loving man, when he's not planning crimes against humanity, obviously. He lives quietly with his wife and five children in a suburb of Tehran. Attends his local mosque, says his prayers, likes flying kites with his children at the beach when the weather's right."

Five more orphans and another widow on my account when I'm done, Gabriel thought. Then dismissed the thought immediately, replacing it with another. *And hundreds of thousands more if I'm not.* Some words of Don's came floating back to him now.

"I'm afraid that sometimes it's a numbers game, Old Sport. Unpleasant

to be sure, but there it is. Kill one to save a hundred. Kill ten to save a thousand."

Or in this case, Boss, kill one to save eight hundred thousand.

Tim unzipped the file case and withdrew a pale-green cardboard folder. It looked new. Its upper right corner bore a red Top Secret stamp and below that, a second, Eyes Only. Both had been placed with pinpoint accuracy and were parallel both to each other and the edges of the card. He pushed it across to Gabriel.

"That's everything we have on Darbandi."

Gabriel opened the folder. The first page was a personal profile including a colour photo taken through a long lens. He could see the candy-striped domes of St Basil's Cathedral behind Darbandi's head, like so many swirls of multiflavoured ice cream. So, taken while he was in Moscow. He wore the same facial expression as in the photo Don had given Gabriel. But did he look like a man capable of designing a weapon whose specific and stated use was to murder almost a million people and destabilise a country to the point of collapse? No. He did not. Or maybe, actually, he did. When had any of Gabriel's missions ever been blessed with a target whose facial features or body matched their warped psychology or twisted actions? *What do you want Wolfe? Vampire teeth or talons for fingernails? Strings of drool and a dead-eyed stare?*

He reflected on the men, and occasionally women, he'd killed. Most had been average-looking. A couple of the men had been handsome, a couple of the women beautiful, though that hadn't stopped him. *Would anything stop you?* he asked himself. *Would you kill a pregnant woman? A child? A man in a wheelchair? Someone lying unconscious in a hospital bed?* Yes, of course. He had killed Marie-Louise Hubert, the corrupt and murderous director of a Cambodian children's charity, by pumping her full of morphine while she lay in a hospital bed poisoned by a customised bio-weapon. The answer emerged from the moral fog inside his head like the spire of Salisbury Cathedral rising out of the morning mist. *If Don Webster ordered me to, yes, I would.*

"Gabriel?" Eli had tapped him on his left arm. She and Tim were looking at him, he with curiosity, she with concern. Bennett was inspecting his fingernails.

"Sorry, miles away," he said, flipping over the pages. "This all looks great, Tim. Eli and I'll study it before we leave."

"Good, good. I'm just sorry there's not more. I have your next orders here, too, from Colonel Webster. He couriered it down here this morning."

He pushed over a plain white envelope.

Gabriel smiled as he took it. Don wasn't a colonel any longer, but his reputation and sterling work commanding 22 SAS had led many of his new contacts to continue using the title, however much Don might protest that he was "plain *Mister* Webster now."

He slid a nail along the flap to open the orders and withdrew a single sheet of paper, which he glanced at for a few seconds.

"What does it say?" Eli asked.

"We're to report to Marlborough Lines tomorrow. A Captain M. Forshaw."

"Army HQ? Why?"

"They have an Iraqi village they've built out on Salisbury Plain and Don's had it tweaked to the layout of Vareshabad."

He looked up at Tim.

"Thank you."

Tim shrugged his thin shoulders.

"Just doing what HMG pays me for. Be careful out there, won't you? We've an embassy in Tehran again, but it's a tricky place to move around in. Hugh?"

Bennett began speaking immediately, as if Tim had fed a coin into a slot. An "I speak your mission" machine.

"Your SIS contact there is Julian Furnish. Officially, he's our Deputy Cultural Attaché. He's been briefed on the operation and stands ready to assist you. You'll collect your kit from him – we'll ship it out in a diplomatic bag."

That appeared to be all he wanted to say, and after a moment's hesitation, Tim resumed the briefing.

"Thanks, Hugh. Yes, so, hopefully, everything will go according to plan. But if it all goes to shit," then Tim blushed and he looked at Eli. "Pardon me, Eli—" She waved it away. "Well, if it all blows up in your face, either literally or metaphorically, get yourself to the Embassy and ask for Julian. He's been briefed you're there undercover and won't be making contact unless you're, what shall we say, *in extremis*?"

Gabriel was beginning to tire of Tim's over-solicitous manner and scrupulous manners around Eli, who Gabriel knew was more than capable of turning Tim's maidenly blush into something the colour of a pillar box. Then he rebuked himself. *The guy's only trying to be helpful. Maybe he really* was *a choirboy. Maybe his dad's a vicar.*

The meeting concluded a few minutes later. Tim offered to accompany them down to the ground floor. As they waited for the lift, Gabriel turned to Tim.

"Did you join the Service straight from university?"

"Yes. Would you believe I was recruited in the old-fashioned manner? A tap on the shoulder during a seminar on Middle East politics."

"If it ain't broke ..." Gabriel said.

Tim laughed.

"Exactly! Although I believe you can now download application forms from the web."

"So is it a family thing?" Eli asked. "Serving your country?"

Tim shook his head, and a ghost of an expression flitted across his face before Gabriel could read it.

"Not really. Unless you count working in a university. My parents are academics, just a little to the right of Karl Marx. They don't really approve of my being a, you know ..." He leaned closer and whispered theatrically, "... *a spy!*" He straightened. "How about you, Gabriel? Does service run in *your* family?"

"My father was a diplomat in Hong Kong."

"So you didn't really see too much of them, I'm guessing. What with all the functions and so on?"

Gabriel thought back to his childhood. He hadn't spent time with his parents. Not after Michael died.

"I left home early. I was what you might call a rebellious boy. I was brought up by a friend of my parents from the age of nine."

"Was that OK?" Tim asked.

"It was good. Great, in fact."

"Is he still with us?"

Gabriel shook his head. Offered a tight-lipped smile.

Tim was clearly enough of a diplomat himself not to press further.

A bleep and a pleasant female voice telling them to "Please take lift number four" interrupted the small talk, which was threatening to become big talk.

Reaching the ground floor, the trio stepped out of the lift and Tim shook hands with them both, Eli first.

Back in the car, Eli spoke.

"I didn't know men like him still existed."

"Oh, there are still a few with manners, even in SIS."

She laughed.

"OK, so back to Shoreditch then off to Army HQ tomorrow."

* * *

Inside the green-glass-and-sandstone building Gabriel and Eli had just left, the analyst with the beard and moustache was talking to Tim.

"Were they those bloody people from The Department?"

Tim looked mildly surprised.

"Well, they were from The Department, Faroukh. I'm not sure they deserve to be called 'bloody people.' They're just doing their job like we all are."

"Where are they off to now, then?"

"Marlborough Lines. Training."

"Huh. All right for some, isn't it? Poncing about on Salisbury Plain while we're stuck inside staring at bloody computer screens all day."

Tim shrugged. He was about to reply when a flicker of grey at the window beyond Faroukh's shoulder made him turn. A bird of prey had landed on the window ledge. It perched there, unable to see the spooks through the shielded plate glass, its head tilted to one side.

"Look!" Tim said. "A peregrine falcon. *Falco peregrinus*. They're roosting all over London now. It's a miracle."

Faroukh snorted. "I'll tell you what's a miracle, Tim. That we get any work done with all these interruptions."

Later, at his flat in Shepherd's Bush, Faroukh pulled out a cheap mobile phone and made a call.

A MATTER OF FAITH

TEHRAN

Although only a thirteen-year-old boy at the time that the Shah was deposed, Abbas Darbandi had been brought up on stories of that glorious moment in Iran's history. His father was a devout Muslim, his uncles both Imams, and his older brothers both served in the Army. They filled the impressionable young boy's head with the glory of the armed overthrow of the Shah's corrupt, Western-facing Iran. And what of its successor? The brutal, theocratic, Islamic Republic of Iran? Naturally, they were in favour. Despite its total power at home, the newborn country needed enemies to bolster its population and distract them from their privations and loss of personal liberty. And what better enemy than Israel? The Jewish state to their west was a puppet of the USA, an affront to Islam, an interloper in the Arab world, and had to be destroyed. The young Abbas swallowed the rhetoric at home, at school and at the mosque as if it were mother's milk.

As soon as he was old enough, he went to university to further refine his already prodigious talents in mathematics and physics. His professors spotted the young man's abilities, and his fervent espousal of the ideas of a radical Shia sect committed to the hardest of hardcore Islamic philosophy: the immediate, total and irreversible destruction of the state of Israel, by whatever means necessary.

Messages were sent to representatives of the security services. Interviews were conducted, in which the young man proved himself a willing, enthusiastic and determined servant of the Republic. And Abbas Darbandi was sent to Moscow, and from there, Beijing.

Alongside his formal studies in Russia and China, Darbandi acquired a thorough grasp of revolutionary politics. Coupled with his flair for nuclear physics, and still brightly burning religious fervour, it made a potent mix.

He returned to Iran with a single, all-consuming idea. To design, build and launch a nuclear missile that would strike at the heart of Israel. So strong was his fervour, he would have been only mildly disappointed to learn that he was at best only the joint author of the idea. That his co-authors were agents of the state, who had spotted his academic talent around his thirteenth birthday.

He worked long hours, returning to his new wife each evening to lecture her on the evils of Israel and its Zionist supporters in America and Europe. And how he, Abbas Darbandi, was going to redraw the map of the Middle East. Over dinners of home-cooked lamb, roasted aubergine and saffron-scented rice, she would nod and smile, asking questions she thought appropriate for a woman to ask her husband, and praising his work.

In time, she bore him five children, two daughters and three sons. And they became part of the audience for his nightly bulletins on his work. He did not entirely forget his role as a father and husband. From time to time, when work permitted, he would take the family to the coast up at Chalus to play on the beach, fly kites and eat delicious picnics of cold grilled chicken and salads dressed with his favourite blend of pomegranate molasses, lemon juice and olive oil.

On the drive back to Tehran, he would always detour through Vareshabad, stopping outside the gates of the facility.

"That's where Daddy works," he would intone. "One day very soon, he will finish the ..." *How he yearned to say it out loud – the bomb!* "... project that will mean great fame for Daddy and a new respect for Iran in the world."

The children, yawning from the hot day at the seaside, would clap and his wife would lower her eyes as she looked at him from beneath her long, dark lashes.

Late at night, after he had taken what was rightfully his from his properly submissive wife, he would leave the bed and go out onto the balcony. Looking over the dark streets of Tehran, he would indulge in a delicious fantasy. That he was, *Whisper it, a Jew! Living in Jerusalem.* A distant siren would sound. He would look to the horizon in a panic. And there, streaking down from the heavens, trailing a plume of holy orange fire, would be a missile. And another. And another and another and another. The mushroom clouds would blossom like rose bushes all over the city. Red fireballs would boil upwards from ruined streets, squares, alleys and parks. Everything obliterated, everything burning. And the blast wave would rush out from the centre of the city and destroy everything in its path. Men, women, children, pet cats, zoo animals, stray dogs, the beasts of the land, the birds of the air – all would become ashes, blown away on the burning wind.

Sometimes the fantasy would produce a state of sexual arousal, and Darbandi would return to bed to wake his wife. Others, it would leave him as sated as if he had already taken her. But of one thing, he was sure. This was his destiny. His God-given destiny. And nothing must be allowed to stand in its way.

TIPOFF

DOCKLANDS, EAST LONDON

High above the rectilinear layout of roads and manicured green spaces comprising the Canary Wharf financial district, three men sat at a glass-topped boardroom table. The men were rich. The phrase "obscenely rich" might have been coined just for them. But these men were not captains of industry. Their families had not acquired their wealth by laying railways across undiscovered lands, excavating harbours or throwing up skyscrapers. They were not media moguls or tech entrepreneurs, transforming whole markets or disrupting traditional industries with a single app. Nor were they financiers, or not in the traditional sense. Had anyone been foolish enough to inquire as to how, precisely, they *had* acquired their billions, he or she would have been met with a thin smile.

"We are in the influence business," they might say. Or, "We work with governments, facilitating global trade."

Both explanations, though minimal, were true. Their families originally came from Russia. They had avoided the recent, and fashionable, route into extreme affluence: selling off, and repurchasing at a knockdown price, previously state-owned assets. Instead, they had concentrated on being of service. When the Soviet state, and then its gangster-capitalist successor, had needed deniable help "disposing of underperforming assets," as their clients might put it, the men and their organisation were there to help. Of course, they had made sure that their clients compensated them for their assistance at the very highest level. And they had joined forces with other, similar organisations around the world.

The umbrella organisation had given itself a name. Aware that they were operating in the real world, and not an adolescent film director's fantasy, they had forgone names with blatantly evil connotations. No Kraken for them. No Octopus. No Black Circle, Widow or Night. Instead, their business cards – for yes, they did proffer them from time to time – bore the word:

Kuznitsa

Some years earlier, one of their senior people in the UK, known only by the code name Strickland, had been killed. The perpetrator was an unknown British security operator. The loss of Strickland could be borne, lightly, if need be. But the plan from which he had been smoothing off the rough edges could not. They had been within weeks of seizing control of a huge central African diamond field and, simultaneously, the financial, military and security apparatus of a sizeable country in that region. Now, that plan was as dead as Strickland, who'd collapsed to the ground in the middle of a remote moor in the Peak District with a five-inch combat knife embedded up to the hilt in his neck.

"So why are we here?"

The speaker, thickset, bearded, leant back in his padded, white leather swivel chair. The man he'd addressed his question to had just risen from his own chair and was now standing at the floor-to-ceiling window, looking down at a superyacht, *his* superyacht, which was moored in a basin of jade-green water between two skyscrapers.

The standing man turned. He was six-foot tall and heavily built. Max considered himself a good dresser. His charcoal-grey suit had been made for him in Savile Row. He had paired it today with a pink silk shirt and matching tie and a pair of handmade John Lobb Oxfords. He was smiling broadly.

"We've got him!" He strode over to the seated man and clapped him on his beefy shoulder. He barked out a laugh. "Our contact inside British intelligence just called me. Strickland's killer. His name is Wolfe."

The third man, older than the other two, peered over gold-framed, half-moon spectacles.

"How can he be sure?"

Max grew exasperated.

"He works in MI6, OK? He heard a whisper that Strickland was killed by some guy working for a group called The Department. They're killers, just like us, but part of the British Government. So he pulled the file on the operation. Happy?"

"Is that why we're paying for the hit instead of him?"

Max nodded.

"Where is he?" the older man asked.

"He's in London, for—"

"London? What the fuck good's that? London?" he shouted. "You summoned me here to be told this man we seek is somewhere in a city of, what twenty-three million people? I could have hazarded a guess at London myself, Max."

The tall man paled. Took a breath. When he could trust himself to speak, he did so in a quiet voice. He hated shouting.

"If you'd permit me to continue. He is in London for a briefing with MI6. Our contact was sure on that point. We have his licence plate. I have arranged a tail. We follow him and when the moment is propitious, we strike."

The thickset man spoke.

"Pro ...?"

"It means favourable," the tall man said, inwardly regretting that his partners did not always match him in the brains department, even if they more than did in ruthlessness, cunning and a willingness to engage in extreme violence.

"Well, why didn't you say so?"

"Forgive me. Next time I shall choose my words more carefully."

Mollified, the thickset man pulled out a gold cigarette case and offered it to the other two. Both shook their heads; the man to his right frowned and pursed his lips but said nothing. The smoker smiled, extracted a cigarette, lit it with a gold lighter and drew in a lungful of smoke before expelling it in a luxurious exhale towards the ceiling.

"Ah, that's good," he murmured, a wide smile on his swarthy face. "Remember when all we had to smoke were *papirosi*, Max? Fucking cardboard tubes to hold, and filled with that stuff they called tobacco? Christ, it tasted like dried cabbage and fucking horseshit. One puff would blow your fucking head clean into the middle of next week, they were so strong. Now I smoke these beautiful Virginia tobacco cigarettes. Smooth as a whore's—"

"Enough!" Max barked. "So. How are we going to kill this Wolfe character then?"

UNWANTED ATTENTION

Gabriel drove fast along the M3 motorway, heading for British Army headquarters at the camp known as Marlborough Lines. Mid-morning, and heading out of London, the traffic was so light as to not count as traffic at all. With the sun behind them, the driving conditions were perfect. In the distance, he spotted a small car cruising along in the middle lane. Gabriel was on the inside lane, though still doing ninety-five.

"Look at this idiot!" he said to Eli, pointing ahead with his right hand. "Completely empty motorway and he's sitting in the middle at, what, sixty?"

"Calm down, Captain Speedfreak. He's not hurting anyone."

"It's bad discipline. He should be on the inside. I mean what's the fucking point of having three lanes if some muppet's going to hog the middle one driving as slow as a fucking hearse!"

As Gabriel shouted this last word he swung the Ford out and overtook the little car at a shade over 100 mph. He left the overtaking manoeuvre until the last minute, so that they passed close enough to the rear and side of the car to see the various stickers plastered inside the glass. "We've been to Legoland." "National Trust." "If You Can Read This, You're Too Close!"

Eli shrieked. Gabriel wasn't sure if it was from fear or exhilaration.

"Whoa! OK, slow down. Now!" she shouted and slammed her palm against the dashboard.

Gabriel took his foot off the throttle and let the car slow down to eighty. His heart was racing and his right leg was jiggling.

"What the fuck just happened?" Eli said, her voice full of anger. "You could have killed that driver. And us, too, while we're on the subject."

Gabriel shrugged. Tried to speak in a casual tone he wasn't feeling.

"He was being a prick. I just overtook him, that's all."

"No, he wasn't! But you were! First you keep tuning out in meetings, then you practically run some little old man off the road. What's going on?"

Gabriel realised there was a part of him that had wanted to do precisely that. To see the little silver hatchback swerve and skid, then turn over and over and over before hitting the crash barrier and bursting into flames.

Shit! What's happening?

"Honestly? I don't know. Look, there's some services coming up. Let's grab a coffee."

He slowed down and switched on the indicator as they approached the first of the turn markers. A high-pitched, extended sound from behind made him look over his right shoulder.

The little silver hatchback, still in the middle lane, trundled past, horn blaring. Its driver, a man in his eighties wearing a tweed cap, turned to his left and put two fingers up.

* * *

Sitting with their coffees, Gabriel and Eli sat staring at each other. She broke the silence first.

"Are you going to tell me what's going on?" The softness was back in her voice. No anger, no indignation. No trace, even, of the flirtatiousness he loved so much.

He took a sip of his coffee to buy time.

"I ... I think it was talking to Tim about our parents. It made me think about Master Zhao. I still miss him, Eli. I mean, *really* miss him. Even after I left Hong Kong and went into the army, he was still there. Here!" He thumped his chest, over his heart. "Then just when I had him back in my life again, she took him away from me."

"Sasha Beck."

"Yes. And her bitch of a boss."

"And you got them, Gabriel. You killed them both. You avenged his death in the best way possible."

"But he's still gone. Can't you see that? They're dead, but so is he!" He was aware his voice had risen, but he couldn't stop himself. Didn't want to.

Eli's eyes flicked over his shoulder, and she pursed her lips in a *shushing* gesture.

Gabriel looked round. A group of well-fed people, the women in pastel hoodies and white shorts, the men in replica football shirts, were looking across at their table. At Gabriel's fierce gaze they looked away, back to their lattes and croissants.

Eli stretched out a hand and gently placed it on top of Gabriel's.

"Listen. You're doing fine. You're working, and you're great fun to be with. But I sense such a sadness in you. Don't let it overwhelm you. My Dad's always quoting from the Torah and the Talmud, old Jewish proverbs, you know. When somebody dies, he likes to say, 'Everything grows with time, except grief.'"

Gabriel didn't pull his hand away. But it felt trapped beneath Eli's, not comforted.

"That's nice. And it's fine for one instance of grief. But grief can grow, if it's for different people. I lost friends when I was serving. We carried on fighting, and when the contact was over, we put them in their sleeping bags, as Colonel Tim Collins said, and sent them home to their loved ones. They could grieve and over time it would lessen.

But what happens to me is different, don't you see? The deaths keep mounting, Eli. Not the targets, I don't give a fuck about them. It's everybody else. It's almost as if someone has it in for me."

"God, you mean? Even though you have a Biblical name, I don't think you're Job."

"I didn't mean that. I don't think. I'm just missing the people I've loved."

Eli frowned.

"Do you miss Britta?"

Gabriel paused before answering. It was a good question. *Did* he miss her? And if he did, *how* did he miss her? He'd proposed to her, after all. But he'd also fought alongside her, in uniform and out of it.

"Taking the Fifth, are we?" Eli asked, teasingly.

"No! I was doing your question the courtesy of considering it properly before answering." He frowned, aware of how pretentious that remark had sounded. "Yes, of course I miss her. We were close. Even before we were together, I liked being with her."

"But you don't miss her as a lover, do you?"

"Wow! OK, you don't beat about the bush, do you?" *What would Britta say? "Run around the bush," probably.* He smiled at the thought.

"No, I don't. It's not the way I was brought up. In my family we liked to talk about everything. And I mean, everything!"

"I don't miss her … in that way. But she was … is … a friend."

"Why don't you call her, then?"

"She's in Stockholm."

Eli stared deep into his eyes and lowered her voice as if speaking to a particularly stupid child. Or a dog, perhaps.

"Gabriel. They do have telephones in Sweden now."

He smiled. God, she was irritating.

"I meant, what would be the point? It's not as if we could all meet up for a drink, is it?"

"Well," she continued in her emotions-for-dummies tone, "the *point* would be that you could say, 'Hi Britta, how's it going? I miss you.'"

Gabriel withdrew his hand, but only so he could use it to cup his chin and stare at the ceiling, frowning as if in deep thought. He decided to adopt the role she'd assigned to him.

"Huh. So what you're saying, and please correct me if I've got the wrong end of the stick, is that I could call her because she's my friend and we could have, what, a chat?"

Eli closed her left eye and pointed her index finger at him, sighting along it with her other eye.

"Bullseye!"

* * *

Outside, in the car park, two rows back from Gabriel's grey Ford, four heavily built men in jeans and navy cotton windcheaters sat in a black Mercedes SUV. The GLS 63 was huge, both inside and out, and the men had plenty of space to stretch their long legs. The car's sculpted front and rear ends bore brand new number plates, though they bore no resemblance to those issued with the car by the dealer.

The man behind the wheel, a veteran of conflicts in the Congo, Thailand, Peru, Nicaragua, Iraq and Syria, was consulting a road atlas. He stabbed a thick finger at Junction 8 on the M3, where the A303 dual carriageway dropped southwest towards Andover and Salisbury.

"Once they leave the motorway, we have a green light to terminate them. Anywhere with the right cover and conditions. Traffic should be minimal. Get them off the road then make sure they're out."

The others nodded. Began the process of checking weapons. Slid out magazines, worked slide-release switches, looked through barrels, checked triggers. They were hard men and used to both death and its rewards. All had fought for their countries before discovering the attractive mixture of on-tap action, freedom to operate outside the laws of war, and bulging bank balances that accompanied work in the private sector.

The man in the front passenger seat jerked his chin at the front window.

"There they are."

The driver reassembled his pistol, seated the magazine with a click, and re-holstered it under his left armpit. As the others did the same, with a pleasing set of clicks and snaps, he started the engine.

MORE UNWANTED ATTENTION

Junction 8 was approaching. Eli flicked on the indicator. After Gabriel's close encounter before their stop, she'd insisted on driving for the rest of the journey. The motorway ahead was empty.

"Absence of the normal," Gabriel said. "Quite nice for a change, don't you think?"

She took the slip road and powered away along another empty road, up a slight incline, before swinging from outside to inside lanes round a slow, left-hand bend. Had she checked her mirror before leaving the motorway, she might have caught a glimpse of the black GLS, which was maintaining a 300-yard gap, leading a small group of cars, vans and a single articulated lorry. But she probably wouldn't have paid it any heed.

"Yes," she might have said in answer to Gabriel's question. "Although there's plenty of abnormal behind us."

* * *

"There they go," the driver of the GLS said.

He flicked on his own indicator and swung the big black Merc off the motorway. He wasn't too concerned when the Ford disappeared from view around the left-hand bend. There were no turnoffs they could take, even if they wanted to, and as he knew their destination, he could always catch up.

Behind him, he listened to the metallic poetry of slides being racked on three Sig Sauer P229s. It was one of the many reasons he appreciated his employers. They didn't skimp on equipment. Whatever he asked for, they provided it. Didn't matter what it was. RPGs. M112 demo blocks. M16s. And demands from their side? Just one thing. Total success, every time. In his five years working for Kuznitsa, he had always met that expectation.

He rounded the bend and regained visual on the grey Ford. It was just passing the Little Chef restaurant on the left. He sped past the restaurant moments later, taking a second to glance right at the airfield dotted with light planes. It reminded him of many a jungle airstrip he'd landed at or taken off from, often in planes not dissimilar to the Beechcrafts, Pipers and Cessnas crouching on the grass now.

* * *

Eli glanced in her mirror. Then she spoke.

"Gabriel, can you see the SUV behind us?"

He started to reach for the rearview mirror. Then stopped. The move would be visible. It would be a tell.

Instead he craned his head forwards so he could look back through the door mirror. He saw a black Merc. One of the big Chelsea tractors. A GL something? Had they renamed it?

"I see it. Black Merc."

"I'm not sure it was there before."

"Must have been. Must've come off the M3."

"I don't remember seeing it. There was so little traffic I was on autopilot."

"Presence of the abnormal?"

"Not sure."

Without his needing to suggest it, Eli began increasing speed. The

Merc paced them, maintaining its distance, though Gabriel suspected it wasn't out of respect.

"Take the left. Now!"

A slip road signposted Micheldever Station and Overton loomed. A hundred yards to go.

"Shit!" Eli said, wrenching the wheel over and simultaneously hammering the brakes to scrub enough speed off to make the turn without rolling the car.

The tyres wailed in protest, and the acrid smell of burnt rubber entered the cabin through the air vents.

She flicked the wheel left and right to negotiate the S-bend before bringing the car to a shuddering halt at a T-junction.

"Right then left!" Gabriel said, keeping his voice calm and clear, despite what was happening to his gut.

A quick glance each way and she was off again.

Gabriel looked in the door mirror, though all thoughts of tells had just evaporated.

"Still behind us. OK. You any good at evasive driving?"

"I guess we'll have to see, won't we? More your thing than mine, but you're there and I'm here."

Alternately accelerating flat out and braking hard, Eli followed Gabriel's instructions like a rally driver.

"Wait, wait, wait ... LEFT!" he shouted.

Eli fed the wheel through her hands as she slewed the car into a skidding turn that had them sliding across onto the wrong side of the road. Then it righted itself under her control of the steering wheel and brake pedal, and they were off again, barrelling out of the bend and gaining speed fast.

She glanced up at the rearview mirror.

"Shit! They're still with us. I can't outrun them in this. Why the fuck couldn't you still have your Maser?"

"Sasha Beck blew it to shit, in case you'd forgotten. I promise to buy something faster when I get the chance."

"Yeah?" Eli said, her arms straight ahead of her on the wheel, right foot jammed down hard on the throttle. "I'm gonna hold you to that."

* * *

"That Jew-bitch isn't a bad driver," one of the Kuznitsa operators, a Belgian, said. Racism was in his blood, although he didn't let it affect his professional judgements. Or his financial ones. He'd fight for anyone, black, white, Jew, Christian, if the price was right. OK, not anyone. The Muslims were beyond the pale as far as he was concerned. They were all terrorists. Or would be, one day.

"Yeah, well, she's not good enough," the driver said. "Get ready. Impact in five ..."

He thrust his boot down on the throttle pedal. Under the bonnet, the twin-turbocharged 5.5L V8 engine, tuned to within an inch of its life by its German midwives, emitted a barrel-chested roar. The four men were pushed back into their seats by the acceleration.

* * *

"This isn't going to work," Eli said.

Gabriel glanced at the speedo: 85 mph and climbing. He wasn't sure of its exact top speed, but the Merc would be good for at least forty-five more than they were.

It was the last thought he had before the impact.

* * *

"One. Brace!" the driver yelled to his men.

He locked his elbows and pushed back against the thickly padded seat.

He rammed the Ford's rear with a bang that clanged inside the Merc's cabin, and gave the wheel a little flick to the right before correcting. Then he hit the brakes and watched.

The Ford's rear end shimmied, then fishtailed.

He closed up again and delivered the coup de grace. Another straight-on ram to the nearside rear wheel.

The Ford spun off the road. Its front hit the barrier beyond the verge, flipped over once then slammed back onto four wheels and careered down a fifteen-foot bank of shrubs and weeds. At the bottom, it smashed through a hedge of hawthorn and disappeared into the field beyond.

He checked his mirrors. *No following traffic. Good. Nice and uncomplicated.* He brought the GLS to a stop on the hard shoulder and began reversing towards the spot where the Ford had gone down the bank.

"Ready? OK, out."

The four men left the Merc and slammed the heavy doors with a series of muffled *clunks*. They slid and clambered down the bank, drawing their Sigs.

* * *

As the Merc rammed them, Gabriel and Eli were each reacting in their own way. Eli had braced herself against the wheel. Gabriel had crossed his arms in front of his face and gripped the rear of the headrest.

The impact tore the steering wheel out of Eli's grip. She was fighting to regain control, Gabriel could see that, but the car's speed, coupled with the slam from over two tons of metal had pushed the Ford into a wild, uncontrollable fishtail. A second impact sent them into a slide, and then the car hit the Armco barrier edging the hard shoulder.

The world revolved outside the car through 360 degrees. The windscreen popped out of its frame when the car thumped back down onto all four wheels and smashed through a thin screen of young trees and into a field.

He looked right. Eli was shaking her head. A cut had opened above her left eye and she swiped at her forehead, smearing the blood.

He leaned down and released her seatbelt latch before doing the same for his own.

"Eli!" he shouted. "Come on. We have to get out."

He pulled and shoved her up and out over the crumpled bonnet. He followed her, banging his shin painfully on the way.

They staggered away from the car. Gabriel knew that they had at best a minute before the crew from the Merc arrived to finish the job they'd started. He spotted a possible way out. A rusting spring-tooth harrow leaning against an oak tree about fifty yards off towards the centre of the field.

"There!" he said, pointing. "Go, go."

Eli was limping, but she managed to keep up with Gabriel as he made his way to the tree, stumbling over deeply ridged tractor ruts.

"Help me work a couple of these prongs free," he said, seizing a foot-long piece of rusted steel that ended in a right-angled hook.

* * *

The driver led his crew down the bank. Then he held up his right hand for them to stop.

"Wait a second," he said. "Do we know if they're armed?"

"Shouldn't be, Boss," the Belgian said. "Blacksmith said they're clean till they get to the base."

"OK, fine. But be careful. I'm not gonna get killed in a contact with two fuckers in a cow field."

* * *

Together, Gabriel and Eli pulled and pushed the rusted steel prong. The point of attachment to the frame of the harrow was a nut and bolt, half-rusted through itself and showering reddish-brown flakes as they worked the steel back and forth. Gabriel snatched a look over Eli's shoulder. No sign of the enemy. But it wouldn't be long. The prong squawked in protest, then snapped off.

Without talking, they moved on to its neighbour, frantically wrestling the steel prong against its fastener. Gabriel glanced up again.

"They're here. Come on, we need this one."

Sawing the prong backwards and forwards they broke it free with a loud snap. They ducked behind the oak tree's thick, gnarled trunk.

"They won't split up. If they come at us from two sides they'll be in each other's field of fire," Eli said. "What's their range?"

"Hundred yards. I can't see what they're carrying. No longs. Assuming Glocks or similar, effective range is only fifty-five yards."

She nodded towards a wood on the left side of the field behind them.

"They'll kill us out here. It's a turkey shoot. In the woods we have a chance."

Gabriel nodded. Held up three fingers. Watched Eli shift her weight, so the muscles bunched beneath her trousers. Two. One.

They sprinted away from the oak tree, each carrying one of the rusted prongs.

From behind them, Gabriel heard a shout. But no shots. Professionals, then. No well-trained soldier willingly wastes ammunition. The woods were only forty yards away. Then Eli stumbled and went over with a scream. He pulled up and ran back to her.

"It's my ankle," she said through gritted teeth.

He hauled her to her feet and pulled her arm over his shoulder. Together, they limp-ran to the woods, hopping and skipping in a bizarre parody of a children's three-legged race. The field was edged with a two-strand fence of barbed wire. Gabriel stripped off his sweatshirt and laid it on the upper strand then rolled Eli over it before vaulting it himself.

A shot ripped through the leaves above them. Then a second and a third. The last one hit the trunk of a tree to their left, sending honey-coloured wood chips flying back towards them. One pointed shard caught Gabriel on the side of the face; he felt the impact but no pain. Too much adrenaline for that.

"Get me over there!" Eli said.

Gabriel followed her pointing finger. A rotting log lay in a wide puddle of stagnant water.

He dragged her to the log and she rolled over and submerged herself into the boggy ground on its far side.

Then he dashed away, off to the side, pushing through the trees before working his way back towards the fence twenty yards from where they had entered the wood.

* * *

The driver swore as the man on his left fired three shots at the running targets.

"Fucking hell, man. Hold your fire. The last thing we want is some farmer calling the cops before we're done."

"I thought I had a shot."

"Yeah, well, wait for my order next time or I dock your pay."

The man offered a reluctant, "Sorry, Boss."

"Right. They're in there somewhere. She's injured – you saw her go over, and she was limping when she got up. He practically had to carry her. Neither of them has a weapon. Remember that village we cleared outside Kinshasa?" The other men nodded. "We do it like that. Spread out, and only fire ahead. I don't want any fucking crossfire. You put a target down, you shout 'One out.' Make sure they're dead. Two to the head whatever they look like. I hear two shouts and we're done. I'll call 'back' and we exfil to the car."

THE FEMALE OF THE SPECIES …

The water was cold on Eli's skin. It smelt sour. Her ankle was sending out jolts of pain every few seconds. She reached down into the water and pressed gently against the flesh all around the joint. It was swollen, but not broken. She was sure of that. Hurt like fuck, though. She could bear weight on the other leg, no problem. And an IDF fighter with one leg was worth four fucking mercenaries any day of the week. Even on a Saturday.

She gripped the hooked steel prong tighter. The tip of the hook was pointed. But that was the end she intended to hold. She checked out the other end. Even better. The jagged break contained three vicious points, all bound in a matrix of rust.

From the other side of the log she could hear the mercs getting closer. Then a voice uttered a command for which she thanked God.

"Spread out."

She heard booted feet crashing off into the woods away from her on both sides. Then a lone guttural voice speaking in German that she mentally translated.

"Die Zeit des Sprechens is vorbei. Jetzt ist es Zeit zu sterben." *Talk time's over. Now it's time to kill.*

She heard the man's boots squishing through the mud as he

approached the log. She readied herself, drawing her knees up and pushing her good foot down into the mud, getting purchase on harder ground beneath.

She waited. Would he vault the log or climb over? It spanned the path completely so he wouldn't go round.

A broad, hairy hand splayed itself out on the top of the log. She saw the tips of the fingers. In slowed-down, hyper-alert combat time, she noticed his fingernails were bitten to the quick.

She thrust upwards on her good leg and brought the prong down like a dagger onto the back of his hand, pinning him to the wood.

He opened his mouth to scream, but she silenced him with a straight-fingered jab into the soft place just below his Adam's apple. His blue eyes bulged, and he began bringing the barrel of the pistol round.

But he was already dead.

Eli smashed the heel of her right hand hard against the underside of his nose. She heard the crunch as the thin bones snapped, and she carried on shoving so the sharp-pointed bone splinters entered his frontal cortex. His eyes rolled upwards in his skull, and he swung round the pivot created by his skewered hand to thump onto his back against the upper surface of the log.

She grabbed the pistol the dead man still clutched in his right hand. *I may be slow. But now I'm deadly*, she thought. *Correction. Deadlier.* Then she looked in the direction Gabriel had taken.

IS MORE DEADLY

The man tracking him was big. Maybe an advantage out in the open, though Gabriel doubted it, but here? In close cover? No. A big body held you back, whether you were in a Bornean jungle or a dense Norwegian pine forest. Or in mixed deciduous woodland on the outskirts of an English market town. A big body was harder to squeeze through small gaps between trees, or stout bamboo stalks. Heavier to pull free of bogs. And more difficult to move silently.

Breathing shallowly though his nose, and somehow finding time to appreciate the loamy scent rising from the ground, Gabriel waited, hunkered down in a thicket of whippy sycamore saplings, dog roses and bracken. He'd smeared his face and hands with mud, and stuck dry bracken fronds, twigs and handfuls of yanked-out soft-leaved weeds into his clothes to improvise a sniper's ghillie suit.

In his right hand, he held the spike-tipped harrow prong. In his left, a piece of wood the approximate size and shape of a large loaf of bread. Straining his ears, he tried to get a fix on his pursuer. Gabriel had led the man away from Eli. He knew the man was alone. Like Eli, Gabriel had heard the order to spread out.

A splash and a muttered oath came from his right.

"Fuck!"

Then footsteps, crunching over a patch of twigs and dried leaves. *Overconfident, my friend. And it's going to cost you.*

Mud-crusted eyes trained on the man who'd appeared five feet to his right, Gabriel gripped the log tighter. He'd left just enough space to his side for the action he performed now. In a smooth back and forth motion, he hefted the log out of the thicket, over the man's head, and into the trees. As the log crashed to the ground, the man drew down on the spot and fired three shots in quick succession.

The deafening reports of the Sig meant he didn't hear Gabriel launch himself out from his hide. Before the man could take a step towards the source of the crash, Gabriel had grabbed his head with his left hand and was swinging his right hand inwards, fingers curled tightly round the steel prong. Like Eli, Gabriel had elected to use the bent end as a handle, which meant the end that pierced the man's neck was similarly jagged.

The man gasped as the point entered his throat and dropped his pistol to scrabble at Gabriel's left hand. The gasp turned to a gurgle as Gabriel pushed his hand forward, tearing the carotid artery and jugular vein. The gurgle was choked off as Gabriel clamped his free hand over the man's mouth. He pulled the prong free, releasing a torrent of blood that washed down the man's chest, and stabbed back again, into his heart. Then he held him tightly, leaning backwards, waiting for the resistance to go from his captive's muscles. It didn't take long.

Gabriel patted the torso down and found a spare magazine for the Sig. He pocketed it, took the pistol and set off back towards Eli's last position.

The fallen log bore witness to Eli's fighting skills. Pinned to its upper surface like a grotesque specimen in a Victorian entomologist's collection was a dead man. *No gun*, Gabriel noted. *Excellent. Two on two. Hardly fair odds.*

A shot rang out through the woodland. Then silence.

Gabriel ran in the direction of the shot. He kept his pistol out in front of him, but couldn't risk delaying by moving stealthily. *To hell with them! I'll kill them all if they've hurt her.*

After ten seconds, he emerged into a small clearing, its floor crunchy with empty beechnut cases. On the far side, a figure lay splayed out, facedown, as if they'd bellyflopped out of a tree.

He stopped dead.

"Oh, fuck! Eli!" he muttered.

Looking around the perimeter of the clearing first, he made his way straight across the centre in a crouching run. Then someone spoke in a sardonic voice from the trees on the far side.

"What the fuck are you doing that for?"

THAN THE MALE?

It was Eli's voice. Gabriel straightened, his insides easing as the anxiety he had been swamped by just a second ago evaporated. She emerged from the cover of a thick-trunked beech, supporting herself on a crutch she'd fashioned from a branch. He ran over to greet her, casting a quick look at the body on the ground. The back of the skull had exploded and what was left of the man's brain was exposed. His pistol lay a few inches from his outflung right hand.

"You got one, too," Eli said, pointing at Gabriel's Sig.

"Yes. We should write a thank you letter to the farmer."

A shot from behind Gabriel shattered the silence. Both he and Eli dived sideways and rolled over into prone firing positions. Each fired two groups of three, closely-spaced shots in the direction of the shooter. Then, keeping their weapons up, they shuffled backwards into the trees behind them, where Eli had been hiding.

"Will he run, do you think?" Eli said.

"Not a chance. Guys like that only go forwards. He knows it'll be his head on the block if he can't report a successful mission to his boss."

"Good. Then you get round to him and I'll keep him busy. Wait! I'll shoot to his right and drive him left. You intercept him."

Gabriel nodded, backed away, then rolled onto his stomach and began working his way round the edge of the clearing, anti-clockwise. He counted shots fired. A Sig P229 held up to 15 rounds, depending on the magazine fitted. He checked his own. Yes, it held the maximum capacity mag. Its original user had fired three, Gabriel, six. That left six, assuming the previous owner hadn't chambered a round then topped off the mag. Plus a further fifteen in the spare mag. He hadn't seen Eli check the other dead man for a spare mag. Counting the round she'd put into his skull, and the six she'd fired as they dove for cover, that left no more than eight rounds. Maybe fewer if he'd been the initial shooter. Twenty-nine rounds between them. Against a single enemy combatant with fourteen in the pistol he carried and one or maybe two spare mags. So up to forty-four rounds.

"It's a numbers game, Old Sport."

Too fucking right, Boss. Two against one. Thirty against forty-four. I just hope the result is two and not one.

Behind him, Eli had started shooting. Single shots, spaced about a second apart. Gabriel counted as he belly-crawled round the clearing, slithering over the boggy ground. He reached eight and waited. His heart was thumping. He took a few measured breaths to bring it under control. Ahead, he heard a crackle of dry undergrowth. He shuffled sideways and pulled some old bracken over his head and shoulders.

Then Eli started up again. Groups of three shots interspersed with double-taps and singles. *You took the second pistol. And hopefully the spare mag. Now you sound like two shooters.*

Under the fusillade of shots, the remaining man quickened his pace. Gabriel heard the distinct sounds as the man's boots hit the ground. He wasn't even trying to keep quiet. Probably figured it didn't matter as his targets were stationary and wouldn't be able to hear him over the noise of their pistols.

Then the man, big like the others, appeared a few feet from Gabriel's nose. He was looking ahead, not down or from side to side. Gabriel let him go past, then rolled onto his back, lifted his head up so he was looking down between his feet, took aim centre-mass, and fired. The bullet entered just to the left of the man's spine. The man stumbled as the back of his jacket exploded outwards with a spray of blood and cloth fragments. He fell to his knees, tried to raise his own pistol, dropped it, then collapsed forwards. Gabriel leapt out of his hiding place and grabbed his former assailant. Rolled him onto his front. No exit wound on his torso, so probably a hollow-point round, unless it had lodged in a bone or taken the scenic route and exited somewhere unlikely, like his groin.

He was still breathing, raggedly, coughing out sprays of bright red, foamy blood. So the round had shredded a lung, even if it hadn't hit any of the large-bore blood vessels in his chest.

"Who sent you?" Gabriel said.

The man's eyes were rolling like a stunned beast's. He was groaning from the pain of his wound. Gabriel tried again.

"Who sent you?"

The man coughed. A gout of blood spurted from his lips.

"Blacks ..."

"Blacks? Which blacks?"

But the man was beyond replying.

Gabriel took the man's pistol and stuck it into the back of his waistband.

Then he walked back to Eli's position. She was sitting propped up with her back to the beech tree.

"Four for four?" she asked, looking up at Gabriel.

"Four for four. Let's get going. You need attention for that ankle and you've a cut on your forehead."

"Me? Have you seen your face recently?"

Gabriel reached a hand up and felt his left cheek. Inspected his fingers. No blood. Mud, yes. But no claret. He tried the other cheek. Winced. His fingers came away red.

"OK, it's a scratch. Let's go."

"Maybe lose the salad first, eh?"

She reached for his collar and withdrew a clump of wild garlic.

Gabriel smiled, then he shook off, pulled out, and untangled his makeshift ghillie suit. He pulled Eli upright and took care to give her time and space to plant her weight over her good foot.

"No, wait. I want their phones," he said. "Give me five minutes, OK?"

"Fine. I'll just sit here on my arse admiring the wildlife."

Gabriel sprinted away from her, heading for the last man he'd shot. Then the first. He circled back to the man pinned to the log, then back through the wood to the clearing, where he retrieved the fourth phone.

"They'll all be locked, but maybe Don knows a man who can," he said. "Now, ready to go?"

"I thought you'd never ask."

* * *

When they reached the mangled Ford, Gabriel reached in through the smashed driver's window and pulled the keys from the ignition. He unlocked the boot and retrieved their bags.

"Wait here," he said.

He unzipped his bag and placed one of the two pistols inside. Then he clambered up the bank beyond the thin scrim of trees and, keeping low, made his way to the parked GLS. The SYUV was empty: no backup man. Thankfully, the driver had left the keys in the ignition. He could have hotwired it without them, but it was a small effort he didn't have to make. He pressed the tailgate release switch and, once the automated gas rams had done their job, threw his bag into the loadspace.

He scrambled back down the bank and repeated the process with Eli's bag, dropping the pistol inside first. Finally, he made the last trip, pushing, pulling, supporting and dragging Eli up the bank with him, ignoring her swearing as her injured ankle caught on the undergrowth.

They reached the car, and Gabriel retrieved a bottle of water from one of the cupholders.

"I'm not drinking from that!" Eli said.

"Nor am I. But we should try to clean ourselves up a little before we arrive at the camp."

"Good point. You look like a wild man of the woods."

"Yeah, well, you're no oil painting yourself!"

They cleaned each other's faces, then dressed their cuts with sticking plasters from the first aid kit stowed behind an elastic cargo net in the loadspace.

Gabriel climbed into the driver's seat, twisted the key in the ignition and turned on the air conditioning. He pushed the engine start button in and felt, rather than heard, the big engine wake up. Beside him, Eli was leaning forwards and massaging her ankle.

"It's not sprained. I don't think so, anyway," she said. "Still hurts like buggery, though."

Gabriel laughed.

"Where did you pick up such salty English phrases?"

"Oh, you know, hang around with Don and his crew of cutthroats and a few choice pieces of idiom rub off on you. Now get this thing rolling and get me out of here."

MARLBOROUGH LINES

Approaching the gatehouse at Marlborough Lines, Gabriel experienced a strong sense of déjà vu. *Back on base!* The militarily precise road layout, the white lettering on the tarmac for PASS HOLDERS and NON–PASS HOLDERS. And an almost perfectly circular roundabout, in the centre of which stood a rectangular block constructed of some kind of pink stone. Gold lettering told the visitor, if he needed telling, that he was approaching Marlborough Lines. Above the lettering, the logo of the British Army: a golden lion atop a crown, in front of crossed swords.

Gabriel rolled to a stop at the barrier and buzzed the window down, waiting for the gate guard to come round the car to ask the usual questions.

"Good morning, sir. How can we help you?"

Gabriel had his Department ID ready and handed it over.

"We're here to see Captain Forshaw. He's expecting us."

The guard frowned, then bent his head to scrutinise Gabriel's ID card. He turned it over but the back was blank, then turned it round again. His brow furrowed.

Not seen one of these before? Gabriel wondered. *Or is this your usual routine?*

"Does your companion have one of these too, sir?" the guard asked, looking past Gabriel at Eli.

Eli returned his stare, turning on that powerful smile that Gabriel had seen work its magic on complete strangers before. Her eyes sparkled like gemstones in her tanned face.

"Yes, I do, sergeant," she said, proffering her own ID.

"Thank you, ma'am," he said.

"Oh, I'm not a ma'am. Just a miss."

Then she winked.

To Gabriel's amazement, the soldier blushed and after a quick scan of Eli's ID, handed both cards back in to Gabriel.

"Wait—" he cleared his throat. "Wait here, please, sir," he said.

While the guard went into the guardhouse to check them out and presumably call Captain Forshaw, Gabriel turned to Eli.

"How do you do it?"

"Do what?" Eli replied, eyes wide, all innocence and butter-wouldn't-melt.

"That!" Gabriel nodded towards the guardhouse.

"I was just being friendly."

"Huh."

"You're jealous!"

"No I'm not! He's just the gate guy."

"Maybe I like men in uniform. He seemed very sure of himself. I like that in a man. And don't forget, Captain Wolfe, I used to be a *samal rishon* myself."

"A staff sergeant, yes, I remember. But you ended up an officer, didn't you?"

"They forced it on me. I told you before I would've preferred to stay in charge of a squad."

"And I bet your men loved you, didn't they?"

"Yes. The girls, too."

Just then, the gate sergeant returned to Gabriel's side of the car.

"Can you both come inside and fill out visitor passes? Then we can let you in and direct you to Captain Forshaw's office. We've rung to let him know you're here."

"I can," Gabriel said. "But my colleague here twisted her ankle. We had a little adventure on the way down here."

The sergeant peered in at Eli. She lifted her leg with both hands to give him a look at the swollen ankle.

"No problem, miss. I'll bring you a form. If you can take a selfie we'll get it off your phone and onto our system. You'll want to have that looked at by the MO."

She smiled at him and fished her phone out.

The formalities dealt with, the sergeant waved them through with directions to the medical centre and Captain Forshaw's office.

"I think you've got a friend for life back there," Gabriel said.

Eli pouted at him.

"Don't worry. I still like you a little bit."

Gabriel pulled the Merc off the perimeter road and parked in front of the medical centre.

"Here we are. Let's get you to the MO."

He jumped down and rounded the front of the car to open the door and help Eli climb out. She banged her injured leg against the door and swore, loudly.

"Fuck it, that hurts like a bastard!"

"Come on, it's only a few steps. Here, give me your arm."

Together they negotiated the double doors, stumbling and bumping hips, before they found the reception area and Eli was able to lower herself, with a sigh, into a chair.

Gabriel went up to the reception desk and explained to the medical orderly on duty what had happened. He returned to the chair next to Eli.

"MO's going to come and get you in a few minutes."

"Good. I need this thing strapping up and a fistful of painkillers."

"Painkillers? I thought with your background, you'd just bite a bullet and gut it out."

Her eyes popped wide.

"Fuck you!" Then she punched him, hard, in the shoulder. Twice. "Gut that out, why don't you?"

Eli's bunched knuckles had located a bundle of nerves called the brachial plexus. The punches had numbed his arm down to the elbow. Gabriel rubbed away at his shoulder, trying to massage some sensation back into the squashed nerve fibres. *That'll teach me to poke fun at an injured ex-IDF and Mossad operator.*

"Miss Schochat?"

A warm male voice with a hint of a Scottish burr made them both turn round.

"I'm Dr Murray," the man approaching Eli's chair said.

He was short: barely more than five six, and trim like a bantam-weight boxer. Ginger hair cut into an old-fashioned short back and sides, with a salt-and-pepper moustache like a toothbrush.

He shook hands with them both and then squatted in front of Eli to take a look at her ankle.

"Let's get you a wheelchair and we'll take a look at that properly. I see you're sporting a plaster, too. We'll have a little peep under that as well while we're at it. Orderly?"

The orderly on reception hurried over.

"Yes, Doctor?"

"Could you scare up a wheelchair for this young lady, please? Quick as you like."

* * *

While Eli was being treated in Dr Murray's consulting room, Gabriel pulled out his phone and called Don.

"Hi, Boss, how are you?"

"Fine, thanks, Old Sport. Tip top. How was the briefing with Tim?"

"Fine. He knows his stuff. Put together a short but informative dossier on Darbandi for us."

"Excellent. He said the same. And did you arrive at Marlborough Lines in one piece?"

"More or less. But we were contacted on the way down. Chased off the M3 by a Merc SUV and then barged off the road. Four occupants, looked like private security. Armed with pistols. New-looking Sigs."

"And?"

"And they came after us. We made it into a wood and killed them all. Eli's got a twisted ankle. She's with the MO now. We took their car, so you may want to recover it and send it for forensic analysis. And we took their pistols. I haven't checked under the boot floor so there may be more weapons in there. Other than that, the car's pretty clean. No documents, no personal items. The plates are probably fake."

"Good work. Glad to hear you're both safe. Whereabouts did they run you off the road?"

"It's a stretch of the A30 just past Micheldever Station. It'll be easy to find. There's a bloody big dent in the Armco and a Ford Mondeo-shaped hole in the undergrowth all the way down the bank and into a field."

"The woods?"

"Head for an oak tree and an old harrow in the centre of the field. From there go into the woods at about eleven o'clock. Body one's pinned to a log through his hand. Two's—"

"That's all right. We'll send a team in with dogs. Did it look like the sort of place hikers might stumble over?"

Gabriel thought for a moment. No obvious paths. The barbed-wire fence.

"I don't think so. It looked like it was enclosed on private land."

"Good. I'll get some people down there ASAP. One last thing?"

"Yes, Boss?"

"Did you or Eli get the chance to talk to any of the men before they expired?"

"I did. I asked him who sent them. All he said was it was blacks."

"Blacks?"

"Yes."

"Which blacks? Africans? West Indians? Americans?"

"I asked him but he'd gone by then. I retrieved their phones, though. Four of them."

"OK. Look, stick to the plan as is. I'll put wheels in motion this end. We'll recover the Merc and the phones, and you can have the car our chap comes down in. Keep me posted. I want regular reports. Especially if anything else ... um ... untoward happens."

Don ended the call. Gabriel looked at the screen, then at the door through which Eli had been wheeled. *Maybe I've got time*, he thought. As the thought entered his conscious mind, an unconscious part sent a shiver of anticipation through him. He tapped for his speed-dial numbers and hit BF. As the distant phone rang, he listened to the long purrs with a mixture of excitement and anxiety. No answer. He started composing a message to leave on her voicemail.

Hey, Britta. It's me.

Shit! That's so lame. Maybe in Swedish.

Hej du. Hur går kriget mot terror?

How goes the war on terror? Really?

Then she answered.

"Hello, you. Long time, no see. Or hear, I mean. How are you? Are you still fighting bad guys for Don Webster? Oh God, sorry. I'm bibbling."

"It's *babbling*. And it's good to hear your voice."

"Yours, too. I thought you were never going to speak to me again."

So did I, Gabriel wanted to say. But he held back. He needed to feel his way back into his relationship with the Super-Swede he'd wanted to marry. Loading her up with guilt wouldn't help.

"I just needed to get away. I went out to Hong Kong. I lived in Master Zhao's house for a year. Well, it's mine now. He left everything to me."

"You know, I never had time to talk to you properly about what happened. And I wanted to. I still want to. I know you lost everyone who mattered to you. I'm so sorry."

"I didn't lose you, though."

"No. You were my *Riddare i skinande rustning*, weren't you? I teased you about it, but you saved me from Lizzie Maitland and her tame pit bull. You saved my life. And not for the first time."

And still you dumped me! Gabriel wanted to shout down the phone at her.

"You would have done the same for me. So how's life in Stockholm. The new job working out?"

"*Oh, ja! Jävla jättebra! Jag älskar det.*"

Britta lapsed into her mother tongue whenever emotions were running high, Gabriel reflected ruefully. *It's fucking awesome, and you love it. Pity you couldn't have taken the job before I proposed.*

"That's great. I'm really pleased for you."

"So are you seeing anyone?"

That's my Britta. Always direct and to the point.

"Oh, you know."

"No, I don't. But now maybe I think you are. Is she pretty? Is she bright? You told me you liked clever girls. Didn't you date an archaeologist once?"

"Petra, yes. But she was an anthropologist."

"Basically the same thing, isn't it?"

"I think so. One's more about the living, the other's more about the dead."

"And what about your living girlfriend? Is she pretty? What's her name?"

Gabriel sighed. Britta had a way of asking social questions as if she were interrogating a suspect.

"Yes, she is pretty. She's Israeli. Her name's Eli Schochat. We're working together. And here she is now. Look, I have to go. Can I call you again?"

"Of course! Don't be a dummy! Whenever. Ciao!"

Gabriel looked at Eli. She was smiling. Limping, and using an aluminium walking stick. But no wincing.

"You're looking better," he said as she sat beside him.

"The doc fixed me up with a bit of strapping and a couple of very nice purple pills. Not sprained, just went over on it. It'll be fine in a day or two." She touched her forehead. "He glued me together!"

"Good. We can rest up and hit the gym or something, then get on with the training when you're properly fit."

"On which subject, the doc wants to see you next."

"Me? Why?"

Eli stretched out a finger and gently pressed the tip against Gabriel's right cheek.

"You have a nasty cut there. It needs cleaning and maybe suturing. Couple of butterfly stitches, maybe."

"OK," Gabriel said, standing. "Wish me luck."

"Who were you just talking to?"

"What, on the phone?"

"No, idiot! Through the speaking tube. Of course on the phone!"

Gabriel hesitated, just for a fraction of a second. But Eli caught it.

"It was Britta, wasn't it?" she asked.

"Uh-huh. You told me to."

"Well?" Eli said, leaning closer and nudging him with her shoulder. "How was it?"

"It was fine. You know, I mean, really, it was OK. Good. We just swapped a bit of news. Then you arrived and—"

"You hung up guiltily."

"No! I just wanted to see how you were."

She leaned closer still and planted a kiss on his cheek, just below the cut.

"I'm teasing. I like you a lot, Gabriel Wolfe, but I know you two have history. You don't think I was a blushing virgin before I met you, do you?"

Before Gabriel could frame a suitably diplomatic reply, she pushed him.

"Go on," she said. "Can't keep the MO waiting."

STITCHED UP

"Pretty little thing, isn't she?" the MO said. "Now, relax your facial muscles. Can't get the bloody thing in otherwise."

He depressed the plunger on the syringe he was holding and injected anaesthetic into Gabriel's cheek. Gabriel winced at the thought of the needle tip hitting a bone beneath the skin.

"I wouldn't let *her* hear you talking like that. She'd rip your arm off and beat you to death with the soggy end."

"Really? I didn't form that impression of her at all. Seemed remarkably pleasant. Especially considering you practically backed over her foot."

"What?" Gabriel almost corrected the MO, then grinned. That was one thing he liked about Eli. She loved to keep information close to her chest. She was playful, too. "Oh, yeah. She's very forgiving."

He watched as the MO threaded a suture onto a curved needle. Steeled himself. Bullets and grenades, knives and bayonets – they were weapons of war, and Gabriel had long ago found an accommodation with the idea of the injuries they could inflict. But he'd never enjoyed the idea of surgery while awake, even though he'd been stitched up more than once by a combat trauma surgeon.

"Now, then," the MO said. "Let's just put this – "

Gabriel felt pressure in his cheek –

" – into there – "

– a tugging sensation –

" – and then we'll have it out – "

– another softer tug –

" – there. Tie it off. Snip the ends, *et voilà*! I think we'll just put one more in for luck. Hold still."

Five minutes later, Gabriel and Eli were driving away from the medical centre, looking for Captain Forshaw's office. Gabriel saw the sign he was looking for and pulled off the central avenue through the base onto a side road. At the end of the road, he drove through a set of gates and into a car park. He pointed at a brick-built block across an expanse of grass, in the centre of which an olive-drab anti-aircraft gun stood sentry on a concrete platform, its fifteen-foot barrel pointed skyward. Gabriel searched his mental database of heavy weapons and came up with a hit: a Vickers QF 3.7-in heavy anti-aircraft gun.

"Come on, then, Hopalong," he said, nudging Eli in the ribs.

Inside the building, which was titled "Training, HR, Learning & Devt.," the layout and furnishings suggested a regional manufacturing firm, or maybe an IT consultancy. Bland corporate sofas in royal blue, grouped around a low table on which Army and civilian magazines were scattered. Brochures and reports in a revolving literature display stand. And a reception desk, staffed by two civilians, a man and a woman, both in grey suits and white shirts.

Gabriel approached the desk.

"Yes, sir," the woman said, with a bright smile. "How can I help you?"

"We're here to see Captain Forshaw. We're expected."

"Can I see your visitor passes, please?"

Gabriel handed his over and went back to get Eli's, which he slid across the top of the reception counter."

"Those both look fine, sir. Thank you. Take a seat, and I'll call Captain Forshaw."

Gabriel did as he was told and settled in to wait. *Stand by to stand by*, he thought. But it turned out they didn't have to stand by at all. The receptionist replaced the handset on her phone and called across to him.

"Sir? Captain Forshaw's free now. Through the double doors, down the corridor, turn left, and it's the third door on the right."

Gabriel pushed through the doors and held them for Eli. Then, slowing his natural gait so Eli could keep up, he headed down the narrow corridor. It smelt of nylon carpet and cleaning fluid. Arriving at the third door – which bore a name plaque: Capt. M. Forshaw – he knocked then pushed open the door and beckoned Eli through.

The woman behind the desk was halfway to standing as Gabriel entered the office. She was in No. 8 combat dress, and the rank slide on the front of her jacket bore the three bullions, informally known as "pips," of a captain. Smiling, she extended her right hand. Eli took it and then it was Gabriel's turn. *Bloody gate sergeants!* he thought.

"Thank you for seeing us, Captain," Gabriel said. "I'm Gabriel Wolfe."

"And I'm Eli Schochat," Eli added.

Captain Forshaw smiled again. Her hair was the colour of ripe wheat, and her eyes were a bright cornflower-blue. She looked like an advertising agency's idea of a typical outdoorsy Scandinavian.

"Please, call me Mary. Can I get you a tea, coffee?"

"Tea, please," Eli said. "It's been quite a day so far."

"For me too, please," Gabriel said.

"Excuse me for one second," Mary said. She picked up her phone and asked the person at the other end for three cups of tea.

When she'd finished, she replaced the phone in the cradle and turned her gaze on Eli.

"I'm all ears."

Eli retold the story of the "mercs in the Merc" as she put it. She was economical, though not with the truth. She neither embroidered nor skimped on essential details.

"... then I hemmed him in and drove him towards Gabriel, who put a round between his shoulder blades."

"That's quite a story," Mary said, when Eli finished. "Down here, excitement usually means someone's broken their leg falling off the assault course. Either that or we get our computers upgraded."

They agreed between them that the training exercise on Salisbury Plain could be held in three days' time to give Eli's ankle enough time to properly recover.

"They have an excellent physio over there," Mary said. "Make sure you go and see him as often as you can manage." Then she winked at Eli. "He's very easy on the eye. Before you go, have they sorted you out with accommodation?"

Gabriel exchanged a look with Eli.

"We thought we'd find a local hotel."

Mary smiled.

"Which is totally fine, of course. I was just going to say they have a few spare houses in the married quarters. I am sure we could sort you out with something."

"We're not—"

"Married? I didn't think you were. But they all have at least two bedrooms."

"That would be lovely," Eli said, beaming.

* * *

The next morning, Gabriel woke to find Eli leaning on her elbow, looking down at him. Her eyes were searching something out in his, he felt.

"Morning," he murmured.

"Good morning."

"Everything all right?"

"Mm-hmm. I want to ask you something."

Her voice was level, and he sensed no teasing in it.

"Go on then?"

"What are we doing here?"

"Here, where? Here in bed or here in Marlborough Lines?"

She slithered on top of him and propped herself up on his chest with her flat palms, slapping him lightly with each word.

"Here. In. Bed."

"Well, I for one have just had a really good night's sleep, and now I'm thinking about letting you ravish me before we go and find some breakfast."

"Which is all very interesting," she said, reaching down under the covers to give him an exploratory squeeze. "And maybe I will. But, seeing as you're playing silly buggers, I'll try again. How do you feel about me?"

"I like you. A lot. Fancy you, I mean. You're cool."

"Cool? What am I, a teenage gamer or something?"

"No, that's not what I meant." Gabriel felt the mattress beneath him turning to quicksand with every word he uttered. "You're sexy, smart, resourceful and very, very lovely. And, Eli Schochat, I think you should be my girlfriend."

"Oh you do, do you? And tell me, do I get a say in this?"

"What? I thought that's what you wanted me to say."

"Maybe you should ask a lady how she feels in return," Eli said, with a grin that stopped Gabriel sinking further into the sand.

"OK then, my lady. Tell me, how *do* you feel about me?"

Eli pushed herself upright, settling her hips down over Gabriel and gently guiding him inside her.

"You're brave. You're gentle. And a little bit lost, I think. You're sexy as hell, but sometimes I see you taking unnecessary risks. I want to be with you. So yes, Gabriel Wolfe." She raised herself up a little before sinking her weight back down onto him. "I'll be your girlfriend. And you can be my boyfriend. Now that's settled, prepare to be ravished!"

FIX BAYONETS!

Gabriel and Eli ate breakfast in the officers' mess, to which they had been given access as visitors. Surrounded by uniformed staff officers, Gabriel felt at home, despite having left the Army six years earlier. The familiar smell of cooked breakfasts, hot toast, and steam from the commercial dishwashers beyond the gleaming stainless-steel counter brought happy memories flooding back.

They'd both consumed plates of fried eggs, tomatoes and hash browns, and, in Gabriel's case, bacon and sausages. Still hungry, they munched their way through a few rounds of toast and washed the whole lot down with two mugs of scalding tea each.

"Strong enough to stand a spoon up in," Eli commented with a smile.

Gabriel finished his own mug and set it down on the table.

"What time's your physio appointment?"

"Nine." Eli checked her watch. "Which means I should get moving. It's eight forty now. How about you?"

"Don's sending someone down to collect the Merc and leave us a car in exchange. But I want to see him. We need to find out who those guys were. And who sent them."

"D'you think there's a mole inside The Department?" Eli asked, frowning.

"God, I hope not. It's unthinkable."

"Well, if it's not one of ours then it must be someone in SIS."

Gabriel sighed.

"Maybe, maybe not. All our operations are overseen by the Privy Council. It's possible a member or someone on their staff saw something they shouldn't have."

"Yeah, what exactly is the Privy Council? Don talked about it in my interview, but he was a bit vague."

"It's basically an interdepartmental committee. I'm not massively sure on the details. But I think there have to be at least four ministers in a meeting. I get the feeling Don still does most of his business working with MI5 and MI6."

Eli stood up, then leaned over to kiss Gabriel on the lips.

"Let's find the mole. And kill it," she whispered.

As she straightened again, he noticed a table of senior officers giving her an appreciative once-over. He felt a pang of jealousy and immediately wondered what it meant.

"See you later, OK?" she said. Then she left, giving, he was sure, just that little bit of an extra swing to her rear as she hobbled past the senior officers.

* * *

After breakfast, Gabriel changed into running gear and was on his second circuit of the base when his phone rang.

"Mr Wolfe?" the base receptionist asked. She'd called his mobile phone so there was no reason to think it would be anyone else answering. Protocol. The Army. The Diplomatic Corps. They ran on it like a car runs on petrol.

"Yes."

"There's a gentleman here asking for you. He says he's here to collect the Mercedes you arrived in."

Gabriel checked his watch. It was 9.35 a.m.

"Tell him I'll be there in ten minutes."

Gabriel jogged back to a T-junction, turned left and arrived at the car park in front of reception at 9.45 a.m.

Identification of his colleague was easy, since he was the only visitor enjoying the comforts of the reception area. Midfifties, stocky, sandy hair cut very short. A sunburnt face in which freckles were still clearly visible. He stood as Gabriel approached, hand outstretched. The man took it, and Gabriel had to exert himself returning the iron grip to avoid having his fingers broken.

"You're Wolfe, eh? Angus Thorne. Heard you got yoursel' in a wee spot of bother yesterday." The man's Glaswegian accent had been softened by travel, Gabriel guessed, but he retained the hard edge his home city had bestowed on him.

"You could say that. Four goons ran us off the road and came after us with Sigs."

"And where exactly are they now? Playing darts in a local hostelry, no?"

"They're communing with nature. Permanently."

"Aye well, circle o' fuckin' life, isn't it?"

Gabriel laughed. It felt good. Being on an army base. A full-English powering his PT routine. Joking about death with a hard man from the Gorbals. For the first time since he'd resigned his commission in 2012, he felt nostalgic about life inside the wire.

"Come on," he said. "I'll take you to the Merc."

When they reached the car, which was parked near a brick wall smothered with white climbing roses, Angus strolled round it, making a visual inspection. He squatted down in front of the massive radiator grille with its dinner plate–sized three-pointed star and ran his finger along the dented plastic where the goons had rammed Gabriel and Eli off the road. Reaching the passenger side, he dropped into a press-up so low his chest was almost on the tarmac. He craned his head up to look underneath. Then he dropped fully to the ground, rolled onto his back and scooched under the car, heeling himself backwards until only his khaki-booted feet were visible. Gabriel waited, impressed with the Glaswegian's thoroughness.

"Ah ha! Got you, you little wee bastard!" Angus's voice carried a note of triumph.

"What is it, Angus?" Gabriel called out.

"Tracker," Angus said as he emerged from under the car and got to his feet.

He held out his palm, on which sat a small, black, plastic box. Gabriel cupped his hands over it to block the sunlight. A red LED blinked at him from the darkness.

"Maybe the techs can do something with it," Gabriel said.

"Oh, I've no doubt. Clever little fuckers can probably lead us straight to whoever sent them."

"You don't want it on while you're on your way back, do you?"

"No. I better give the eggheads a call, hold on."

Gabriel walked off a short distance while Angus called Technical Services Division. Above him, the sun shone out of a sky streaked with cirrus clouds. A commercial jetliner was leaving a crisp, white contrail that feathered at its trailing end as high-altitude winds took it. *That'll be us soon. Wonder which way Iran is from here.* He inhaled deeply and caught the scent of roses mixed with hot bitumen from the carpark. The tarry smell did nothing, but the roses whisked him back to his parents' garden in Hong Kong. He had been playing with plastic soldiers in a patch of dirt, surrounded by huge, fragrant old roses. An excited shout made him look up.

"Gable! It's me! I love school!"

His four-year-old brother Michael had just returned home from his first day at school. His grey-and-maroon uniform, so immaculate at the breakfast table, was less so now. His shorts had a patch of mud on the left leg, his white shirt was half-untucked and one sock had fallen down around his ankle.

The two boys squatted together in the shade of a twenty-foot-tall South China Maple while Michael unfolded his day, from the "welcome circle" – "I said 'My name is Michael and I like animals'" – to afternoon break and, finally, hometime.

As the memory faded, Gabriel's thoughts returned again to a hot afternoon playing with Michael in the park at Victoria Harbour. Just a year later, and already Michael was so confident. Running for the ball, shouting instructions to his older brother about where to place the kick. Shouting instructions. Why was that important? *Why is that important, Michael? Why? What are you trying to tell me?*

Angus's rough voice jerked Gabriel back to the present.

"Got the keys then, Boss?"

Gabriel felt a momentary stab of panic. *How long have I been standing here in a trance?* Clearly not long, as Angus made no reference to it. *Or are you deferring to me because I'm officer-class?*

"Yeah, sure."

Gabriel pulled out the keys and blipped the fob for the doors and the tailgate, which opened with low hum. It looked like the maw of a great beast, ready and waiting to swallow him whole. Together, the two men pulled up the carpeted boot floor, lifted it out and set it down on the tarmac.

"Well, well," Gabriel said. "Lucky they were in a hurry to come after us."

They were looking down at two Heckler & Koch MP5Ks. Stubby sub-machineguns capable of emptying 30 rounds into someone in two seconds. And an Accuracy International AT308 sniper rifle. All black, from the stock to the muzzle brake.

"Aye, well, I'm sure you could've coped with those. You used a couple of do-it-yourself bayonets is what I heard."

Gabriel laughed.

"Something like that."

"Good for you! I was an infanteer. Second Battalion, Scots Guards. You know our job? 'To close with and engage the enemy at close quarters with rifle, grenade and bayonet?' Bayo-fuckin'-net, I ask you! You ever use yours, Boss?"

Gabriel shook his head.

"Never."

"I'll tell you a story. I was in the Falklands War. Battle of Mount Tumbledown, OK? So, we were contacted by the Argies and it all got a bit kinetic for a wee while. Bullets flying everywhere, you know. Crack-thump, crack-thump, crack-thump. We had a general-purpose machinegun putting down suppressive fire, grenades, the whole fuckin' works. Anyway, after about ninety minutes, we were nearly there, you know? I mean, we'd beaten them back to where they were ready to surrender. But we were still taking fire. We were really low on ammunition, and our captain gave the order to fix bayonets. Fifty yards ahead of our squad's position, we spotted a trench. My mate, Willie Andrews, just stands up and shouts, "Cover me!" like in a fuckin' Western. Then he ran towards the trench. I followed him, giving covering fire as we ran.

"Now Willie was a tough little fucker. Christ only knows how he and me made it into a fuckin' Guards regiment, but there ye are. Used to box back at home, and didn't mind whether it was at a club or with his bare fists in a wee vennel between two rows of houses. Not a bad soldier, and a pretty good mechanic as well. But what he excelled at, was killing. We joined up together, but he never really wanted to, not at the start. Just two wee lads from the Gorbals looking to get out, you know? Make something of ourselves. But in battle, well, he used to get the old red mist. Like one of those Viking warriors. The ones that used to get bevvied up and then go into battle in a fuckin' trance and slaughter as many of the enemy as they could manage. What did they call them again?"

"Berserkers."

"Aye! Berserkers! Well, Willie was our berserker. He gets to the lip of the trench and gives them a few rounds with his rifle. And then he shouts at them, even though I'm pretty sure they're all dead or as near as. This is what he shouts, OK? Word for fuckin' word. 'I am Colour Sergeant William McKenzie Andrews of the Second Battalion of the Scots Guards, and I am here to deliver the Queen's message. And the Queen's message is this, you fuckers!' And then Willie jumps down into the trench and he's just going up and down with his bayonet like a fuckin' sewing machine. After he's done them all, he comes to rest and he looks up at me out of the trench, and his face is spattered with blood, you know? I mean, pretty near covered. His face is like a devil.

And he says to me, 'How did I get down here?' He's got no idea of what's just happened."

Gabriel nodded his appreciation of the story. He had many similar ones of his own. They weren't pretty. Or even always particularly heroic. Certainly not the kind of story the popular press liked to trumpet in their blaring banner headlines about "our brave boys and girls" as the current journalistic fashion had it. They were much happier with the big picture stuff: acts of bravery, daring rescues, successful raids, even troops building schools or handing out sweets to local kids. They knew the great British public would get twitchy if they knew the reality of war. That sometimes the job involved killing as many people as you could, as fast as you could, before they did the same to you. You used grenades and bullets. When the grenades and the bullets ran out, you used bayonets. If you didn't have a bayonet, then a tomahawk, a knife or your bare hands would have to suffice.

Angus climbed into the front seat and Gabriel took the back. Together they methodically searched the interior. Finding nothing of interest apart from the road atlas and a couple of Ordnance Survey maps, Gabriel handed Angus the keys and received a set in return. The black plastic fob bore the four linked rings of the Audi logo.

"Please tell me this is something with more poke than my Ford Mondeo."

Angus smiled.

"I think you'll be happy. Now, take care of yourself and that wee Israeli lassie. I'll be on my way."

The two men shook hands, then Angus was slamming the door, starting the engine and trundling the GLS out of the carpark and back to MOD Rothford.

Gabriel watched him go, shading his eyes against the sun. And one thought revolved in his head. *Why is it so important to remember that game in the park with Michael?*

He arrived back at the house at 11.00 a.m. to find Eli already there.

They sat opposite each other at the simple kitchen table, mugs of fresh-brewed coffee steaming before them.

"What are you going to do about replacing your repmobile?" Eli asked.

"I thought I'd book a few test drives. Find something fun and fast—"

"And flashy," Eli said with a smile.

"And flashy."

"Yeah, well hurry up. I can't have my partner behind the wheel of a grey car for much longer."

A thought occurred to Gabriel.

"What time's your next physio?"

She looked at her watch.

"Twelve. Why?"

He grinned.

"Maybe I'll follow your advice."

CALL THE COPS

Detective Chief Superintendent Calpurnia "Callie" McDonald watched the monitor in the observation room as the newest member of her team, Detective Inspector Jean-André Malo interviewed a middle-aged Libyan man. The small group of experienced officers she led – The Special Investigations Unit – pursued what everyone referred to as "the really bad 'uns." They had conducted a three-month surveillance operation on the Libyan before arresting him. He was running a human trafficking operation, bringing women into the UK from the Gulf states, selling them into slavery for rich Saudi families living in London, having them raped by male family members and then, when the children were born, delivering them into the hands of sex traffickers. Her phone rang. Frowning, she pulled it from her trouser pocket and glanced at the screen.

"Bloody hell!" she said. "I don't believe it."

She excused herself from the cramped room and found a quiet stairwell off a corridor.

"Hello, Mr Webster. To what do I owe the pleasure? It must be five years since we spoke."

"Six, in fact, and do please call me Don. Otherwise I shall feel obliged to call you Detective Chief Superintendent McDonald, which is quite a mouthful."

Callie smiled. She also nodded with appreciation that Don had taken the trouble to find out about her promotion.

"OK, then, Don. And you'd better call me Callie. What can I do for you?"

"Do you remember when we helped you clear up that little bit of business?"

"What, you mean when we handed you a list of civilians and you killed them all?"

Don chuckled, causing the short hairs on the back of Callie's neck to rise.

"That's the one! Pulled the Met's fat from the fire, didn't we?"

Callie had to agree, reluctantly, that the secret assassinations of the remaining *Pro Patria Mori* conspirators had been the least worst option. If the politicians or, God forbid, the press, had discovered that senior law officers were acting as judge, jury and executioner on Britain's streets, the fallout would have flattened Scotland Yard, the High Court, the Department of Justice and dozens if not hundreds of careers.

"You might be right at that, Don."

"I said back then that perhaps you might not be averse to some mutual aid down the line."

Callie could sense what was coming. Her stomach clenched.

"I remember. You also tried to poach my detective inspector."

"Nothing so crude, Callie. I merely suggested that, as we had interests in common, we might share intelligence from time to time, or work together."

Callie was growing impatient.

"And now, what? You want some intelligence? You want to share some?"

"Actually, I need some help."

"What sort of help?"

Don must have caught the suspicion in Callie's tone. She admitted to herself she had made no effort whatsoever to hide it.

"Oh, completely legal, ethical and above board. No need for men in black bursting in and shooting everyone. One of my teams was attacked. We suspect the attackers were mercenaries. We need to find out who hired them, and why."

"You don't have that sort of capability in your organisation?"

"Ha! Not as such. We are rather the shoot-first-ask-questions-later department. Tell me, does the delightful Detective Inspector Cole still work with you?"

Callie's hackles rose.

"Yes, she does. Why?"

"Perhaps she might be a useful asset on this investigation."

Callie sighed. Nodding to a colleague using the stairs, she waited until he'd gone through the door. Counted to three.

"I'll assign whoever I see fit, Don. As I'm sure you do on your own operations."

"Oh, of course. I was merely enquiring."

Yeah, right, you wee little liar. Plus, I have a feeling suggestions from you are more like orders.

She sighed. "What have you got for me?"

"We have the car they used, a Mercedes GLS. Four pistols: Sig Sauer P229s. Two Heckler & Koch MP5K sub-machineguns. An Accuracy International AT308 sniper rifle. Four mobile phones, locked." A pause. "And four bodies."

"Well, that should give us plenty to be going on with. Where are you keeping all the evidence?"

"Let me see, it's eleven now. I'd say, if you look outside your office window, you'll see a large refrigerated truck parked on the double yellow line. It's all inside. Except the GLS. That'll be with you shortly."

Callie's eyes widened and her mouth dropped open. *I've been played.* She inhaled deeply through her nose and let it out in a controlled exhalation through her mouth. *Two can play at that game.*

"Excellent. That means we can make a start straightaway. I'll call you when we have something."

"I'll await your call, Callie. Thank you again."

He ended the call.

Callie stood with her back to the cool concrete wall of the stairwell. She closed her eyes. *No. This was not what I signed up for. I'm not running the investigations branch of some fucking Government death squad.*

No? said another voice, which might have been that of Stella Cole, her DCI. *You were pretty happy when Don helped you finish off the* non-Government death squad. *You owe him.* Then she opened her eyes again and spoke aloud.

"Hang on a minute. A gang of heavily armed men attacked two British citizens working in service of the Crown. That's pure, one hundred percent legitimate police work!"

NOT QUITE OUR CLASS OF PUNTER

With the Audi key fob swinging from his right index finger, Gabriel headed for the visitor parking area. When he arrived, it was to see twenty-odd spaces occupied by cars in every colour of the rainbow, if the rainbow in question ran from black through midnight-blue to gunmetal, grey, silver and white. He squeezed the fob's door-unlock button as he got within blipping distance and watched for a pair of orange indicators to signal which ride was his. He heard the quiet *plunk* of a central locking system but couldn't see any winking lights. He frowned, and tried again, drawing closer to the row of identikit rear ends.

Lock-*plunk*-unlock-*plunk*.

Now he did see the orange glow from a pair of rear indicators. They were reflected in the pearlescent black paint of a Mercedes S-Class saloon's rear wing. He hadn't seen them at first because the car they belonged to was about two feet shorter than the Merc, and the Jaguar XJ saloon on the other side. Sitting between them, like a pint-sized gangster between two brawny minders, sat an Audi RS3 hatchback. The paint may have been a yawn-inducing metallic grey, but Gabriel was grinning. Two tailpipes the size of the Channel

Tunnel peeped out from beneath the rear end. And a spoiler protruded from the top of the rear windscreen.

Don had once told Gabriel that he liked his people to be able to get wherever they were going as fast as possible. Advanced driving courses were mandatory for new recruits unless they had joined from the relevant branch of the police. Couple enhanced skills in pursuit and defensive driving with a small but impressive fleet of punchy off-the-shelf motors, and you had the recipe for a highly efficient way of covering the ground. And, when circumstances permitted, a certain amount of don't-ask-don't-tell fun and games.

Inside the Audi's leather-scented cabin, his back and thighs cushioned by quilted bucket seats, Gabriel started the engine. Five minutes later, he was turning left out of the main gates, pointing the feisty little hatchback's nose towards Swindon, and waiting with eager anticipation for the A303 and the fast A-roads across the North Wessex Downs.

Once on the dual carriageway, he pulled out into the outside lane and floored the little car's throttle. With a yowl almost as satisfying as the bellow from his old Maserati's V8, the Audi picked its skirts up and surged forwards, pressing Gabriel back into the contours of the seat.

Sixty-three minutes later, he exited a roundabout flanked by a Holiday Inn Express and a branch of Costa Coffee and pulled into the carpark of a Ferrari dealership.

The showroom reminded Gabriel more of a contemporary art gallery than somewhere to buy a car. The white walls were hung with expensive, limited-edition modern art prints that *suggested*, while never doing anything as vulgar as *depicting*, speed and power. Much red in evidence, which picked up the *Rosso Corsa* paint of the cars artfully arranged on the sparkling white granite floor. As he entered, a slender blonde in her midtwenties looked up from her lectern and cast her eye over him. The smile appeared a brief moment later, as if he'd ticked enough boxes on a checklist headed, "Client or Clown?" Having clearly decided that he was at the very least worth a greeting and not the bum's rush, she came out from behind the protective shield of the aluminium and blond-wood tower and clicked her way over to him on high heels the same shade of red as the paintings and the cars.

"Good morning, sir," she said, extending her hand for him to shake: cool, dry, fingers tipped with metallic-red nail varnish.

"Good morning."

Gabriel noticed her gaze flicking from his eyes to his watch. The Breitling his father had given to him when he'd joined the Parachute Regiment in 1999 now lay somewhere beneath metres-deep red mud in a Cambodian killing field. In its place, on a black alligator strap, was buckled a rose-gold Bremont 1918. Gabriel had treated himself to the English-made timepiece to mark his return to The Department after his self-imposed exile in Hong Kong and then his travels in the US and Cambodia tracking down an old comrade's murderer. It had cost him the thick end of sixteen thousand pounds, and perhaps Ferrari salespeople were trained to recognise the different brands and their price tags.

"How can I help you?" she asked, hazel eyes now locked on to his own.

"I'd like a test drive, please."

"Any particular model?"

He felt he was playing poker with a battle-hardened gambler. One who was alive to the tell that would scream "timewaster" and lead to his early ejection from the game. He turned and pointed at a convertible, its metallic, kingfisher-blue paintwork reflecting its surroundings like a mirror.

"That one, please."

She smiled a polite smile and looked past his right shoulder.

"There's Anthony," she said. "He deals with new customers."

She raised her eyebrows and within seconds, a young man dressed in an immaculately tailored, dove-grey, two-piece suit and highly polished black monk strap shoes appeared at Gabriel's left elbow.

The blonde spoke again.

"Anthony, this gentleman has expressed an interest in the 488 Spider."

She turned on her heel and retreated to the sanctuary of her lectern.

All the time she had been speaking, Gabriel had listened to the way she stressed certain words, and paused before others. "Deals with," came out sounding as if the next word might be *trash* or, possibly, *athlete's foot.* In articulating the word *gentleman,* she managed to suggest that the casually dressed man in front of her was more likely to be a tramp who had stolen someone else's watch and clothes, or perhaps a door-to-door salesman offering poor-quality cleaning products. He decided on the spur of the moment to have some fun.

"You're interested in the 488, is that right, sir?"

"Yeah," Gabriel replied with a smile, dropping his accent a few rungs down the social ladder. "I read a review in some magazine or other. At the airport. The bloke what wrote it reckoned it was, you know, the mutt's nuts. So I thought, well, why not give it a whirl?"

"Well, the 488 is certainly a thoroughbred sportscar, sir. If I may ask, are you aware of the price?"

"Two 'undred and twenty grand, right? It was in the article."

"And you're comfortable with that amount?"

Gabriel leaned towards the man and poked in the soft flesh between the shoulder and ribcage. Just hard enough to hurt. He winked.

"Lottery numbers came up, didn't they? Been doing the same ones since I was in the army. I'm fucking minted, aren't I?"

The salesman winced as Gabriel's finger found a pressure point. But he was maintaining his composure. Just.

"Congratulations, sir. But I'm afraid we don't have a car available for a test drive today. In fact, Ferrari are very selective about whom they allow to buy certain models. To protect their brand equity. For someone with your ... obvious good fortune, I'm sure a Lamborghini or even an Aston Martin or a Bentley would be a far more suitable choice."

Was that a hint of a smirk on his clean-shaven face? Satisfaction at having given this ex-squaddie the brush off? Gabriel countered.

"Oh, yeah. No. I see what you mean." Gabriel stared intently at the salesman's right pupil. Then the left. He flicked his eyes back and forth between them. "After all," flick, "we can't have," flick, "the riff-raff tooling," flick, "around in a," flick, "Ferrari, now can we?"

The salesman blinked. His left pupil was twice the size of the right, now.

"Er, no. Exactly. I'm glad you understand, sir."

Gabriel continued, now breathing in time with the salesman. He added minute forwards and back movements of his head to the eye movements and murmured a second set of instructions among the normally voiced banter.

"Of course I understand. *You just realised you want to help me.* Bad for business to *Go get the keys* have someone *and open the big glass doors* like me sitting behind the wheel of a 488 Spider. I'll just toddle off and *and let's test drive the 488 Spider* find a Lambo to test drive. *right now.* What's that on your forehead?"

Gabriel darted his right index finger out and tapped the salesman once, lightly, between his eyes. "Do it now," he murmured.

The salesman blinked again and looked at Gabriel as if seeing him for the first time. He smiled.

"Wait there, sir. I'll just go and get the keys and we can take the 488 out for a spin." He turned to the svelte blonde who appeared to be engrossed in her phone's screen. "Christina? Could you ask Dave to open the doors, please?"

Gabriel watched with amusement as she left her station, frowning, to find "Dave." He checked his watch while he waited. A burly man in his forties appeared from somewhere at the back of the showroom. He wore a scarlet overall with the Ferrari prancing horse logo embroidered in black on his left breast pocket. Without a word to Gabriel, he took a set of keys from his hip pocket and bent by the plate glass sliding doors at the front of the space and began unlocking the chromed bolts securing it to the highly polished floor. He straightened and eased the massive sheet of steel-bound glass back in its rails, then repeated the process on the other side. When he'd finished, the entire front of the showroom was open to the air, and the smells of an English spring wafted into the air-conditioned room: new-mown grass and some elusive, floral, fresh scent Gabriel always thought of simply as home.

The salesman reappeared, a set of keys on a scarlet leather fob dangling from his finger. He handed them to Gabriel.

"Here you are, sir. Take it easy out of the showroom, won't you?"

Gabriel eased himself down into the Ferrari's snug bucket seat and buckled the seat belt. He waited for the salesman to do the same. The car started with a crisp bark as its V8 caught on the first turn of the starter motor. He gentled it out of the granite and glass palace, across the tarmac forecourt and onto the road. Finding his way to a quiet stretch of road, he checked behind and ahead, then floored the throttle.

As the car leapt forwards with a howl from the exhausts, the rev counter's needle jerking right then falling back as he zipped through the gears, he turned briefly to the salesman and uttered a short phrase.

"You're awake."

The man shook his head sharply and then, as he came out of the hypnotic trance Gabriel had put him into back in the showroom, jerked back in his seat. His polished manner deserted him, and, in an accent not so very far from the one Gabriel had adopted, swore.

"What the fuck? What's going on?"

Braking hard for a roundabout before swinging left then right then left again to exit at maximum revs, Gabriel laughed.

"I said I wanted a test drive. Now we're having one. Hold on tight!"

Over the salesman's screams, Gabriel flipped the gear change paddle to drop down a gear and then floored the throttle again to accelerate wildly past a pensioner trundling along in a little car the metallic pink of a Christmas chocolate wrapper. Coming straight towards them at roughly double the little pink car's speed, an oncoming supermarket truck sounded its airhorns in a series of belligerent honks. Gabriel gripped the wheel tighter and flicked the Ferrari back onto the correct side of the road. The truck roared past on his right, airhorns still blaring, and the car shimmied in its wake.

Gabriel looked sideways as he braked from a hundred and sixty to a more manageable ninety and took the car round a sweeping left-hand bend. The front of the salesman's suit trousers was a darker grey than the rest. Hurriedly, he clasped his hands over the damp patch.

"Look, I'm sorry for what I said back there. But please, you have to slow down. I'll get the sack if I bring this back dented."

Gabriel nodded, as he accelerated into a long straight section of road. He could see a tractor up ahead.

"Fine."

"But you're speeding up!"

"I know. I meant fine, I won't dent it, not fine I'll slow down."

His sightline was better than his passenger's and he could see that the road ahead was clear to overtake. But he saved the manoeuvre until the last possible moment, racing up behind the tractor and then jinking out from behind the massive rear tyres to sweep past it, exhausts howling, wind dragging its fingers across his scalp.

Ahead, he saw a sign for a roundabout with the fourth exit that would take them back to the showroom. As he reached it, the last car on the roundabout took the exit for London. He glanced to his right and saw what he had hoped to see: nothing. He flicked the wheel left and right and, as he took the car onto the curve of the roundabout, pushed harder on the throttle until the rear end stepped out of line. The wide rear tyres squealed in protest as he controlled the drift and made a complete circuit looking sideways out of the passenger window. Finally, he indicated left, and shot out onto the wide road leading back towards Swindon.

Ten minutes later, he pulled up on the tarmac forecourt of the showroom. He pulled the key from the ignition and handed it to the white-faced salesman.

"I'll leave it, thanks," he said with a grin. "Bit too showy."

And then, leaving the Ferrari's thoroughly test-driven engine ticking as it cooled in the warm spring air, Gabriel strolled back to the Audi and drove back towards Marlborough Lines. Over the acrobatic vocals of a new jazz singer he'd discovered called Cecile McLorin Salvant, he spoke aloud.

"Buy British, Wolfe."

STRIKING SPARKS

While Gabriel had been scaring the pants off the Ferrari salesman, Max was enjoying the brilliant sunshine reflecting in dazzling spears off the mirror-like surface of the sea. The superyacht's captain had just informed his boss that they were in Spanish waters when the latter's phone rang. He glanced at the display and frowned. *Shit!* He put his flute of champagne down on the polished walnut deck.

"Blacksmith! How are you my friend?"

"I'm fine, Max. How are you?"

"Oh, you know, the champagne could be colder, and the weather could be warmer, but other than that, not too shabby."

"Good. Well, now we've got the pleasantries out of the way, how did it go with Wolfe and his little friend? They're both dead?"

Max ground his teeth together.

"No."

"No? What the fuck do you mean, *no*? I served them up to you on a silver platter! How many men did you send after them?"

After a few years of service, members of Kuznitsa came to think of themselves as being not so much outside the law as above it. They held a similarly dismissive view of the concerns of others. So to be interrogated by this low-ranking intelligence analyst caused the man who called himself Max no small amount of anger. Though at its core was a glowing ember of shame. How *had* it gone wrong? He inhaled deeply through his nose and let the breath out again, slowly.

"Four." To offer a longer answer would be to sound weak. Apologetic.

"Four," Blacksmith repeated, in a tone lacking the earlier outrage. "And now they're all dead, I suppose?"

"It's the conclusion I am forced to draw, yes."

Blacksmith sounded petulant.

"I thought I could trust you, Max. I thought you understood why this was so important to me. Why do you think I didn't ask you for money for my information? Why do you think—"

But Max had had enough.

"Listen to me. You have your little reverse-crusade going on against the West. Good for you! Me? I'm not interested in ideology. We put a squad on Wolfe and his little friend, and somehow, they came off worst. We still want him dead, but right now I have other fish to fry. You want to strike a blow against Western imperialism? You need to look elsewhere."

And with that, he ended the call. A slender, leggy blonde in a pale-yellow bikini had been hovering a few feet away. When she saw he was free, she sidled closer.

"Max," she cooed. "You've been ignoring me."

He encircled her waist with one arm, and emptied his glass of champagne.

"I'm all yours now, baby."

* * *

Blacksmith had left the building as usual at 12.30 p.m., mentioning with a smile to a colleague that he was going to try a new place for lunch. Once outside, he headed for a quiet little park half a mile from the office. Little more than a lawn surrounded by flower beds and a few benches.

After Max hung up on him, he held the cheap pay-as-you-go mobile to his ear. He listened to the silence. Heard the roar of his blood. How dare that, that *criminal* hang up on him? After he'd practically gift wrapped Wolfe. He recalibrated his plan. If non-state actors weren't up to the job, maybe it was time to turn to their opposite numbers inside the wire. *State* actors. And one state in particular. A state implacably opposed to the existence of the state of Israel. A state he knew intimately. A state that Wolfe was headed to very shortly.

He called a number he had memorised during his first week on the Iran desk.

While he waited for his call to be connected, he practised breathing deeply and slowly, trying to calm the fluttering storm of butterflies in his stomach. This move would have to be definitive. And it would have to perfect. One whiff of what he was up to, and he'd spend the rest of his life staring at the walls of a very unpleasant cell indeed.

"Embassy of the Islamic Republic of Iran, how may I direct your call?"

"I would like to speak to the Ambassador please."

"Who may I say is calling?"

"My name is Kaveh."

"And you are calling from?"

"I work within British intelligence. I have information vital to the security of the Islamic Republic of Iran."

The receptionist paused. He could hear her breathing. And he could imagine the internal dialogue playing in her brain.

A crank. Like they warned us against in our training

But if he's genuine and I don't put him through, I will be committing a terrible mistake.

The Ambassador must not be disturbed by frivolous intrusions.

He will be furious if he learns I did nothing.

Blacksmith knew how it would play out. He had no desire to

speak to the Ambassador. It was merely the opening gambit. He waited.

"I'm sorry, Mr Kaveh, sir. The Ambassador is in meetings all afternoon. Let me put you through to our Head of Security."

Perfect!

Blacksmith waited while the call was put through. This time, the person answering had a deep, male voice, which dripped with suspicion.

"Good afternoon, Mr Kaveh. You say you have information?"

"I do."

"And you say you work for British Intelligence. Which branch?"

"Secret Intelligence Service. The Iran desk."

"Why are you wasting my time? You are a fantasist, a, who is it, Walter Mitty?"

Like a seduction, these initial contacts had to be played according to a strict set of rules.

"No, sir. I am not. I am an intelligence analyst. And I have information vital to the security interests of the Islamic Republic of Iran. It has to do with Abbas Darbandi."

There, that should do it.

While he waited for the security man to make his next move, Blacksmith looked down at a dirty grey pigeon that was hopping closer to his bench. Its left foot was deformed, the toes curled up and apparently clawless. He kicked out viciously at the diseased-looking bird, and was gratified to feel the soft contact as his toe connected with its side.

"I'm afraid I do not know of this Abbas Darbandi. There must be a mistake."

"Mr Darbandi is your top nuclear scientist. He works at Vareshabad, running the programme to develop a nuclear warhead."

Your move.

"Perhaps we should meet, Mr Kaveh."

"The bandstand in Battersea Park. I'll be there at 6.30 p.m. this evening."

"Fine. How will I recognise you?"

"You won't. But I'll recognise you."

* * *

At 6.32 p.m., Blacksmith approached the black, green and red wrought-iron bandstand from the north. The park was buzzing with commuters, mums with pushchairs, joggers, winos, tourists and students. Standing on the southern edge of the octagonal structure, dressed in a light-grey silk two-piece suit and a collarless white shirt buttoned at the throat, was the man he had come to see. Maziah Gul, Head of Security at the Iranian Embassy and also holder of the position equivalent to the SIS title "station chief" for the Iranian Ministry of Information and Security. In plain language, the chief spook.

Blacksmith approached him from the side, getting within ten feet before the tall Iranian turned to face him. He held out his right hand.

"Head of Security Gul. I am Kaveh."

"Prove to me that you are who you say you are and you work where you say you do," Gul said.

Having anticipated this most basic of vettings, Blacksmith had come prepared for his meeting. From the inside pocket of his jacket he produced his SIS ID and a folded sheet of paper. He handed them to Gul.

"My ID. Which you can photograph and check out later. And a standard intelligence profile of one of your people. Please take it. You'll discover it is genuine."

Gul raised his finely curved eyebrows just a fraction.

Good. You're surprised. But also gratified and relieved. Not a wasted trip.

He took the paper, unfolded it, glanced at it, then refolded it and placed it carefully in the inside pocket of his own jacket. He took a photo of Blacksmith's ID with his phone.

"If this is all genuine, I will be here tomorrow. Same time," Gul said. Then he turned and walked away, skirting a group of mums

dressed in jogging gear and warming up behind pushchairs equipped
with spindly bicycle wheels.

* * *

Twenty-four hours later, the two men met again. Gul's demeanour
was noticeably different. If not friendly, then not overtly hostile
either.

"What is it you want to tell me?"

"Forgive me, but it is not you I want to tell."

Gul frowned and his eyes darkened until they were almost black.

"What do you mean? I warn you, do not play games with me."

"I am not playing games. But the information I have, I will only
reveal its detail to someone inside MOIS in Tehran. If you can set up
a call, I will explain everything."

"You need to give me something more. I have to present a credible
case."

Blacksmith sighed.

"Let me put it this way. If you send me away now, I will find
another way to speak to the right people. But speak to them I will.
When I do, I will tell them of your lack of cooperation. And believe
me, Head of Security Gul, when they learn of what I know, and
discover you prevented me from telling them sooner, they will not be
pleased with you. I can imagine they might recall you to Tehran."

Blacksmith watched Gul's facial muscles warring with each other.
Half wanted to explode with rage, drawing lips back from teeth. Half
wanted to remain impassive. The latter half won. Just. Gul didn't
speak for almost a minute. Blacksmith was patient. He could afford to
be. He and his family had waited a long time already. Finally, Gul
broke his silence.

"Very well. I will let you know when I have set up a call."

LET'S GET INTO CHARACTER

Back on base, Gabriel changed into shorts, T-shirt and running shoes and left the house at an easy jogging pace towards the base perimeter. After ten minutes, he found an unoccupied assault course. Smiling, he sprinted for the first obstacle, a net-climb, and leapt onto the knotted ropes. He reached the top and paused, looking west over the surrounding countryside and the distant trees hazed with blue. He folded himself over the top bar and scrambled back to ground level.

Twenty minutes later, having thrown himself at each of the obstacles the course's designers had installed to test soldiers' fitness, he sprawled on the grass, chest heaving, face damp with sweat. He sighed deeply. In many ways, life on base was simple. You did what you were told to do, or briefed to do. Your three squares were laid on and cleared away for you. You worked, you played, you slept.

Yes, slept.

In truth, he hadn't been sleeping so well recently. Nothing to do with the job. Even incidents like being contacted by armed mercenaries in the depths of the English countryside didn't stop him getting a decent night's rest. *They* didn't. But something else was interfering with his sleep. And it had to do with Michael.

He closed his eyes and let himself become absorbed by the

floating orange-and-blue blobs inside his eyelids. Breathing deeply and rhythmically, he tried to feel his way to the key that would unlock the memory he could feel but not access.

We're at the park. Down by Victoria Harbour. Mum's there. She's reading a book. Michael and I are playing with a rugby ball. He's so good, even though he's a little kid.

"Kick it, Gable! Kick it higher!"

"I don't want to. The park's not big enough."

"Baby!"

"I'm not a baby!"

"Kick it, then."

Mum looks up. Tells us to keep quiet.

"There are other people who want to enjoy the sun without two little boys shouting and disturbing everyone."

Michael sticks his tongue out.

I check Mum's not looking and put two fingers up at him.

His eyes widen in shock. It's very naughty to do that. It means, you know, "F-word off."

"Do we need to call the MO?"

The woman's voice snapped the fragile thread linking Gabriel to the past. He opened his eyes, blinking against the bright light, to find himself looking up at a female soldier in combat dress, a major's single crown on her shoulder boards. He stood, shading his eyes against the sun.

"Sorry, was I in the way?"

The major smiled and shook her head.

"I was watching you. Not bad for a civilian."

Gabriel smiled back. She had blue eyes that contrasted with her raven-black hair, which was twisted into a pleat across the back of her head.

"I like to keep in shape."

"Which you most certainly are." She held her hand out. "Sal Morris."

"Gabriel Wolfe."

"I said civilian, but you used to serve, didn't you?"

"Is it that obvious?"

She shrugged.

"What is it people say? 'It's the little things'? You carry yourself like a soldier, and those weren't weekend warrior moves you were pulling on the assault course."

Gabriel held his hands up in mock surrender.

"Guilty as charged."

"Which regiment?"

"Paras then SAS."

She nodded, looking him up and down.

"Figures. So what are you doing down here in the glorious confines of Marlborough Lines."

I'm preparing to go undercover in Iran to assassinate a civilian scientist who's building a nuclear bomb that will destroy Israel.

"I work for the Ministry of Defence now. You know, swapped the sword for the pen. Here for consultations on procurement policy. We have some free time and they said I could use the course."

"Huh. Procurement. Riveting stuff."

Gabriel could see the major trying to find something interesting to say, or ask, in response to his conversation-killing statement, then give up. He took pity on her and gave her a face-saving way out.

"I know, right. Listen, don't let me keep you. Unlike me, I'm sure you have something interesting to do."

She smiled, probably grateful she wouldn't have to force herself to make small talk about arms procurement.

. . .

After saying goodbye, Gabriel waited until he was alone again, then called Fariyah Crace. She picked up on the first ring.

"Hello, Gabriel. How are you?"

"I'm fine. How are you?"

"Oh, you know. Preparing papers for two conferences at opposite ends of the country. Trying to catch up on my reading. Dealing with hospital paperwork. And, if I'm lucky, seeing patients. I told Simon I might be able to squeeze him and the children in for a half hour three weeks next Friday."

Gabriel laughed. Her unflagging good humour was one of the qualities he loved about the soft-spoken Muslim psychiatrist whom he credited with having saved his life. Not from an enemy's bullet, but possibly one of his own.

"So, I was wondering—"

"Whether, amongst all this well-organised chaos, I had an hour when I could see you?"

He shrugged, even though he knew she couldn't see the gesture.

"Something like that. You did once say I was your favourite patient. Or do you say that to all the boys?"

Now it was Fariyah's turn to laugh.

"Professional ethics prevent my answering that, Gabriel, as you well know. I would like nothing better than to see you. But there is a small problem. My time at the Ravenswood is booked solid for the next month at least."

Gabriel's heart fell. He knew it was selfish, but he had grown used to the idea that whenever he needed her insights, Fariyah would be magically available.

"Oh," he said. "No, of course, I mean it was stupid of me to—"

"So, if you would like, I could see you at home. I have a consulting room. Well, it's a conservatory, but it has two very comfortable chairs and a lovely view over Hampstead Heath. As you like acting on the spur of the moment, how about this? Can you come this evening? Say about seven-thirty? We could talk for an hour or so, then perhaps you would stay for dinner. I'm sure you and Simon would get on and I know the children would love to meet you."

"Yes. Yes, please. I have a couple of days before my next—"

"Jaunt?"

"Jaunt, and I'm kind of at a loose end, so yes, please. What's your address?"

* * *

Eli returned to the house in the married quarters at 2.30 p.m., looking red-faced but more relaxed than Gabriel had seen her since the encounter with the mercenaries. Like him, she was dressed in running gear: pale-grey vest, khaki shorts.

"How was the physio?"

She smiled.

"Really good. And you're not going to believe it. What sort of treatment do you think he did on me?"

"Oh, this being the Army, probably bent it backwards and forwards a few times and told you to get over yourself."

"Nope. Acupuncture."

Gabriel was genuinely shocked. He'd grown up in Hong Kong, where all forms of Chinese medicine weren't just commonplace but often preferred to Western treatments. But here?

"That is, actually, very surprising. What was it like?"

"Amazing! He stuck the little needles in my foot and around the ankle and then gave me a magazine to read for ten minutes while he went off and saw someone else."

"And it worked?"

"Well, it feels a hell of a lot better than before. He gave me exercises to do as well, obviously, and he did some massage and manipulation on it, but, yeah, it really feels better."

"Which is excellent. We can carry on and hit our deadline."

She nodded.

"How was your day?"

Gabriel told Eli about his spur of the moment trip to Swindon. When she'd finished laughing, he told her he was going to visit Fariyah Crace in Hampstead.

"Good," she said. "You can tell her about your present-not-present moments. Did she ask you to stay?"

"For dinner, yes. But I guess if I drink too much they'll have a spare room."

"Just be back in good time tomorrow, OK?"

"Yes, miss."

"So what now, Boss?"

"Now, we have some reading to do. Our covers arrived by courier while you were being stuck with needles."

"Sex first," she said. "Then showers. Then reading."

On the dining room table, Gabriel spread out their travel documents: passports, visas, airline tickets; their British Council accreditations; business cards; and backgrounders on their new identities. Eli picked up a couple of business cards, turned them over then back again and began to read out loud.

"Melina Arifakis, Editorial Director, and Robert Denning, Publisher. Both of The Copernicus Press, who apparently publish books on ancient civilisations. Huh. Making me Greek was a smart choice. Similar colouring. Enough to throw the Iranians off the scent, hopefully."

Gabriel made some coffee, and they settled down to read through their backgrounders, learning CVs, personal histories, relationships and significant life events. Then they moved on to role-playing, interviewing each other as if for a job.

"This is always the part of the job I find weird," Gabriel said.

"What do you mean?"

"It's like we lose ourselves. As if we're not real people, just characters in a play."

"Welcome to the undercover world. I thought you'd be used to it by now."

Gabriel cast his mind back, over different missions, different identities. His favourite alter ego was Terry Fox, the aggressive ex-squaddie with a taste for bare-knuckle fighting. He'd enjoyed his time in Estonia masquerading as Fox. He'd got a job as a nightclub bouncer, while tracing the Chechen kidnappers of the family of a British pharmaceutical executive.

"Let's just say it's one more level of complication I could do without."

"Fair enough. Robert."

They spent a couple of hours reviewing their cover stories and reading the dossier on Darbandi. The afternoon's work finished, Gabriel went upstairs to change. He put on the only clothes he had with him he considered vaguely suitable for dinner with an eminent psychiatrist and her family: clean jeans, a white shirt and a navy linen jacket.

Two hours and twenty minutes later, Gabriel pulled into the drive of Fariyah and Simon Crace's house in Prince Arthur Road, Hampstead. As he climbed out and stretched, his kidneys made their presence felt with an ache around his midriff. *So much for Audi engineering*, he thought ruefully, as he massaged the afflicted area. *That suspension might be fine for a racetrack, but it doesn't do too well on crappy London streets.*

He looked up at the house. Technically, he supposed a local estate agent would describe it as an end-terrace. But it fitted that description only so far as it was, indeed, at the end of a terrace of houses. Much as he might legitimately describe himself a civil servant, being both civil and a servant of the crown. In fact, now he came to think of it, even civility had its limits, as the growing list of Britain's enemies now pushing up daisies would attest, if they were still capable of speech.

At ground level, a bay window looked out over the parking area, where the RS3 now sat plinking and ticking as its overstressed engine and exhaust cooled. To Gabriel's left, a flight of 18 stone steps rose to the front door, which filled a gloriously gothic pointed archway rimmed with alternating sand and dark-red bricks. His eye met two further storeys as his gaze ascended to the roof, where a pair of dormer windows with scalloped lead flashing confirmed that the owners had "gone into the loft" as the jargon had it.

He'd stopped on the way through Hampstead village to pick up a bottle of white burgundy and a second of elderflower fizz. Having no children of his own, and virtually no experience of other people's, he'd made a stab at presents he thought might be suitable for Fariyah and Simon's. In an upmarket stationer on Heath Street named Bunthorne's, the only shop still open, he'd bought black Moleskine notebooks and Lamy fountain pens, in bright shades of ice-blue, apple-green and buttercup-yellow.

"I'm sure they'll love them," the eager, bespectacled shop assistant said, though for Gabriel it was more of a shot in the dark than anything else. Did kids even *know* how to write anymore? Weren't they all blogging? Or on Instagram? She'd seemed young enough to be one of Fariyah's children herself though, so maybe she was right.

He mounted the stone steps, feeling unaccountably nervous, and stopped on the half-landing to take a couple of breaths and to close his eyes briefly to focus on lowering his heart rate. Then, eyes open again, he continued up to the front door and rang the bell.

MEET THE FAMILY

Fariyah answered the door a few seconds later. Over the time he had known her, Gabriel had become fascinated with the range of colourful hijabs she wore. Today's was a soft rust, shot through with glittering yellow threads that picked up a gold tone in her coffee-brown skin. Her almond-shaped eyes were twinkling with what looked like genuine pleasure at seeing him, and he felt his shoulders dropping and relaxing.

"Gabriel," she said, smiling. "Welcome to my home. Come in."

Knowing she wouldn't touch a man not part of her family, Gabriel made no move to hug or kiss her, but stepped past her into the cool of a black-and-white tiled hallway. An eclectic mixture of art covered the walls, from small black-and-white drawings to colourful watercolours and oils. The effect was humorous, rather than jarring, expressing an almost exuberant attitude to collecting and displaying pictures the owners were attracted to.

"Thanks. I brought these," Gabriel said, holding up the bags from Bunthorne's and the off-licence.

"We're all down the end," Fariyah said. "Let's see what booty you've brought in the kitchen."

She led him to a big kitchen painted robins-egg blue and spacious enough to accommodate a large, scrubbed-pine table and six chairs as well as a couple of saggy sofas upholstered in bright floral fabrics. The large room smelled deliciously of lamb, cumin and garlic. More pictures adorned the walls, including a large family portrait photograph taken against a white background. One wall was covered from knee to head height with framed certificates for music exams passed, usually, Gabriel noticed, with distinction: piano, violin, saxophone and guitar. A white-painted pillar, clearly the remains of a long-gone dividing wall, was marked with an ascending column of overlapping pencil and pen marks: short horizontal lines with accompanying dates, heights and initials: A, J and P.

Sitting at the table, hunched over a maths textbook, was a teenaged boy, a floppy fringe of deep-brown hair obscuring his eyes. On the sofas checking their phones sat two girls. One looked to be about 18, the other younger, though Gabriel couldn't figure out by how much. And standing at the stove, tasting something from a wooden spoon, a man in his early fifties wearing a green apron. He returned the spoon to a space beside the hob and wiped his hand on his apron before offering it to Gabriel.

"Hi, Gabriel. I'm Simon. Let me introduce our brood." He pointed to the boy sitting at the table. "This is Alexis."

Alexis looked up and Gabriel was struck immediately by his resemblance to his father. Although he had Fariyah's colouring, his bone structure was exactly the same as his father's: high cheekbones and a narrow, angular jaw. He stood and shook Gabriel's hand.

"Pleased to meet you, Gabriel," he said with a shy smile that revealed braces, before resuming his homework.

Before Simon could introduce her, the older girl got up from the sofa and came to stand closer to Gabriel, sticking out her hand.

"Hi, Gabriel. I'm Persia. I know men find it impossible to judge children's ages, so I'm sixteen. Alexis is fourteen going on twenty-five and Juno," she pointed at the younger girl who had stayed sitting but was regarding Gabriel with a smiling, open face, "is twelve."

Gabriel instinctively liked the rest of Fariyah's family, with their friendly faces and easy social skills. He remembered having none of the same ease as the child of the British Ambassador in Hong Kong, instead being browbeaten and sometimes plain beaten into behaving appropriately. My turn, he thought.

"Hello all of you. Simon, Persia, Alexis and Juno. I brought these," he said for the second time, proffering the two bags, one paper, the other plastic.

Persia took them from him while her parents looked on. She seemed to be quite happy playing the role of hostess. Or at the very least *aide de camp* to the true hostess, Fariyah.

"Thanks," she said smiling. "Now, this one clinks. Let's assume it's wine and, ooh!" she said, peering inside, "sparkling elderflower, lovely!"

She looked inside the paper bag from Bunthorne's and this time the smile was genuine surprise rather than the arch display Gabriel felt she'd put on for the drinks.

"Wow! Come and look, you two. Gabriel's a stationery geek like us."

Alexis and Juno stood to crowd round their elder sister as she retrieved the notebooks and fountain pens. Each chose a colour without squabbles, then, after effusively thanking Gabriel, retired with the notebooks to begin writing immediately.

Fariyah spoke.

"That was really generous, Gabriel. And completely unnecessary—"

"No it wasn't!" Juno called from the sofa.

"—but thank you. Let's get some drinks poured, then perhaps you'd like to come through to the conservatory and we can have a chat."

Simon opened the wine, which was already cool, having come from the off-licence's fridge, and poured two glasses, handing one to Gabriel, who gratefully took a large gulp. Then he opened the elderflower and poured a long glass for Fariyah, before adding a slice of lime and rough chunks of ice from a bulbous, cream, upright freezer in the corner.

* * *

Sitting facing Fariyah in a huge wicker armchair padded with more floral cushions, Gabriel set his glass down on a side table with a *clink*. Waiting. Fariyah took a sip of her drink then copied Gabriel. She smiled. And waited.

"Shall I start?" Gabriel asked, rubbing at the back of his neck and feeling unaccountably nervous.

"Why not? You're between operations, I'm guessing?"

"Yes. The last one was personal. This one is official."

"Tell me, how did the personal one go?"

Gabriel smiled at the memory of his final meal with Terri-Ann Calder and JJ Highsmith. The widow and her imposing yet gentle Texas Ranger friend.

"It went well."

"Do you remember last time we talked about your need for redemption? And that ultimately God – or whoever you choose to believe in – judges us on our actions, not our desires? How do you feel now?"

Gabriel scratched at his scalp before running his hand over his hair and down onto the back of his neck again.

"Better, I think. I did what I promised I would. I investigated my friend's death. His murder, as it turned out. I put things right. I brought some sort of resolution to Terri-Ann's pain. And I didn't get anyone killed."

Fariyah's finely arched eyebrows lifted very slightly.

"Nobody?" she asked.

"I didn't *get* anyone killed. We should probably leave it there."

Fariyah smiled and nodded.

"We probably should."

Gabriel recalled her telling him the first time they'd met that she'd worked as an army psychiatrist. It explained her realistic attitude to his work and the business of killing. It was one of the things that helped him be open with her.

"But there's something else. Something bothering me that I can't quite put my finger on."

"Tell me."

"It's about Michael."

"Your brother."

"Yes."

"Do you still have trouble believing his death wasn't your fault? That would be completely understandable."

Gabriel shook his head and took a hurried sip of the wine.

"Not exactly. I mean, part of me does, but I've accepted that I was only a child. Like he was."

"Then what's troubling you?"

Gabriel frowned and sighed, trying to articulate the strange feeling he'd been experiencing that Michael was trying to tell him something. From so long ago and so far away. Something important.

"I remembered how he was always so confident when we played rugby together. He was always trying to boss me around. I know it's important but I don't know why."

Now it was Fariyah's turn to frown.

"That's very interesting. Perhaps because you've begun to make peace with yourself for your perceived – and I stress the word *perceived* – shortcomings as a brother, as a friend, as a leader, you're becoming more open to new ways of seeing the world. And about your own history."

Gabriel shrugged.

"Maybe I am. But how can I get to this, this, *thing* I have stuffed away in my head like a loose round at the bottom of a kitbag?"

"A very apt analogy. Are you worried if you touch it, it might go off in your face?"

"Honestly? I don't know. How could it be any worse than first forgetting I had a brother and then discovering I caused his death?"

Gabriel caught a warning look in Fariyah's dark-brown eyes. He smiled, ruefully, reflecting not for the first time that seeing a shrink was a bit like taking truth serum. There wasn't any point trying to deceive them. Or yourself, come to that. "OK, OK, discovering I was playing with him when he died?"

"Maybe you're right," Fariyah conceded. "How about this? I know you like to work fast, and as we may not be seeing each other for some time, are you willing to be hypnotised?"

Used to employing the self-hypnosis techniques taught him by Master Zhao, Gabriel assented at once.

"Ready when you are, Doc," he said with a smile.

He settled back into the chair's comfortable embrace and prepared himself mentally and physically. He deepened his breathing, falling back on the simple ten-second breath. *In for four, hold for one, out for four, hold for one. Rinse and repeat.* And he let his shoulders become heavy, focusing on unwinding each muscle group in turn, from the sternocleidomastoid that connects the jaw to the neck and shoulder, the trapezius, the wing-like latissimus dorsi, and down through the intercostal muscles of the ribcage to the abs and lower back, the quads, hamstrings, calves and, finally, his feet and toes. As he tensed then released each group of muscles, he felt a familiar warmth and weight descending on him, and he realised with pleasure that his anxiety had abated.

Fariyah began speaking. He knew it was a specialised sequence of verbal commands, but that helped rather than hindered him: he *wanted* to go under. *Needed* to.

"Focus on your breathing, Gabriel, but also listen to the sounds in the room. The birds outside the window. The cars driving by at the end of the garden. Any planes in the sky. Do you hear them?"

"Yes."

"Picture the number nine and say 'ten' in your head."

Ten ... ten ... ten ...

"Picture eight and say *nine*."

Nine ... nine ...

"Think of the fifth letter in the alphabet. Make it a big painting of that letter."

E

"What colour is it?"

"It's bright green."

"Picture seven and say *eight*."

Seven ... no, eight ...

SIBLING RIVALRY

Fariyah's voice came from far away.

"Do you hear the birds singing?"

"Yeah."

"Picture zero and say *one*."

Birdsong ... zero ... B ... Fariyah's voice is here but I'm not there. Where am I?

"Can you hear me, Gabriel?" Fariyah's voice asks inside his head.

"Yes."

"You're nine years old now. A boy again. And we're in Hong Kong," Fariyah's voice says. "In the park by Victoria Harbour. Tell me what the weather's like."

"It's hot. The sun is shining. I'm really sweaty."

"What can you see, Gabriel? What can you see?"

Gabriel looks around. There's Mummy, sitting on the bench with her book. He waves. She waves back and smiles. She's so beautiful. The most beautiful lady in the whole world. The grass is turning brown in the heat. But it's still good for playing rugby on. There's a big flower bed on one side of the park. It's planted with big fluffy white roses. They smell sweet, like peaches. He tells the lady inside his head. She asks him another question.

"Michael's there, and your Mum. Her name's Lin, isn't it?"

"Yes. But I call her Mummy."

"You two boys are playing with your rugby ball."

"We love it. Michael's really good, even if he's a little squirt."

"He likes telling you what to do, doesn't he?"

He looks over at Michael. He's sticking his tongue out and waggling his fingers in his ears.

"Yes. He's always trying to boss me around."

"Even though you're the older one?"

"Yes. He says I have to do what he tells me."

"So you kick the ball for him to catch. Then what?"

"He says I'm not kicking it high enough. He says, 'Kick it higher, Gable. You're useless.'"

"What's happening now?"

Gabriel looks down at the grass. He sees his right heel hacking out a divot to support the ball. Sees his two hands holding the orange ball, placing it carefully in the dent, tilting it back a little. Then he backs up. Looks at the ball. Backs up some more. And runs. Michael is shouting at him to make it a good one.

"I kick it as high as I can."

"What happens, Gabriel? When you kick the ball so high?"

"It flies up in the sky. Right over Michael's head. It's gone in the water. Michael couldn't catch it."

"Now what? What are you telling him?"

Michael is laughing. He's pulling his T-shirt over his head and treading the heels down on his trainers to push them off. He turns his back on me and walks to the harbour wall at the edge of the park. Mummy hasn't even looked up. She told us to play quietly but that was ages ago.

"Nothing."

"Nothing? Why, nothing? Are you sure? Don't you want the ball back?"

I don't want to see this next bit. I don't want to!

"Yes, but Michael's bossing me again."

"What is he saying?"

"He says, 'I'll get it. Watch me, Gable.' He's climbed over the wall and dived into the water. He's ... Michael! No! Mummy! Come quick! Michael's ... I can't see him, he's ... No!"

The lady in his head sounds worried. Not cross, exactly. But she doesn't sound so friendly anymore.

"Listen to me, Gabriel. Come back with me. I'm going to count to three and when I say 'three' you will wake up and be here with me. One, two, three."

* * *

Gabriel opened his eyes and sat bolt upright in the armchair. He was panting and staring at Fariyah. He spoke, though in his head his voice sounded leaden and flat.

"It wasn't me."

Fariyah shook her head, smiling softly at him.

"It appears not."

"But how come I thought I'd ordered him into the water to get it? If he made the decision, why did I blame myself for all these years?"

Fariyah clasped her hands in her lap. Looked down at them, then up at Gabriel.

"Perhaps, as his older brother, you felt it was your duty to protect him. To look after him. Your subconscious found it impossible to accept that he had dived in voluntarily, so it fabricated a story that fitted with your moral outlook. I know you took personal responsibility for Smudge's death, though that, too, was not your fault."

"Maybe not my fault, but he was one of my men. He was my responsibility."

"I know. And I think that is simply an aspect of your character, an unchanging aspect. It is part of what makes you the man you are."

Gabriel furrowed his brow, clasping his hands together as if in prayer and bringing them to his pursed lips. *How could I have got it so wrong? Blaming myself for Michael's death when all along it was him who decided to go in after the ball?*

Fariyah was consulting a notebook. Then she looked up at him. She looked troubled. *Oh no, what now?*

"Something wrong, Doc? I mean apart from my memory?"

"Not wrong. But there's something you said a couple of appointments ago that I wanted to check with you. It has to do with Michael. Normally we would have got to this within a month or so, but your ... unpredictable ... schedule means that months can turn into years."

"Go on, then."

"Can you tell me that story again about when you realised you hated him?"

Gabriel scratched at his scalp. Reaching back into his memory twice over, he located, first, the time he'd talked to Fariyah about his intense feelings of jealousy when Michael was born, and second, the incident that seemed to mark the beginning of those feelings of possessiveness towards their mother.

"It was my third birthday. It's my earliest memory. I remember it clearly because the cook made me a big birthday cake, and my Dad gathered all the staff for a tea party that afternoon. I was in my bath after the party. Mum was sitting on a towel chest, feeding Michael. Breastfeeding him, I mean. You know, he was just this little baby. All red and wrinkly. I climbed out and punched her legs. Then, later, after she'd put us both to bed, I went into the nursery and looked into his cot. He was all wrapped up in a little blue blanket and I remember wanting to kill him. Wanting him to be dead so I could have her all to myself again."

Fariyah's normally smooth forehead furrowed again.

"Mothers normally only breastfeed until six months. Maybe a year if they're able. Your description of Michael makes him sound younger. But can you see the problem with this picture?"

"What, you mean apart from a psychopathic toddler wanting to kill his baby brother?"

"Yes, apart from that."

Gabriel looked up at the ceiling. A broad-bladed fan revolved slowly, wafting cooler air down across his forehead. Through an open window, a sudden gust of wind brought the scent of roses into the conservatory from the garden beyond. The same scent as he'd smelled in the carpark at Marlborough Lines. The same scent given off by the roses down in Victoria Park and outside his boyhood bedroom. Something was battering at the doors of his conscious mind. Something about the baby. About the toddler. The little baby. And the three-year-old toddler.

The truth came like a slap.

He looked at Fariyah, the synapses in his brain all firing at once, so that he felt illuminated from within by a bright, white light.

"I was too young!"

Fariyah nodded, her face impassive.

"You were three. The baby was somewhere between newborn and a year old. Michael wouldn't be born for another year."

"But how? First the harbour and now this?"

She shook her head.

"There's no easy answer to that question. But let's take a step back here and look at what we know. One, you were in no way responsible for Michael's death. You need some time to process that, but I think that's tremendously positive. Guilt is a destructive emotion, as I think you know, and this is a huge burden you can lay down. Two, it appears that there was a third child. A middle child."

"Of whom I have no memory. Or only that one. Did it die?"

Fariyah sighed, then she smiled a small, tight-lipped smile. Coming from her, it seemed an impossibly sad expression.

"It looks as though he, or she, might have. Otherwise, they would have grown up with you and, even if you were living with Master Zhao, you would have known about them."

Gabriel shook his head. He reached for his glass and drained it. It had warmed up in the time he had been sitting with Fariyah and tasted acidic.

"I ... I need to find out what happened. This is just, I mean, I came to see you because of Michael and now there's, you know, I had another brother, or a sister. At least for a little while."

"It sounds as though you need to do some research in Hong Kong. Or perhaps our old friend Google would be the place to start." She checked her watch. "I think that's plenty for today. Let's end it here and join the others. I can smell something lovely coming from the kitchen."

* * *

Gabriel drank only water at dinner. He supposed the lamb stew and rice Simon had cooked tasted delicious, though he could barely register the sensation as he put each forkful into his mouth. The talk ebbed and flowed, and the three Crace children were lively conversationalists. If he contributed, he forgot instantly what he had said. After a dessert of rose petal jelly and tiny cups of thick, sweet coffee with almond biscuits, Fariyah stood and motioned to Gabriel to join her as she left the kitchen.

Standing in the hall, she looked into his eyes. Her forehead below the smooth folded edge of the hijab was furrowed with concern.

"Are you all right?"

Gabriel inhaled deeply then sighed the air out in a rush.

"I'm not sure, to be honest."

"Would you like to stay here tonight? We have plenty of room."

"I think I'm going to head back, if it's OK with you? The drive will do me good and that coffee was strong enough to wake the dead. Sorry, bad choice of words."

"It's fine. Go, then. But drive carefully. And call me when you can. I'm always here for you, Gabriel, you know that."

Gabriel returned to the kitchen to say goodbye, then left.

As he twisted the key in the ignition, he checked the mirror, then reversed into the road and pulled away, resisting the almost-overpowering urge to slam his foot down on the throttle.

With each passing mile, the traffic lessened. He tried and mostly succeeded in keeping his speed below 100 mph. Then, on the A303, he was alone. The digital clock on the dashboard said 11.30 p.m. He checked his mirror. No black SUV racing up behind him, gaping maw threatening to swallow him whole. He looked forwards. No red lights in the distance. The road ahead swept down and to the right in a long, sweeping curve. Now he did what he had been resisting since Hampstead.

With a yowl from its turbocharged engine, the RS3 leapt forwards under the urging of Gabriel's right foot. Someone at The Department had specced, or added, a head-up display. Seeming to float twenty feet in front of the windscreen, green numerals registered the car's increasing speed. Whoever had added the head-up display had also removed the speed limiter. Steering into the bend, Gabriel watched the ghostly numerals shimmer through 155 mph and continue ticking up. At 170, the engine was roaring. Gabriel held his arms firm, without locking his elbows, and powered on down the road and exited the bend at 174. Then it happened. An audible snap inside his head like a safety catch being flicked off.

He had the same, mad desire that seemed to afflict him more and more these days. To stop steering into the bend and let the car run off the carriageway. Onto the hard shoulder. Then into and through the barrier, until it all ended in a spectacular crash that would make his and Eli's previous adventure behind the wheel look like a fairground ride, and he, Gabriel Wolfe, would be rendered into his constituent parts, to join Michael, his unknown sibling, his parents, his dead friends and comrades and Master Zhao, and all his many targets.

"No!" he shouted.

He gripped the wheel tighter and eased off the power until the small bomb in which he was encased slowed through the triple-figures and broke the ton – in the right direction this time. The road straightened and he resumed an 80-mph cruising speed, letting his breath normalise. When the adrenaline coursing through his bloodstream had dissipated, he pulled over and brought the car to a stop. Then he opened the driver's door, rushed round to the nearside of the car and threw up onto the long grass beyond the Armco, holding onto the sharp-edged metal barrier for support. Blowing his nose and dabbing the tears from his eyes, he climbed back into the cabin.

He leaned back and closed his eyes, gently massaging his stomach.

When will it end? Just when I thought I'd come to terms with Michael's death I discover I was one of three children.

He kept his eyes closed and slowly drifted into a place somewhere between waking and sleeping. Waiting for the pain in his gut to subside and the voices in his head to quieten.

A sharp rapping on the window jerked him out of his semi-trance. He opened his eyes and looked right to see a traffic cop peering in, his silver beard glistening in the light from his torch, which he was shining directly at Gabriel's face.

GOING TOO FAST

Gabriel checked the rearview mirror. A police car in chequered trim was parked a few yards back. He buzzed the window down. If the cop had been alerted to his passage through this part of Wiltshire at over twice the legal limit, Gabriel would need the famed "Get Out of Jail Free" card possessed by all Department operators.

"Everything all right, sir?" the cop asked, his voice not unfriendly, though his eyes were narrowed with suspicion, or maybe it was just in response to the bright light of his own torch.

Suddenly, Gabriel had an uncomfortable thought. *What if he's not a cop? What if he's with the same crew who barged us off the road?* He scanned the front of the cop's hi-vis vest but couldn't see a telltale bulge that would indicate a firearm.

"Yes, officer. Sorry. I had dinner with friends and something must have disagreed with me. I had to stop to be sick."

"Dinner?"

"Yes. In London."

"Whereabouts in London, sir, if you don't mind my asking?"

Gabriel realised what the cop was doing, but his mind was fuzzy and he couldn't think fast enough. Hesitating would look bad.

"Hampstead."

The cop smiled.

"Nice. And you left your friend's house when?"

"Er, not sure exactly. Ten thirty?"

The cop made a great show of consulting his watch.

"Well, you've made *extremely* good time. It's only eleven forty-five now, so you made it from Hampstead all the way to here in just an hour and a quarter."

Gabriel started mentally preparing himself for what would come next, visualising the scene where he handed over the white rectangle of plastic with a Government crest on it and a phone number.

"There wasn't much traffic."

"There can't have been! That's, what, a seventy-mile trip? Let's see." The cop looked upwards. Then back at Gabriel. "If my maths is correct – and I did get an 'A' in my GCSE – you averaged fifty-six for the journey."

"Is that good?"

"Good? It's bloody amazing! Stick to the speed limits all the way, did you, sir? In Hampstead and round the North Circular?"

Honesty is the best policy. Gabriel smiled and aimed for a sheepish look.

"I may have gone over it once or twice, officer. When the roads were empty, you know?"

The cop scratched his chin. He was still squatting at the window and Gabriel was willing to bet his quads were screaming.

"OK, look. Let's not muck about," the cop said, finally. "Car like this? Middle of the night? Empty roads? You've been caning it. From the noises coming from under the bonnet I'd say your engine's just short of melting point. I can't smell any alcohol on you and you seem to have your wits about you. But for the rest of your journey, I want you to stick to sixty, OK? Where are you headed?

"Marlborough Lines."

"Soldier?"

"Ex. I'm with the Ministry of Defence now."

"Fine. I'm going to follow you to the turnoff. We'll call it one public servant helping another, shall we?"

So, for the remaining portion of his journey, Gabriel trundled along like the pensioner he'd railed at on his previous drive down the A303. He switched the cruise control to 59 mph, with his Battenburg-liveried escort maintaining a fixed, if discreet distance behind him. When he turned off, the cop roared past, giving him a double-toot on the horn and a wave.

He was in bed beside Eli twenty minutes later.

"How'd it go with Fariyah?" she mumbled. She smelled of massage oil.

"I'll tell you tomorrow. Go back to sleep."

"OK, Boss. Night."

"Night."

But Gabriel didn't sleep. Not until much, much later.

* * *

The following morning, he roused Eli and, while they dressed, explained about his session with Fariyah the previous evening.

"That's amazing. She's really good, isn't she?" Eli said through a mouthful of toothpaste foam.

"That's one way of putting it. But now what? I mean, I thought my life was complicated enough, but now it's like a fucking great jigsaw where someone ripped the picture off the box.

She spat into the basin, then turned and put a hand on his cheek.

"Let's talk more tonight over a bottle of wine. Right now, we need breakfast. What time did Sam say we had to be at the Plain?"

"Eight thirty."

"OK. It's seven now. Come on. Let's get going."

BRIEFING ROOM 17D

TEHRAN

Its present occupants would have denied the fact strenuously, had they known it. But Briefing Room 17D at the Iranian Ministry of Intelligence and Security on Delgosha Alley could have been lifted directly from the CIA's headquarters in Langley, Virginia. Or, for that matter, from MI6's in London, Mossad's in Tel Aviv, the FSB's in Moscow or countless other security service buildings from Ankara to Tokyo. That is to say, unimaginative institutional decorators, or those who wrote the rules they followed, had selected for the walls the sludgy green of stagnant pond water. The boardroom table that almost filled the fourteen-by-fourteen-foot space was of highly polished mahogany. The seats were mesh-backed, black leather, swivel numbers. And a matrix of four plasma TV screens entirely covered one wall from waist-height to the ceiling. In the centre of the table a black plastic conference-calling module crouched like a giant black spider, from which someone had pulled all but three, fat legs.

Facing the black screens sat General Omar Razi, head of the

MOIS. Next to him sat the third-most-powerful cleric in Iran, Ayatollah Sharpour Al-Khemenah.

"General Razi, sir. I have Blacksmith on the line. Shall I patch him in?"

Razi came from an old Persian family who had served the Shah during his reign and the previous members of the Pahlavi dynasty who had ruled Persia/Iran for two and a half thousand uninterrupted years. After the 1979 revolution, they had skilfully manoeuvred their way back into the corridors of power. His father had also been a military man, though in a frontline combat regiment rather than in the intelligence role he once told his son was little more than "creeping about listening at keyholes." Nevertheless, he respected the old man, and had heeded his words that, "One should always be courteous to those under one's command. Shouting is for bullies and weak men."

Now, he leaned towards the microphone placed on the polished wood in front of him.

"If you would be so kind."

"Very good, General."

The black spider clicked once, then, as though he were sitting in the next-door office, the man known as Blacksmith, came on the line.

"Good afternoon, gentlemen. I hope you are all well," he said in Farsi.

Razi rubbed at his nose. Despite the vetting they had devoted to the Englishman, he was never entirely comfortable holding conversations with him. If he turned out to be a plant by the British, then Razi would very quickly get to experience all the delights of the MOIS basement that he himself had been instrumental in developing. The fact that the mole spoke Farsi perfectly did nothing to reassure him.

"We are fine, thank you, Blacksmith. In the room with me I have His Excellency Ayatollah Sharpour Al-Khemenah."

The long-bearded cleric sat silently, his bony, liver-spotted hands folded on the table in front of him. His skin was papery and his eyes were deeply hooded, a feature that had earned him the reverential nickname, *'Eqab*: "The Eagle." Though nobody in possession of this knowledge would ever dare to utter the name in his presence, or that of any cleric for that matter. He looked at Razi and nodded. Just the slightest tilt of his turbaned head, but Razi had been waiting for the signal: *Begin.*

"You have something for us?" Razi asked, speaking into the mic, but keeping his gaze locked onto the cleric's.

"The British Government has received intelligence, which it regards as completely credible, that the Islamic Republic of Iran is within sight of its strategic goal of developing, if not actually firing, a low-yield nuclear warhead. It has also identified Dr Darbandi as the principal architect of the technological breakthrough."

"And?" Razi asked, maintaining a calm exterior yet fighting down a writhing sense of anxiety mixed with anger that threatened to burst free of his chest. Who had betrayed them?

"And they are moving to take Dr Darbandi off the board."

"Stop talking in riddles. Speak plainly."

"An assassin, General. They are sending an assassin to kill Dr Darbandi."

Razi burst out laughing. The cleric remained impassive, although between his luxuriant beard and hooded eagle's eyes, there wasn't a great deal of his face left visible from which to draw conclusions about his mood. His long fingers remained motionless on the polished wood of the table.

"This is a joke, surely. How could the British even find him, let alone infiltrate an agent – an assassin! – into Iran? Why it's—"

The voice that interrupted the general was impatient, which perhaps explained the breach of protocol.

"Entirely possible, General. My apologies, but you should prepare for the assassin."

"Then tell me. Who is this, this assassin?"

"His name is Wolfe. He is ex-Special Forces. The SAS, General. A very dangerous and resourceful man."

The cleric leaned across and whispered in his right ear. Razi nodded, and smiled. He spoke in English for the first time.

"His Excellency says if the British send a *goorgh* to us, we shall meet it with a *sheyer*."

Blacksmith answered, also in English.

"A lion to catch a wolf. Almost Koranic in its poetry."

The cleric frowned at the only word in the Englishman's sentence he vaguely understood.

"Be careful, my friend," Razi said, switching back to Farsi. "You are offering us a valuable service, but that does not give you the right to utter blasphemies."

"My apologies General, and also to you, Your Excellency. I meant no offence."

"In view of the service you are rendering, we can overlook your ..." Razi paused. "... unfortunate language. We will need background on the assassin, Wolfe."

"Yes, General. I have prepared a dossier. I can hand it over to Head of Security Gul in person here in London."

Razi looked at the cleric. He nodded imperceptibly, little more than a one-degree tilt of the turban. The meeting was over.

THE THIN BLUE LINE

Callie sat, head sandwiched between her hands, her cheeks squashed inwards by her palms. On her desk was a short report, detailing Stella's preliminary findings. They didn't amount to much.

The Mercedes had been supplied new by a main dealer in Manchester. According to the sales rep who closed the sale the customer was – the classic layman's description – "average." Pressed, she had admitted the gentleman might have had a tattoo on his hand.

Which hand?

The left. Or the right.

Which, Callie felt, just about covered it.

An email to the Department of Vehicle Licensing and Administration had yielded a single hard fact, but one of negligible value. The new owner was a company registered in Panama: Rovy Ltd.

Some fast-tracked forensic accounting had revealed that Rovy Ltd was wholly owned by a corporation registered in Delaware: Sarastro, Inc. And Sarastro, Inc. was owned entirely by an offshore family trust in Guernsey. The trust was administered by a firm of lawyers – Cecil, Francis, Meyrick (Partners) LLP – domiciled in the Bahamas. And the beneficial owner of the law firm was another family trust, based in the Cayman Islands whose sole trustee (name withheld) was a resident of Bahrain and a director of a firm called ... Rovy Ltd.

The physical evidence was just as inconclusive.

The CSIs who had crawled all over and into the GLS had recovered multiple fingerprints from at least seven individuals. Those of Gabriel Wolfe, Eli Schochat and Stella Cole had been quickly eliminated. The remaining prints, all of excellent quality, had yielded precisely no hits in the British police database. Requests had been sent to Europol, INTERPOL and the FBI. Results pending.

Hairs and epithelial cells from the car's interior had been sampled for DNA. Results pending.

The four bodies had been sent to front of the queue in the morgue, where the pathologist had begun work. Cause of death in all four cases had been straightforwardly established. In his usual, dry style, the pathologist gave these as:

1. Brain injury from penetration by the victim's own nasal bones.

2. Both carotid arteries and both jugular veins torn open by sharp metallic object. Stab wound to heart, which penetrated right atrium.

3. Gunshot wound to the head. 9mm hollow-point round.

4. Gunshot wound to chest. Left lung partially destroyed. 9mm hollow-point round.

Tissue samples had been sent out for DNA testing. Results pending.

Bodies had been fingerprinted and prints sent for identification. Results pending.

The station's armourer had test-fired all the weapons and was running tests to cross-check the striations on the bullets against police and security service databases. Results pending.

The phones had been sent to an external lab. Results pending.

A translator had been sent photos of the Russian tattoos. Results pending.

Callie had begun her career in Edinburgh. Not the world's

roughest city to be sure, but even so, she'd dealt with – and solved – her fair share of murders. But nothing like these. And what was even more infuriating, solving these killings wasn't even her job. The, what, perpetrators? Doers? Hitters? Killers? Well, whatever she ought to call them, they were already known. One, to her personally. And apparently it was all perfectly fine and dandy.

Don, fucking – *Sorry Mum* – Webster wanted to know who the dead men were and that was it. Which was the real source of her anguish. Because she had nothing to tell him. Despite all those infuriating "results pending" notes, in her heart, and with her copper's intuition, Callie could save everyone a whole lot of trouble with her own, bleak assessment. *They're ghosts.*

She thought back to her latest trip to the morgue. The pathologist had revealed each man's face in turn. Callie thought it would be a wee while before she'd forget the ruined visage of the man who'd been impaled on needle-pointed shards of his own skull. Then their torsos.

"Look at them, Callie," he'd said. "These were fit men. Extremely fit. Very little body fat. Plenty of scars, either from edged weapons, shrapnel or bullet wounds. Plenty of tattoos. Tanned, but not from a sunbed. You can see they were somewhere hot wearing short-sleeved shirts."

"Soldiers?" she'd asked him.

"Men of action, certainly."

She stared at him, willing him to abandon his customary caution. He sighed and spoke again.

"In all likelihood, yes. Either current or former military personnel. Will that do?"

* * *

She muttered into the space between the heels of her hands.

"Our four corpses are ex-soldiers. Mercenaries, probably. If and when we discover their identities, we'll learn that they have no criminal records, either here or wherever they came from. Their careers after leaving the army will be blanks."

She called Don Webster. Might as well get it out of the way, then at least she could spend a little of her dwindling day doing something more productive.

"My dear Callie. What can you tell me about our four soldiers of fortune?"

"Apart from the fact that I tend to agree with you about their career choice, almost nothing. We're fast-tracking DNA results, fingerprints and ballistics, and we've requests out with our international colleagues but to be honest, Don—"

"You think we're going to come up empty-handed?"

Inwardly she thanked him for saying "we" rather than "you."

"I'm afraid so. The car was a bust, too. It's registered to an offshore company that basically seems to own itself through a tangle of other equally opaque entities."

"Hmm, mm-hmm. Is there anything at all you can give me? I appreciate that I did rather spring this upon you."

Callie sighed and ran a hand through her hair.

"The facts, such as they are, are these. The offshore company is called Rovy Ltd. It's registered in Panama. The man who originally bought the car had a tattoo on one of his hands. The four DBs downstairs have a lot of ink, too."

"What sort?"

"You know, the usual. Naked girls, skulls, guns, a couple of tribals, yin and yang, the usual shit. Oh, and one of them has some Russian words and a rather well-executed picture of Saint Basil's Cathedral in Red Square."

Don paused. Mm-hmmed again in that breathy way Callie had learned meant he was thinking.

"Thanks, Callie," he finally said. "Let me know if anything turns up from your tests, but please don't worry if nothing does. I have a feeling the gentlemen I sent you were very carefully selected for their anonymity."

He ended the call. Callie stared at the screen until it faded.

"Bloody spooks," she said.

Then she picked up her phone again.

NEVER DISCUSS RELIGION OR POLITICS

Gabriel checked his watch: 8.30 a.m.

"Bit colder in Iran than I'd been expecting," he said to Eli, with a grin.

Five minutes earlier, they'd climbed out of an army-supplied Land Rover that Gabriel had parked beside two identical vehicles on the outskirts of a village of dusty, white houses. They walked to the central square, where an army officer in battle dress and a second man dressed in chinos and a lightweight summer jacket with open-necked shirt were standing talking to a woman dressed in a sea-green hoodie and boot-cut jeans over a pair of turquoise and grey Converse baseball boots. Sam.

As they drew closer, Gabriel recognised the man in civvies. It was Hugh Bennett, their SIS liaison. The officer, a captain, introduced himself as James Gaddesden.

"Aha!" Sam said, a smile lighting up her heart-shaped face. "My favourite Department operator. Ever ready with an original quip about magnetic watches and invisible submarines. And you've brought a friend."

Sam turned to Eli and stuck out her hand. The two women shook.

"Eli Schochat. Late of Mossad."

Gabriel noticed Gaddesden's lip curl fractionally. But Eli was asking Sam a question, and he refocused on his partner.

"What did you mean about magnetic watches?"

Sam smiled.

"Gabriel here, and your boss Don Webster, added their names to a very long list of people who visited me in the Quartermaster's room in Vauxhall Cross and thought it amusing to make James Bond jokes."

While the two men looked on, grinning, Gabriel held his hands up in surrender.

"Guilty as charged. But you have to admit, Sam, you do have the best toys. It's just we both felt you were keeping the really good kit back."

Sam prodded Gabriel in the chest, hard, though she was still smiling. The skin at the corners of her eyes, which were the colour of wet slate, crinkled with good humour.

"One, they're not toys." Prod.

"Two, I seem to remember you took some of my really good kit with you." Prod. "Or are depleted uranium pistol rounds not sufficiently exciting for you?"

"No, no. The DU rounds performed brilliantly. I apologise. It won't happen again."

Hands in pockets, affecting a casual pose, Eli spoke.

"So if *I* can ask a question, Sam?"

"Of course. Go ahead."

"When Gabriel and I go over to Iran ..."

"Yes?"

"Will we both get jet packs, or only him?"

Sam's mouth dropped open as the other two guests guffawed. Gabriel joined in and was amazed at Eli's poker face.

"You're just as bad as he is! Jesus! I'm going to have a word with Mr Webster the next time I see him. I'll send his next lot off with spud guns and a catapult."

Bennett interrupted.

"Hilarious though this all is, I wonder whether we might make a start?"

He phrased his words as a question, but there was no mistaking the implied rebuke. *We didn't come up here to listen to a pair of off-the-books comedians bantering about secret agents.*

Collecting himself, Gabriel nodded. Gaddesden began. He told them he worked in what he described, vaguely, as "Strategy." Thinking that during his own service, he and his mates would have regarded Gaddesden as a "desk jockey," Gabriel asked him what his job entailed.

"Basically, we're war planners. Everything from getting a pallet of water to a bunch of guys in the desert to taking over a country. And, of course, everything in between. We helped reconfigure this little place to match what we know of Vareshabad. Shall we go?"

Together, the three men and two women walked down the central street, which ran arrow-straight for a quarter of a mile between low-rise apartment blocks built of the same, white-painted concrete as the houses on the edge of the village. The strategy guys had gone to great lengths to make the place feel real. Cars and trucks were parked on the street, mostly painted white and authentically dented and dusty. Here and there, children's bikes lay on their sides against the kerb. But the absence of any other people gave the assemblage of buildings and artefacts the feel of a ghost town. Gabriel shivered despite the early-summer warmth. *Absence of the normal. But what's normal about a man working towards the destruction of a whole country, a whole people?*

At the far end of the street, between a mocked-up petrol station and a two-storey dwelling, its walls pockmarked with bullet holes, someone had planted a rudimentary street sign.

< Jerusalem 1246 m
Nuclear bomb factory 4 m >

"Someone's got a sense of humour," Sam said.

"It's the chaps in logistics," Gaddesden replied. "Whenever they get a brief to create a special location, they delight in hand-painting appropriate road signs."

"It's because they don't get to blow it all to shit," he added. "Unlike you chaps." He glanced at Eli. "And chapesses, of course."

She smiled.

"Chapess. I like it. Sadly we won't be blowing it to shit, either."

"No?" Gaddesden said, the surprise evident in his voice.

"More of a surgical strike," Gabriel said, hoping to prevent Eli from revealing the exact purpose of their mission.

"We're going in to kill a scientist," Eli said, smiling sweetly at the captain, and including Sam in the sunny expression.

Gaddesden frowned.

"Assassinating a civilian? Not quite cricket, is it?"

Eli turned to face him directly, keeping the searchlight-bright smile on full power.

"Cricket? No, not really. But then again, nor is blowing up a city with a nuclear missile. So tell me, *Captain Strategy*," Gabriel heard the barely veiled contempt in her voice, and he was sure the others had, too, "What would you suggest we do with him? Smack him on the wrist and ask him politely to cease and desist?"

Gaddesden smiled back, but there was a hard edge to it that Gabriel didn't like.

"Of course not. But you Israelis are never ones for jaw-jaw when you can go for war-war, are you?"

Eli took a step closer to the captain. Gabriel's pulse ticked up by a few beats per minute.

"I beg your pardon?"

Her voice had lost its playfulness and even if the captain couldn't hear it, Gabriel could. He'd heard once before the tone she was using now. The man on the receiving end died a few minutes later, his forehead neatly drilled by a 9mm pistol round.

"I'm sure the captain was joking," Gabriel said, realising how pathetic that sounded even as the words left his lips.

"Yes, come on Gaddesden," Bennett said laying a palm on the

captain's right shoulder. "No need for politics. We're all on the same side."

But Gaddesden wasn't to be placated. He shrugged the spook's hand off with a jerky movement. His face had paled and Gabriel could see the increased muscle tone running from the crown of his head to the toes.

"That's just it, though, isn't it?" Gaddesden continued, writing his own sick note as far as Gabriel was concerned. "We aren't all *on the same side*."

He put air quotes round the final phrase, and Gabriel realised with a sinking feeling that this conversation was only going to end one way. He'd already decided not to intervene unless Bennett did. Two against one – even when the one was Eli Schochat – wasn't exactly cricket, either.

"Meaning?" Eli asked.

"Meaning," Gaddesden repeated, as if speaking to a slow or perhaps stupid person, "that when it suits them, they're allies, and when it doesn't, they'll do deals with the Russians, the South Africans, the Saudis or whoever they think can protect their precious Jewish—"

The move, when it came, was deceptively simple.

Eli hooked her right foot around Gaddesden's left and delivered a lightning-fast, open-palm strike into Gaddesden's solar plexus.

His breath left his lungs with a sharp "Oof!"

He flew backwards, over Eli's foot, and landed on his arse in the dirt, then rolled onto his side, clutching his stomach and mewing as he fought for breath.

Gabriel found it interesting that Bennett, though obviously shocked, didn't move to help the captain. Instead he drew Sam back a few paces, saying, "Better let this one play out."

Eli turned to Gabriel.

"Everything OK?"

"With me? Fine. You?"

"Yep."

Then she turned to Gaddesden, who'd got to his knees, and was panting with the effort of breathing as he staggered to his feet. He balled his fists and took an ill-advised swing at Eli's head.

Which wasn't there.

He'd telegraphed the punch so completely that before his fist had even started on its forwards run from his shoulder, she was sliding sideways and rotating her body out of the way.

As his fist passed harmlessly through the air a foot from the tip of her nose, she counterattacked.

A flurry of punches to his side put him on the ground, and this time Eli followed them in. She knelt on his chest, grabbed his right wrist and yanked his arm high into the air over his shoulder, before jabbing her straightened fingers into the soft place just beneath the angle of his jaw. Just when Gabriel thought she was going to kill Gaddesden, she stopped.

Gaddesden was almost weeping from fear and the battering he'd just taken. Eli leaned closer and whispered something into his ear. Then she stood, turned her back and stalked off, dusting her palms together.

She called over her shoulder. "I'll see you later."

Gabriel dearly hoped she meant the remark for him.

Bennett and Sam were helping the shaken Captain Gaddesden to his feet. His face was scarlet. Half embarrassment, half exertion was Gabriel's estimate.

"See what I mean?" he asked the remaining three members of the recce group while holding his hands wide.

"What *I* see," Bennett shot back, "is a somewhat arrogant, possibly anti-Semitic and definitely ill-informed army officer, who really ought to have learned better manners at Sandhurst, getting a pasting from a young lady he had gone out of his way to insult. She was using Krav Maga, by the way. If you don't end up shitting your liver out tonight, it's Eli's restraint you'll have to thank."

The atmosphere having been irreparably damaged, they toured the mocked-up nuclear facility in more or less complete silence, Gabriel only breaking it to ask questions about access roads, the staff carpark and a few other details of the building's layout.

After walking a final circuit round "Vareshabad," Gabriel and Sam said goodbye to Bennett and Gaddesden and walked back to one of the two remaining Land Rovers. Gabriel gave Sam a lift back to Marlborough Lines, where she was to discuss equipment with him and Eli.

"SEND THE MISSILES"

TEHRAN

Darbandi reviewed the latest data, poring over the green-and-white-ruled printer paper, analysing the test results one last time before making the call that would cement his place in history. Yes. Everything confirmed his initial thought. The warhead could work. The warhead *would* work. In perhaps as little as a week, it would be ready.

He pulled the yellow desk phone closer, lifted the receiver and dialled a number he had memorised long ago. The Minister of Defence and Armed Forces Logistics answered after three rings.

"Yes?"

"Minister, it's Darbandi here. I have the latest test data in front of me. *Melkh* will work. Send the missiles, please."

The Minister paused. Darbandi looked up and watched a fly buzzing in random geometric figures a few inches below the slowly revolving blades of the ceiling fan. *I wish I could exterminate you as easily as the Jews*, he thought.

"You are sure?" the Minister finally asked. "I have to report to the Supreme Leader every time there is a new development on Project *Melkh*. I would not like to raise false hope."

Darbandi frowned. Just recently, he had begun to doubt the Minister's commitment to *Melkh*. He was a careerist. Concerned more with his next political appointment than with his country's destiny. But Darbandi was not to be thwarted by a mere office-holder. *Melkh* was his. And nothing must be allowed to stand in its way.

"Do you doubt me, Minister?" he asked, silkily. He knew the Minister was aware that Darbandi had been blessed personally by the Supreme Leader ten years earlier. To cross such a man as he would be unwise, not to say career-limiting.

"Of course not," the Minister snapped. "But I need to be sure. As I said—"

"And as *I* said," Darbandi interrupted, "send the missiles." He paused for a moment. "Please."

FAIRBAIRN-SYKES

The Land Rover having been built for utility rather than speed or, indeed, refined road manners, Gabriel kept to a stately 50 mph as he drove back from the Plain to Marlborough Lines.

"That was quite a performance from young Ms Schochat," Sam said after a couple of miles.

Gabriel turned to look at her for a second before returning his eyes to the road.

"He deserved it. Though I hope he doesn't report it. If we end up in hot water with the brass for fighting during a mission briefing, it'll put a kink in Don's day. And I really don't want that to happen."

Sam smiled as she continued to look straight ahead.

"Oh, I shouldn't worry. He brought it on himself. And there were three witnesses. If nothing else I suspect he'd be far too embarrassed to have to explain how he lost a scrap with a mere female."

The irony dripping from the final two words made Gabriel smile.

"He did look a bit shocked, didn't he?"

"You think? He looked like a schoolboy who'd kicked a cat and got a faceful of claws for his trouble."

"So you think we'll be OK?"

She laid a reassuring hand on his thigh for a second.

"Yes. Now tell me, what did you have in mind for the mission? And if you say 'exploding fountain pen,' I'll tell the brass about your little escapade myself."

Gabriel grinned. Resisting the temptation Sam had put in his way, he projected an array of edged weapons onto the road unwinding in front of him, much like the RS3's head-up display. Then he scanned the knives and swords one by one until he located the precise weapon for the job.

In the closed world of Special Forces, two knives are known worldwide as killers' weapons. One is the US Marine Corps' KA-BAR. The other is the British Fairbairn–Sykes fighting knife. Developed by two former members of the Shanghai Municipal Police, the Fairbairn-Sykes is what's commonly known as a *stiletto*, equipped with a narrow, strong blade designing for stabbing rather than slashing. Gabriel had, from time to time, used one in the SAS, and he pictured one now. He imagined himself using the knife. He picked it up and hefted it in his right hand. Feinted left then thrust through the ribcage and into the heart.

Yes. The Fairbairn-Sykes would do it. And, crucially, its wound signature could easily be mistaken for that of a robber's dagger. He'd take his man down, remove his watch and wallet and leave a crime scene that would suggest a vicious mugging gone wrong rather than an assassination by an operator working for a hostile foreign power.

"A Fairbairn-Sykes, please."

"That's it? You don't want a pistol? A rifle? Plastique?"

He shook his head.

"Not for this one. We need to make it look like a mugging gone wrong."

"I'll get you a couple. One each, just in case. Hmm," she said, tapping the tip of her nose.

"What is it?"

"You're going to laugh."

"I promise I won't."

"I just bought a couple of new toys to trial. But I think they'd be perfect for you and Eli. Especially in your guise as publishers."

Intrigued, Gabriel glanced at Sam.

"Go on."

"Tungsten-alloy striker pens."

An image flitted through Gabriel's brain. A spam email he'd deleted, though not before reading all the way through to the end and clicking through to the landing page on the company's website. The owners of ExecTactical, Inc. were promoting various ranges of survival and personal defence equipment suitable for office workers to carry about with them, open-carry firearms being frowned upon in the glitzy offices of merchant banks, lawyers and accountants. The email was offering something called an "Executive Tactical Striker," a fully functioning ballpoint pen whose barrel and tip were machined from a single piece of tungsten-alloy. Under attack, the besuited owner had only to pull the implement from his or her pocket or purse and stab their assailant's head, keeping their thumb over the non-business end for added power. "Drop a two-hundred-pound attacker like he was a sack of potatoes!!!" ran the company's breathless headline.

Gabriel widened his eyes, took his right hand off the wheel and slapped his thigh.

"I *knew* it!" he cried. "You *do* have top-secret toys! Yes, please. We'll take two."

Then he burst out laughing. Fearing a slap, or worse, from the quartermaster, he was relieved when she joined in.

"OK, I deserved that," she said, finally. "But it would make me feel a little more comfortable to know you and Eli at least had backup weapons. And, interestingly, the alternative name for Tungsten is Wolfram so it seems rather fitting."

Back at Marlborough Lines, Gabriel parked the Land Rover in the motor pool and together, he and Sam walked across the base to the house in the married quarters.

Eli was in the kitchen making a pot of tea and from the smell of it, toast as well. She turned when Gabriel led Sam into the kitchen and smiled at them both.

"Hi. How did it go?"

"It was fine," Gabriel said. "To be honest, as it was only the exterior, there wasn't a massive amount of useful information. But it was good to see the place where Darbandi works in three dimensions."

"Did that idiot say anything after I left?"

"Nothing you need to worry about. I think you bruised his pride as much as his kidneys."

"Speaking of which," Sam added, "you missed what Bennett said to him. I nearly died."

Eli smiled.

"Go on then. Tell me."

Sam roughened her voice in a passable imitation of Bennett's gruffly posh tone.

"He said, 'If you don't end up shitting your liver out tonight, it's Eli's restraint you'll have to thank.' Classic!"

Eli inclined her head in acceptance of the praise. Bennett had been on the money, though. Unlike other forms of unarmed combat, Krav Maga was designed to disable, permanently injure or kill the opponent. The Marquess of Queensberry would have fainted at some of the moves Eli and her colleagues had practised.

"One thing, though," Sam said. "What did you say to him when you put him on the ground for the second time?"

Eli caught a slice of toast as it popped up out of the toaster and spread some butter and jam on it before answering.

"I told him I was like my country. Loyal to my friends and ruthless with my enemies. He needed to decide which one he was."

* * *

After Sam left to drive back to London, Gabriel called Don.

"What's up, Old Sport?"

"We were wondering whether you'd made any progress identifying the mercs or their masters?"

"Afraid not. D'you remember that Scottish Detective

Superintendent we met a few years back when we helped the Met clear up their little vigilante problem?"

Gabriel raised his eyes to the ceiling, searching his mental database of official and semi-official contacts. Found the Scot, with her efficient haircut and slash of red lipstick.

"Yes. What was her name? Caroline? Cassie?"

"Callie. McDonald. I *reached out* to her, in the modern parlance, sent her the evidence and asked for assistance. She's looking into it, but to be honest, we don't have time to wait for the cops. She told me what I already suspected, and I think you did, too. That they're – or rather, were – mercenaries. One might have been Russian, but it's not enough to go on. We need to keep the train rolling. You and Eli ship out tomorrow. Sam bring you your paperwork?"

"Yes, Boss."

"Good. Listen, once you're on that plane you'll be on our radar but off the comms. Stay in character until you're back home."

With that, and a gruff "good luck," Don ended the call.

* * *

That evening, after dinner, Eli brought the bottle of Chianti they'd shared into the sitting room. She poured them both another glass and sat on the sofa before beckoning Gabriel to join her. She'd folded her legs up under her and stretched her arm wide along the back of the cushions.

"Come on," she said. "Tell me what's going on. What you found out when you talked to Fariyah."

Gabriel took the proffered glass, and a large mouthful, then sat next to Eli, leaning into her and relaxing as her hand began caressing the back of his neck. He explained how Fariyah had hypnotised him and he'd remembered that Michael had been all too eager to dive in to retrieve the ball. And how she'd uncovered the cavernous hole in the timeline Gabriel had constructed to explain away the presence of the mysterious third Wolfe sibling.

When he paused, she didn't immediately jump in to fill the

silence with explanations, reassurances or questions. He liked that about her. He waited, listening to her breathing, feeling her chest expand and contract against his own ribs.

"I was an only child," she finally said.

"I didn't know that."

"Why would you? I never told you much about my family last time. But you weren't, although you became one when you were, what, nine?"

"That's right."

"Why do you think your parents never told you about the middle child?"

Gabriel shrugged. He looked down and realised he'd placed his left hand on Eli's thigh. It felt comfortable there. Not a sexual thing, just a companionable gesture. He left it in place.

"I don't know. I suppose they didn't want to upset me. He, or she, can't have been more than a year or so old. Perhaps they thought it was for the best. Given my reaction when Michael died, that was a good call."

"Why? What happened?"

Gabriel explained how he'd become almost catatonic for a fortnight, before waking with absolutely no memory of Michael's ever having existed. The resulting stress had led directly to his parents sending him to live with Zhao Xi.

Eli sipped her wine. Then she placed the glass down and turned to kiss Gabriel gently on the lips before pulling away a little.

"You have to go back to Hong Kong. As soon as possible. Find the grave. Maybe there are people still living there who knew your parents. Friends of Zhao Xi's. That lawyer you mentioned, for example."

"I know. That's where I'd got to as well. As soon as we're done in Iran, that's my plan. You could come. See the house. Maybe we could travel around a little?"

She smiled, and brushed a stray strand of her auburn hair out of her eye.

"I would love that. Really. As soon as we can, yes?"

"Yes."

"Good. Because I have a feeling we're going to want a proper break after this business. And it all starts tomorrow. What time's our flight?"

"Ten past nine in the evening."

Gabriel took another mouthful of the Chianti. He felt that what he had with Eli might be important. As important – *More, maybe*, he thought – than what he'd had with Britta. More, anyway, than just the playful boyfriend-girlfriend thing they'd agreed on just a couple of days earlier. But that meant he needed to be honest with her. He'd discovered with Fariyah just how good he was at keeping secrets from himself. He didn't want to start a new relationship off by doing the same thing with his partner. He put his glass down and turned so he was facing Eli. He sighed, deeply.

"There's something I have to tell you," he said.

She matched his body posture, turning a little and readjusting her legs so she could sit facing him on the sofa.

"Oh my God, what? You're not gay, are you? Or dying of cancer?"

She was trying to keep it light, he could see that, but he didn't miss the micro-expression of real concern that flitted across her face.

"No and no. Listen, you know I'm seeing Fariyah. Well, how it started was, I was having these nightmares, flashbacks, suicidal thoughts, the works."

"PTSD? I assumed that was it. I'm not stupid, you know."

"I know you're not. But the other thing that kept happening was, I kept seeing one of my men. Do you remember I told you that time at my place in Salisbury about how out of my patrol, there was just me left?"

"Yes. The others were Smudge, Dusty and, oh, I'm sorry, who was the fourth guy?"

"Damon. We used to call him Daisy because his surname was Cheaney."

"Go on," she said, putting a hand out to touch his knee.

Gabriel frowned and ran his hand over his hair, scratching at his scalp.

"A couple of years after I left The Regiment, I started doing this sort of work again, and I began seeing Smudge. We had to leave him behind on our final mission. We were in Mozambique. A search and destroy. But we were betrayed, and ambushed by a warlord's men. My last sight of Smudge was his dead body crucified on a tree by machetes through his hands. After that, he started turning up. You know, in the street, in an art gallery once, all kinds of weird places. I used to talk to him and he used to help me. I thought I was going mad, Eli, I really did."

Gabriel could feel tears pricking at the corners of his eyes. He sniffed loudly, and knuckled his eye sockets to stop them flowing, afraid that if they did, they might not stop for a very long time.

She shuffled closer and embraced him though their facing positions made the gesture awkward for both of them.

"But you went to see Fariyah, didn't you? That took guts, Gabriel, you know that, right? Lots of people just bottle it all up."

He sniffed again, feeling that the spasm of grief had passed, for now.

"I did, you're right. She helped me understand why Smudge kept appearing. In the end he sort of faded away. But I still hear his voice from time to time."

"Maybe that's a good thing. You said he was a friend. Friends never truly die. I believe that. I mean, yes, obviously, their bodies go. But they live on inside of us. Here." She said, placing her flat palm over Gabriel's heart.

He covered her hand with his own.

"Maybe you're right. I just ... He's not really gone completely, and I wanted you to know. What you might be getting into if we're, you know ..."

"Together?" She smiled "You can say it, you know. It doesn't mean we have to start shopping for furniture, or having a joint bank account."

Gabriel drew in a deep breath and let it out in a huff. He felt better for having confessed to Eli. Had he really expected her to run screaming into the night, yelling that she was dating a lunatic? No. Of course not. He pictured Fariyah's face, an ironic smile playing on her lips, as she asked him the same question.

"So, you're OK with that?" he asked Eli. "Me being, you know, not completely mentally on point?"

"Of course I am, you fool. But I have to tell you, if you start trying to beat me up in your sleep again, I may have to retaliate properly."

"Like you did with poor old Gaddesden?"

"Worse!"

MAX

BARCELONA

Max paid the bill in cash. Nine hundred and fifty euros, including the service charge. The restaurant was the most expensive in Spain and the third-most expensive in the world. Its chef, renowned among the super-rich for his flair with food and equally fiery temper, had emerged from the kitchen twenty minutes earlier to greet the evening's diners. He had complimented Max's companion on her beauty and shaken Max's hand. Max wondered whether he would have done so if he'd known how many men's lives that hand had snuffed out.

On the drive along the coast road, back to his house overlooking the ocean, he remained silent, guiding the vintage Ferrari around the curves with a lover's touch on its thin-rimmed, wooden steering wheel.

"What's the matter, darling?" his young companion asked.

"Nothing. Please be quiet. I need to think."

The woman clammed up as Max knew she would. He glanced

sideways to see her fingering the new diamond necklace at her throat. He looked ahead, then down at the water. A long, silver streak glittered on the mirror-smooth surface all the way to the horizon, where it pointed at the moon.

Diamonds. By now Kuznitsa should have been enjoying the bounty of that field in Mozambique. And the pleasure of having an entire mineral-rich African country under its control. That it was not caused Max and his partners no small amount of anger. That the blame could be laid at the feet of a single man intensified that anger. That the man was still alive focused it onto a single, white-hot point. And Max could feel it, boring a hole through his skull and into his brain. The money and the power, those he could live without. He had plenty of other ways of increasing his stock if he so chose.

No. It was the – he hated even thinking the word – it was the *shame*. The tarnishing of his reputation. The trashing of his honour. Without them he was nothing. Lower than a *suka* – a prison bitch.

Beneath his fine silk Brioni suit and sparkling white handmade shirt by Turnbull & Asser, his back, chest, shoulders and arms were covered with ink that delineated his progress through the Russian prison system, the Russian army and the Russian *Mafiya*. Cats, an eight-pointed star, a hooded executioner (applied after he'd killed his own brother for breaking the criminal code), a Madonna and child, skulls, suns, ships, and a crucifix. He wore them with pride, and everyone who saw them knew him to be a man of power. But power, he knew, could be lost as well as gained. Respect, also. To be bested by this British agent? It could not be allowed to stand. People were already whispering. He heard them in his sleep. On waking. While shaving. And the whispers always went the same way.

Max is losing it.
Max isn't the man he used to be.
Maybe it's time to move against Max.
The old Max would never have allowed this to happen.
He ground his teeth together. Nor would the new Max.

* * *

Later, he stood on the terrace, leaning over the balcony and looking out at the ocean and the huge, silver moon, hanging there as if to mock him with its trail of diamonds across the water. The noise of the crickets singing at the moon made it hard to focus his thoughts on his next move. The air around him was scented with a lemony perfume. From the herbs he'd brushed against on his way out from the bedroom, he assumed.

He scrolled through his contacts and tapped the screen.

"Hello, Max," the voice at the other end said.

"Hello, Nils. How's business?"

"Busy. Am I about to get busier?"

"If you have time, yes."

"For you, Max, always. Name?"

"Wolfe. First name, Gabriel."

"Dossier."

"All I have is a photo and a few details. He works for British intelligence. I'll email it to you. Usual fee?"

"You know my rates, Max. Usual plus fifty percent for security people."

"I'll send you half in the morning. Tell me, if all we have is his name and a photo, how will you locate him?"

"Don't worry about that. It's all part of the service."

* * *

Max was as good as his word. At 7.45 a.m. the following morning, Nils Kristersson checked his account at the Oslo branch of Nordea Bank Norge. and was pleased to see that his balance had swelled by $375,000 overnight. He showered, singing an old Norwegian folk song as he lathered his cropped blond hair, then dressed, sliding his six-foot frame into black jeans, a white shirt and a new black leather jacket before snapping on his stainless-steel Rolex.

Fifteen minutes later, he was sitting in his favourite cafe in the City Hall Square sipping a perfect black coffee and eating a toasted cheese and smoked ham sandwich. On the screen of his laptop, a brief profile of the man he had just been hired to kill.

* * *

While Kristersson was reading the profile of his latest target, Blacksmith and Gul were standing talking for the third time, in a different park, in a different part of London. Bright sunshine turned the leaves of the beech trees shading them translucent. Birds filled the air with all manner of trills and warbles that, under normal circumstances, Blacksmith would have enjoyed, ornithology being something of a passion with him.

"Under what name is he travelling?" Gul asked.

"I don't know."

"No matter. What does he look like?"

"Here."

Blacksmith handed over a colour photo, printed from one he'd taken on his phone on the day Wolfe and his Jewish sidekick had visited the Iran desk. Gul scrutinised the photograph. Pursed his lips. Nodded.

"He is travelling alone?"

"No. With a partner. An Israeli. Ex-Mossad."

He handed over a second photo.

Gul took and pocketed the sheet of paper. Then he looked hard into Blacksmith's eyes.

"Why?"

"Why?"

"Why are you doing this? Why are you betraying your country?"

"It's not my country."

Gul smiled, though the expression didn't reach his eyes.

"Very well. Why are you betraying the UK?"

"Because the UK betrays me through its support for Israel. I help you stop Wolfe, Darbandi finishes his work. Iran destroys Israel. I am happy."

"As simple as that."

"As simple as that."

"Very well. In fact, life is more complicated. But your help – if it proves useful – will bring us closer to achieving our aims. Do you have more information to share? The Islamic Republic of Iran is both loyal and generous to its allies."

Blacksmith smiled.

"Let's deal with Wolfe first."

YOU CAN'T JUDGE A BOOK

TEHRAN

The receptionist at the Tehran Grand Hotel looked up from her leather-bound guest book as Gabriel and Eli approached the front desk. A burgundy-and-gold-uniformed porter stood a respectful few paces behind them with their luggage stacked neatly on a gold-coloured, wheeled trolley. The receptionist smiled, her full lips parting slightly to reveal large, even, white teeth.

"Welcome to the Tehran Grand Hotel, sir, madam," she said in flawless, unaccented English. "Checking in?"

A gold pin on her left jacket lapel gave her name as Yelena and her title as Assistant Manager.

"Yes, that's right," Gabriel said, pushing a pair of round, tortoiseshell-framed glasses higher on the bridge of his nose.

"You are here on business?" Yelena asked.

"The Tehran International Book Fair. Our company has space on the British Council's stand."

"Very good. We have many guests attending the fair also. May I take your passports, please?"

Yelena disappeared through a door. After a few minutes, she returned their passports.

"Thank you, Mr Denning, Miss Arifakis. May I ask you to sign the guest book?"

After they'd added their details – all fictitious – to the leather-bound journal, Yelena bent to her computer and set about assigning rooms, activating keycards, explaining about the hotel's Wi-Fi and the usual little details Gabriel felt were designed mainly to prevent guests getting what they really wanted, which was to their rooms.

The porter showed them to the lifts, then their rooms, which were adjoining, on the fifth floor. After an extravagant guided tour in which no facility, however insignificant, escaped his pointing finger and smiling explanation, Gabriel was able to tip him and close the door behind him.

"Fucking hell, I thought he'd never go!" Eli said, rolling her eyes. "I need a shower and something to eat. Want to join me?"

"In the shower or the restaurant?"

Eli started unbuttoning her blouse.

"What do you think?" she asked with a grin.

* * *

The book fair was scheduled to start in two days' time. So the next morning, after a breakfast of coffee, eggs, and bread rolls flavoured with raisins and coloured a startling yellow by turmeric, Gabriel and Eli set off on foot for their scheduled rendezvous with a messenger sent by Julian Furnish.

"There's a nice little place to go for a coffee and a cake. Kind of a tourist stop. Fereydoon Sandwich at the corner of Eshqyar and 4th Streets," he'd said when they spoke on the phone before leaving England. "Be there at 9.30 a.m. the day after you arrive, and I'll have one of my chaps drop you off your little cutlery set."

Gabriel and Eli had dressed in light summer clothing, but even so, the heat in Tehran's concrete and steel city centre was oppressive. They'd decided to walk. As they wandered along, they gazed up at the skyscrapers, mosques and occasional trees as if they were merely goggle-eyed tourists here to sell a few books and do a little sightseeing, and not stone killers tasked with assassinating the architect of the country's nuclear weapons programme. The capacious black nylon laptop bag Gabriel was carrying quickly produced a patch of sweat against his right side.

From the hotel, their route took them along Sepand Alley, a narrow street lined with mobile phone shops and cafes, then into Qarani Street, Sanaēe Street and Shahid Motahari Street. With each turn, the businesses grew bigger and brasher. Banks dominated the start of their journey, only to be replaced with electronics shops, grocery stores and bookshops. After an hour, they reached the junction of Eshqyar and 4th Street

"There it is," Gabriel said, pointing to a shabby-looking shopfront, above which signs blared out in garish orange, yellow, blue and brown Farsi script. Gabriel translated aloud.

"Fereydoon Sandwich – shish kebab, kofte, meat sandwich, lamb, chicken, falafel."

He'd worried they might stand out, he in his blue-and-white-striped seersucker suit and Eli in a conservatively cut cotton trouser suit in a pale-beige, but the place seemed to be attracting as many westerners as locals. They took their place in the queue and, once inside, looked around for a table. A handful of white plastic tables stood along one wall, mismatched plastic lawn chairs shoved underneath them.

An enormously fat man wearing chef's whites and a red-and-white chequered cap was running the show behind the counter. He called out to Gabriel, first in Farsi, then in English.

"Shema ak jedwel ma khewahad?" – You want a table?

Gabriel resisted the urge to reply in Farsi. Instead, he spoke loudly, as Englishmen had been doing when talking to foreigners since time immemorial.

"Yes, please. For two?"

He held up two fingers as well.

The fat man waved stubby fingers at a table at the far end of the shop. He signed that they should seat themselves and someone would come to take their order. Gabriel placed his laptop bag out of sight under the table. While they waited, Gabriel leaned across to Eli.

"Hungry?"

"I am, actually. That hotel breakfast wasn't up to much, was it?"

"Lamb sandwich OK?"

"Sure. And a coffee."

A young guy with a slight beard came over to their table holding a pad. He smiled and stood waiting for their order.

Gabriel pointed at a garish colour photo of lamb koftes wrapped in flatbreads and signalled for two, receiving an enthusiastic nod from the waiter in return.

"And two coffees, please?" he said, loudly, in English.

Eli laughed, and when the waiter had departed she leaned across to Gabriel.

"My God, it's harder for you to speak English than Farsi!"

The cafe was thrumming with conversations, shouting from behind the counter, the hiss of coffee machines and the sizzle of raw meat being slapped down onto hot metal. Gabriel inhaled deeply. The air was rich with spices, the aroma of grilling lamb and chicken and, perhaps owing to the large number of prosperous-looking Iranian businessmen, pungent aftershave.

Eli leaned across the table and murmured a question.

"Do you want to talk about Darbandi? It's probably safer here than in our room. It's bound to be bugged."

Gabriel laughed as if she'd told a joke.

"Sure, why not?" he said with a smile. "I say, do it tomorrow. We'll spend the morning at the fair, to show our faces, then we'll hire a car, head out to Vareshabad and pick him up when he leaves the car park. Plan A: We follow him and ambush him on a quiet stretch of road. Dump the body and get back to the Grand to grab our things and head for the airport."

Eli nodded.

ANDY MASLEN

"Agreed," she said.

"How do we explain our presence in Vareshabad if we're stopped?"

Eli shrugged, then smiled over Gabriel's shoulder. He turned just as the waiter arrived bearing their order on a tray. They waited while he placed the hot sandwiches and coffees before them. Once he'd left their table, Eli took a bite of the lamb wrapped in flatbread.

Her eyes widened.

"Oh, God, that is delicious! Try yours."

Gabriel took a bite. The lamb was so hot it was almost sizzling. The smell of the meat juices, combined with fried onion, green chilli and coriander made him smile, despite the topic of their conversation.

"Excellent. Pity their leaders couldn't make sandwiches instead of nuclear bombs."

They paused for a while, enjoying their food and taking sips of the strong, black coffee. Putting her sandwich down and wiping her lips on a paper napkin she plucked from a red-and-chrome dispenser, Eli spoke.

"We'll just play the amateur archaeologist card. Coupled in your case with the dim Englishman card. We say we were sightseeing and got lost. We were looking for an archaeological site that's mentioned in our book."

It was thin, and they both knew it. At best, they'd end up being escorted back to the book fair with strict orders not to stray from the exhibition hall. At worst ...

"Hi, you guys!" a man in his early twenties said, plonking himself down at their table.

He shrugged off his laptop bag – capacious, black, nylon – and pushed it under the table. He wore a pale-grey business suit over a white shirt, no tie, which seemed to be the fashion for businessmen in Tehran. His hair was cut into a fashionable style, slick with some kind of wet-look gel and combed back from his forehead.

"Hi!" Gabriel said, smiling broadly and re-seating the glasses on the bridge of his nose. "How are you?"

"I'm good, good. All ready for the fair?"

"Mm-hmm."

The young man smiled.

"Great! I brought that contract you wanted. Here."

He fished inside his jacket and extracted a white envelope with "Robert Denning, Copernicus Press" typed on the outside. Gabriel took the envelope and slid it into his inside pocket.

"Thanks. Was there anything else?"

"Nope. Listen, I'd love to stay and chat about books, but my boss needs me back at the office. Enjoy Tehran."

Then he reached under the table for his bag, slung it over his shoulder and was gone. Gabriel finished his coffee and stood up. He grabbed the other bag, slipped the strap over his head, then went up to the counter to pay the bill.

* * *

As they walked back to the hotel, they resumed their earlier conversation. Moving among the morning crowds through Tehran's bustling streets, it was easy to talk without being overheard. Gabriel and Eli were both taking pains to monitor their immediate and not-so-immediate surroundings. Keeping track of faces, making sure the same ones didn't appear more than once. Checking number plates on cars. Occasionally doubling back and looking for pedestrians momentarily interested in shop windows or stooping to tie their shoelaces. Gabriel had discussed with Hugh Bennett the possibility of their being tracked by Iranian security. It seemed unlikely. But not out of the question.

"Vareshabad is swarming with Revolutionary Guards. What if he has one with him as a bodyguard in the car?" Gabriel asked.

Eli smiled and shrugged. Ran a finger behind her ear to replace a strand of hair.

"Plan B. We do him at his house. Get rid of the bodyguard first. He won't be expecting trouble. Probably sees it as a boring babysitting job for the egghead. I had to do it myself once. You try to kid yourself it's vital, but it's dull compared to frontline work or covert stuff."

Gabriel smiled as he mimed opening a book – *Publisher talk*, he conveyed with his hands. *Nothing to worry about.*

"Fine. Let's say he does have a bodyguard. So we get to Darbandi's house before they do and ambush them there. We wait till they arrive. They park. The muscle gets out of the car first, checks the coast is clear, then goes round to open the door for the egghead."

"And while his back is turned we come out of the shadows. I put the bodyguard down and pull the body clear. Darbandi's a scientist. An evil scientist, but not a soldier. He's trained for lab work, not street fighting. His brain will just freeze," Eli said, also putting on a little dumb show of her own with her hands.

"Then I freeze him permanently."

"Exactly. Once he's dead, how do you want to handle things?"

"We set the scene so it looks like a violent robbery. Then we basically get in the car and drive straight to the airport. If for some reason we can't go to the airport, we head for the British Embassy. While I drive, you text Furnish to say we're en route. When we get to Jomhouri Avenue, send a second text saying we're there and he'll get the gates opened. We drive in. Gates clang shut behind us. They drive us to the airport in an embassy car and we're out of the country and sipping G&Ts in Business Class."

"Business? I didn't realise Don was so generous with the expense account."

Gabriel grinned.

"He isn't. I upgraded us at Heathrow."

Eli returned the smile.

"What it is to have money!"

A man's shout interrupted their banter.

Gabriel looked up to see a uniformed policeman glaring at him and Eli, and resting his right hand on the butt of his pistol.

JUST ANOTHER DAY AT THE OFFICE

Gabriel looked straight at the cop. Then down at his feet. He wanted to smile, but felt it would be counterproductive.

"Take two steps back," he murmured to Eli.

She complied, as the cop strode towards them, gesticulating with his left hand while keeping his right resting on his pistol.

"What is it?" she said in a low voice.

"Relax. We were jaywalking."

As the angry cop reached them from the middle of the road, Gabriel plastered a huge social smile on his face and placed his right hand over his heart. He waited until the cop reached the end of what was no doubt a frequently delivered speech, then apologised, first in halting Farsi.

"Metasef, metasef!" *Sorry, sorry!*

Then again, loudly, in English:

"I am humbly sorry, Excellency. My friend and I did not intend to break your law. We will wait for the signal to cross. Please forgive us."

Mollified, and no doubt confused by this foreigner's use of Farsi and over-the-top apology, he removed his hand from his gun butt and stroked his moustache.

"It is fine," he said in slow but perfect English. "Be careful. Tehran drivers too fast."

Gabriel nodded in agreement, offering an anxious frown to show he had learnt his lesson. The cop about-turned and marched back into the centre of the road junction, where he resumed his officious handwaving at the cars, trucks and motorbikes that swarmed around him like locusts.

"Fuck me, Wolfe, you're a cool customer," Eli said.

"Cops, waiters and secretaries. It always pays to treat them with courtesy."

Back at the hotel, having stopped to buy a set of screwdrivers, Gabriel and Eli took the stairs to Gabriel's room. Once inside, with the door locked and the security chain on, Gabriel dropped the laptop bag onto the bed. He unzipped the main compartment and took out the ageing black computer within. It was thick, and heavy. He turned it over and placed it on the turquoise and gold silk counterpane. As Eli watched, he began removing the ten stubby black screws holding the casing together.

Something about the repetitive sequence of movements triggered a memory. He was sitting in an air-conditioned house on the edge of a compound built deep in the Brazilian rainforest. Before him on a table, a dismantled professional video camera, into which he was wedging blocks of C-4 before pressing silvery ball bearings into its yielding surface. The bomb he was making was designed to end the lives of a couple of politicians, as well as their entourage and a dozen or more journalists. The mission had ended in carnage. More dead bodies in one place than Gabriel had ever seen, outside of Bosnia in the midnineties. He shuddered, willing himself to unsee the spreadeagled corpses.

Eli touched him lightly on the arm.

"You all right? You just zoned out for a minute."

He looked round at her and smiled.

"Yeah, yeah. I'm fine. Just concentrating on the job in hand."

Eli frowned.

"Don't bullshit me, Wolfe. I can tell when you're lying. What's going on?"

Gabriel continued working the tiny screws out from the black plastic casing, but he answered Eli's question.

"I was thinking about another time, another place. Brazil. I was brainwashed by the leader of a suicide cult. His name was Christophe Jardin, though he had all his disciples call him Père Christophe. He had me make him a bomb. I was supposed to blow up a press conference and myself with it."

Eli's lips curled upwards a little.

"Clearly, he failed. So is that it? You were just taking a long walk down Memory Lane?"

Gabriel so wanted to lie to her. Desired nothing more than to offer her a bland, suburban smile and say, "Of course, darling. Just reminiscing about that camping trip to the Dordogne we took that glorious summer in, when would it have been, '03?" But although lying came easily enough in service of the Crown, something ingrained in his character made it much harder when he was facing someone he cared about. *Loved?* he thought. He sighed deeply, and it must have sounded so heartfelt that Eli's brow crinkled with concern.

"You're right. I did zone out. It keeps happening. And seeing Fariyah didn't make it stop like I'd hoped. I'm worried. What if I screw up this hit because I go flying off into Neverland just when I need to be focused?"

Eli took the screwdriver from his unresisting hand. She placed them on the bed then turned back to face him. Cupping his cheeks in her soft hands she looked directly into his eyes.

"You won't mess up. Whatever's going on in your head, we can work it out together. Fariyah can help. I said I'd come with you to Hong Kong after this, and I meant it. We'll do some digging and we'll find out what happened. So stop worrying about letting me down. I trust you, Wolfe. With my life."

Then she pulled him towards her and kissed him, hard, on the mouth. When she finally released him, he sat up straight and nodded a couple of times. The speech had worked. He felt clearheaded again.

"OK. Come on, then. Let's get this bloody thing open."

A few more moments' work with the screwdriver, and Gabriel was prising the back of the laptop, to find nothing more than an array of silicon chips, circuit boards, plain, black plastic squares and a rectangular battery. His heart jumped in his chest.

"What the fuck?" he said. "There's nothing here."

He picked up the laptop and inverted it, giving it a shake. He turned it back.

"Let me look," Eli said. She picked it up and brought the uncovered innards of the computer up to her eye. She frowned. "Give me a flat-head screwdriver."

She inserted the blade into the edge of the largest circuit board and pressed down. With a snap, the edge lifted. She put the tip of her index finger into the gap and pulled upwards. What Gabriel had taken for a collection of separate components came away in her hand in a single piece. Beneath the cleverly constructed cover were two Fairbairn-Sykes knives and two very ordinary-looking grey metal pens, complete with pocket clips.

"Ta-daa!" Eli said. "Sam's a very clever woman. I bet this thing even boots up."

Gabriel looked closer. The rectangle of components Eli had placed beside the laptop was connected to the case by a ribbon of rainbow-coloured wires. She was probably right.

They took out the knives and the striker pens, then put the laptop back together, closed the lid and left it on one side. Eli held her pen up to the light. Turned it this way and that. Then went to the desk and scribbled a note on the hotel's branded notepaper. She held it up for Gabriel to see. In a flowing script, she'd written:

Melina Arifakis

· · ·

Then she flipped her grip so that she was holding the pen like a dagger, with her thumb over the non-writing end. She came over to the bed, raised her hand high above her head and slammed it down onto one of the pillows.

Gabriel found he could imagine, vividly, what such a blow would do to a human skull.

"I hope nobody asks for your autograph," he said.

The next job was to hide the knives. The laptop bag also contained two slim, black leather document cases, preloaded with authentic-looking papers. They emptied them out and used the Fairbairn-Sykeses to slit the lining where it met the zip. In went the stilettos. Using a tube of Super Glue, they carefully stuck the lining back in place. The assorted publicity flyers and contracts camouflaged the cases' true purpose admirably.

At eight thirty. the following morning, Gabriel and Eli exited the revolving door of the Tehran Grand Hotel and walked to the book fair. Each carried a brand-new pen in an inside pocket and a slim document case, in the bottom of which, beneath the lining, lay a knife no publisher in their right mind would want to have on them. They registered using the terminals in the vast lobby, watched by a couple of bored-looking security guards in maroon uniforms. Gabriel and Eli exchanged a look. *No guns.*

As they waited for the printer next to the terminal to spit out their name badges, Gabriel turned to Eli. He knew how much she hated wearing formal clothes, and today she was dressed to kill in a cream trouser suit over a sea-green silk blouse. Her feet were encased in three-inch-heeled shoes a few shades darker than her suit. Like him, she carried, slung across her chest, a black leather briefcase.

"You look very smart," he said.

She shot him a look. A look he knew. It translated, roughly, as, "One more word and you'll be eating through a straw for a month."

"Very ... professional," he added.

She leaned closer, bestowed upon him a smile of the purest saccharine sweetness, and spoke.

"It's a good job I like you so much. Otherwise, what I did to that jerk on Salisbury Plain would look like foreplay."

"I love you, too," he said, grinning.

With a grating buzz, the badge printer finally condescended to speak to the terminal, and out crept two name badges. At a kiosk just before the four sets of plate-glass, double-doors that gave way into the main exhibition space, they collected two badge holders on purple lanyards and completed their cover. Robert Denning and Melina Arifakis, here to sell a few books in Tehran, capital city of the Islamic Republic of Iran, sponsor of terrorism all over the world, deadly enemy of Israel and home to Abbas Darbandi. Just another day in the life of an academic publisher.

A row of tables stood between them and the exhibition hall. Behind each table, a pair of uniformed staff stood, searching bags. Gabriel and Eli exchanged another look. When it was their turn, they removed the black leather document cases they both carried, unzipped them and then, smiling and mumbling "Hello" in English, held them out for the bored-looking security staff to inspect.

Gabriel affected nonchalance as the contents of his bag were scrutinised. The woman's bronze-varnished fingernails walked across the edges of a set of papers – draft foreign rights contracts, publicity flyers for 'Persia: Jewels in the Desert, part of the Civilisations of Antiquity series by Copernicus Press, England' and lists of stands to be visited. Finding nothing to excite her interest, she offered Gabriel a brief smile and waved him through. He noticed Eli receiving the same treatment. *Thanks, Sam*, he thought.

The hall could have accommodated a fleet of jets, and everywhere earnest groups of suited men and women in conservatively cut outfits – some in suits, others in long dresses or niqabs – were wandering along the aisles, or standing chatting to publishers, printers, data firms, designers, booksellers or each other at the brightly designed stands. Despite – or perhaps because of – Iran's strict codes on behaviour in the street, the prevailing sound was excitable chatter and laughter.

"It's like being in the world's biggest library where they forgot the 'Silence!' signs," Eli said as they walked.

The British Council stand occupied a house-sized space on a corner between two of the hall's main thoroughfares. Union flags were in evidence, though placed discreetly on the corners of the display panels. In deference to the host country's suspicions of Western influence on its people, Gabriel supposed. A dozen or more booths, replete with tables covered in white cloths and groaning under the weight of books, dotted the space. The staff were easy to spot. They resembled the British Airways staff he was used to encountering in the airline's executive lounges at airports. Charcoal-grey or navy suits, white shirts, red-white-and-blue ties or neck scarves. Each wore an enamelled union flag pin on his or her left lapel above a name badge.

Gabriel and Eli crossed from the purple-and-gold flooring of the aisle onto the soothing deep-blue of the British Council's own carpet. Almost at once, a smiling young woman in her late twenties approached them. Her long, blonde hair was gathered into a bun at the nape of her neck.

"Good morning!" she said brightly. "Can I help you?"

"Hi," Gabriel said, extending his hand. "Robert Denning, Copernicus Press."

Eli mirrored his movements.

"Melina Arifakis. How do you do?"

The woman's smile didn't falter by a millimetre.

"Hello. I'm Sophie. Publisher liaison. Your stand is over this way. Please."

She extended her right arm, and Gabriel and Eli allowed themselves to be ushered towards a table near the back of the stand. A pile of books stood beside translucent document holders full of multicoloured flyers and a glass goldfish bowl half-full of business cards. Beside the bowl, an iPad Mini had been propped up against its pristine white box.

"Well," she said, the smile apparently glued onto her cheeks, which were matte with foundation, "I'll leave you to settle in."

Then she spun on her heel and went to help a pair of visitors clutching bright-yellow tote bags bulging with brochures and sample books. Gabriel and Eli hung their document cases by their straps over the backs of two blue-upholstered side chairs.

Three hours later, Gabriel and Eli stepped back from the table. She glared at him.

"Give me a knife."

"Why?"

"Because I'm going to cut my throat. This is literally hell."

Gabriel laughed.

"Just because that librarian from the university wanted to ask you about academic discounts?"

Eli's mouth dropped open.

"I was in her clutches for, what, half an hour? I thought I was going to die on my feet from boredom. Come on, we've done our duty here. Let's go."

Gabriel shook his head.

"Not together. Sorry, but you should wait another thirty minutes before leaving. It'll be less conspicuous."

She groaned.

"Fine. I'll meet you back at the hotel. Get the hire car sorted out, then come and pick me up. I want to kiss you good luck but as we're both happily married to other people, that would be inappropriate."

"How about a publisher's air-kiss? That should be OK."

Eli placed her hands on his shoulders and they touched cheeks briefly on each side.

"Be careful," she whispered.

"Always. See you shortly."

* * *

Gabriel left the stand and made his way to an Avis branch, a fifteen-minute walk from the event hall. The queue of people waiting for cars stretched out the door. All were looking at their watches and rolling their eyes at each other. He made a quick calculation. Judging by the speed with which the single sales guy was processing customers, it would take him thirty minutes to get to Gabriel. Still plenty of time to drive out to Vareshabad before the day's end.

He called Eli.

"There's a queue. It'll be at least half an hour before I get a car. Then allow, what, twenty minutes to get to you. I'd order some food if you haven't already."

"Fine. Want me to get you something, too?"

"I'll have whatever you're having. And a coffee."

THE JAWS OF LIFE

LONDON

Callie called the forensics officer Stella had requested be transferred to join the new unit.

"Hi, Lucian. Callie here. You busy?"

He laughed.

"Me? Nope. Why would I be busy? I was just sitting here playing solitaire."

Callie smiled.

"Excellent. In that case, go on down to the garage and get yourself some overalls. There's a Mercedes SUV there that's suspiciously clean. Take it apart and don't stop until you find something."

She ended the call.

"I'm going to find something, Don, and when I do, it'll be lunch on you. Again. With twenty-year-old malt."

* * *

Lucian stood up and rolled his neck and shoulders to ease the tension that had been building all morning. He'd spent the previous three hours scrutinising insect larvae through a high-powered microscope, and his eyes felt like marbles that had been rolled in glue, then sand. He turned away from his desk and headed for the door.

"Where are you off to?" a woman at the next desk asked him. "If you're going to the canteen you couldn't get me some cheese and onion crisps, a pork pie and a strawberry and kiwi Fanta, could you?"

He smiled. Julie was pregnant and brought her food cravings to work.

"Sorry, Jules. I've been sent down to the garage by our glorious leader. It's welder's gloves and angle-grinder time."

She grinned.

"Which you should love, what with you being so butch and everything."

He poked his tongue out and headed through the door, which *whuffed* shut behind him on its pneumatic closer.

The garage echoed to the sound of air hissing from impact wrenches as they spun the wheel nuts free of cars, vans and trucks, pop music from the radio, and the good-natured banter of people who enjoyed working with their hands, especially if the subject material had four wheels and an internal combustion engine.

Lucian found a face mask and zipped himself into a spare Tyvek forensic suit. He looked down. White Gucci loafers would attract grease and swarf, not to mention well-earned jabs of caustic wit from the mechanics and forensics officers working on the cars and bikes parked in a long row on the oil-stained concrete. He stashed them in an empty locker and replaced them with a pair of shin-high leather work boots with steel glinting through the ripped toecaps like bone beneath skin.

A young guy with sandy hair and a wide streak of grease across his forehead wandered over.

"All right, Lucian? Don't often see you down here?"

"Hi, Terry. I'm looking for the Merc SUV that came in the other day. Callie sent me down to have a go at it."

"It's been swept cleaner than a suite at the Paddington Hilton. You won't find anything."

Lucian compressed his lips and frowned.

"Yeah, I don't think sweeping was what she had in mind."

Terry pointed to the end of the row of vehicles.

"It's at the far end. Keys are on the rack. Knock yourself out."

Lucian collected the keys, labelled with a brown paper tag on a loop of string, and stopped off at the rack of heavy-duty equipment stacked on industrial racking on the long wall of the garage. He selected a set of huge pneumatic shears commonly known as the Jaws of Life.

He lugged the tool over to the Mercedes and screwed the brass coupling onto the nearest air supply. First, he did a walkaround.

"AMG GLS. Nice."

He pulled on a pair of leather work gloves and ran his hand along one gleaming flank, now glittering with grey fingerprint powder. He opened the driver's door and inserted the key to switch on the electronics. Then he pressed the button to drop all the windows. He turned the key to the OFF position.

The heavy cutters hissing, he manoeuvred the massive jaws around the driver's side windscreen pillar and hit the green CUT button. The compressor behind him deepened its hum to a more purposeful note. He watched with satisfaction as the cutting edges closed around the A-pillar, which emitted a jagged, metallic squeal, then severed it as if it were made of cheese. He repeated the process five times. The B/C and D pillars took more bites to cut through, but each parted with the same sudden bang as the final cut chomped through the steel. Finally, he cut through the supports for the rear tailgate.

"Hey, Terry," he called. "Give us a hand with this, would you?"

Terry trotted over and together they pushed the entire roof off, shattering the front and rear screens, which crashed inwards with a hiss of crazing safety glass. The roof, looking like a monstrous, flat-bodied insect, fell onto the far side of the car with a bang that raised heads the length of the garage. A mocking cheer went up, as if someone had dropped a plate in the canteen.

Next, Lucian opened all four doors. The blades made short work of the hinges and corrugated rubber cable sleeves connecting the doors' inboard electronics to the battery.

Four hours later, what remained of the Mercedes was a sorry picture far removed from the triumph of engineering and styling its manufacturer had shipped from the factory. The car itself resembled a stripped-out dune buggy. All the body panels were stacked in a pile ten feet from the rear. Lucian had dismantled each door into outer skin, inner frame and door cards holding the arm rests and switchgear. The bonnet and tailgate were propped against a wall. The seats were lined up as if for an impromptu film show. And the boot floor, spare wheel and toolkit were pushed well back into the corner of the garage where Lucian had been working.

Wiping sweat from his forehead, he bent to examine the floor-mounted rails to which the sumptuously padded leather seats had so recently been bolted. Beneath the driver's seat he found a single penny. 2015. Moving across to the front passenger seat, he added the cap of a ballpoint pen. Black. Then he clambered into the rear passenger compartment, lay down on his front across the transmission tunnel and stuck his face close to the floor pan. A structural member ran transversely across the space. He curled his fingers beneath it and tried to feel his way along, but the thick leather gloves were too stiff. He pulled them off with his teeth in frustration and tried again. He felt thick smears of grease, a few specks of grit and ... nothing.

"No!" he muttered. "Not after all this. Nobody's *this* clean."

Twisting onto his side to increase his reach by a few precious inches, he poked his index and middle fingers into the furthest corner where the seat squab would have met the back rest. In family cars, it was the spot where he usually found chocolate buttons, white with age, or half-sucked boiled sweets, melted into blobs of jewel-coloured sugar. The tip of his index finger encountered something flexible. A piece of plastic perhaps. No. Too flexible to be plastic. He pushed his fingers harder into the gap, wincing as a sharp metal edge dragged across the first knuckle of his middle finger.

"Fuck!"

With a scissoring action, he closed his fingers around the thin, flat object, pad of middle finger on top of nail of index. Clamping them together as tightly as he could, he withdrew his hand. His fingers slipped off. He tried again. This time, the object stayed put inside in his improvised pincer-grip.

He sighed with relief and brought it all the way out. Sucking at the jagged tear across the top of his middle finger and tasting the iron tang of his own blood, he looked at what he held in his fingers.

It was a business card. The paper was coated in a silky finish, and was creased and oily with his own finger marks. But it was perfectly legible.

Max Novgorodsky

Kuznitsa

F765/TRF.maxN

"Hello, Max," Lucian said with a smile. "Is this your car?

* * *

Callie phoned Don the moment Lucian had left her office with the single piece of hard evidence that might be worth a damn.

"We've got something. A business card."

"And I'm guessing you're not calling to tell me it belongs to Paula in Mercedes Corporate Sales?"

"Nope. It says Max Novgorodsky. Kuznitsa. And then this code. Foxtrot seven-six-five forwards slash Tango Romeo Foxtrot dot Mike Alpha X-ray – those three in lower case by the way – November."

"Callie, that's absolutely fantastic! Where was this business card?"

"Under the rear seat. Looks like it might have slipped down there out of someone's back pocket. One of my forensics officers pretty well tore the car to pieces to find it."

"Please extend my personal thanks to him or her."

"It's a he, and yes I will. Thank you."

"Any idea what the code means?"

"Not yet. But my forensics guy's also an IT expert when he's not cutting up cars into tiny pieces. He's on it now. And yes, I will let you know the moment he has anything."

ROOM SERVICE

TEHRAN

Back at the hotel, Eli launched the tracker app on her phone and tapped the icon for Gabriel. She'd designated her partner with a simple white G in a blue circle. The map rendered itself in a few seconds and Eli found she was looking at a section of Tehran. The blue-and-white spot was pulsing once a second over the Avis branch, which was indicated with orange text.

She picked up the room phone and ordered two club sandwiches, a Coke and a coffee on room service.

"Certainly, madam," came the courteous reply. "It will be with you in about ten minutes."

Eli returned her gaze to her phone. No movement. Her suitcase was resting on the straps of a wooden foldout stand. She unzipped the case and began packing. Every few items, she paused and check the phone's screen.

Hope they've got aircon over there.

A soft knocking at the door interrupted her thoughts.

"Room service!" said a female voice.

She crossed to the door and placed her eye to the spyhole. A young woman stood waiting, holding a tray with a glass of Coke and a coffee, and two plates covered by gleaming metal domes. *Five-star fancy!* she thought as she turned the chromed knob a foot below the peep-hole.

She opened the door, smiling, ready with a folded bill to tip the waitress.

But the woman had gone. In her place stood a heavily built man in a bottle-green uniform. He shoved her hard in the chest with both hands and stepped into the room as she stumbled backwards. A second man, dressed in a grey suit and white shirt, followed him in and slammed the door shut behind him.

Uniform was reaching for the pistol at his belt. He should have had it already drawn before shoving Eli. Underestimating their target was their first – and last – mistake. In the act of stumbling, she'd twisted round and righted herself with an extra-long step towards the desk. In a single movement, she swept the striker pen from her pocket and closed with him. His gun arm was on its way up so Eli stepped inside his reach and helped it on its way, knocking his wrist wide with her left hand where it collided with his accomplice's face.

Her knee came up, smashing into his groin. Not once, but twice. And she smacked the point of the striker into the centre of his forehead. He dropped like a demolished tower block. Straight down into a tangled heap of bent limbs. She turned to the plainclothesman, who'd drawn his own pistol from a shoulder holster. A stubby suppressor lengthened its barrel by a few inches. He hadn't been able to shoot for fear of hitting his partner. As the man fell back, he had a clear shot, but Eli had one too.

She grabbed his gun hand and twisted violently, turning his arm outwards and exposing the soft tissue on the underside of his wrist. Down flew the striker pen, puncturing the skin and ripping through the blood vessels serving the hand. He screamed with pain and dropped the pistol. But Eli wasn't finished. She pushed him away and leant way back before kicking up and breaking his lower jaw with a loud snap. He moaned in pain, a deep lowing sound like a cow, clutching his ruined face with both hands. Still in motion, Eli swept her foot round against his left knee, delivering a punch to his throat at the same time. He fell back onto the bed. She stooped to grab the pistol then straightened.

Grabbing a pillow, she stuffed it down hard over his face, jammed the suppressor against it and fired twice. The pillow exploded, releasing a sickening smell of burnt feathers.

Behind her, she heard the uniformed man move. She turned to see him clawing his way upright, using the door handle for support. Blood was streaming from the deep hole in his forehead, blinding him. He'd found his pistol and was trying to clear the blood from his eyes with his right sleeve.

She covered the distance from the bed to the door in three fast paces, pistol gripped in her right hand. But as she reached him, he dropped a foot or two and scythed out his right boot, catching her below the knee and sending her to the carpet. She lost her grip on the pistol and dropped it.

He'd cleared blood from a stripe of skin across his eyes giving him the look of a monstrous bandit. Teeth bared, he drew down on Eli.

ONE OUT, ALL OUT

The blow Eli had dealt to her attacker's head had opened a fast-bleeding wound, but it had also knocked his perceptions seriously askew. The barrel of the gun was pointing off by a few degrees. Not much. And at point-blank range not enough to matter. But at six feet – the distance from the muzzle to Eli's torso – too much. He fired. The sound was deafening in the enclosed space. The round went wide, hitting the wall and gouging out a chunk of plaster. He may have spent his last few moments drawing breath trying to figure out what had gone wrong with his first shot. But he didn't get a chance for a second.

Eli flipped herself upright like a gymnast, which she had once been as a fifteen-year-old schoolgirl, and launched a ferocious attack. His eyes were masked in blood again, but still presented an excellent target. In a sequence of stabbing moves, her clawed fingers destroyed them utterly. To prevent his screaming, she jabbed her straight fingers hard into the soft place between his Adam's apple and the supra-sternal notch where his collarbones met. He coughed and wheezed, struggling to drag air into his lungs. Then it was over. Eli took his pistol and hit him on the side of the head so hard the crack as the thin plate of the temporal bone shattered was clearly audible. He fell back, his head thumping on the carpet. She reached under the bed for the suppressed pistol, curled her hand round the grip and dragged another pillow off the bed.

* * *

After killing the second man, she sat on the bed and called Gabriel.

"Hey, has my food arrived yet?" he asked. "I'm still ten minutes from the front of the queue and the clerk's clearly been—"

"Shut up!" she said, panting, her knee jiggling from the adrenaline now that the fighting was done. "I've been blown. *We've* been blown. Two heavies just burst in here. They're both dead. I'm getting to the embassy. You should do the same."

"That's very interesting Melina. Do they have my contact details?"

"What? Of course they do!"

"Well, not to worry. I'll just have to go to the meeting on my own. I'm sure I'll manage even if you do have to go back to the office."

"Gabriel, wait. You can't go alone. It's too dangerous."

"Oh, I wouldn't say that. We're just talking about a contract, after all. I have to go. Ciao, darling. See you at the airport."

And he ended the call.

Eli stared at the little white and red phone icon. Then the screen grew tired of her scrutiny and faded to black.

"Fuck!" she muttered. "Just do the job and get yourself to the embassy."

She went into the bathroom and examined herself in the mirror. Her face was spattered with blood and her hair had come loose. She pulled out the scrunchie now only hanging from a single hank of hair and refastened her bun. A scrub with a cold flannel took care of the blood spatters, though her cheeks were flushed. Two minutes later she'd concealed the evidence behind freshly reapplied foundation and lipstick.

"Time to go," she said to her mirror-self. "I hope to God you'll be OK, Wolfe."

Back in the bedroom, she collected her phone and slid it into her inside pocket beside her passport. She shoved the suppressed pistol into her document case. Then she dragged the body of the plainclothesman away from the door and left, hanging a "Please do not disturb" sign on the polished handle. Nobody was running towards her. She suspected MOIS had instructed the hotel management to keep clear and tell their guests likewise.

Turning away from the sign for the lifts, restaurant and reception, she walked fast down the corridor to the far end, where the fire escape door beckoned. Once through, she raced down the concrete steps, taking them two at a time, and reached the ground floor without encountering another soul. The door from the stairwell was tucked away in a corridor between the kitchen and the lobby. Eli emerged into the marble-floored space at the opposite end from the reception desk. Turning her back, she left through a set of plate glass doors that led out onto Mansour Street. Her mind was working in overdrive as she weighed up her options.

Taxi or walk?

Three-quarters of an hour or ten minutes?

Freedom to move or concealment?

Walk.

The direct route would take her left onto Shahid Motahari Street then right onto Larestan Street. Eli turned right then left onto Valiasr Street. A longer walk but if MOIS agents were waiting they'd more likely be two blocks to the east.

Her document case was snug against her front. She kept her right hand inside, gripping the butt on the pistol. Knowing her cover was blown, she had no illusions about what awaited her, an Israeli, a Jew and a woman, if she was caught by the Iranian secret police. Anyone trying to stop her reaching the British Embassy would be dead before they hit the ground.

The pistol was an ageing Sig Sauer P226. She'd checked the magazine on the way down the back staircase: a 20-round model, which meant it was chambered for 9 x 19mm Parabellum rounds. Assuming the MOIS man had arrived with a full mag, she had seventeen left. Sixteen ought to be enough to get her clear. And if not? She wouldn't allow herself to be captured.

Walking purposefully, but not so fast as to draw attention to herself, Eli made her way steadily down Valiasr Street. A wide boulevard, it was lined with drab concrete apartment blocks in shades of rose pink and beige, car dealerships, cafes, department stores, banks and office buildings. Plenty of people milled about or sat outside cafes, chatting and drinking coffee or mint tea.

The traffic was heavy and loud, car horns adding to the clamour. Eli crossed and recrossed the street, being careful to wait for the green signal or the officious white-gloved wave of a traffic cop on duty at the centre of the busier junctions. Aiming for the interested look of a tourist, she swivelled her head every few seconds, as if to take in another of Tehran's architectural wonders. Each time she brought her gaze down and to the front, she scanned the pavement behind and beside her. Nobody was following her, on either side of the street.

Her destination was only half a mile away. She remained on high alert but somewhere, a spark of hope had ignited. Her hand felt sweaty on the pistol's grip. With her left hand, she pulled out her phone and sent a short text to Julian Furnish.

Aborting. Admit in 15.

She crossed College Bridge into Hafez Street. No more shops, just an open area planted with palm trees and hundreds of scarlet roses. As she walked past the display, inhaling their sweet perfume, she remembered randomly that the rose was the national flower of Iran. *Who knew?*

Left on Ghazali Street, skirting the impressive compound of the Russian Embassy, its gardens home to even more roses, plus tulips, carnations and bird of paradise flowers. Right on Pars. Left on Nofel Loshato Street. Right on Ferdowsi Avenue. The pavement ahead and behind was empty.

* * *

By the time she reached the metal gates of the British Embassy, the Iranian police guard on duty had moved aside to allow the Deputy Cultural Attaché to emerge. Eli walked straight up to him. He placed an arm on her shoulder, smiling broadly.

"My dear Ms Arifaki. Taking a break from the book fair? Come inside. We'll have tea and talk about literature."

He turned to the cop.

"Metshekerem." *Thank you.*

Then he ushered Eli inside the compound, the gates clanging together behind them as they walked.

"We've been blown," Eli said. "Gabriel's still in play. He's headed to Vareshabad."

TARGET APPREHENDED

Gabriel reached the outskirts of Vareshabad at 4.30 p.m. The logistics people at Marlborough Lines had done their homework. The real village bore a striking resemblance to its breeze-block and white-paint counterpart in the wilderness at the centre of Salisbury Plain. Though as Gabriel had observed at the time, the temperature difference was striking. England in late May was enjoying balmy temperatures in the midtwenties Celsius. In the scrubby desert in Northern Iran, currently midway through a spell of freakishly high pressure, it was hot enough to fry an egg on the bonnet of Gabriel's hire car. The drive had taken an hour, and even with the white Nissan's air conditioning going full blast, the interior of the car was still only cool rather than cold, and the air puffing out of the vents smelled of mould. But as he stepped out of the cramped cabin and slammed the door closed with a tinny clang, the full force of the Iranian climate hit him.

The heat was dry and intense, like stepping in front of an open furnace. He knew he was sweating, but it was evaporating off his skin as soon as the beads of moisture appeared. He took a bottle of water from his bag and swigged half of it down. He ripped the document case's lining away from the zip, reached inside and closed his fingers around the leather-wound hilt of the slim-bladed stiletto. Nodded to himself and let go. He didn't zip up the case again. Next, he checked his inside breast pocket. His fingers touched the cold, blunt metal end of the striker pen. *Backup. I'd rather have Eli.*

Owing to his having arrived in the hottest part of the day, the dusty streets were deserted. Not even a dog had ventured out. Every house wore shutters over its street-facing windows, their blank faces lightened only by the occasional pot of scarlet geraniums by the front doors.

He climbed back in and reversed to the turning he'd just passed. According to the map, in half a mile or so, a track would lead him around the western edge of the village and up into the hills. He looked to his left as he drove. The village itself was small. Only a few dozen houses. He assumed most of the residents had jobs at the nuclear facility outside the settlement. He could see it shimmering in the heat haze on the far side of the village, along a straight, metalled road. He reached the last house, then was past it.

The map was right. To a degree. A track did indeed lead into the hills from the village, but its purpose clearly had very little to do with easing the passage of motorised vehicles. Its broken surface might have suited livestock or strolling farmers, but the Nissan was finding it heavy going.

After fifteen minutes of torturously slow driving, at no point during which did Gabriel have the luxury of keeping the steering wheel still, he reached a wider stretch. Unclenching his stomach muscles, he drove along for a few more minutes before reaching the end of the track: a roughly oval space a kinder soul than he might have described as a turnaround.

He climbed out. Then winced at a sudden squawk of protest from the area of his kidneys. He put on the foppish Panama hat he'd brought all the way from a shop in Winchester, rolled up in its own stiff cardboard tube. The shade cast by its wide brim and a pair of sunglasses allowed him to stop squinting.

From the sheaf of papers in the document case, he withdrew a map marked with fictitious archaeological sites in and around

Vareshabad. He put another two bottles of water, the Fairbairn-Sykes and a pair of binoculars into a daysack he'd bought earlier. Then he started climbing into the hills along what appeared to be a goat track, to judge from the scattered clumps of dry droppings. He dropped to one knee and looked closer. Yes. The tracks imprinted on its dusty surface confirmed his initial impression. So not everyone worked on building a nuclear bomb, or cleaning and cooking for those who did.

He reached a barren patch of rocky land scabbed here and there by patches of brownish-yellow lichen growing on immense flat stones. Rounding a corner, he found what he was looking for. A stand of perhaps a dozen short, twisted trees growing out over a precipice. Along every branch, small, green fruits were emerging from behind browning flowers. Beyond the trees, a sandy ledge gave a perfect view of the nuclear facility. He sat with his back to one of the trees and pulled out the binoculars. In keeping with his admittedly thin cover, these were not military-spec, but a still-serviceable pair of Nikons such as an amateur archaeologist on a field trip might own.

Bringing the rubber cups snug against his eyes, he adjusted the focus, closing first one eye then the other and tweaking the ridged knob until he had a pin-sharp view of the bomb factory. Against an almost painfully clear blue sky, the place had the look of something a child might construct out of white building blocks. A white sphere occupied the central space, flanked by low rectangular buildings, with narrow cylindrical towers off to one side. The access road was a wavering black strip all the way from Vareshabad to the gates, which Gabriel could see were defended by a tall, glinting wire fence, and armed guards standing in towers mounted with what looked like light machineguns.

He checked his watch. He'd arrived an hour earlier. He had no idea if nuclear weapon scientists kept office hours but he imagined Darbandi would be putting in plenty of overtime. If he left work late, so much the better. There'd be less traffic on the road and fewer people around. He consulted his memorised briefing note on Darbandi. Unusually for a man living somewhere as hot as Iran, Darbandi did not drive a white car. His was black. A Mercedes E-class. Presumably the German air conditioning was sufficiently well engineered to cool the man down after a hard day planning genocide.

The registration plate was etched into Gabriel's mind, too: 71Q333-11. Black-on-white, it was a private plate, the 11 signifying Tehran city. As he was engaged in an activity deemed illegal under international law, Darbandi did not use a red-on-white government plate, to which he was presumably entitled. More of the plausible deniability so loved by the people Gabriel and his colleagues at The Department regularly went up against. And, he supposed, The Department itself.

By 6.45 p.m., the worst of the heat was gone, and Gabriel began to enjoy the cooler temperature, out here, in an oasis of calm. If only for a short while. He took the Fairbairn-Sykes from his daysack and turned it in the sun, so that the edge glinted. Soon it would be buried deep into the vital organs of Abbas Darbandi.

A shout in Farsi from behind him jerked him out of the focused state of mind he'd dropped into as he watched the gates.

"Ha tew! Cheh kear ma kena?" *Hey, you! What are you doing?*

Staying seated, Gabriel slipped the knife into his jacket pocket, lowered his binoculars and turned slowly, assembling a well-meaning if puzzled smile. Suddenly aware of the distant *tonk-tonk* of goat bells, he found himself facing a powerfully built man in his early or middle forties, dressed in a traditional white kaftan over baggy trousers and sturdy leather sandals.

The man had startling green eyes that glared at Gabriel from a face seventy percent covered with a ferocious reddish-brown beard and moustache. In his left hand, he carried a long staff, by the look of it carved from a single tree branch. His right hand was empty. But it was the object strapped over his back that Gabriel fixed on. An ancient rifle that could easily have dated from the turn of the twentieth century.

As Gabriel got to his feet, the goatherd, if that's what he was, dropped the staff. He unslung the rifle and brought it around and up to his shoulder. Despite his predicament, Gabriel found time to identify the rifle properly. A Lee–Enfield .303. It may have been old, having been launched in 1895, but it could still snuff out a man's life –

his life – perfectly well at ranges well beyond the ten feet now separating him from his aggressive new companion.

Gabriel let the binoculars drop to his chest then raised his hands and spoke, clearly but not loudly.

"Letfa. Shelak neken!" *Please. Don't shoot!*

In response, the man worked the bolt back and forth to load a round from the short steel magazine into the breech. He jerked the rifle's stubby muzzle at Gabriel, then swung the barrel back down the path. His meaning was clear. You're coming with me.

Gabriel walked ahead of the man, then flinched as his captor jabbed the muzzle into his back, right between the shoulder blades. Gabriel kept his back bent and his head down. He raised his hands and placed them on the back of his head as he walked back down the path. The rifle's muzzle was digging painfully into his back. Which was perfect.

TARGET ACQUIRED

In a single, fast, flowing movement that Eli's Krav Maga instructors would have approved of, Gabriel ducked and rolled anticlockwise, sliding around the business end of the Lee–Enfield. He completed the turn, grabbed the wooden fore-end with his left hand and pushed it out wide, and stepped in towards his captor. Now the rifle was useless. An encumbrance.

As the man's eyes widened, Gabriel pulled the striker pen from his breast pocket with his right hand. He clamped his thumb over the top, brought it up, then smacked it down, point-first on top of the man's head. His green eyes, so sharp a second earlier, lost focus and rolled up into his head until only the whites were showing. He staggered sideways for a second. A second was all Gabriel needed. He dropped the striker, grabbed the stiletto from his jacket pocket and stabbed the man under his ribs and up into his heart.

As blood surged from the ruined pump to fill his chest cavity, the man died. He collapsed into a heap, blood spurting from the crater the striker had punched through his skull, and the small hole in the front of his robe, which was rapidly changing from white to scarlet.

"Shit!" Gabriel hissed. Then again, louder this time. "Shit!"

Then he dragged the body back to the stand of trees, between the two nearest until he reached the drop-off. He looked over the edge. It was an uninterrupted, near-vertical drop across more of the weirdly flat rocks to a thick patch of greyish-green bushes smothered in orange flowers.

"I'm sorry, my friend," he said, meaning it. Then he uttered, almost as a prayer, the mantra Master Zhao had taught him. "I honour your life."

Then he rolled the corpse over until gravity took hold of it. He watched as it tumbled over the rocks, gathering speed until it crashed into the centre of the flowering bushes. Their blossom-laden branches shook angrily for a few moments, then were still again.

Heart pounding in his chest, he returned to his observation post and brought the binoculars up to his eyes again. *Fuck! Have I missed him?* He scanned the road from the fortified gates of the facility all the way back to the village. He couldn't see any cars at all. No, wait! Yes. But it was white. A small hatchback. He kept waiting and watching. Five minutes later, relief flooded his system. Cruising up to the gate from the factory side was Darbandi's long, black E-Class. The licence plate matched. He could even see the target's face through the windscreen.

Gabriel ran back to the hire car and started the engine. He threw it into gear and spun the steering wheel as he accelerated out of the turning circle, racing to intercept Darbandi. The potholed goat track did its best to rip the car's suspension from the chassis, but Gabriel didn't have the luxury of slowing down. Instead he floored the throttle so that the car almost seemed to skitter over the crests of the holes. Clamping his jaws shut, he gripped the wheel until his knuckles turned bone-white, and powered down the hill towards the spot where it joined the road.

As he reached the metalled road, he slowed a fraction. He turned to his left and saw, between two widely-spaced houses, Darbandi's car driving through the centre of the village.

Good. I'll let you leave by the main road then get in behind you.

Ahead, as the houses thinned and then ended, Darbandi accelerated away from Vareshabad. Gabriel had a moment's worry as he realised the big Mercedes could easily outrun his overworked little Nissan, then relaxed. *He's a scientist. He'll just get to the limit then sit back and enjoy the drive home. Put on his favourite tunes and think about what his wife's made for dinner.*

And that's exactly what Darbandi did. At 60 mph, he levelled off, and Gabriel was sure he saw Darbandi lean over as if fiddling with the stereo.

"Now you're mine," Gabriel said aloud, realising how hot the interior of the car was and leaning over to locate the knob to switch on the air conditioning.

When he returned his eyes to the road, it was to see Darbandi's brake lights glowing bright red. He was slowing hard, and in a few seconds, Gabriel had made his decision.

Darbandi came to a halt. Gabriel pulled up fifty yards behind the Mercedes's rear bumper and got out, the Fairbairn-Sykes tucked into the back of his waistband. He mentally rehearsed his Good Samaritan speech as he closed with the Mercedes.

"Hemh cheaz rewbh rah aset? Matewnem kemeketewn kenem?" *Is everything all right? Can I help you?*

He watched as the driver's door opened. Darbandi climbed out. He looked back down the road at Gabriel and held his hands out wide.

Gabriel frowned. Motorists who broke down rarely emerged from their cars smiling.

TARGET CAPTURED

Gabriel strode on towards Darbandi, retrieving the knife from his waistband and preparing to attack. Instead of retreating to the safety of his car, Darbandi leaned on the boot and folded his arms across his chest, the smile seemingly glued to his face.

Puzzled, Gabriel broke into a run.

The rear driver's side door opened.

A man climbed out.

And pointed a pistol at Gabriel.

Then he gestured with the barrel at a spot on the road a few feet in front of Gabriel.

He spoke in English.

"On the ground!"

This was no sun-ravaged goatherd with a Boer War-era bolt-action rifle. The man, dressed in a suit and white shirt, looked fit, alert and ready to put a bullet in Gabriel's torso without a moment's thought.

Gabriel stopped running. The distance between them was twenty yards. Had it been twenty feet, and his opponent's pistol in its holster, he would have sprinted on and killed him with a single knife-thrust. A US police report he'd read had concluded that inside twenty-one feet, a fast assailant armed with a knife would reach an officer before he or she could unholster, raise, aim and fire their service weapon.

Twenty yards.

Less than half the effective range for what he could now see was a Sig Sauer P226 – ironically, his own favoured short. It didn't matter whether the Iranians favoured the 9 x 19mm Parabellum, the .40 S&W or the SIG .357 round. At this range, any of those lethal projectiles would blow a fist-sized hole in him.

He tossed the knife to one side, out of reach. No need to wait for the command. Then he got to his knees before lying face-down on the boiling-hot road surface. It smelled of tar and burnt rubber.

The bodyguard's footsteps were unhurried as he closed the distance to Gabriel. Gabriel could hear the metallic taps from the man's cleated boots. The striker pen felt reassuringly uncomfortable as it pressed into his ribs. Expecting to be hauled to his feet and frisked, Gabriel was ready. He'd let the man get him halfway vertical, stagger a little and pull out the striker in that split-second. Game over.

He caught a movement out of the corner of his eye. A pair of black boots had arrived in his peripheral vision. He tensed every muscle, ready to fight. He heard a scuffing sound as one boot disappeared. Then a blinding flash of white light and a grenade of agony detonated inside his skull.

Then.

Blackness.

* * *

Later.

Pain.

* * *

Gabriel's eyes fluttered open. The pain in the right side of his head was making him nauseous. He tried to reach up and touch his pounding temple. But his hand wouldn't move. He was sitting on a hard, wooden chair in front of a simple wooden table. On the other side of the table, an empty chair waited.

He looked down, then inhaled sharply at the combination of a stab of pain and a roiling wave of nausea that left him sweating and swallowing hard. His wrists were tied to the chair with green plastic cable ties. He moved his ankles experimentally. Nothing doing. And he'd been stripped while unconscious.

The room was oversized for a torture chamber, he thought. Not that he had any experience. Perhaps twenty feet by thirty. Stained concrete floor. Grey-painted walls, also smeared with substances that could have been blood or shit. Fly-specked ceiling in the centre of which hung a single pendant lamp from a chain. One door. A coat-rack to its left.

The room smelled of pain and fear. He didn't need to guess his location. He'd arrived at the Ministry of Intelligence and Security. He looked back at the door.

You must prepare yourself, Wolfe Cub, his old mentor whispered in the space between Gabriel's temples.

A key scraped in the lock.

His pulse jerked upwards and there was nothing he could do to bring it down again.

He watched as the door swung inwards. He inhaled sharply, then began to clear his mind of Gabriel Wolfe and fill it with Robert Denning.

Two burly men walked in, closed the door behind them, then hung their jackets on the coat rack. One carried a length of green hosepipe. They approached him, their faces expressionless. Then they began to beat him. First a few blows from the hosepipe. Then punches to the kidneys and groin. They repeated the routine until Gabriel saw black curtains swing shut over his vision.

* * *

He came to. Below the jabbing spikes of pain from his head, he felt a dull ache in his groin, and echoes of the same sensation in the region of his kidneys. Long red welts covered his torso.

The door opened. He watched as it swung inwards. Trying to prepare himself once more.

Revealed in the rectangle formed by the open door, stood a man of average height and build, a bulging canvas holdall dangling by its handles from his right hand. His olive-green uniform, bedecked by medal ribbons, was immaculate. His glossy back hair, cut militarily short, gleamed in the light. It was as luxuriant as the bushy moustache that completely hid his upper lip. His eyes were also obscured, by black-lensed, aviator-style sunglasses. *Take away the tache and you could almost be my twin*, Gabriel thought.

He put the bag down, removed his stiff-peaked officer's cap and hung it on one of the hooks on the coat rack. The jacket came off next. He hung it next to the cap and slapped a few specks of dust from one sleeve.

Then he picked the bag up again, walked to the table, pulled out the other chair, dusted the seat with a handkerchief and sat down, placing the bag at his feet. He spread his hands, palms down, on the plain wooden table between him and Gabriel. They were hard hands, thick fingered, with knuckles that appeared to have been broken and healed many times. *A regimental boxer?* Gabriel wondered.

"My name is General Razi," the man said. "Everything that happens, or does not happen, to you from this point in your life forwards is at my pleasure. I would encourage you to co-operate."

"I don't know why I'm here," Gabriel croaked out. "I came to Tehran for the book fair. I'm a publisher."

Razi smiled.

"Are you a religious man, Gabriel?"

SEARCHING IN THE DARK

LONDON

Lucian looked out of the window. His apartment had a view across the Thames to Canary Wharf. At this time of night, the towers of the financial district were largely dark, though the red lights on their tips shone through the cloudless sky across the river.

If Kuznitsa were an organisation capable of issuing business cards, it probably had an internet presence. Not a visible web presence, though. He had a feeling organisations who sent heavily armed mercenaries after state security operators liked to keep to the shadows.

He opened his laptop and launched a browser. Not the regular web-surfing tool the general public – and even the police – used to find basic corporate information. This tool was the TOR browser, used exclusively for searching the dark web. Despite the occasional media piece on this illicit area of the internet, most people really didn't have much of a clue what went on down there. Lucian, as a forensics officer, knew only too well. Sometimes he wished he didn't.

There was no point searching for Max Novgorodsky. Nor for Kuznitsa. The individuals and organisations who swam in these deep, dark, cold waters tended to obscure such basic facts as their names.

But he'd recognised the code he'd typed into his phone from the business card. Not in its specifics, but in its format. The previous year, he'd worked on a case spanning three continents involving law enforcement agencies from five countries. They'd been digging into a human trafficking ring, and in the process had discovered and then cracked a secure communications code. The line of letters, symbols and digits on Max's business card fitted the personal identifier format perfectly: capital letter-one or more digits-forwards slash-three capital letters-dot-a text user name rendered as three lower-case letters plus a capital. The three capital letters after the slash represented the owner's home base, which Lucian knew was The Russian Federation.

He typed the code into the browser's search box.

F765/TRF.maxN

Hit the return key.

And nodded.

Buried deep below the innocuous surface web – with its cat videos, auction sites and the kind of porn most people knew about, even if they claimed never to view it – Max Novgorodsky and his kind had profiles as brazenly self-promoting as the most avid Facebook user's. Business was business, after all. And in a globalised world, not everything could be handled face to face. Of course, without their ID code, they were harder to reach than the bottom of the Marianas Trench, but then, that's why Lucian had taken a hundred-grand Mercedes GLS and reduced it to a pile of scrap metal.

Here was the owner of the business card in all his poisonous pomp.

Max Novgorodsky. Managing Director, Europe, Middle East and Africa, Kuznitsa.

Formerly of the Gradlovsk Street Brigade, the Red Army, and State
Correction Institute (Maximum Security), Nizhny Novgorod.
Specialities: arms dealing, human trafficking, extractive industries,
political operations.

The space for a photo was occupied by a dark-grey silhouette on a
paler grey circular background. Who'd want to show their face, even
on the dark web? They knew the police swam in these waters too,
from time to time.

Below that was a button labelled *Contact*. He resisted the urge to
click it. The designers of this particular interface had included a
pingback mechanism that alerted users when someone was even
thinking of making contact. As one Drug Enforcement Agency agent
had discovered to his cost on the previous year's mission.

Lucian took a screenshot and typed up all the information into a
new document. The copy and paste function didn't work on the dark
web. One more safeguard, even if minor, to keep its occupants and
their activities private.

Lucian reversed out of the dark web, closed Tor and snapped the
lid of his laptop shut. He checked the time: 2.15 a.m. He hesitated, but
only for a moment. Callie had been explicit on the subject.

"You find something, you call me, d'ye hear? I don't care if it's
three in the bloody morning or I've just left for my bikini wax
appointment. You call me the moment you have something."

He smiled at the memory. Her soft Scottish burr hardened up
when she was under pressure, which, he reflected, was most of the
time, and she had a choice turn of phrase. He called her.

"This better be good, Lucian. D'ye know what time it is?"

"Well, it's before three, Boss."

"Go on, then. Make me a happy wee girl."

He heard the sharpness come back into her voice. The blur of
sleep had vanished.

"I've found Mr Novgorodsky. He's ex-Red Army, and what looks
like some kind of Russian gang before that. And he's spent time in a
Soviet prison."

"You're two for two, Lucian. Come and see me first thing and I'll give you a sticker."

"Thanks! How's my chart looking?"

"Nearly full. Now please, and I mean this in a kind and caring way, fuck off and let me get a couple more hours' sleep."

* * *

The following morning, after Lucian had briefed her on his findings from the night's trawling in the dark web, Callie called Don.

"We've identified Mr Novgorodsky. He's Russian. Ex-con. Ex-Red Army. We have a route to contacting him, but my forensics guy says it needs handling carefully. You need to be ready for anything once you send the message."

"Which we are. Thank you, Callie. Can you send me the report? I think we'll take it from here, if you don't mind."

"After what Lucian told me? No, I don't mind at all. We'll go back to catching serial killers and terrorists. Much simpler."

BY ALL THE PROPHETS

TEHRAN

Gabriel looked across at the man who now controlled every aspect of his life. The man so similar to him in height and stature and yet who possessed every scrap of power in this temporary relationship. He could see himself reflected in the man's sunglasses. A pair of tiny, pale, naked men looked out at him from the opaque lenses as if submerged in deep pools of black ink.

"Why do you keep calling me Gabriel?" he asked. "My name is Robert Denning. I told you. I am a publisher, and I'm over here for the Tehran Book Fair. I don't know why you are doing this to me."

"I am calling you Gabriel because that is your name. And I am doing *this*," Razi leaned across the table and slapped Gabriel hard, "because you are an assassin and I must discover as much about you and your orders as I can manage."

He was frowning, but he spoke softly and patiently, as if to a slow-witted child.

"It was somewhat arrogant of your parents to name you after an angel, but then, I have never found westerners to be over-blessed with humility before God. Speaking of the Creator, it's interesting how the founders of the world's religions grounded their prophets in a simple world their adherents could understand, don't you think? Take Mohammed, peace be upon him. In his early years, it was reported that he was a shepherd. Then he became a merchant."

"I don't know what you want me to say. I'm a publisher, not a spy."

Razi smiled. He leaned over to the canvas holdall by his left foot. He straightened, and placed a copper-headed lump hammer on the table. The face was pitted and gouged by much use. Then he laid a six-inch steel nail beside it.

"Or take Jesus, as another example. A carpenter. A man who worked with his hands. With tools just like this one."

He unbuttoned his right shirt cuff and folded it back on itself. Repeating the movement twice more, he smoothed the rolled cotton over his bicep. Agonisingly slowly, he performed the same routine with the left cuff. His forearms were covered with dense, curling black hair. Almost apologetically, he smiled at Gabriel.

"It's new. I don't want to spoil it. My wife would give me a hard time, I can tell you."

Then he stood. Gabriel watched out of the corner of his eye as Razi rounded the table and came to stand behind him. He closed his eyes and resumed his inner chanting of the mantra against despair his old friend and mentor Zhao Xi had taught him.

Pain passes like clouds on a windy day, pain passes like clouds on a windy day, pain passes

Razi placed his hands on Gabriel's shoulders and pushed down hard. Gabriel could smell his aftershave. Razi shouted in Farsi.

"Ali! Der aaneja. Hala!" *Ali! In here. Now!*

The door opened, and a heavily built man entered. He was dressed in the western style: grey two-piece suit, dress shirt open at his bull neck, black shoes. Only the Kalashnikov slung across his massive shoulders made him look like anything other than a successful Middle Eastern businessman.

like clouds on a windy day,

Razi issued a brief instruction.

"Dest khewd ra ber rewa maz neguh darad." *Hold his hand out on the table.*

pain passes

The man called Ali drew a knife. Its blade whispered against the cable tie that bound Gabriel's left hand to the arm of the chair. For a split-second, Gabriel's hand was free before being secured in the six-footer's iron grip. He slammed Gabriel's hand down onto the table, exactly half-way across, and leaned down on it, pinning it in place.

like clouds on a windy day, pain passes like clouds on a windy day, pain passes

Razi re-entered Gabriel's field of vision. He picked up the nail in his thick fingers and turned it this way and that in the harsh light. Then he rested its four-sided point on the thin skin on the back of Gabriel's hand. He felt for a moment with the index finger of his other hand then repositioned the point. His fingertips were cool against Gabriel's sweating skin.

"Please!" Gabriel screamed. "Don't hurt me! I'll tell you anything. OK, fine, I'm not a publisher. You're right. I'm a, uh, a spy. For the

British Government. I'm spying on your, your secret agents in Tehran. Robert Denning is just my codename. I'm actually called, called, Rick Stone. You have to believe me. Don't hurt me! I'll tell you what you want to know."

like clouds on a windy day, pain passes like clouds on

Razi smiled. But he did not relax his grip on the nail. Or the hammer.

"Indeed you will, Gabriel. But not until you have shed every last scrap of your humanity. Now," he said, repositioning the nail point a fraction. "We place it there. Between the metacarpal bones. In my profession, one must study an extraordinary amount of anatomy, you know. Take the man we were just speaking of. Jesus. Every statue, every icon, every painting, etching and silverpoint drawing got it wrong. You cannot crucify a man with nails through his palms. Believe me when I tell you this. Even a light body has enough weight to simply drag the nails through the flesh and out between the fingers. No. The correct way to crucify a man is to place the nails behind the wrist, you know? Between the radius and the ulna. Then he can hang there as long as you wish. Or," an apologetic smile, "until his leg muscles are too weak to support his weight. And he suffocates. On the other hand, if you do not wish to kill a man, then you have greater latitude in where you position your nails."

a windy day, pain passes like clouds on a windy

Gabriel looked into black lenses, at the pathetic figure he saw trapped there. He forced himself to cry.

"I told you. My name is Robert Denning. I am a publisher. I came here with The British Council to attend the Tehran Book Fair."

"No," Razi said in a singsong voice, extending the single syllable

to three. He picked up the hammer. Gabriel closed his eyes. Inhaled
deeply. And let it out in a hiss.

day, pain passes like clouds on a windy day pain passes

"You are an assassin – "
    like clouds on a windy day, pain
He raised the hammer a foot above the table top.
    passes like clouds
"– sent by the British –"
    on a windy day,
Government—"

pain

Razi smashed the hammer down onto the nail head.
    Gabriel screamed.
    Razi bellowed.
    "And you came here to kill Abbas Darbandi!"
    Razi issued another order in Farsi.
    "Ma ra terk ken!" *Leave us*!

Gabriel was panting. Salty sweat stung his eyes as it mixed with the
tears, real ones now.
    He looked at his left hand, fastened to the table like a large exotic
insect in an antique collection, bleeding heavily onto the scratched
and stained wood. When he could trust himself to speak, he grunted
out another variant of the answer he had been giving for, how long
was it? One day? Two? More? He'd lost count.
    "My name is Robert Denning. Please! I have no idea what you're

talking about. I'm a publisher. We do books on ancient civilisations. That's why I'm in Iran. We have a new book coming out on Persia. I work for Copernicus Press. Why won't you believe me?"

Gabriel had no more need to fake tears.

Razi smiled. His hand moved to his shirt pocket.

"It is said that Siddārtha Gautama, the prince who metamorphosed into the Lord Buddha, had dreams of becoming a surgeon before his enlightenment. Did you know that?"

A silvery scalpel appeared in Razi's fingers as if produced out of thin air by a magician.

"I don't know why you are doing this to me," Gabriel gasped.

"I wonder, did he ever practise with one of these, do you think?"

Razi reached towards Gabriel's bleeding hand and took the middle finger in his own.

ANATOMY LESSON

Razi placed the tip of the scalpel blade beneath the edge of Gabriel's fingernail and stroked, left to right, pushing just enough so that blood welled out over the blade and flowed in rivulets onto the table.

The throbbing pain in Gabriel's hand turned from a dull orange to a blinding, searing, yellow-white.

He groaned and felt the world lurch sideways for a second. In the far corner of the room, he saw a black-skinned man emerge from a water stain on the roughly plastered wall. A man wearing an assortment of camo items and a sand-coloured SAS beret. A man he'd buried a couple of years earlier after recovering his mortal remains from the Mozambican forest.

Smudge, mate. I could do with some help here.

Stay strong, Boss. Stay strong, yeah. You can beat this.

Then Smudge vanished back into the wall.

Maintaining his inner chant – *pain passes like clouds on a windy day* – he straightened and focused on the two tiny Gabriels.

Razi stood.

"Anatomy, Mr Wolfe. We have plenty of time to explore the subject."

Then he turned and left the room, shutting the heavy steel

behind him with a clang. Despite the red-hot agony threatening to unman him, Gabriel scrutinised the way the torturer walked. The slight drag to the left foot, the stiffer swing to the left arm.

Blinking away the tears that were clouding his vision, Gabriel stared down at his left hand. The pain was like a scream in the centre of his brain. So loud it drowned out every other thought. He closed his eyes and searched for a place Master Zhao had taught him to find *in extremis*. He focused on his breathing. *Use the ten-second breath, Wolfe Cub*, Master Zhao's voice instructed. *Like you did with Fariyah. In for four. Hold for one. Out for four. Hold for one.*

Over and over again he followed the simple but grindingly hard ritual breathing sequence until he felt an odd calm descend upon him. The pain from his wounds was still there. Still a red-hot needle sweeping back and forth in his fingertip. Still a drill-bit boring through the flesh, bones and tendons of his hand. But remote, now, also. Something he could observe from a distance. Not far. But far enough to think.

He opened his eyes.

Looked at his injured hand.

And pulled it towards him.

He bit back the scream as fresh dark blood welled up around the nail's dully gleaming shaft. Then he pushed it away.

To the left – grunt with pain.

To the right – swallow back the vomit threatening to burst from his throat.

Then in small, agonising circles – ignore the lake of blood spreading to the edges of the table.

He let out the air trapped in his lungs with a sound halfway between a sigh and a groan. Tensing every muscle in his body and concentrating on his left arm until the tendons and muscles stood out against the grimy skin in thick ropes, he swore under his breath – "Fuck, fuck, fuck, fuck, fuck!" – leaned forwards, then wrenched his hand up.

He turned his head to the side and spewed a thin stream of watery, yellow bile onto the bare concrete floor.

Blood welled out of the ragged-edged hole and began dripping steadily from his hand to join the puddle on the table. Experimenting, he waggled his fingers, swearing under his breath as a fresh wave of agony washed over him. They moved at his command and he was momentarily distracted by the sight of the glistening silvery rods of his tendons moving back and forth in the centre of the red hole.

Panting, he reached for the nail, intending to free it from the table and use it against his torturer. A scrape of key in lock from the door ended that plan before it had begun. Panicking just for a second, he realised what he had to do. He clenched his teeth, placed his palm back over the nail head and hissed out a breath as he jammed his hand back down until it slapped against the tabletop. In the moment of agony, he saw black curtains swinging shut across his eyes and fought back the urge to let them shut completely. They parted and he felt cold tears on the edges of his eyelids.

In walked his tormenter. Razi was brushing crumbs from his lip with a white cotton handkerchief. He smiled as he sat down.

"Well, Gabriel. Shall we begin again? Why did you come here to kill Abbas Darbandi? Who sent you?"

"Please let me go. You've made a mistake. If it's a ransom you're after, I'm sure my employers will pay whatever you ask for."

Razi shook his head and retrieved the scalpel from an inside pocket as if reaching for a fountain pen. He leant forwards and picked up Gabriel's ring finger. Gabriel winced as the pressure pushed the raw edges of the hole through his hand against the nail. He watched as the tip of the blade moved closer to his finger tip.

In a low, steady voice, his own, not that of the panicky, stuttering Robert Denning, he leaned a few degrees forward.

"Stop! My name is Gabriel Wolfe. I work for the British Government. We know all about Darbandi's work on your nuclear weapon."

Razi withdrew the scalpel. He removed his sunglasses.

Gabriel saw that he had golden-brown eyes with long, almost girlish lashes.

"Who betrayed us?" Razi asked. "Tell me and you will die quickly and relatively painlessly."

Gabriel heaved a huge sigh, filling his lungs with fresh oxygen and blowing it out. He mumbled under his breath.

Razi leaned closer, tilting his head a little to the side.

"What? What did you say?"

Gabriel drew in as much air into his lungs as could manage and screamed it out – a full-throated yell of defiance – as he yanked his hand free of the steel nail. He grabbed a handful of the man's thick, black hair. Using all the remaining energy at his command, he pulled Razi's head up then slammed it down.

The bridge of Razi's nose met the nail-head with a dull, wet crunch before slipping sideways, permitting the rest of the steel shaft to disappear into his left eye socket and penetrate deep into his brain.

Gabriel snatched the scalpel from Razi's hand, which was twitching spasmodically. In three swift movements he sliced through the cable ties binding his right hand and ankles. He staggered round the table, stood behind Razi, who was jerking like a landed fish, leaned down and slit his throat from ear to ear, cutting through both carotid arteries, both jugular veins and the windpipe. Razi died without making any more sound than a wheezing gasp as the last of the air in his lungs issued from the rent in his throat. A flood of bright red blood flowed out of his neck and across the tabletop, before running off the edge to spatter the floor.

It took Gabriel five minutes to strip him and then dress in his clothes, checking that the key to the door was in his trouser pocket. The pistol in its highly-polished, brown leather holster might come in handy later, but for now it was the wrong weapon. Gabriel pulled Razi's head off the nail with a wet, sucking noise. Rigor mortis hadn't set in yet and it flopped back on the neck, opening up the cut into an obscene gape through which Gabriel could see the front of the spinal column. He dragged the corpse round the table and positioned it, face down, in the chair he had so recently occupied himself. Using the scalpel, he dug a hole through Razi's left palm and pushed it down over the nail. The left side of the body was disfigured by scar tissue that puckered the skin at the bicep, hip and thigh. Burns, maybe. Or blast trauma.

He picked up the scalpel again and walked to the door. Standing on the hinge side, he called out in Farsi, in a rough approximation of Razi's voice.

"Ali! Der aaneja. Hala!" *Ali! In here. Now!*

The key scraped in the lock again and the door opened, hiding Gabriel.

The big man entered, shoulders relaxed, hands loose by his sides. No Kalashnikov this time. His head swung left and right, looking for his master.

As he turned right, Gabriel sprang at him and, in under a second, executed a quartet of deadly moves ...

Arm across the forehead.

Lean back.

Slice hard, left to right.

Let the body fall against the wall, and stand clear of the jetting blood.

Panting, he slammed the door closed behind him.

How much time he had, he didn't know. Torturers didn't keep regular hours and, in his experience, hated to be disturbed. So he was counting on at least thirty minutes more before anyone noticed the guard's absence and dared knock on the door.

He wiped his undamaged palm down over his face. His clean-shaven face. Then he looked over at Razi s naked body.

"I'll show you knowledge of anatomy, you bastard," he said.

He pulled Razi's head back, ignoring the red mush filling the eye socket, and cut away the skin of the top lip, retaining the moustache. He stuck the disgusting scrap of tissue to his own lip and held it there until the congealing blood was dry. Once he'd finished, he lowered the head back down onto the tabletop.

On the way out, he lifted the peaked hat from the hook on the wall and settled it low over his forehead. The sunglasses enhanced the deception. He squared his shoulders, puffed out his chest, stuck his wounded hand into his pocket and left, locking the door behind him. He walked down a corridor, mimicking the general's posture and gait. The words of an MI5 surveillance instructor came back to him now.

"People think its faces that give us away. But they're easy to alter. What really marks your target out is their body language. Think gait, posture, stature. How does the target use their arms? What's the stride length? Are they relaxed or twitchy?" She'd used the phrase "human architecture" to describe the sum total of information you could pick up about a target without seeing their face or hearing them speak.

Gabriel kept his head down and his right hand resting on the butt of the pistol. He walked fast, letting his left foot drag a little, stiffening his left arm. He could see a stairwell at the far end of the corridor. He pulled the fire door open with his right hand and began climbing.

He turned a corner on the first half-landing only to almost collide with a fat, uniformed guard coming the other way, taking the steps two at a time.

"Sorry, General," the man said breathlessly in Farsi.

He was about to move past, then he stopped and turned.

Gabriel knew what the guard was experiencing before the man did himself. A sense of dislocation. Of things being not quite as they should be. Maybe the moustache had slipped. Perhaps he simply recognised Gabriel. Gabriel drew the General's pistol and jammed it hard into the guard's soft midsection before pulling the trigger.

The bang was still loud, but the man's belly made an effective suppressor. With his mouth open wide in a perfect *O* and his eyes staring, he fell back against the wall. Not wanting to risk any more noise, Gabriel leaned over him and dealt him two vicious blows with the pistol butt, aiming for and hitting his left temple. The thin bone snapped. The noise was within acceptable levels. The man died with a gasp. Gabriel moved past him, holstering the pistol.

He reached the ground floor and exited the stairwell through another fire door. The corridor into which he emerged was a better decorated version of the one in the basement. He strode on, ignoring the occasional uniformed guards who appeared from offices or around corners. They caught sight of the moustachioed man in the dress uniform, snapped to attention, looked away, or both. He glanced up at signs screwed to walls until he saw the word he was looking for.

خروج

Kherwej. Exit.

He turned left into a brightly lit corridor and saw a rudimentary reception area straight ahead. A security guard in black with a Kalashnikov over his shoulder. A glassed-in booth housing two more men. And beyond them, a pair of glass doors through which sunlight streamed, illuminating motes of dust floating in the air.

Willing his pulse to settle, and ignoring the rivulets of sweat running from under the peak of his cap, he stroked the moustache to push it back against his top lip and strode onwards.

From behind him a man shouted in Farsi.

"Sir! General Razi!"

IMPERSONATING AN OFFICER

Gabriel carried on walking. *Glad to see my impersonation is working.* He noticed the man ahead looking at him then straightening up. He waved his right hand dismissively at whoever was calling out for him.

"The report, General. The one you asked for."

Hearing fear in the man's voice, Gabriel slowed fractionally and held his right hand out behind him, snapping his fingers. Three dry pops. He felt a sheaf of papers being thrust into his palm, closed his fingers on them and marched on.

He heard the man turn, then footsteps echoing off the stone walls. Ahead the security guard was now standing to attention, eyes heavenwards.

Useful, given I'm only borrowing a bit of your boss's face, Gabriel thought.

The men in the cubicle were doing their best to look efficient, both standing erect in the tiny space and staring straight ahead. As Gabriel neared the glass security barrier, one bent and pressed a button on the console in front of him. The thick sheet of glass slid sideways. Keeping his head down, as if reading the report, Gabriel strode through.

Five paces.

He could see cream Mercedes taxis in the street beyond the flight of stone steps leading to the street. He held his breath.

Four.

A pigeon waddled along the top step, pecking at grit just outside the doors. He forced himself to unbunch his shoulders.

Three.

Two men in the same crisp, olive-green dress uniform as Gabriel's crested the steps and approached the doors. Gabriel stared down at the report, trying to ignore the sweat trickling into his eyes.

Two.

The men took a door each and held them open for him. Saluted as he left the building.

"General Razi, sir!" they said in unison.

One.

He stepped out into the searing heat of Tehran. Blinked in the sunlight. Descended the steps, feeling a flare of pain from his left hand with every jolting pace. And left the confines of the Ministry of Intelligence and Security behind him.

A taxi screeched to a halt as he reached the pavement on Delgosha Alley. The driver jumped out and raced round to the passenger side and held the rear door open for Gabriel.

"Salâm, hal-e shoma chetore, ser keredh?" *Hello, General. How is your health?*

"Salâm."

The man continued in Farsi.

"Where do you wish me to take you, General, sir?"

"National Jewellery Museum."

"Yes, sir, General."

The ride took 20 minutes, thanks in part to the driver's liberal use of the horn, tailgating and rash overtaking. Perhaps sensing that this particular cream Mercedes carried the sort of person they wouldn't want to anger, the other drivers braked, swerved or pulled in to let him pass. Gabriel felt his thirst mounting, along with his fatigue, and realised he was down to the dregs of his energy.

The driver pulled up to the kerb on Ferdowsi Avenue, waved away any suggestion that the General might pay, and repeated his performance with the door.

Once the man had disappeared back into the traffic, Gabriel turned away from the museum entrance and headed north to the junction where Ferdowsi Avenue met Jomhouri Avenue. Every step produced a sharp flash of pain in his concealed left hand, which was throbbing in time with his heartbeat.

Reflexively touching the stinking piece of skin adhering to his top lip, he crossed the road and approached the deep-blue, spike-topped gates of the British Embassy.

A lone guard stood outside. Not a member of the British armed forces, he belonged to the Iranian police.

As Gabriel approached, the guard caught his eye, straightened his spine as if electrified, and snapped off a sharp salute.

"Open them now," Gabriel said in Farsi to the guard.

The man turned and pressed a button set into the wall. With a series of clangs, the multiple locks opened and the gates began an agonisingly slow journey sideways on well-greased metal rollers. As soon as a man's width had appeared between them, Gabriel slipped through and walked up to the main doors.

Now he did meet British soldiers. Two Royal Marines in blue Parade Dress uniform standing each side of the Embassy front door. Gabriel came to a stop before them, ignoring curious stares. Each man carried an SA80 rifle and they were levelling them now.

Before they could speak, Gabriel reached up and dragged the remains of General Razi's face from his lip and dropped it to the ground. He swept the peaked cap from his head and spoke.

"My name is Gabriel Wolfe. Please tell Julian Furnish I am here. He's expecting me."

Then he tottered forwards and collapsed into the arms of the left-hand Marine.

SMUDGED INK

Gabriel came to in a white-painted room. Above him, a ceiling fan rotated, wafting cool air down onto his face and neck. He turned his head and saw that he was lying in his own bed.

Outside, he could hear his father giving one of the staff instructions about a garden party.

He looked down towards his feet. His left hand lay on top of the bedclothes. From wrist to knuckles it was bandaged. He turned the hand over. In matching spots on his palm and the back of his hand, blood was seeping through to the outer layer of the crepe bandage. The tip of his middle finger was dressed with a sticking plaster. He felt nothing from either wound site. In fact, he felt delightfully pain free all over. He raised himself up on his elbows and examined the spot inside his left elbow where a canula had been inserted. A tube lead away from his arm to a bag of clear fluid hanging on a stainless-steel drip-stand. *Cool!* he thought. *Intravenous gin.*

He could taste the Tanqueray coursing through his blood vessels.

The door opened. His mum was standing there.

"Gabriel, you have a visitor," she said, smiling.

His old friend walked in.

"Hello Smudge, mate. Are you on the gin, too?"

"Nah, Boss. You know me. I like a proper drink."

Smudge came over from the door, rubbing the alcohol sanitiser gel over and through his twisting fingers. He sat on the edge of Gabriel's bed and raised his glass of whisky.

"Cheers, Boss."

"Cheers."

They clinked glasses and drank.

"How's everything?" Gabriel asked.

Smudge smiled and rubbed his jaw.

"Fine. Thanks for taking me home to Melody and Nat. How about you, though? Got yourself in a right mess, didn't you?"

"I had to try though, didn't I?"

"'Course you did! And fair play, Boss, you got pretty close. Just a shame twenty yards wasn't twenty feet. So what're you going to do now"

"Get better. Regroup. Try again."

"Yeah, but you need to shut that fuckin' mole down, don't you?"

"The boss is working on it. But we haven't got much to go on."

"What about the bloke with the ink on his wrist?"

"What bloke?"

"One of the ones that attacked you and Eli. Who is very easy on the eye, by the way." Smudge winked. "It was the one you stabbed in the throat. He had a tattoo on the inside of his left wrist. It was a Russian phrase."

"What did it say?"

Smudge drew in the air with his index finger. Three words in Cyrillic script appeared at the end of his fingertip in smeary black ink.

убей их всех

"*Ubey ikh vsekh*, Boss. It means 'Kill 'em all.'"

Gabriel smiled at his dead friend.

"I didn't know you spoke Russian."

Smudge laughed.

"Don't be daft, Boss. Of course I don't. But you do."

He drained the rest of his whisky, stood up and walked away.

"Bye, Smudge," Gabriel called out.

"Get some sleep, Boss," Smudge's disembodied voice called back.

ROOM AT THE TOP

Lieutenant Colonel Massoud Jamshidi, Deputy Director of MOIS, was used to the leisurely pace of interrogations conducted by his boss. Only the very valuable assets fell into General Razi's capable hands, and weeks might pass before they were granted their final peace. But even the general needed to eat from time to time. To sleep. To catch up on events outside the four walls of the "pressure cooker" as they called the grimy, windowless, concrete cube where suspects spent their final days.

When his boss didn't appear for their regular evening meeting, Jamshidi became concerned. He reasoned with himself that perhaps this Wolfe character was going to experience a night like no other in his miserable life. The General was renowned for his cruelty and his ability to work for days on end without apparently needing to sleep. With that thought producing a smile on his moustachioed face, he left for home. Even though they had lost the Israeli woman, the Englishman was the bigger prize.

Jamshidi's anxiety returned the following morning, when the General was once again conspicuous by his absence from the daily 8.00 a.m. briefing.

He left his office and hurried along the corridor back towards the security desk by the front doors. The soldier on duty snapped to attention, eyes at the prescribed forty-five-degree angle to the horizontal, staring fixedly at a spot above Jamshidi's head.

"Have you seen General Razi this morning?"

"No, sir. Not since last night."

"Last night? What do you mean? General Razi stayed here last night."

The soldier appeared uncomfortable. Contradicting a senior officer was bad enough, but setting yourself in opposition to the Deputy Director would rarely end well.

"Well, man?" Jamshidi barked. "Spit it out."

"Sir, I'm sorry, sir, the general, he left yesterday at 5.00 p.m."

"You're sure? You saw him?"

"Yes, sir. Clear as I'm seeing you, sir."

Jamshidi turned on his heel and strode back down the corridor towards the door that led to the general-purpose interrogation rooms and "the pressure cooker." A worm of anxiety was squirming forcefully in his gut. Razi had left without checking in first? It *could* happen, he supposed. But it hadn't ever. Not in the five years he had been serving under the General.

He stopped outside the pressure cooker. The door was closed. He tried the handle. Locked.

He pulled his phone out and called Razi. He feared that somehow he had missed the General through an oversight of his own, and that he was about to hear the distinctive ringtone from beyond the door. Instead the phone went straight to voicemail. Jamshidi ended the call without leaving a message. He was starting to feel something was very badly wrong.

Like all senior MOIS officers, Jamshidi had a master key. He fished it out of his pocket now and, with trembling fingers, inserted it into the lock. The tip of the key jittered against the silver lock before sliding home, and Jamshidi swore under his breath.

He pushed the door open wide and stepped through, wrinkling his nose at the smell. Blood, stale sweat, excrement and the sharp reek of vomit. Wolfe, naked, lay face down on the table, his hand nailed to the wooden surface. Despite himself, Jamshidi smiled. *Ah, yes, the General's trademark. He probably gave him the "prophets" speech, too.*

Something about the sight of the unconscious prisoner rang an alarm bell in Jamshidi's mind. He moved a few paces closer. Then his hand flew to his mouth.

The scars on Wolfe's side, that was it. Rumpled tissue on his left bicep, hip and thigh as if a giant hand had taken a few fistfuls and scrunched the skin between powerful fingers. Jamshidi had seen those scars before. In a Turkish bath on Parisooz Alley. An establishment used by all the senior officers of MOIS. Including General Razi.

He ran to the table and lifted the nailed man's head back, wincing at the wet sucking sound as it came free of the congealed blood sticking it to the tabletop.

Then he screamed as his brain tried to process the disfigured features staring back at him. The ruined eye. The broken nose. The obscene, red moustache of raw, weeping flesh.

The features, already turning a hideous shade of yellowish-green, screamed back at him.

Yes! You are right! We are the dead face of your boss and Director, General Omar Razi! Now, in the name of Allah, do something!

Jamshidi turned to run, noticing the second corpse slumped behind the door. Just a guard. He didn't even stop.

Back in his office, he called the commander of the Revolutionary Guards at Vareshabad.

"I'm sending you another hundred men," he said as soon as Major Darius Esfahani answered.

"Thank you, sir. But why? My men and I are more than capable of protecting the facility with our current strength."

"Just take them. I want 24-hour patrolling. Put a bodyguard on Darbandi at all times."

Esfahani's voice tautened. An experienced soldier picking up on a superior officer's tension.

"Are you expecting an attack, sir?"

"Yes. No. I don't know. I have to go."

Just the thought of the call he had to make next brought him out in a sweat. He felt himself shaking as he dialled the number for the Minister of Defence and Armed Forces Logistics.

RECUPERATION

"Gabriel? Can you hear me?"

Gabriel looked up into the eyes of the angel and smiled. If this was death, it wasn't too bad at all. The angel was beautiful. No, that wasn't really the right word at all. Beautiful was for actresses or models. The angel was ... was radiant. Her face was framed by a corona of red hair through which rays of blinding white sunlight shone, illuminating each individual strand so that he could actually see the life-force pulsing along them like current along white-hot wires. The angel ...

... checked her patient's pulse with two fingers pressed over the inside of his right wrist. She noted his vital signs down from the monitor. Then visually checked the drips feeding into cannulas inserted into veins on both arms. She ...

... smiled down at him. In her swirling blue eyes, he could see his own face reflected, small, like a child, dressed in his own white angel's robe. Or was it a vestment? A raiment? What angels wore, anyway. She spoke from far away, and he believed he had never heard such a loving sound from any woman's lips in his entire life. Not his mother, not Britta Falskog, not Fariyah Crace, not Eli Schochat. Nobody. He reached out to her, feeling his growing wings tickling beneath his arms as they unfurled, and spread his fingers wide and the angel ...

... took his hand gently from her breast and replaced it by his side. She smiled. The morphine was doing its job and the benzodiazepine was joining in with its own tranquilising song. She leaned over him and said ...

"... someone's feeling better. Can you hear me, Gabriel?"

"I'm an angel, too," Gabriel croaked, smiling up at the radiant creature bending over him. His throat felt dry. And the angel said ...

"I somehow doubt that. But you're on the side of the angels and that's good. Now, rest."

And Gabriel closed his eyes and rested. Somewhere, perhaps in his old life, his left hand was hurting. But there was no pain. No pain. He slept.

* * *

He woke.

Lifted his head.

The spinning sensation wasn't pleasant so he lowered his head to the pillow. He tried rolling his head to the side. Better. A window, shaded by a Venetian blind. Closer in, a tower of electronic devices, tubes, wires and fluid-filled bags hooked to a pole.

Beeps. A soft ticking.

The other side.

A door. Its small, square window also shaded.

The room smelled of disinfectant. Like the sickbay at school. But which school? There had been so many. He felt as if he were adrift on the ocean. On a soft inflatable bed.

He looked down. A sheet was pulled up to his waist. He was wearing a white smock, or gown of some kind. Thin tubes ran into both arms. He followed their sinuous length back to the pole festooned with plastic bags of fluid. His left hand was throbbing, one throb for every beat of his heart. A bandage separated his fingers from his wrist. His watch was missing. *Now I don't know what time it is.*

The door opened and slowly he turned his head to observe the arrival of whoever was behind it.

It was his angel. Only now she didn't seem to shine anymore. Her, what was the word? Her *radiance* had left her. She was still very pretty. Red hair. He'd always loved that. She came to his bedside. Looked down at him and spoke in a soft voice.

"How are you feeling, Gabriel?"

Gabriel inhaled deeply, then wrinkled his nose at the tang of the disinfectant.

"First I thought I was in my childhood home. Then I thought I was dead."

"Ah." She smiled. "That would have been the morphine. Well, that and the diazepam. It's a common side effect with that combination of drugs. You were on a fairly heavy dose. The doctor thought it best. While you healed. We also had to give you a lot of fluids. You were very dehydrated."

He looked down at his left hand again. At the bandage, in the centre of which a small spot of red stood out like the bull's eye of a target.

"Where's Eli? Is she OK?"

The angel – *no, not angel, she's a nurse* – the nurse smiled.

"Eli's fine. Unlike you, she knows how to take care of herself. A couple of bumps and bruises but otherwise, A1."

"So they got her too?"

"I couldn't say. Above my pay grade, as they say. All I do know is she's here at the embassy and she's perfectly well."

"I want to see her."

"I'll go and fetch her after I've emptied your urine pouch."

"What? What do you mean?"

"We catheterised you when you came in."

He shook his head, sending the room spinning for a moment.

"What? But how long have I been here? They only picked me up yesterday. Or the day before."

The nurse, whose name according to her badge was Hannah, sat beside him, perching on the edge of the mattress. She took his right hand in her own.

"Three days. You've been through a rough time. Dr Bedel thought it best to keep you thoroughly medicated."

Gabriel's mind was whirling as he tried to process what Hannah was telling him.

"But, you have to get me out of," he waved his hand over to his left side, at the drug delivery paraphernalia, "all this. Eli and I have important work to do."

"I know. And I also know that Mr Furnish told me it would have to wait. That you were to be treated. Mended. Your poor hand."

She stood and gently disengaged her hand from his; he had been gripping tightly.

"Here," she said, placing a straw inserted into a bottle of water to his lips. "Have a drink. It'll help your sore throat."

Gabriel sucked hard at the straw, groaning as the cool water slid over his tongue.

"Let me go and get Dr Bedel," Hannah said. "We'll see what he has to say. And I'll call Eli. And Mr Furnish."

Gabriel sank back into the soft embrace of his pillow, which folded around his head. *Shit! I ballsed that up badly.*

Then another thought shouldered its way into his internal conversation.

No you didn't. They knew your name. They knew we were coming. There is *a mole. Who knew about the operation?*

He began a list of possible suspects. He began with Don's name, then crossed it out angrily. Then, reluctantly, added it back in again.

Don Webster.

The members of the Privy Council.

Sam Flack.

The spook, what was his name, Hugh Bennett.

The army officer. James Gaddesden.

Tim Frye on the SIS Iran desk.

Any colleague of Frye's who'd helped prepare the briefing.

Julian Furnish.

Eli Schochat.

Himself, Gabriel Wolfe.

He reviewed the group's members and mentally crossed off the ones he trusted with his life.

~~Don Webster.~~

The members of the Privy Council.

Sam Flack.

The spook, what was his name, Hugh Bennett.

The army officer. James Gaddesden.

Tim Frye on the SIS Iran desk.

Any colleague of Frye's who'd helped prepare the briefing.

Julian Furnish

~~Eli Schochat.~~

~~Himself, Gabriel Wolfe.~~

Great! So a suspect pool of just too bloody many.

As he wondered whether he should really be including Furnish and the SIS people, the door burst open and Eli rushed in. She crossed to his bed in a couple of strides and knelt beside him. Clutching his right hand with both of hers she brought it up to her chest and held it there, leaning forwards to plant a long, hard kiss on his mouth. When she withdrew, her eyes were glistening.

"I thought you were dead. Then when you staggered in here between those guards I thought you were about to. Oh, my poor Gabriel. What did they do to you?"

He shuffled back so he could prop his head up a little.

"It's OK. I mean, they roughed me up and nailed my hand to a table, but, you know, you should have seen the other guy."

Eli sniffed and laughed, then coughed.

"I saw part of him."

"Oh. They picked that up, did they?"

"Well, they could hardly leave it on the path, could they? It was disgusting. Like a, I don't know, a big hairy caterpillar."

"It belonged to General Razi, late of the Ministry of Intelligence and Security."

"Was he the one who ...?" Eli pointed at Gabriel's bandaged left hand.

He nodded.

"Good. And he's not ...?"

Gabriel shook his head.

"He gave me a lecture about the right and wrong way to use nails if you wanted to kill a man. I gave him a practical demonstration."

"We were betrayed, you know that, right? Those four goons back in England were the first attempt. That didn't work so whoever it is upped the ante. Contacted the fucking Iranians. This is serious."

"I know. Have you spoken to Don?"

"Yes, but he says the cops have come up with nothing. Or not precisely nothing, but nothing we couldn't have told them ourselves."

"So what about Darbandi?"

"He said we had to abort—"

"We can't!"

Eli smiled.

"He said we had to abort this specific op. Get back to England and meet him. We can't risk another attempt until we find the mole."

"I was making a list when you came in. There are too many people. It could be any one of at least a dozen. I say we go in for a second attack. The Iranians won't be expecting it."

"Of course they will! You escaped wearing half their interrogator's face, remember? They'll have Darbandi locked down at Vareshabad until he's finished. I would."

Gabriel slumped back. She was right. Of course, she was. The meds were interfering with his thinking.

"What then?" he asked.

"Like I said. We fly back to England. Regroup. Find the mole. Then we start again."

They were interrupted by the door opening again. Julian Furnish poked his head round.

"Aha! You're back with us. Pretty impressive escape, I must say. The Iranians will be spitting feathers. Though not the chap whose tache you pinched, obviously."

Gabriel grinned.

"He won't be spitting anything anymore."

Furnish stood at the end of the bed, hands in pockets, looking as though patching up escapees from MOIS was just part of his daily routine.

"Well, we'll get you up on your feet and then spirit you and Eli here back to England. No need to worry about the Iranians now you're here. But I did want to ask you what went wrong."

Eli twisted round before Gabriel could answer.

"All we know is our covers were blown. The Iranians knew we were coming."

"Fair enough. But Gabriel's been inside MOIS and survived. We'd like to know a bit more about that. It's not exactly an everyday occurrence. Would you be up for an informal interview later today?"

Gabriel felt he had no option but to agree. They settled on a 3.00 p.m. meeting in Furnish's office.

CROSSING OFF NAMES

At 2.30 p.m. Gabriel gingerly climbed out of bed. The nurse, Hannah, had stopped by thirty minutes earlier.

"We'll sort you out with some oral painkillers," she'd said, as she disconnected him from all the tubes and monitors. "But Dr Bedel's happy with your rehydration, and there's no infection in your hand. You're a strong man, Gabriel Wolfe. And a very lucky one."

He walked stiffly to the adjoining bathroom and closed the door behind him. Holding his bandaged hand above him like someone hailing a cab, he showered, grateful to be sluicing himself free of the filth he felt still clung to him from the torture cell.

Someone, Hannah, he assumed, had laid out a razor and a can of foam on the sink and he spent five minutes carefully shaving, relaxing for the first time in days, and enjoying the sensation of the blade sweeping across his skin. Lastly, he cleaned his teeth.

He dressed in the clothes that had been laid out for him on a side chair. Underwear, navy chinos, a soft white shirt and a pair of tobacco-brown boat shoes. *Thanks, Eli.*

At ten to three, he left the sick bay and walked along a short corridor, following signs to reception.

"Yes, sir," the receptionist, a young woman with olive skin and huge brown eyes, asked. "How can I help?"

"I'm meeting Julian Furnish at three o'clock. Could you point me in the direction of his office, please?"

"Certainly, sir. Take the lift to the second floor and Mr Furnish is third door on the left."

Gabriel thanked her and made his way to the lift.

Outside Furnish's door, he inhaled once, then knocked briskly and entered.

Sitting behind the desk, Furnish looked like an everyman middle manager. Only the array of telecoms equipment on the righthand corner of his desk gave a hint as to his true profession. A slim, tanned, athletically built woman in her early forties wearing a cream silk suit sat facing Furnish. Her hair, the colour of polished teak, was cut short in a sleek bob. Both she and Furnish stood and smiled at Gabriel.

"Gabriel! You're looking much better," Furnish said. "Please, take a pew. This is Sarah Hunt."

The woman sat down as Gabriel did, turning to shake hands.

"Hi," she said. "I work with Julian. MOIS is my area of interest, so he asked me to attend this chat."

"Hi. I only hope I can give you some useful information."

"Oh, I'm sure you can," she said. "The fact you survived is something of a miracle. In fact, if you don't mind my diving straight in, how on earth did you escape?"

Before Gabriel could answer, Furnish interrupted.

"Let's get some refreshments sorted out first, Sarah. Poor old Gabriel's had nothing but sugar water and intravenous smack for the last three days."

"That would be wonderful." Gabriel said, suddenly realising how hungry he was.

Furnish picked up the receiver from a standard desk phone and waited a few seconds.

"Alice, could you bring in the sandwiches and drinks, please?"

A moment later the door opened and a plump woman in her midthirties appeared carrying a large tray.

"Where do you want it, Julian?" she asked.

"Over here, please, Alice. No need for Gabriel to be jumping up and down every time he wants another sarnie."

She placed the tray in the centre of the desk, smiling at Gabriel.

"Will that be all, Julian?"

"Yup. Thanks. I'll give you a buzz if we need anything else."

Once she'd left, Julian gestured at the plates of sandwiches, bottles of beer and flask of coffee.

"Dig in," he said, unnecessarily.

Gabriel took a ham sandwich and demolished it in three bites. He reached for a beer and washed down the sandwich with a long pull on the cold lager.

"Oh, my God, that's good," he said finally.

"Good stuff. So, back to Sarah."

Sarah smiled and waited while Gabriel ate another sandwich.

"Sorry for jumping in before," she said as he polished it off.

He shook his head, swallowing the last bite.

"It's fine. Really. I'd do the same in your position. Have you heard of SERE training?"

She frowned for a second, grooving two parallel lines in the tanned skin above the bridge of her nose.

"Survival, Evasion ...?"

"Resistance and Escape. I did a course with the US Marines in San Diego a while back. It helped."

She made a note in an A4 pad she'd balanced on her knee.

"Can you take us through your experience. From capture right through to the point you reached the embassy?"

Gabriel recounted his journey from the road outside Vareshabad to the taxi journey from Delgosha Alley to the Jewellery Museum and then the final, agonising walk to the British Embassy.

Sarah noted down the torture techniques and asked him to go

back over Razi's speech until she had it down verbatim. She asked about the internal layout of the building, the dimensions and condition of the torture cell, and the number, physical condition and dress of all the staff he'd seen.

"Can I ask a question?" Gabriel said, when they reached what felt like a conclusive end to the debrief.

"Of course," Furnish said. He had been silent throughout Sarah's gentle but persistent questioning.

"Who else apart from you and Sarah knew what Eli and I were doing in Tehran?"

Furnish shook his head.

"Sarah was outside the loop. This was strictly need to know. It was just me out here."

"How about the young guy who delivered our kit."

"Davoud?" Another shake of the head. "No. He was just running an errand."

"Fair enough."

Then Furnish narrowed his eyes.

"Looking for the mole out here? It's a reasonable place to start. But an incorrect one, I'm afraid. Tell Don I'm happy to co-operate in any and all ways with his investigation, up to and including a polygraph. Believe me, I want to catch whoever sabotaged the operation as much as you do."

Gabriel shrugged his shoulders. Furnish was a long shot at best but he'd have felt he was neglecting his duty if he hadn't probed just a little.

"No hard feelings, I hope."

Furnish smiled.

"None at all. As I said, it was a reasonable idea. Now, if you're done, Sarah," he looked at Sarah, who nodded, closing her notepad, "then I think we should let you get some rest. I'll sort out transport and flights for you and Eli and we'll have you back in Britain as soon as we can. Probably in the morning if I can scare up a friendly BA pilot."

* * *

Sarah accompanied Gabriel from Furnish's office. In the lift, she pressed the button for the third floor then turned to him and spoke.

"I'm so sorry I made you relive your experience. But the intelligence you gave us was really useful. We can incorporate it into briefings we give our field agents here."

"That's OK. Hey, at least I'm out here looking in and not in there, well, not looking out but ..."

She smiled.

"I know what you mean. We've sorted you and Eli out with a room here by the way. I'm sure you'll be glad not to be going anywhere near the sickbay again. I'll show you the way."

At the door to the room, she knocked.

"Come in," Eli called from inside.

"I'll leave you to it," Sarah said, offering her hand again. "Thanks again."

Inside, Gabriel barely had time to close the door behind him before Eli enveloped him in a hug.

"Easy, Tiger," he said, laughing, then wincing at the pain in his ribs her embrace caused.

She relaxed the pressure a little and drew him with her to the bed, manoeuvring him into a seated position beside her.

"We are so owed a holiday after this shitstorm is over," she said.

"Agreed."

"So what did the chief spook want?"

"Full debrief on what goes on inside MOIS."

"What about him? Do you like him for the mole?"

Gabriel shook his head.

"It was always a long shot. He practically begged to submit to a lie-detector test."

Eli snorted.

"Huh. Beating a polygraph's child's play. It's the first thing they taught us at Mossad."

"I know, but it just doesn't stack up. If there's a motive, then I can't see it, and I've had plenty of time to think about it."

"So what now?"

"We're flying home tomorrow."

DON'S HOUSE

A VILLAGE IN ENGLAND, ONE WEEK LATER

The Department arranged for a reconstructive plastic surgeon to operate on Gabriel as soon as he arrived back in the UK. No tendons or bones were damaged, except superficially, and the results were, according to Mr Raphaelson, the hand surgeon, "more than satisfactory." Had General Razi wanted to crucify Gabriel, and placed the nail behind his wrist as he had explained, the surgery would have been more complex. Apart from some localised swelling and an oddly precise circular bruise on the back of his hand, Gabriel was free to operate as normal. The tablets Raphaelson prescribed did a decent enough job of numbing the pain, and whatever discomfort was left over Gabriel coped with on his own or with the help of a bottle of Armagnac, a present from Don.

* * *

Nursing a glass of the warming spirit now, Gabriel sat beside Eli on a cherry-red, brass-buttoned Chesterfield sofa in Don's sitting room. Don faced them, occupying a matching armchair. Christine Webster had greeted Gabriel and Eli at the door and taken them through to meet Don, then excused herself, saying she had a meeting of her book group.

The French doors were thrown open, admitting the early evening sunshine, which spilled across the carpet and illuminated motes of dust in the air. The glinting airborne particles reminded Gabriel uncomfortably of the reception area at MOIS. Outside, a blackbird was warbling and the breeze was ruffling the delicate leaves of a birch tree. The smell of new-mown grass drifted into the room.

"Better give me your report," Don was saying. "You first, Eli, then you, Old Sport, if you wouldn't mind."

"Obviously we were blown," Eli began. "I'd ordered room service while I waited for Gabriel to bring the hire car, and two goons turned up at my door. One in uniform, Revolutionary Guard. One plain clothes, probably MOIS. Both now dead."

"Anything before that? Any warning signs?"

She shook her head.

"No. None at all. We got ourselves set up at the British Council stand and everything was going to plan."

"Were you followed after the room service business?"

"No. I think it was too soon for them to realise they were down two men."

Don looked at Gabriel and nodded.

"I surveiled the facility at Vareshabad. I saw Darbandi leaving, apparently alone. Followed him. He stopped. When he got out, he sat back and smiled. He had a bodyguard. The guy'd been hiding. Crouched down in the back. A plainclothes agent like Eli's. They took me to MOIS. Fairly forceful interrogation, as you know. I stuck to my cover story then escaped."

"And nobody saw you while you were there?"

Gabriel cast his mind back. The hot climb to his position. The boredom of watching and waiting. The dry heat. The smell of the desert plants. The total absence of life.

"No. I was alone the whole time."

Don brought his hands together beneath his nose, as if praying. He huffed a breath out and looked at Gabriel and Eli in turn.

"This is very bad," he finally said, in a level voice. "They knew why you were there, and they knew where to find you."

"Someone betrayed us," Eli said, in not such a level voice. Her eyes flashed. "A traitor! And I've got a pretty good idea who."

Gabriel turned to her.

"And that would be?"

"That twat I dumped on his arse on Salisbury Plain. What was his name?"

"Gaddesden. But I think you're wrong."

"Why? You heard what he said. He hates Israel. Hates Jews!"

"Even if that's true," he patted the air as she opened her mouth to speak again, "OK, *given* that it's true, he didn't have enough information. He didn't know our covers, or that we'd be at the Tehran Grand."

"He didn't have to. He could have told them we'd gone there to kill Darbandi, and given them our real names. You said Razi knew yours. They would have put extra security on Darbandi and that's how they picked you up. And me. We arrived in Tehran together, after all."

Gabriel shook his head.

"It doesn't work. Even if he'd told them we were coming and why, he could only have given them a description of our faces. There would have been dozens of people looking enough like you and me for it to be impossible to know who was who. Even if they did pick me up just because they were being extra careful with Darbandi, they wouldn't have known you were my partner."

Don took a sip of his own drink before speaking.

"I think it's best if I arrange for Captain Gaddesden to be interviewed, informally, of course. But I have to tell you, whatever his political opinions, I don't see him as our problem child. This has the tang of a security operation, not something cooked up by an army officer with a subscription to *The Guardian*."

"Who then, Boss?" Gabriel asked.

"Ask the old Latin master's favourite question: *Cui bono*? Who benefits? We're talking about treason. About blowing a top-secret security operation aimed at one of Britain's enemies, organised at the request of the Israelis. That's a big thing to get in the middle of. Whatever Gaddesden's politics, I don't see a motive powerful enough. Who would stand to gain if a mission to remove Darbandi from the game failed? And I don't mean the Iranians. Who *here*?" He stabbed his index finger into the arm of his chair. "Who on Gabriel's list?"

Gabriel stayed silent. Eli, too. He thought about each person on his list of suspects. Don had set up a whiteboard in a corner of the room, between the fireplace, currently filled with a huge arrangement of dried flowers, and a bronze sculpture of a dancer. The whiteboard looked incongruous, as if a management consultant had wandered into a gathering of antiques dealers. Gabriel crossed to it and uncapped a black pen, releasing the aroma of pear drops. He wrote the list of suspects on the left.

Don Webster.
    Privy Council.
    Sam Flack.
    Hugh Bennett.
    James Gaddesden.
    Tim Frye
    Tim's Colleagues
    Julian Furnish
    Eli Schochat.
    Gabriel Wolfe.

Then he wiped four names off, leaving:

Privy Council
    Sam Flack.

Hugh Bennett
Tim Frye
Tim's Colleagues
Julian Furnish

Don stared at the list when Gabriel had finished with the deletions. He spoke.

"Nobody on the Privy Council has access to operational details. Yes, they have overwatch, but it's at the strategic level. They don't approve individual missions or personnel."

Gabriel wiped off the first item.

Sam Flack
Hugh Bennett
Tim Frye
Tim's Colleagues
Julian Furnish

"Did Julian know who was coming out?" Eli asked.

"He knew your cover names. But not the nature of your mission. We like to keep MI6 at arm's length wherever we can once our operators are in the field."

"I asked him more or less straight out in his office. He denied everything, which I know means nothing, but we can probably cross him off," Gabriel said, wiping his name off the list.

Sam Flack
Hugh Bennett
Tim Frye
Tim's Colleagues

. . .

He sighed and scrubbed at his scalp until his hair stood up in spikes. It didn't make any sense.

"If this were an op against the Russians, and it was still the Cold War, I suppose I could just about understand it. But Iran? Who believes in *them*? I can't see it."

"I still think it's something to do with being anti-Israel, not pro-Iran," Eli said. "OK, Boss, I go with your opinion on Gaddesden. He's a jerk, but not a traitor. Soldiers are trained to follow orders. I think he was just blowing off steam. Look, why does someone betray their country? Because that's what we're talking about. One, it's ideological. Philby, Burgess, Maclean, Blunt – they were Communist fellow-travellers. They thought the Soviets had it right and we had it wrong. Two – blackmail. Sex or money. That's not the Iranians' style. In fact, none of this is their style. They just don't engage in this kind of activity. We had a whole department at Mossad devoted to understanding their methods."

Now it was Don's turn to stand. He walked over to Gabriel and held out his hand for the whiteboard marker.

"May I?"

Gabriel handed it over and sat facing Don, like a student in a tutorial in his professor's rooms.

"We don't have time to investigate everyone. We need to nip this in the bud and get you back to Iran before Darbandi's finished. In order, this is how I see it."

He wiped the board clean and then rewrote the names.

Frye.
  Other Iran Desk.
  Bennett.
  Flack.

"I've known Sam Flack a very long time. She's happily married, two kids at an ordinary London comprehensive school. Manageable mortgage. No bad habits. And her husband's Jewish. I know none of that means she couldn't have done it, but I'm not looking at her."

He wiped her name off the board.

Frye.
  Other Iran Desk.
  Bennett.

"I don't know Hugh Bennett very well at all. He's been at MI6 since graduating from Oxford. But like Julian, he didn't have enough of the details to betray you. And to be honest, this goes for all the spooks: they love the Israelis. Without them we'd have no allies worth anything in the Middle East. Yes, we sell toys to the Saudis and anyone else not on the blacklist, but as for intelligence-sharing, it doesn't happen. Without the Israelis, our counterterror operations in the Middle East would be severely limited – and remember, that's the real threat."

Another swipe with the felt eraser.

Frye.
  Other Iran Desk.

"It wasn't a big space," Gabriel said. "But apart from Tim, I counted at least four people sitting at computers when we went in for our briefing."

Don smiled.

"Happily for us, one of those people was detailed to report to me on your movements. I don't like leaving anything to chance, Old Sport. Not after you went AWOL during that business with Lizzie Maitland."

Gabriel thought back. Don had ordered him not to follow the

woman who'd been persecuting him, and he'd disobeyed. Flown straight to the US and almost got himself and Britta Falskog killed.

"Is Tim your source?" Eli asked.

"No. He isn't. So he could be our problem child. Or it could be one of his other colleagues. Of whom there are, in fact, eight, though two were on a training course the day you were there, one was off sick and one was in meetings at MI5 all day."

"So of the five we saw, including Tim, one was your guy. That leaves us with four targets," Eli said.

"Let's stick to *suspects* at this point, shall we?" Don said.

"Fine. Suspects. What now?"

"Well, believe it or not, MI6 are very touchy about this sort of thing. They like to handle it themselves. I don't think we have the luxury of waiting for them to get their shit together. So I have a different course of action in mind. But I'm going to have to eat a little slice of humble pie to make it happen."

"What about the cops, Boss?" Gabriel asked. "Have they got anywhere with the mercs?"

"Yes, they have. They found a business card belonging to a chap called Max Novgorodsky. It appears he works for an organisation called, and I hope I'm pronouncing this correctly, kuznitsa. They Googled it. It's Russian and it means—"

"Smithy," Gabriel said.

"What?" Eli said, interrupting Gabriel's own interruption.

Gabriel turned to her.

"It means forge. Like a blacksmith uses." A morphine-dream swam into Gabriel's consciousness. Russian! "One of them had a tattoo on the inside of his right wrist. I missed it at the time but it said 'Kill 'em all' in Cyrillic."

Don frowned and rubbed fiercely at the end of his nose as if he had an itch.

"We have a quartet of highly trained, well-equipped mercenaries, of whom at least one was Russian, tooling around in a top-of-the-line Mercedes owned – probably – by a man with a Russian-sounding surname and a business card for a Russian company called Smithy or

Forge. Anyone want to contradict me if I say we have a few Reds under the bed?"

Gabriel and Eli both shook their heads.

"People like that don't come cheap," Gabriel finally said. "At least five hundred a day plus expenses. So that's two grand for the four of them, plus all the weapons they had with them. And the car was at least a hundred grand."

"So whoever was after you – or rather, trying to stop you dealing with Darbandi – has deep pockets," Don said. "Which complicates matters when I look at our list of suspects. None of them is exactly a millionaire."

"Are you watching them, Boss?" Eli asked.

"Not yet. That's what my humble pie-eating is all about. But we can't afford to wait while we track our mole down. You need to get back out there and finish what you started. Why don't you give your old boss a call in the morning?"

ALL OUR FORCE, PURSUIT AND POLICY

After Gabriel and Eli left, Don pulled his phone out and called Callie. His Irish setter, Fingal, had just padded in from the garden, claws clicking on the polished wooden floorboards. He reached down absent-mindedly and scratched the dog behind the ear while counting the rings. He'd just reached the point where he expected Callie's recorded voice to click in, asking him to leave a message, when the woman herself answered.

"Don! I just can't seem to get rid of you, can I? Sorry for the delay in answering. I was just getting ready to go out."

"Somewhere nice, I hope. Not another meeting."

"No. We've tickets to see Shakespeare at the Barbican Theatre. *Troilus and Cressida*."

"Well, let me keep this short. I wouldn't want to make you late for the Bard. It's about Max."

"Oh, yes? Max 'we'll take it from here' Novgorodsky, you mean?"

"Yes. And I'm sorry if I came across as high-handed. It turns out we're not quite so equipped to penetrate the dark web as I'd imagined."

"Well, that's quite all right. Do you want to come in and chat? I'd love an excuse to change tomorrow morning's schedule, believe me."

"Would ten be all right?"

"Ten would be perfect. You've just got me out of not one, but two meetings."

"Then I'll let you go. Enjoy the play."

* * *

The following morning, Don drove his Jaguar into the carpark behind Paddington Green police station and found a space. Collecting his briefcase from the boot, he made his way through reception and security and up to the seventh floor, where the Special Investigations Unit had its base.

Callie was waiting for him when the lift doors parted. She smiled, and as he shook her hand he thought how attractive she was when she wasn't scowling at him.

"How are you, Don?" she asked as she led him through a pair of card-operated doors and into an open-plan office.

"Very well, thank you, Callie. And you?"

"Mustn't grumble. Though if I have to sit through another bloody meeting this week, I swear I'll do more than bloody grumble."

He smiled. A kindred spirit.

"You have my sympathies. It's the PowerPoint I can't stand. Bloody civil servants reading to me off a screen when I've already reached the end of their stupid slide."

"I know!" she exclaimed turning to him, eyes wide. "In my day – Oh God that makes me sound about a hundred years old – but anyway, we were taught to keep it short and simple. Say what you have to say, ask questions, then shut up and listen."

Continuing to share examples of what they most disliked about admin, they made their way to Callie's office, where a young black man dressed in clothes Don felt sure Gabriel would admire was waiting for them.

Callie turned to Don.

"Don Webster, meet Lucian Young. Lucian is the best forensic scientist in the Met. And Don – " In the microscopic pause, Don wondered how Callie planned to introduce him, " – works in another branch of law enforcement. Don't you, Don?"

Wondering whether her pursed lips and narrowed eyes signified disapproval or an arch sense of humour, Don simply smiled at Lucian and extended his hand.

"Pleased to meet you, Lucian."

Lucian smiled.

"Likewise. And I'm flattered by Callie's description, but really I have an excellent team under me."

"As do I," Don said. "Which is rather why I'm here. It's about that business card you found."

Five minutes later, coffees procured and a laptop occupying centre stage on the circular table in the corner of Callie's office, Don turned to Lucian.

"We need to get to this chap. He may have ordered, or was ordered to arrange, an attack on two of my people. From what Callie told me, it's probably not wise to just send him an email. I wondered whether you had any ideas?"

Lucian blew his cheeks out and picked the card off the table, where Don had placed it.

"The challenge, obviously, is to make contact without revealing that we're the law. Any computer connecting to Max over the dark web will be forced to give up its IP address. From that he could narrow down the PC to a city using publicly available tools. But he'll have people who can get right to a physical address. We could cloak it, but that would send a warning signal to Max that something wasn't kosher."

"Don't his kind routinely keep their identities secret?"

"They do, of course. It just means there'll be another level of security to get through before we get anywhere near Max."

"How about using a phone instead of a PC?"

"I haven't managed to unlock the mercenaries' phones yet. And any contract mobile we use will reveal enough information about its owner for Max to trace them. Checking bona fides is fine if it comes back registered to an Albanian drug smuggler or a Colombian cartel boss ..."

"But less so if it says Metropolitan Police."

"Exactly."

"So can we set up a fake account? Or buy a burner?"

"We could do that. In fact, it's how we figured out the comms format that Max is using."

"But?"

"But then we face the same problem as with a cloaked IP address."

"What about if we had the computer or phone of someone who was already a contact?" Callie asked.

"Then we'd be home free," Lucian answered. "Just message him about a new job, or the existing one if you know the basics."

Don leaned back in his chair, making the wooden frame creak. He pinched the skin at the bridge of his nose and closed his eyes.

Finding Max was important. But it wasn't as big a priority as completing the operation against Darbandi. And from what Lucian had been telling him, an operation to infiltrate Kuznitsa would be expensive and time consuming. He sighed and opened his eyes again to find both Callie and Lucian looking at him.

"Here's what I think," he began. "We need to find the mole first and get his, or her, phone. Then we use that to contact Max and take things from there."

"And how do you propose to find the mole?" Callie asked.

"We'll play the hunter with all our force, pursuit and policy."

"Are you quoting Shakespeare at me, Don?"

"*Troilus and Cressida*. It seemed appropriate. How was it, by the way?"

"It was fine. What do you mean, 'We'll play the hunter'?" she asked, fearing she already knew the answer.

"I need eyes on a couple of people who work at MI6. Discreet, deniable eyes, but eyes nonetheless."

He gave her a description of the targets, one codenamed 'Hare', the other 'Rabbit', and, after listening to her complaints, references to protocol, and mini-lecture on due process, thanked her warmly, got up, shook hands again, and left.

Callie glared at Lucian, who was grinning.

"Typical. He plays the hunter, but with *our* force, pursuit and policy."

* * *

"Stella! Got a minute?" Callie called from her office door.

Detective Inspector Stella Cole left her desk and joined Callie and Lucian in her office, closing the door behind her. She sat opposite her boss.

"What's up?"

"I'll tell you what's up. We've to put a couple of MI6 intelligence analysts under surveillance. I want you to take one of them."

"Who?" Stella asked, as if spying on spies was second nature to her.

"Here."

Callie pushed a sheet of paper across the desk to Stella, who picked it up, read it then handed it back.

"Rabbit? Why not his real name?"

Callie shrugged.

"Above my pay grade. Maybe Don *Bloody* Webster enjoys playing secret agents."

Stella grinned. She'd met Don once, briefly, a few years earlier. He'd seemed more the friendly uncle type.

"When?"

"Start right now, please. Get yourself over to Vauxhall Cross and when you see him, stay on him. If he just takes himself off home, go back tomorrow. And you keep going back until we have him. I've got his home and mobile phones tapped, but to be honest, I'm not really expecting him to be that stupid. No. It'll be a face-to-face meeting."

THE SANDS OF TIME

The next day, while Don was talking to Callie and Lucian, Eli called her old boss at Mossad, Uri Ziff.

"Elisheva!" he'd said, when she identified herself. "How are the British treating you?"

"Well. Although I need somewhere nicer to live."

"And the work?"

"Is good. And also why I'm calling you."

Eli explained how their initial attempt to get to Darbandi had failed, and why. Given that The Department was working to help Israel, could Israel now work to help The Department?

Ziff answered immediately.

"Of course. Why don't you come here? Bring your partner. We will equip you, and together we will work out a new plan."

BIRD'S EYE VIEW

US surveillance satellite "Groucho" completed its thirty-thousand-and-nineteenth orbit. On its thirty-thousand-and-twentieth circuit of the blue-and-green planet, its cameras picked up movement in the desert of Iran between Nojeh Air Base and a small town called Vareshabad north of Tehran. A convoy of slow-moving vehicles was tracking east along the Tehran-Saveh Freeway.

The pictures relayed back to the National Security Agency HQ at Fort Meade, Maryland made for interesting viewing. At the heart of the procession of vehicles, four huge, wheeled transporters crawled along. Each bore upon its back a long cylinder whose profile identified it incontrovertibly: a Soviet-made Pioneer medium-range ballistic missile. Fore and aft, the missiles were escorted by a motley collection of armoured vehicles, also of Soviet manufacture. Motorcycle outriders led the way and brought up the rear: mosquitos to the larger vehicles' bumblebees, beetles and locusts.

Once the on-duty intelligence analyst monitoring the feed identified the convoy, she kicked it up the chain of command. Twenty minutes later, it had found its way onto the desk of the Director, NSA, known throughout the organisation as DIRNSA. From the expanse of mahogany in DIRNSA's office, the intel passed to his boss, the

Director of National Intelligence in Washington, DC. The DNI frowned and sent it onward to her boss, the National Security Adviser.

The National Security Adviser informed the White House Chief of Staff of the situation.

Having been informed of the development, the Chief of Staff ran, literally, along the corridor to the Oval Office where, uncharacteristically, the President happened to be in residence. Advising his boss that discretion was advisable, he left to convene the relevant parties in the Situation Room.

The President read the report. Looked at the screengrabs. Looked again at the analyst's three-sentence comment at the bottom of the first page.

Cannot avoid conclusion Iran is routing four medium-range, nuclear-capable missiles to its research facility at Vareshabad for arming. No threat to USA. Most likely target of any attack: Israel.

The President laid the report aside and frowned. Then he spoke to the empty room in a low growling voice.

"Discretion be fucked!"

He marched out of his office and along the thickly carpeted corridor towards the Situation Room. There, he found his Chief of Staff, the National Security Adviser, the Joint Chiefs of Staff already convened.

The Chief of Staff spoke first.

"Mr President, sir. We thought we'd make a start. DIRNSA is onboard a military flight heading in as we speak. We need to discuss the options, and outline the available scenarios. Then we can answer any questions you may have, sir."

The President stuck out his lower lip and glared at the men in the room.

"I only have one question."

"What's that, sir?"

"Has anyone called the Israelis yet?"

"No, sir. As I said, we thought it best—"

The President's face suffused with blood.

"I don't give a rat's ass what you thought. Give me that phone."

The Chief of Staff handed the secure phone over.

"This is the President. Get me the Israeli Prime Minister on the line. Now."

Then he sat down in one of the padded leather chairs to wait.

His friend's voice travelled along the secure line as clear as if he had been sitting right there.

"Wallace. Always a pleasure. But this is an unscheduled call. What's happening?

"Listen, Saul. I just saw an intelligence report. From one of our spy satellites, OK? And it concerns you."

"What is it?"

"It's the Iranians. They've got four medium-range nuclear missiles on the move. Sounds like Israel's the target."

"My God! And this is credible? The intelligence, I mean. You believe it?"

"Me? Of course I believe it! We have eyes-on, Saul. A bird's eye view from, whatever, like ten miles up. It looks like it was taken on someone's iPhone for Chrissake. No offence."

"Thank you. I have to go. You understand? But, thank you."

The President looked at the phone in his hand. He shook his head.

"Go and kick some ass."

TELEPHONE DIPLOMACY

Arlene Mackie picked up the phone on her desk.

"Director, ma'am? I have the office of Mossad Director Peretz for you."

"Put him through."

The line clicked a couple of times.

"Director Mackie?"

"Speaking."

"Connecting you with Director Peretz now."

Two seconds of complete silence followed, followed by a click and a buzz.

"Arlene. How are you?"

"I'm fine Daniel. How are you? How's Avigael, and the children?"

"All fine, thank God. And Raymond?"

"He's fine, thank you. What can I do to help you?"

"We have a problem. I need your help clearing an airborne operation over a few friendly countries' airspace."

"Strictly speaking, that's the State Department's role."

"I know. But this is urgent. We both know how slowly the diplomatic wheels grind."

"I'm listening."

* * *

OFFICE OF THE UNDERSECRETARY, NATIONAL INTELLIGENCE ORGANIZATION, ANKARA, TURKEY

"Sir, I have the Director of the CIA on the phone for you."

"Very good. Put her through."

"Undersecretary Özdilek. Thank you for taking my call."

"Anything for our friends at the Central Intelligence Agency, Director Mackie. How may I be of assistance?"

* * *

OFFICE OF THE AGENCY EXECUTIVE, NATIONAL SECURITY SERVICE, YEREVAN, ARMENIA

"This is Demirdjian."

"Good morning, sir. I have CIA Director Arlene Mackie on the phone for you."

* * *

OFFICE OF THE DIRECTOR, STATE SECURITY SERVICE, BAKU, AZERBAIJAN

Director Hasanov nodded as the most powerful woman in the global intelligence community outlined her requirements. When she finished –

"... and free return passage over Azerbaijani airspace."

.   .   .

– he nodded, even though she couldn't see him. This was a coup. He could assist the CIA at no cost, thus building both his country's international prestige and his own, within the domestic corridors of power. Then he answered.

"Of course, Director. As a member of the NATO Partnership for Peace programme, Azerbaijan is always ready to help our allies, especially America."

* * *

OFFICE OF THE DIRECTOR, INSTITUTE FOR INTELLIGENCE AND SPECIAL OPERATIONS (MOSSAD), TEL AVIV, ISRAEL

"Director, I have CIA Director Mackie for you."

"Thank you, Rachel. Please put her through."

"Daniel?"

"Arlene. What news?"

"It's all set up. You have clearance to overfly Turkey, Armenia and Azerbaijan. Both directions. The Azerbaijanis will also offer support on the ground."

"Thank you. We'll move straightaway. Come and see me soon."

"I will. Shalom, Daniel."

"Shalom, Arlene.

SHALOM

TEL AVIV

Another city, another hotel room. But at least this time, Gabriel felt he and Eli were safe from the attentions of the local spooks. Mainly because they were on the same side. He'd wanted to experience something new as they climbed into the back of the taxi at the airport, but on the thirty-minute drive to the Crowne Plaza hotel, he'd been disappointed.

There wasn't anything *wrong* with Tel Aviv. But as they drove under gantries, whose blue-and-white signs pointed the way to Tel Aviv-Yafo, what he saw looked depressingly familiar. An initial expanse of flat scrubland outside the airport's perimeter gradually giving way to low-rise and then high-rise developments. Lots of cranes. A concrete barrier on the meridian of the highway dotted here and there with graffiti. Advertising hoardings towering over the road promoting razors, local TV stations, cars, lipsticks. The sky, a leaden grey as they emerged into the hot, soupy air outside the arrivals lounge, gradually changed to a sapphire blue as they neared the city proper.

Sitting in the hotel dining room the following morning, dressed for business in a light-grey linen suit, Gabriel looked across the table at Eli. He had to admit, she looked happier than he'd seen her for a while. Her face was radiant. It wasn't just the few hours of sunshine she'd enjoyed by the hotel pool the previous day. She looked like she belonged. Which, he reflected, she did, of course. Her eyes were sparkling and her smile was relaxed. She'd dressed in loose, sage-green trousers and a white shirt. A turquoise necklace and matching earrings set off her tan. And she was wearing makeup. Not a lot. But enough for him to notice.

"What do you recommend for breakfast?" he asked her.

"Here? Only one choice. My favourite. *Shakshouka.* Come on, let's go to the buffet."

Shakshouka turned out to be eggs poached in a tomato sauce served in individual cast-iron frying pans. Gabriel and Eli collected one each and returned to their table with the eggs and mugs of coffee. He sliced off a piece of egg and dipped it in the sauce, which was rich and spicy. Below the onions, peppers, chilli and oregano, Gabriel detected cumin and smoked paprika. Crumbled feta cheese and a scatter of chopped parsley gave the whole dish a bright, sparky edge.

"Mmm. Good," he said, after swallowing. "I could get used to this in the mornings."

Eli smiled back.

"I'll share my mum's recipe with you when we're back in England."

* * *

Thirty minutes later, Gabriel and Eli were riding in the back of an armoured Mercedes, being driven to Mossad headquarters.

Eli turned to him. "You know," she said, "we're headed to one of the world's best-hidden buildings."

Gabriel nodded.

"I looked it up last night. Some writer, a guy called Patrick Tyler, I think, published the location in a book. He said it was between the Glilot highway junction, a cinema and a shopping centre."

Eli's smile widened.

"I know. It isn't. Tyler got his information from a retired Mossad operator." She put air quotes round the final three words. "He wasn't retired at all. He's still there. He works in counter-intelligence."

Gabriel smiled.

"So unlike our own, dear SIS, you don't have photos all over the web of your sumptuous riverside accommodations?"

"Nuh-uh. Nor do we have terrorists shooting RPGs at them."

"Seems sensible."

"You think?"

Their banter was interrupted by the driver, who leaned back and announced that they had arrived.

Gabriel had experienced security checks at the CIA, the FBI, MI6 and 10 Downing Street. The Israelis had seemingly taken all the techniques used by their counterparts, combined them, refined them and added a few of their own. He emerged from the small room convinced that if he'd entered Mossad with any secrets about his person, he was certainly free of them now. Eli was waiting for him. She was standing beside a woman who appeared to be in her early forties. Compared to Eli's casual outfit, hers was pure Fortune 500 CEO. A sharply tailored, pinstriped suit over a snowy-white shirt. Her black hair was pulled back from her face, which was marked by a long, silver scar over her right eye. They turned as Gabriel arrived. Eli smirked.

"Feeling OK?"

"Tip top! Better than a weekend at a spa. Clean and tidy inside and out."

"Gabriel, I'd like to introduce Deputy Director for Operations, Dinah Mizrahi."

Dinah extended her hand and Gabriel took it. Her grip was firm but not the over-compensating bonecrusher adopted by some powerful women he had met.

"Shalom, Gabriel. Welcome to Israel, to Tel Aviv, and to Mossad."

He smiled back.

"Shalom, Deputy Director Mizrahi. Tevdh shheskemt l'ezevr lenv." *Thank you for agreeing to help us.*

Her eyes popped wide.

"I am not used to being thanked in Hebrew by foreign agents. But you are most welcome, Gabriel. After all, as you are already working on our behalf, it would be discourteous not to."

Then she turned to Eli and smiled.

"Your partner has such good manners, Eli! Now. Why don't you come to my office and we can discuss what to do about Mr Darbandi?"

Mizrahi's office occupied a corner of an open-plan space in which, as everywhere, analysts and agent handlers stared at monitors, made calls, sent and received emails and gathered by whiteboards or huddled round documents and screens in meeting rooms.

Standing waiting to greet them was a man in his early sixties. Trim and fit looking, with an open, tanned face demarcated by heavy black eyebrows, he smiled broadly as Gabriel and Eli entered ahead of Mizrahi.

He held his arms wide, and Eli stepped into his embrace. They kissed on each cheek before releasing each other.

"Eliya!" he said, holding her by her shoulders. "You look well. But that British weather. You are as pale as a lily. Look at you!"

She laughed.

"Gabriel, this is my old boss—"

"Not so much of the old, please!"

"My *former* boss, Uri Ziff. I worked for him for three and a half years. And he thinks he's my dad! Really, Uri, my colour is fine. Maybe you need to get your eyes tested."

Ziff rolled his eyes and made a dumb-show of screwing his knuckles into them before blinking them open and scrutinising her even more closely.

"No. If anything, you look paler. What can we do to tempt you back? A corner office like Dinah's? Nice fat expense account? Gold-plated Uzi?"

Gabriel enjoyed watching Eli and Ziff sparring. For a moment, everything felt normal. No shadowy Russian gangsters after them. No double agents wishing destruction on Israel and their deaths as a by-product. No missing siblings.

Mizrahi called them to order, and once coffees had been requested and brought, the real business began.

"We learned yesterday that Darbandi will be finished in a matter of days. No longer than a week," she said. No smiling now. Her face a mask of seriousness. "Vareshabad is defended from aerial attack too well for an airstrike to be effective. His laboratory and the workshops are many storeys underground."

"We want to go back in and do it in person," Gabriel said. "But he's heavily protected by Revolutionary Guards, several of whom Eli and I had the pleasure of meeting on our last visit."

"And that is where we can help you," she said.

"We're going to need help getting there, too. I have a feeling swanning in through the arrivals lounge at Tehran International isn't going to work this time."

Ziff smiled.

"Leave everything to me. I have a meeting with Director Peretz this afternoon."

"You can't tell us how you're going to distract the Guards?"

It's best if you don't know. You'll find out when the time is right, I promise."

Ziff paused, and his heavy brow seemed to gain even more weight as his black eyebrows drew together.

"Gabriel, you know of my country's history."

"Of course."

"Then you know that Iran's stated desire to wipe Israel from the map is not simply expressed in this one man, this one bomb?"

"Yes."

"We want to do more than just kill Darbandi."

"Meaning?"

"We intend to send a message to the Iranians that we will prove a fearsome adversary if they try to restart their nuclear weapons programme."

Gabriel could see that Ziff was sounding him out. Probing for a sudden bout of conscience. If he was, he would be disappointed. After his experience in the MOIS building, Gabriel Wolfe was no friend of Iran or its twisted ideology.

"And when you say 'a message' ...?"

"We want to put Vareshabad beyond use. A phrase that has some resonance for your country, too, I believe."

"You're talking about the IRA weapons dumps. Yes. It went beyond sawing the odd Kalashnikov in half. I think most were buried under a few hundred tons of concrete."

"We can't really truck that much construction material across the desert, but we have an alternative. A bomb."

Gabriel was just about to suggest that the size of bomb they would need to utterly destroy a plant the size of Vareshabad would be about as cumbersome as a concrete mixing truck when he had a flash of insight. A bright, white flash.

"You're going to nuke it, aren't you?"

Ziff blew his lips out with a flapping noise. Then nodded.

"Yes, but not with some showy mushroom cloud. Though believe me, there are plenty of people here who would like nothing better than to do just that. No, we have built a low-yield, hybrid device, part conventional high-explosive, part nuclear. It's—"

"A dirty bomb. You're going to put Vareshabad beyond use by irradiating the fuck out of it, aren't you?"

Ziff smiled. Though, somehow, from his lugubrious features, it emerged without a trace of humour.

"Aptly put, my dear friend. Yes. The initial charge would do little more than put a kink in the Iranians' plans. Thirty kilos of high-explosive would do a certain amount of damage, but nothing that couldn't be rectified. But wrap that thirty kilos in a quantity of fissionable material – in this case, Cobalt-60 – and you turn the entire plant into a hotspot that will kill anyone venturing inside the perimeter."

Eli spoke.

"We're going to take the bomb in with us?"

"Yes."

"And we're not going to come back looking like a pair of glow-in-the-dark soldier dolls?"

"No, Eliya. Don't worry. The device is shielded with a coating of lead and a composite material we have developed. You could make the return journey twice, and a Geiger counter would not so much as chirrup."

"They'll have missiles, too. Probably at or near Vareshabad," Gabriel said. "We should try to destroy them as well."

Ziff nodded.

"We've developed a very effective time-delayed magnetic mine armed with C-4. We'll send you in with some.

"How will we get into Iran?" Gabriel asked.

"You'll land just outside Chalus on Iran's Caspian Sea coastline. There's a perfect spot for the chopper to set down, and you can ride straight off and get going."

"Ride?" Gabriel asked, raising his eyebrows.

CARGO HOLD

The IAF C-130 Hercules took off from Ramat David Air Force Base southeast of Haifa at 6.30 a.m. local time. Onboard were its crew of pilot, co-pilot, navigator, air engineer and air loadmaster, a squad of four mechanics and six technicians, also members of the IDF, and two passengers: Gabriel Wolfe and Eli Schochat. They were garbed in lightweight desert camouflage. Each wore combat webbing loaded with M26 high-explosive grenades, Gerber Mark II daggers (similar in shape to the Fairbairn-Sykes) in nylon sheaths, and Glock 17 semi-automatics in chest-mounted, sand-coloured nylon holsters.

Three hours earlier, Gabriel and Eli had stood on the night-cool tarmac of the apron beside Uri Ziff, watching as two Triumph Tiger off-road bikes were ridden up the ramp and lashed to the cargo rails with nylon straps. The bikes were painted in a broken pattern of beige, white and a pale grey: tanks, seats, engines, wheels, the lot. The tyres were made of a sand-coloured rubber compound. Nothing on the bikes had a glossy or metallic surface. No mirrors. No polished forks. Nothing that would glint in sunlight, giving away its rider's position.

Gabriel turned to Uri.

"Nice bikes."

"You approve! Good. We have thirty altogether. We asked Triumph for a few modifications. They were most helpful with the upgrades."

"What did you have upgraded?"

Uri winked.

"Everything."

Gabriel smiled as he watched a corporal carry two IWI ACE assault rifles up the ramp and stowed them beside the bikes. He turned at the noise of an approaching articulated lorry, painted white and with no insignia or official markings of any kind. Even the licence plate was a regular civilian type: seven black numbers grouped two-three-two on a reflective yellow ground.

"What's in that?" he asked Ziff.

"Your advance party. When you and Eli are within one mile of the facility at Vareshabad, stop and watch the sky."

Then Ziff smiled, before clapping Gabriel on the shoulder.

"Come on," he said in a hearty voice. "Let's get you and Eli boarded. You're riding up front with the pilots."

In the cabin, Ziff introduced Gabriel and Eli to the pilot and co-pilot. Both men wore civilian pilots' uniforms: navy-blue suits with three gold rings at the wrists, white shirts and plain, navy-blue ties.

While the pilots went through their pre-flight routine, checking in with the control tower as they flipped switches and looked at the displays in front and overhead, Gabriel turned to Eli.

"Next stop, Baku."

In front of them, the pilot signed off on the radio.

"Thank you, Tower. Out."

He twisted round in his seat to speak to Eli and Gabriel.

"OK, we're cleared for take-off."

* * *

Just under four hours later, the plane touched down with a screech from its tyres at Baku Kala Air Base, local time 11.30 a.m. As soon as it had taxied to a stop, Gabriel and Eli unstrapped themselves and were

heading through the door and into the main passenger cabin. One of
the IDF men had already sprung the door, and a team of ground staff,
all dressed in military uniforms, were wheeling a stairway over to the
plane. It clanged against the side, causing the IDF soldiers to yell
something down at the men.

Gabriel and Eli descended the stairs, into baking heat, then walked
to the rear of the plane. They watched as the cargo ramp descended
with a great hissing from its hydraulics before clanging down onto the
concrete. Like military air bases the world over, Baku Kala was built to
a fairly standard pattern. Runway, taxiways and an apron fronting a
few low-rise, brick-built offices and corrugated iron hangars. Beyond
the hard surfaces reflecting the heat in shimmering waves, a few low-
growing trees swayed lazily in a warm breeze blowing off the sea a few
miles to their east. A couple of helicopters, four- and five-rotor blade
models, sat on the tarmac like dragonflies resting after the hunt.

From the dim interior of the cargo space, two IDF mechanics rode
the camouflaged Tigers down and over to Gabriel and Eli, where they
heeled out the kickstands and killed the engines. A second man
arrived a minute or so later carrying the steel cases containing the
rifles.

Gabriel walked round one of the bikes, kneeling down to open
each of the panniers and additional storage bins strapped and bolted
to its frame. From his crouch, he looked up at Eli.

"Mines, ammunition, spare petrol, water. Got your gold?"

Ziff had given each of them a roll of gold Krugerrands before they
left Tel Aviv.

"You used to carry something similar in the SAS I believe?" he'd
said to Gabriel. "In case you were captured by tribespeople or local
militias?"

"Twenty gold half-sovereigns," Gabriel answered. "Plus a blood
chit."

Ziff frowned. "A blood ...?"

"Chit. It's just a piece of paper with a Government crest telling any
civilian who helps an escaping soldier that they can present it at a

British embassy or consulate and claim a reward. English, Arabic and Farsi, to cover all the bases."

Eli patted a pocket on her chest just to the right of her pistol.

"Though our chances of being able to buy our way out of Iran if it goes sideways are, I think it's safe to say, minimal."

Gabriel nodded as he straightened.

"Maybe, but it's better than nothing."

A third IDF soldier arrived from the cargo hold with a squat, desert camouflage Bergen rucksack on his back. He eased it off his shoulders and settled it with great care onto the right rear rack of one of the Tigers before lashing it to the frame with more webbing.

Gabriel jerked his chin at it.

"Toss you for who gets to ride the bomb-bike."

Eli grinned and shook her head.

"Israeli bomb, Israeli bike. I'll ride it."

"Technically it's a British bike, so I think I should ride it."

Eli turned around until she was facing Gabriel. She squared her shoulders and frowned.

"I'll fight you for it," she growled.

He took a step back, hands aloft.

"No, I'm good. I saw what you did to Captain Gaddesden, remember. Just don't crash it."

"Fuck you! You look after your bike, and I'll look after mine."

A polite cough from behind them made Gabriel and Eli turn.

An officer of the Azerbaijani army, dressed in combat gear and wearing a pair of aviator-style sunglasses, was standing stiffly to attention. In slow but perfect English, he addressed them.

"Greetings. Welcome to Azerbaijan. I am *Polkovnik-leytenant* Kerem Mammadzi of the *Pirekeshkul* Army Corps. I am your liaison here in Baku. Welcome to my country. We are honoured to be assisting you."

"Thank you," Gabriel said, before shaking hands.

"Yes, thank you," Eli echoed, offering her own hand.

"When you are ready, please ride over to that helicopter," he said, pointing at an ageing chopper parked on the concrete about two hundred yards from where they were standing.

His face twitched as he said this, then he strode back to the Soviet-era 4x4 waiting for him with its engine running.

Did he just wink?" Eli asked Gabriel, grinning.

"Nah. Dust in his eye."

They walked to the bikes, mounted them and set them vertical before pushing the kickstands away with synchronised *clunks*.

Gabriel thumbed the starter button and smiled as the engine caught before settling into a steady, if throaty idle. Beside him, Eli did the same. He looked right, nodded at her, then toed the gear selector into first and pulled away. It felt good to be back on a bike. He'd last ridden one in Cambodia, although that had been a dinky little machine compared to this 800cc monster.

A few seconds later, he and Eli reached the helicopter and rode round to the ramp at the back. Gabriel went up first, giving the throttle a quick twist to generate enough speed before closing it off and braking the big bike to a stop. Eli roared up the ramp behind him. They spent a few minutes lashing the bikes to the cargo netting on each side of the fuselage before walking back down the ramp to meet Mammadzi.

He looked almost apologetic. He waved a hand at the rotor blades.

"It is not the most modern aircraft. A Soviet model. The Kamov Ka-27. You have studied it?" Gabriel and Eli shook their heads. "Well, no matter. It is reliable. What do you say, bulletproof?" He smiled. "Not literally," he added, unnecessarily in Gabriel's opinion. He thought a well-aimed slingshot would be enough to penetrate its outer skin.

"What's its top speed?" Eli asked.

"Oh, about one hundred and thirty knots. The journey will take roughly two hours."

"And we're sure the Iranians don't monitor the Caspian Sea?" Gabriel asked.

"I am assured at the highest level that our neighbours to the south have been told we are running a brief naval exercise purely to test airworthiness of some of our helicopters. If the Iranians do spot you before you are landed, they will not attack. I am sure of it."

With that reassuring speech to comfort them, Eli and Gabriel remounted the cargo ramp, found a couple of thinly padded seats and strapped themselves in. The interior of the helicopter smelled strongly of aviation fuel. Gabriel frowned.

"Don't strike any sparks. We're flying in a fuel-air bomb."

Eli pointed at her Tiger.

"Don't worry. I'll be riding something much worse."

Five minutes later, the Kamov lifted off the apron with a jerk that set the two Tigers swaying in their harnesses. Gabriel and Eli exchanged a look. *Hope we get there in one piece.*

As the Kamov wheeled away to the southeast, the IDF technicians were busy with electric tugs, unloading the sixty matte-grey containers that had been driven onto the Hercules back in Tel Aviv.

Mammadzi had wanted to stay and observe, "purely out of academic interest, you understand." But the ranking IDF officer insisted on the protocol agreed to over the phone between CIA Director Mackie and Director Hasanov of the State Security Service. Disappointed, yet unable to disobey, Mammadzi stalked back to his 4x4 – *My shitty Soviet GAZ-67!* – and ordered his driver, more harshly than he deserved, to drive away.

CONTROL ROOM

TEL AVIV

Ziff and Mizrahi had been joined by Director Peretz, in a dimly lit room the size of a suburban sitting room, two floors below ground level. Stacks of plain, black servers seemed to be communicating with each other, winking with rows of green and red LEDs. The computer hardware filled every available square foot of floorspace, apart from that occupied by two black, metal-and-plastic workstations and large, comfortable-looking chairs upholstered in black mesh. The workstations bore an array of monitors, displaying a variety of graphs, charts and outputs from digital still and video cameras. Wide, curved screens took up most of the central space, where the forward-facing area of the canopy would be if the workstations were actual aircraft.

Sitting at the stations, wearing the beige uniform of the Israeli Air Force, were two drone operators, one male, one female. They wore headsets with small mics on black plastic wands that curved along their left cheeks. Their right hands rested on joystick-style controllers; their left hands on similar units to control the drones' throttles. Keyboards occupied the spaces between the pairs of controllers.

"Is this going to work?" Peretz asked, turning to Mizrahi.

"It's been tested with two hundred. The software has triple redundancy baked in."

"That's not what I asked, Dinah."

"I know, Dani. I'm sorry. Yes, it's going to work."

"It had better. For all our sakes."

* * *

Forty-five miles southeast of the control room where the three most senior Mossad directors watched the screens, Saul Ben Zacchai sat in a conference room beneath the Knesset in Jerusalem. The space was insulated and protected against electromagnetic, audio and visual surveillance, even by Mossad. He was not alone. Ranged around the table were the members of *Va'adat HaSarim Le'Inyanei Bitahon*: Israel's security cabinet.

These thirteen individuals constituted the political, military, intelligence and legal apparatus that would allow Israel to go to war. The prime minister himself, the ministers for defence, internal security, justice, finance, the interior, transport and intelligence, education, immigrant absorption, construction, energy and water resources, plus the attorney general and the chief of the National Security Council.

The prime minister banged his fist down on the table.

"I am not going to sit here on my arse waiting for the Iranians to launch a nuclear missile at Jerusalem! I said before, and I will say it again now, a pre-emptive nuclear strike at Vareshabad is the only way to save the city. To save Israel herself!" Another fist slammed down onto the table to emphasise the final word.

The defence minister spoke.

"*Nobody* round this table wants to sit on their arses. But launching a strike while our operation is still in progress? At least give them a chance."

The prime minister's pale-grey eyes widened.

"A chance? They already *had* a chance! And what happened? Our operator was almost killed, and the British agent was captured and tortured."

Nobody saw fit to remind the prime minister that "their" operator was now working for the British. They knew what he meant.

"Are we sure the Iranians are ready?" asked the attorney general.

"Believe me. I have satellite intelligence delivered to me personally by the president of the USA himself. The Iranians are maybe only days away from launching a strike against us."

"If I may, Prime Minister?" This was the minister for defence again.

The prime minister nodded. He had two spots of colour high on his cheekbones. His ministers worried when these red bullseyes appeared. It usually meant trouble.

"Go on, Ben, you know I value your counsel."

"Have the missile armed and put on standby. Initiate the targeting sequence. But please, wait until we hear from Peretz. It will all be over by tonight. One way or another."

The prime minister didn't answer at once. He was weighing up his options.

Strike now and destroy the Iranians' nuclear weapons programme at the source. Save Jerusalem. But reveal to the world, incontrovertibly, that Israel did indeed possess theatre nuclear weapons.

Or hold fire and trust Mossad to achieve the same ends by covert means. And risk their failing, and allowing a nuclear strike against Israel. Against which the country had anti-missile defences. Which themselves might fail.

He looked around the table. At twelve expectant faces. Each one bearing a variation of the same expression: resolve, tempered with anxiety. Brows knitted together, eyes narrowed. Tongue tips occasionally flicking out to moisten dry lips. He'd known these men and women a long time. Had served with two of them. The preceding hour of discussion had been heading towards a majority in favour of staying his hand. Waiting it out.

He shook his head. He'd reached his decision.

The prime minister looked around the table. He made sure to lock his gaze onto each of the twelve pairs of eyes in turn. Then he spoke.

COUNTDOWN

"Prepare the strike."

Everyone started speaking at once. He patted the air for silence. It had no effect. He stood up, bolt upright and roared at them.

"Be quiet! I will *not* go down in history as the man who let our people's birthright be obliterated. You've all read the intelligence reports. They have the missiles. They are days away from arming them with nuclear warheads. They *will* strike. So we strike first."

He sat, breathing heavily, his face flushed red.

"Saul, please think," the attorney general said. Out of all of them, he had known their boss the longest. Since they were nineteen-year-olds doing military service together.

"Do you want, then, to go down in history as the man who ignited a nuclear war in the Middle East? Please, let Peretz have the rest of the day. We promised him. If he reports that his people failed, then yes, we should strike."

The prime minister sat back in his chair and covered his face with his hands, scrubbing at his cheeks as if he would erase the high colour painted there.

"Until four o'clock this afternoon, our time. That's how long they have. After that, I want our Jericho in the air."

A LITTLE RIDE THROUGH THE DESERT

CHALUS, NORTHERN IRAN

The chopper touched down in a bouncing landing that rattled Gabriel's teeth in his jaw. He checked his watch: 2.00 p.m. local time. The rear ramp jerked downwards, admitting bright sunlight into the dim cargo hold. Donning wraparound sunglasses, he and Eli grabbed their rifles and slung them across their backs. They unstrapped the Tigers and wheeled them down the ramp and onto the hard-packed ground, Eli taking particular care with her bike and its innocuous-looking camouflaged Bergen. Gabriel ran round to the front of the chopper and waved at the pilot, who waved back before lifting off again and swinging the ageing machine due north, over the sea and towards home.

Gabriel looked around. The pilot had picked a good spot. No signs of human habitation. Or animal, come to that. Just a flat, sandy plain sloping gently up and away from the sea, with a cracked and weedy strip of tarmac heading southeast towards Tehran. A few olive trees grew beside a clump of rocks, and their spindly branches waved in the breeze blowing off the sea. It smelled of salt, overlaid with the heady aroma of aviation fuel.

"Ready?" he asked Eli, who was fastening a camouflage bandanna over her nose and mouth.

She nodded.

He adjusted his own bandanna, resettled his sunglasses on his nose and started his bike. Eli did the same.

With a spurt of sand from his rear tyre, Gabriel moved off, bringing his boots up onto the footpegs and changing up through the gears.

They crested the rise that led away from the sea and got their first decent look at the terrain. A hundred and twelve miles or so of scrubby desert, grassy plains and, in the far distance, snow-capped mountains, blue-grey in the haze. No roads. No settlements. Nothing. All to be covered as quickly as possible, without breaking the bikes or detonating the bomb nestled behind Eli's right calf.

As he reached sixty miles per hour, Gabriel changed up from third to fourth. He didn't kick it into the highest gear, wanting a reserve of torque in case the bike hit a patch of soft sand. He heard Eli matching him, and they rode on at the agreed top speed, ten feet apart, leaning forwards a little to counter the wind. The two triple-cylinder engines generated a weird, thrumming beat as their thrashing pistons came into, and went out of, sync.

The bikes' already forgiving suspension had been specially tuned for desert riding, and although Gabriel could see the front forks dipping and rising almost to the full extent of their travel, the effect on his hips and spine were kept to an acceptable minimum. Even so, stretches of hard, bumpy ground had him standing up in a half-crouch to avoid the kidney-bruising jolts transmitted up into the seat.

After an hour, they stopped for water. They'd covered fifty-four miles. Another fifty-eight to go. He checked his watch as they pulled away after the stop: 3.05 p.m. *Should be there by four fifteen*, he thought.

INITIATE STRIKE SEQUENCE

While Gabriel and Eli were mounting their bikes for the second half of the ride to Vareshabad, Lieutenant Colonel Sara Moreno of the IDF leaned towards the desk-mounted mic in front of her and gave an order.

"Strike Controller, Command. Initiate strike sequence, confirm."

"Copy, strike controller confirms. Initiating strike sequence."

She sat back and breathed out. *What have I just done?* she asked herself.

All around her, technicians, engineers and some very senior military personnel were moving through a well-rehearsed set of activities. Half a mile to the west of her padded leather chair, and fifty-eight feet below ground, a Jericho ballistic missile armed with a one-megaton nuclear warhead woke up.

DRONE SWARM

VARESHABAD

Gabriel glanced sideways. Eli was looking straight ahead. She'd tied a second bandanna around her forehead and knotted it at the back. Her hair was pinned back in a bun, but a stray hank had come loose and was whipping around in the slipstream created by her head. She looked across the gap between them and nodded. He imagined her smiling behind the sand-crusted bandanna covering the lower half of her face.

A wind-rippled sand dune rose before them. Standing on the footpegs and opening the throttle wide, Gabriel powered up the slope. At the top he gasped. Spread out before him like a multicoloured handkerchief was a vast field of roses. Squares of red, white, pink and apricot. He brought the bike to a stop and flipped the gear lever until the bike was in neutral. Then he sat back and pulled his bandanna down under his chin. He inhaled deeply through his nose. The wind was blowing towards him and on it rode the sweet, peach fragrance of the roses. Eli drew up alongside him and uncovered her own face.

"Mmm," she said. "Beautiful."

"Do you ever wish the people we go up against would just stick to flower farming, or hymn-singing, and not world domination?" Gabriel asked.

"Yes. All the time. We could retire and have lots of babies. But until then, we have a bomb factory to disable. So come on. Stop daydreaming. We've another good hour's riding before we get there. I just sent a message to Uri. I told him we'd be in position by four fifteen."

Skirting the rose fields, Gabriel and Eli rode on. They reached the point where they were to wait at 4.10 p.m. and dismounted. The rocky outcrop they'd spotted was no higher than fifty feet. But carved by wind, or possibly prehistoric peoples, a cave led downwards from the sandy surface at a shallow angle. They wheeled the bikes down a few yards then returned to the shade of the entrance. Eli sent a short, coded message to Ziff then turned to Gabriel.

"Now we wait," she said.

"And watch," Gabriel replied.

He took a pair of Zeiss compact binoculars from a pocket and brought them up to his eyes, pushing the yellow-lensed sunglasses up onto his forehead first. The white construction-set buildings of the weapons factory at Verashabad stood out clearly against the sapphire-blue sky. Although heat haze rendered the point where the ground met the sky a fuzzy, blurred line, the outlines of the blocks, spheres and cylinders were sharp.

He felt Eli's arm round his waist and looked left. She was looking into his eyes. Her expression was serious.

"What is it?" he asked.

"Don't let them capture me," she said.

"I won't."

"I mean it. If it doesn't go to plan, and you see them take me, I want you to shoot me."

"Don't be stupid."

"I'm not being stupid."

"You'd be worth more to them alive than dead. You know that. There'd be a prisoner exchange."

She shook her head.

"You don't know them like I do. You don't know what they're capable of."

Gabriel pulled off his left glove and held the back of his hand up to her face.

"I think I do."

"I'm sorry. That's not what I meant. But they'll see me as a triple affront to their ideology. An enemy agent. An Israeli Jew. And a woman."

Gabriel pulled the glove back on. Leaned over. And kissed her.

"It won't come to that. Eli, I love you. And I'm not going to shoot you. I'm not going to see you hurt, either. We're going to rock their world, kill Darbandi, then ride out of there waving our cowboy hats in the air, OK?"

She smiled at him. Leaned forwards and kissed him fiercely on the mouth. When she pulled away, she swiped the back of her hand across her eyes.

"You just said you love me."

"Did I? Fucking hell. I must be suffering from heatstroke!"

She punched him on the bicep.

"Did you mean it?"

Gabriel looked her in the eye, marvelling at the way glints of gold interwoven among the grey-green strands of her iris blazed in the sun.

"Of course I meant it, you idiot."

"Good. Because I—"

"What the fuck's that?" Gabriel asked, looking up before Eli could finish her sentence.

It sounded as if an attack by killer bees were imminent. A harsh buzzing filled the air. Gabriel turned a full circle before locating the source of the noise, which was growing louder with every passing second. He pointed to a grey cloud advancing on them from the north, from the direction they'd just ridden. It had to be a couple of hundred feet across and flying at maybe twice that altitude.

"What the hell is that? A swarm of locusts?"

Eli shaded her eyes with one hand and squinted.

"I think it's our way in."

A few seconds later, the leading edge of the swarm reached them. Craning his neck, Gabriel understood why Uri Ziff had been so cagey about the precise nature of the Israelis' plans. The first ten or twenty members of the swarm buzzed overhead. Each individual was roughly six feet across, configured into an X-shape, and lifted by whirring rotor blades at each of its four extremities. Dangling from a wire loop beneath its centre was a small, white, finned projectile. As he gaped at the drone swarm, he tried to count the identically configured craft. After estimating his way to fifty he gave up as hundreds more flew over the cave mouth, headed on a straight-line course to the Iranian nuclear weapons factory. The noise was intense, as the swarm of Israeli drones continued to pass overhead.

"There must be at least three hundred of them," Eli shouted.

Gabriel nodded, still staring. Trying to imagine the effects on ground troops when this monstrous, mechanised horde arrived and started delivering their payloads.

They stood, shoulder to shoulder, watching the drone swarm cover the final mile of its journey to Vareshabad.

MINI-SPIKE

The female drone controller – the sensor, in the parlance – swivelled in her seat. She looked up at Director Peretz.

"Ten minutes to target, Director. Look."

She pointed at her screen. Relaying video from a forward-mounted camera on the lead drone, it showed the collection of white buildings that Gabriel and Eli were seeing 1,243 miles to the east. The video was a little jerky, but Peretz could imagine he was back behind the controls of his beloved F-16, flying sorties over Lebanon.

"Very good. When we get there," – he realised that "we" wasn't really the right term, but somehow having a pilot's eye view of the terrain made it seem appropriate – "wait for the defensive forces to begin shooting. Then attack. I want as many of them out in the pen as possible."

"Yes, Director."

"Tell me again about their armaments."

"Each drone carries a single munition. A modified high-explosive warhead derived from the Mini-Spike missile normally carried by our infantry. No guidance systems, no rocket motor or fuel. Just an injection-moulded plastic body with tail fins to impart spin. They only weigh two kilos instead of four. When we hit the fire button on the joystick, the whole swarm drops its payload. Three hundred detonate-on-impact warheads. Even if the guards hit twenty percent, which is unlikely, the remaining drones should still clear the way for our two agents on the ground."

"Let's hope so," Peretz said.

MELKH

VARESHABAD

As well as commanding a garrison of 175 Iranian Revolutionary Guards, Major Darius Esfahani was a keen student of Middle Eastern history. He found it fascinating that the project the scientists were engaged in had been codenamed "Melkh." *Locust.* Not that his superiors, or his men, had asked him, but had they, he could have told them that the largest ever recorded locust swarm in the region was in 1915. The Ottoman Syria locust infestation, to give it its full title, had virtually destroyed the summer harvests in Palestine, Lebanon and Syria. The name, he felt, was apt.

Esfahani had just completed his afternoon walkaround of the facility when something pricked at his awareness, making him look up. He frowned. A low, dark-grey cloud was advancing from the northwest towards Vareshabad. No. Not a cloud. It was far too low. And far too small. And it appeared to be composed of separate ... what? He couldn't tell. He called over a corporal who was manning an observation post and asked for his binoculars. He brought them up to his eyes and adjusted the focus knob between the barrels.

His brain struggled to process the confusing signals his eyes were sending Then, when he realised what was almost upon them, he mentally recited a short prayer. *O, Allah, protect me against them however You wish.*

He turned to the corporal, who was standing to attention by his side. "Sound the general alert! Now!" he said.

The corporal ran back to his post and hit the alarm button. Esfahani raced to the armoury and grabbed a short-barrelled assault rifle, an unlicensed copy of the American M4 carbine.

* * *

In the drone command centre in Tel Aviv, Peretz authorised the two operators to begin their attack sequence. They spoke to each other, and the controller, a disembodied voice elsewhere in the building, in terse fragments:

"Control, two friendlies waiting outside strike zone. Confirm?"

"Copy, sensor confirms."

"Copy, pilot confirms."

"Approaching target. Ground forces, vehicles, all buildings live targets."

"Pilot copies."

"Sensor copies."

"Ground forces readying weapons, small arms, RPGs."

"Pilot copies."

"Sensor copies."

"Pilot, Control, request weapons loadout?"

"Copy. I have three hundred Mini-Spikes, on three hundred Hornet drones in the target vicinity."

"Pilot, Control. You are cleared hot on all targets. Confirm?"

"Copy, pilot confirms. Sensor, prepare to spin up all weapons."

"Copy. Pre-launch checklist. PRF code."

"Entered."

"Launch triggers armed."

"Armed."

"Code weapons."

"Coded."

"Weapons status."

"Weapons ready."

"Pre-launch checklist complete."

"Pilot, Control. You are clear to engage target at your discretion."

"Pilot clear to engage target. Sensor, ready?"

"Copy.

"Master arm is hot. Three, two, one, rifle."

* * *

The swarm arrived just as Esfahani emerged from the concrete bunker housing the armoury. He looked up and felt a great fear descend on him. Hundreds of drones, hovering a thousand or more feet overhead. Without thinking, he raised the carbine to his shoulder and began shooting. The rifle's fire selector switch was set to AUTO, and he emptied the magazine in a few seconds.

All around him, his troops were gathering. Those on duty were already armed. Those arriving from the barracks or the mess hall were following his own movements: rushing to the armoury before emerging armed with carbines like his own, light machine-guns, sniper rifles, even a couple of rocket-propelled grenades – whatever came to hand first.

"Fire at will!" he screamed, slamming a new magazine into the receiver of his own rifle.

The noise was deafening. In seconds, the air had turned a grey-blue and Esfahani's lungs were full of pungent smoke. The smell of burnt propellant and the ejected brass cartridge cases intensified. A shout went up as one of his men scored a hit and a drone crashed out of the sky. Then the man, and the five closest to him, were vaporised into a pink mist that quickly combusted in the explosion as the drone's payload detonated on impact.

Realising that whoever had sent the drone swarm – *The Israelis,* was his first thought – would be following up with ground troops or an airstrike, Esfahani ran for his office. He needed to get word to Tehran.

* * *

From their vantage point, Gabriel and Eli watched the attack. They saw the sparkling muzzle flashes of the small arms. RPGs left their characteristic white smoke trails as they shot upwards before the fuel ran out and the projectiles returned to earth, detonating harmlessly way beyond the facility's perimeter fence.

* * *

For a few seconds, the scene on the monitors in front of the two operators remained one of intermittent muzzle flashes and the occasional brighter burst from an RPG. Then, as three hundred Mini-Spikes reached the ground and detonated, the screens turned white. When the onboard video sensors started operating again, the scene had changed. Each warhead had left a black starburst on the ground. Bodies, and body parts, lay everywhere, fires raged, and smoke drifted left to right across the picture.

Peretz's phone buzzed on his hip. He looked at the screen before answering. His lips compressed. He turned to Mizrahi and Ziff who were both standing to his right.

"It's the PM," he said.

He tapped the screen.

"Prime Minister."

"What's happening Daniel?"

"We've just attacked. Three hundred warheads dropped onto the facility."

"And the agents?"

"Waiting for our signal, sir."

"Well, fucking give it! It's almost three. You have till four, then I'm launching *my* attack. A Jericho. We'll show the world that Israel does not wait for annihilation. We act!"

The call ended, Peretz took the phone from his ear and stared at the fading screen. He turned to Ziff.

"Send the codeword. They need to go now. We need confirmation that Darbandi's dead *and* that the missiles are destroyed by four our time, or he's going to launch a pre-emptive nuclear strike. And then, God help us all."

"What? He's going to use a nuclear missile when our people are in there?"

Peretz sighed, hating the situation he'd been placed in.

"Uri, you know as well as I do that, weighed in the balance, two lives do not count against eight and a half million."

"Then, we should tell them."

"No, my friend. What if they cut and run? They don't need to know about the PM's plan. It will only ... distract them."

"They won't cut and run, as you put it. They're professionals. They have a right to know."

"No, Uri, they do not. They have a right to the information that I, as Mossad director, deem it necessary for them to know. Now, send the code."

FACTORY VISIT

VARESHABAD

Eli looked down at her phone. A single word scrolled left to right across the top of the lock screen.

לִתְקוֹף

Attack.

She pocketed it again and spoke.

"We go now."

Ahead of them, they could see the orange fire and thick, black smoke from Vareshabad boiling up hundreds of feet into the air. Even from a mile away, the noise of the bombardment had been immense. As the warheads hit the ground and detonated, the individual flashes had combined into a distant light show, bright despite the harsh sunlight. Jets of burning chemicals speared into the sky, burning in bright greens, blues and pinks and trailing white smoke.

They started the Tigers, kicked them into gear and roared across the remaining mile of scrubland towards the white factory, which was now obscured by the cloud of oily black smoke.

A couple of the drones must have hit the gates with their missiles. The metalwork was twisted and blackened, burst apart and ripped into a tangle of sharp-pointed steel brambles. The guard post to the left had taken a direct hit. Nothing remained but a black starburst on the tarmac and a scattering of unpleasant, charred gravel, black on the surface and red at its core.

Gabriel pulled his bandanna down. Then immediately wished he hadn't. The smell of burnt flesh was everywhere. He felt a sudden urge to vomit, and took a shallow breath, trying not to imagine particles of carbonised human being entering his lungs.

"Darbandi'll be in the underground levels. Or they'll be trying to get him out."

Eli nodded.

"Go in together or split up?"

"Split up. By the look of all this," he swept his arm round at the devastation wreaked by the drone swarm, "the guards ought to be no problem. Radios to Channel 3. And watch yourself, OK?"

She nodded again. "You, too," she said, then replaced her own bandanna.

They dismounted, and ran towards the complex of buildings, pulling back their rifles' charging levers as they went.

The drone swarm and their deadly eggs had reduced what had been a hive of activity to a charnel house. Body parts lay everywhere. Some recognisable, many just pieces of blackened meat.

Where the factory's defenders had avoided direct hits, they had nonetheless been flung against walls or blasted up into the air to be caught on electricity pylons, cooling towers or communications masts. The air was thick with the familiar yet horrific stench of a full-scale military attack. Combustion gases from the high-explosive warheads, the sharp tang of gunsmoke, the coppery stink of freshly spilled blood. Fires burned where combustible supplies or vehicles had been heated to ignition by the explosions, adding an acrid overlay of burning rubber, plastic and chemicals.

Gabriel saw Eli veering left towards a roadway that led to the rear of the complex. He headed for the largest of the white blocks. The double glass doors at the main entrance to the factory had been shattered in the drone attack. Millions of twinkling fragments covered the ground. Without slowing, he leapt through the empty steel frame, swinging the muzzle of his rifle through a sixty-degree arc.

He was in some sort of reception area. No cut flowers or fancy furniture. Just a rudimentary desk and a steel security barrier. Beyond both, a single door surmounted by a pair of security lights – red and green – seemed to offer access to the innards of the building.

As he strode towards the gates, readying himself to vault them, the door opened and a man wearing the bottle-green uniform of the Revolutionary Guards appeared, an assault rifle at his hip. His eyes met Gabriel's. On his face a mixture of expressions appeared to be warring for supremacy: fear, surprise and aggression. Baring his teeth, he loosed off a burst from what Gabriel saw was an AK-47, or some sort of copy. But in the time it had taken for the guard to process the fact that he had an intruder to deal with, Gabriel had dived sideways behind the reception desk. The guard didn't have time for a second burst. Gabriel fired along the ground under the desk, hitting the guard in the ankles and sending him, screaming, to the floor. Gabriel's next burst hit him full in the face, smashing his skull in a welter of blood and brain matter.

Then Gabriel was on his feet again. He used the dead man's rifle to shoot out the door lock then kicked hard to send the door swinging back against the wall. He shouldered the AK and moved through the door. He found himself in a white-painted corridor. At the far end, twenty feet away, a lift awaited. The walls were plain all the way down the narrow space, no doors to left or right. He ran down the corridor, finding a brief moment to hope Eli was doing as well as he was.

At the lift, he pressed the button to go down. The doors immediately slid apart with a hiss. He stepped in and scanned the control panel. The floors indicated ran from 2 through 0 to -2. He stabbed a finger at -2, figuring that if he were going to protect a bunch of nuclear scientists, he'd push them as far down into the bowels of the earth as possible. And if he didn't find them there, he'd work his way up on foot until he found Darbandi.

The lift jerked into motion, and Gabriel took a few deep breaths as it descended. Tucking his arms in tight against his ribs, he went down on one knee against the left side of the lift, bracing his back. He aimed both rifles at the door. Anyone wearing a uniform or carrying anything more dangerous than a clipboard would fall under a combined burst of 7.62mm and 5.65mm full metal jacket rifle rounds.

The lift stopped with a bump.

Gabriel let his latest breath out in a hiss.

The doors opened.

* * *

In Tehran, General Arom Garouhd replayed the conversation he'd just had with Major Esfahani, the commander of the Revolutionary Guards out at Vareshabad. The Major's final words had been chilling.

"We're under attack! A drone strike. Hundreds. My men are all dead or soon will be!"

Then Garouhd called the commander of the Iranian Air Force, Brigadier General Reza Ebram, and asked for immediate help. Both men knew what was at stake if Vareshabad fell. Their own positions to begin with, if not their heads.

Within twenty minutes, six twin-engine Mikoyan MiG-29s were taking off from Mashhad tactical fighter base and heading west towards Vareshabad, a flight of some 553 miles. The Russian-supplied fighters were primarily designed for air-to-air combat, but they were the nearest planes Ebram had available.

* * *

From his vantage point flying through a cloudless sky at 20,000 feet, *Sarvan* – Captain – Karim Mansourian saw the smoke and flames that had engulfed the factory at Vareshabad several minutes before he overflew the site. He radioed back to base to confirm that Major

Esfahani had been telling the truth. But as he turned to fly over the site a second time, dropping to just 3,000 feet, he could see no massed troops, no heavy armour, nothing to indicate an attack was in progress.

Then, off to the northwest, he caught a flicker of movement, as if a flock of starlings were wheeling over the desert, the outlines of the amorphous shape shifting and changing as individual members adjusted their position to avoid a collision with a neighbour.

He banked sharply to port and gave chase, issuing a sharp order at the same time.

"Green Flight. Intruders to northwest. Follow me. Confirm."

"Two."

"Three."

"Four."

"Five."

"Green Six."

* * *

Keeping close to the side of the massive white building, Eli ran down the roadway, rifle at the ready across her body, fire selector set to AUTO. All she encountered were more mangled corpses and shattered vehicles, where the Mini-Spikes had landed. The quality of the smoke was different here: whiter, with a sharp chemical tang. Wishing they'd thought to bring breathing apparatuses, she ran on, holding her breath while skirting the thickest part of the cloud.

A scream brought her whirling round to her right, finger tightening on the trigger. A Revolutionary Guard, bleeding from a long diagonal cut on his forehead, was coming straight for her, a knife clenched in his right fist. She raised her rifle and shot him centre-mass. He tumbled over, arms outflung, his abdomen torn open and spilling blood and slithering intestines onto the ground.

Breathing heavily, she pressed on, looking left and right, waiting for a face matching her mental picture of Darbandi.

She came to a stop in the lee of the vast white sphere they had first seen while waiting for the drone swarm to do its deadly work. Up close, she could see that far from being a smooth, white ball, it was scabbed with rust and streaked with brownish, oily slicks that issued from the riveted joints between its steel plates. Intricate pipework enveloped its base, making her think for a second of an egg in a nest. One of the Mini-Spikes had hit the centre of an electricity substation hidden on the far side of the sphere. Blindingly bright, blue-white arcs fizzled and danced all around the huge transformers, occasionally leaping to a nearby set of overhead power lines. The ocean-smell of ozone was so intense it made her sneeze, twice.

That doesn't look good, she had time to think, before moving on, deeper into the complex of buildings. *You think? None of it does.*

A roar above her head made her look up. Six jet fighters, in close formation, howled over the site. She ducked under a section of pipe so fat it totally obscured her body. She tried to raise Gabriel on the radio, but only heard the rush of static. *Stay out of sight, Gabriel. They'll be reporting an attack, but without a visible enemy they should return to base.*

* * *

Sarvan Mansourian realised what he was flying into about five seconds too late. He pulled back hard on the control column, but not in time. As if controlled by some central intelligence, the drones shot outwards in all directions, increasing the volume of the cloud of whirring metal and plastic a hundredfold.

He fired his 30mm cannon, and may have hit one or more of the little machines, but then one burst through the fine wire mesh protecting the gaping square air intake of his port engine. Fifty milliseconds later, the fan blades ground it into fragments, which were sucked back into the compression chambers. The engine detonated with a huge bang, of which Mansourian only heard the beginning. Along with the $22 million-worth of the finest aero-engineering Mikoyan could supply, he disintegrated in a fireball.

The planes to his left and right banked away from the explosion, but the scattering drones caught them, too. The right-hand pilot panicked and hauled his control column hard over to port, thus ensuring his plane collided with his neighbour's. Burning drones fell from the sky along with the wreckage of the three Iranian fighters. The other pilots, saved by their positions at the rear of the formation, were able to pull up into vertical climbs before rolling away from the mid-air carnage and heading back to Mashhad.

Once the planes had flown off, Eli emerged from her hiding place. Shading her eyes against the sun, she looked up, trying to find them. A series of bright flashes to the northwest, followed by hard-edged thumps, told her all she needed to know.

THE FIRE GOES OUT

LONDON

The brunette mum in her late thirties pushed her stroller along the pavement opposite the headquarters of Britain's Secret Intelligence Service. The local council had thoughtfully provided a bench with an excellent view of the main exit, so from time to time, she parked up for a bit and read a book. The activity didn't bother her baby, snug beneath a brushed cotton sheet and shaded from the sun by a white broderie anglaise clip-on parasol. Mainly because she was made out of plastic. Though she would wet her nappy and cry if asked.

The following day, a Lycra-clad blonde alternated sprints and more relaxed sessions of jogging along the same stretch of pavement.

The next, a dowdy figure of indeterminate gender shuffled past, hair a matted grey tangle, clad in a charity shop raincoat that reached almost to the pavement.

And each day, somewhere between 5.30 p.m. and 6.30 p.m., keeping well back, one of this motley crew followed a member of staff from the gate all the way to the tube station, where they passed him off to a colleague who boarded the same train.

On the sixth day, the brunette was back on duty.

* * *

While the young mum walked her baby outside, Blacksmith called Gul. He'd become twitchy over the last few days, so had dumped his first burner phone in the Thames and bought another. It was a risky move but he felt he was running out of safer options.

"It's Blacksmith. Why haven't you called me? Did you kill Wolfe and the girl?"

Gul paused before answering, and the silence told Blacksmith all he needed to know.

"You didn't, did you? You screwed up. After I gave them to you on a plate!"

"It is not that simple. I need to see you."

"Why? I have nothing more to give you."

"Please. Indulge me."

Blacksmith noticed a ragged fingernail and worried at it with his incisors before finally tearing it off down to the quick.

"Fine. The first park we met at. Six tonight."

* * *

Stella closed the book. She'd read the acknowledgements, the foreword, the dedication, epigraph, about the author page and book club questions helpfully provided by the publisher. But now the book was well and truly finished. She huffed out a sigh of frustration.

Come on. A body could die of boredom here.

She checked her watch – 6.00 p.m. – and readied herself for the final half hour when the target was likely to appear.

And then she smiled a grim smile. *Hello again, my treacherous little friend.*

He'd appeared through the pedestrian door to the side of the main gate, nodding at the guard in the bulletproof glass cubicle. Looking both ways, he darted across the road and took a right, walking right past Stella, who at that moment was attending to her charge, leaning in so her face was obscured by the parasol.

As he passed her, she straightened, let him get thirty yards ahead and walked after him. He led her on a half-mile tour of the less busy streets of Vauxhall before entering Battersea Park through a black-and-gold, wrought-iron gate. Staying further back, she bent over the stroller again and this time muttered into the stem of the parasol.

"Rabbit has entered Battersea Park from Prince of Wales Drive. Repeat. Battersea Park from Prince of Wales Drive. Cover the other exits."

Then she meandered her way past a duckpond and some swings as she tracked her quarry into the centre of the park. He was heading for a Victorian bandstand. An octagonal, wrought-iron construction of black, green and red. Standing off to one side, a man waited. His suit was smart, but not cut in the English style. And his high-collared shirt was buttoned to the throat without a tie.

She sat on a bench giving her an excellent view of the bandstand and pulled out her book again, opening it at random. The target approached the tieless man and they started talking. Arguing, she realised. The target pointed at tieless man, then jabbed a finger in his face. Clearly, this was a mistake. Tieless man responded by grabbing the target's jacket lapels and hauling him close enough that their noses were touching. He said something, then he thrust him away so hard he stumbled, and fell. Tieless man turned on his heel, though not before Stella had taken a series of pictures of him talking to the target.

Stella stood up, and pushed her buggy towards the target, walking quickly and plastering a look of concern onto her face. He'd just got to his feet when she arrived.

"Excuse me, are you all right?" she asked. "I saw what just happened. Shall I call the police?"

His face was white with anger or shock, but he managed to stammer out a few words.

"No, thank you. I'm fine."

"Oh, OK. Well in that case," Stella reached under the blanket covering the doll and brought out a Sig-Sauer P250 fitted with a suppressor. She held the dinky little pistol close to her side and pointed it at his midriff, "I wonder whether you'd mind coming with me instead."

Something happened to the target. His shoulders slumped. He looked defeated. His blue eyes looked pleadingly into Stella's.

The punch was amateurish. An analyst's attempt at an operator's move. As his fist moved through empty air to the side of her head, Stella coshed him on the side of the head with the pistol, catching him under the arms and letting him down gently as his knees buckled. Within seconds, his hands were cable-tied together behind his back and Stella was waving away a couple of curious bystanders who were already raising their phones.

"Police! Put those away or lose them! He's a terrorist."

Something in her voice persuaded them to comply. Or maybe it was the threatening couple of pounds of black metal in her right hand. She spoke into the parasol stem again.

"Rabbit in the trap. To me, everyone. At the bandstand."

While she waited, she retrieved two smartphones and a simple feature phone from Rabbit's pockets. *Work, personal and burner*, she thought. *Got you.*

WHERE IS HE?

VARESHABAD

Gabriel looked up at two more Revolutionary Guards. Their rifles were aimed at the back wall of the lift. At head height. Simultaneously, they looked down at Gabriel. And simultaneously they fell backwards, blood spurting from the monstrous wound cavities blown open in their chests as Gabriel hit them with a burst from his two automatic weapons. Dying, one man squeezed the trigger and sent a spray of bullets into the ceiling and behind him. Gabriel heard a woman scream. He jumped to his feet, scanning the room, which was about the size of a school gym, and packed with equipment and computers. But there were no more Guards. Just a huddle of people in white coats, their eyes wide as they clutched each other. As he ran to them, a woman in the centre of the group collapsed sideways, blood pouring from a massive chest wound.

"Where is Darbandi?" he shouted in Farsi.

A man in his midforties answered in a trembling voice.

"They took him."

"Who?"

"The guards."

"When?"

"Just now. There is a stairway. Over there."

Gabriel ran for the door. He tried to raise Eli on the radio but all he got on Channel 3 was static. He was too deep. Or the Iranians had installed electromagnetic shielding. He didn't know which. He had no time to care. He took the stairs two at a time. He dropped the Kalashnikov. It was slowing him down and he wanted a free hand.

When he reached the ground floor, he kicked the door open, holding his rifle at waist height. But the reception area was as empty as it had been when he'd left. The Guard's corpse was spreadeagled in a lake of congealing blood. Gabriel tried Eli again.

"Eli, come in. Over."

"Yeah, I'm here. Did you get him? Over."

"No. Just a bunch of frightened-looking scientists. They said a couple of Guards took him. Get outside. We need to stop them escaping. Over."

"On it. Out."

Gabriel ran for the exit.

According to the aerial photos he'd seen, there was only one road into the complex. If the Guards were going to spirit Darbandi out, that's the way they'd have to go. He ran for the ruins of the gate and took up position beside a wrecked armoured car. The blackened torso of a Revolutionary Guard with one remaining arm clutching an AK-47 lay behind it.

A burst of automatic fire echoed off the side of the building he'd just left. Then an answering burst. And another. Single shots, too, so someone was using a pistol.

Gabriel's mind whirred through his options.

Shit! It's Eli! Do I go and help or wait here for Darbandi? She'll be firing from cover. Wait.

He unclipped one of the high-explosive grenades from the webbing across his chest, flipped off the safety clip and pulled the pin, keeping his fingers tight over the spoon.

The firing continued. He tensed, holding the grenade at his side.

From the roadway between the buildings he'd watched Eli run for, a big, black car burst into the open. It was Darbandi's Mercedes. The side windows were open and he could see the muzzles of a couple of AK-47s poking out.

Gabriel let the spoon fly from the grenade and tossed it into the path of the Mercedes.

With a sharp, percussive bang, the grenade exploded as the car sped over it. The car bucked, and Gabriel heard the frantic roar of the engine as the rear wheels lost traction as the grenade lifted them clear of the ground. Then it slammed down and kept coming.

Fuck! Armoured.

He stood directly in its path and opened up with his rifle, firing directly at the windscreen, hoping to scare the driver into a swerve. Head on, they couldn't return fire, so he stood his ground and fired at the glass until the magazine was empty.

And, of course, his rounds had no effect beyond starring the toughened glass with dozens of silvery-white craters.

In the seconds remaining before the car reached, then passed him and escaped onto the road leading back to Tehran, Gabriel turned and grabbed the AK-47 from the outflung arm of the corpse by his side.

He jumped aside and fired as the car swept past, holding the trigger down and keeping the muzzle at the level of the side windows. Which were still open. The faces inside were a blur and the Kalashnikov bucked in his hands, spitting out hot brass cases with a loud rattle, but he held it steady as the Mercedes roared between the smashed gates. Now the car did swerve. It slewed off the road and careered through a patch of scrub, heading for open desert. Through the untouched rear window, he could see someone twisting to reach between the front seats to steer the car.

"Gabriel!" It was Eli shouting from behind him. "The bikes!"

He turned to see Eli running towards the two Tigers, rifle slung across her back, panic in her eyes. Realising in an instant what she meant, he raced back to meet her.

* * *

Major Esfahani propped himself up on his elbows. He was lying in a pool of blood that stretched from his hips to his feet. Yet he felt no pain. *Adrenaline has a way of doing that to a soldier*, he thought. Since time immemorial, men have fought on with horrendous wounds, unaware that they were missing limbs, internal organs or parts of their skulls. Realising that his own lack of pain was caused not by brain chemicals but by an absence of injuries, he looked left and right. And shuddered. Beside him, a headless corpse – a Second Warrior by the look of it – lay spreadeagled, its chest cracked open, broken rib-ends showing white through the ruined flesh.

Esfahani got to his feet and looked around for a weapon. A blood-smeared AK-47 lay just beyond the dead man. He grabbed it, checked the magazine, and ran towards the main gates.

He rounded the corner of the office building and stopped dead in his tracks. Two figures in camouflage were running towards sand-coloured motorbikes by the gates.

"Infidels!" he screamed, raising the AK-47 to his shoulder and pulling the trigger.

DEATH OF A PATRIOT

Running to meet Eli by the Tigers, Gabriel's attention was entirely on her and the need to get after Darbandi. It was only as he got within thirty feet that the movement from the roadway between the buildings caught his eye. At first, he couldn't process what he was seeing and thought the staggering black figure was Smudge, putting in one of his increasingly rare visual appearances. Then reality reasserted itself. The soldier with the hairless head burnt black by an explosion, blood running down from lurid red cracks in the skin, was real, not a hallucination. And it – he – was raising a rifle to his shoulder.

"Get down!" he yelled at Eli.

Only amateurs look round. Eli was a professional. She dropped to the ground before rolling and reaching for her pistol.

The blackened soldier loosed off a burst but his aim was wild.

Gabriel's was not. His own pistol drawn, he cradled the grip in both hands and shot the man in the chest. He fired again as the man staggered, hitting him in the right arm and tearing a chunk of muscle away with a spray of red.

Eli jumped to her feet and ran back, making sure of the kill with two rounds to the head, blowing a bright pink hole in the blackened skull. The she turned to Gabriel and gave him the thumbs up before rejoining him at the bikes.

"Come on," she said. "We need to catch him."

Gabriel swung his leg over the Tiger's saddle. In a single, continuous movement, he started it, kicked it into first and slewed it round in a tight circle.

Together, Gabriel and Eli raced after the Mercedes, which had a few hundred yards' start on them. But as Gabriel raced after it, he realised the car wasn't accelerating. Instead it was trundling along at barely more than 20 mph. In an instant he realised what had happened. He'd hit the driver, who'd slumped over the steering wheel. The figure he'd seen in the back seat was leaning forwards to steer but they had no access to the throttle pedal. The dead man's foot could so easily have come down hard on the pedal, but instead it had clearly slipped to one side or simply been pushed back by the internal spring.

Within a few seconds, Gabriel had caught up with the Mercedes. With a bang from its underside, the car hit a huge flat rock protruding from the loose sandy soil of the riverbank. Its nose reared up for a second, then it plunged six feet down a steep incline into what would have been the main channel of the watercourse.

Gabriel rode after it, standing up on the footpegs and jumping the bike down onto the riverbed. He saw Eli's bike flying out and down twenty feet to his right. The Mercedes trundled across the expanse of gritty sand before coming to rest with its wide, chromed grille munching at the sandy slope of the far bank. He jumped off the bike, letting it fall onto its side, unshouldered his rifle and ran towards the stationary car. Eli approached it from the rear, carrying her own rifle at the level of the rear screen. Bulletproof it may have been, but anyone sticking their head or weapon out of one of the open side windows would get a burst of fire that would either drive them back inside or kill them outright. Nobody moved.

Gabriel reached the car first. He saw what had happened at a glance. A Revolutionary Guard lay slumped over the steering wheel, blood still leaking from a gaping wound in the side of his head. In the rear seats, a second Guard sat with his head against the window. He'd taken a bullet to the throat and bled out. And there, wedged between the front seats, a bruise already forming on his forehead where it had smashed against the rear of the driver's headrest, was the man he had come to kill. Abbas Darbandi. The man's face was speckled with blood from the dead. His teeth gleamed through the red mask.

With a convulsive twist of his torso, Darbandi threw himself backwards and grabbed a pistol that lay beside him on the back seat. He stuck the gun out through the window.

Gabriel squeezed his own trigger. Nothing happened.

He looked down at the black barrel of the pistol pointed at his gut.

The shot was immensely loud.

TWO-UP

As Gabriel looked down and waited for the bolt of agony, Darbandi's right hand flew away, trailing blood and still gripping the pistol. Darbandi screamed and carried on screaming, clutching the stump of his right wrist, from which thin jets of bright red arterial blood were jetting up onto the roof lining of the car.

Gabriel couldn't figure out what had happened. Until he looked to his right.

Eli was getting to her feet from a kneeling position. She slung her own rifle, which clearly hadn't misfired, across her shoulder and ran to him.

"Don't kill him," she panted.

"Why?"

"We need to know where the missiles are."

She yanked the door open and dragged Darbandi out and onto the dried-up, sandy soil of the river bed.

Then she sat astride him. He was clutching his right wrist to his chest. The combined effects of adrenaline and the elastic properties of the blood vessels she'd just shredded with a bullet meant he was in no real danger of bleeding to death. Not if he co-operated.

"Where are the missiles?" she yelled into his face, gobbets of spittle flying from her lips and hitting his right cheek. She used both English and Farsi.

Darbandi was shaking his head, his eyes rolling in his skull, white showing all the way round his dark-brown irises.

"This isn't going to work," Gabriel said.

"Yes, it is. It has to," Eli said.

She pulled her Gerber from its nylon sheath, showed the blade to Darbandi, then stabbed down into the soft place between his left shoulder and his pectoral muscle. He screamed.

"Where are they?" she shouted.

Darbandi grimaced up at Eli, and tried to buck her off. He uttered an oath in English.

"Fucking Jewish cockroach! I'll never tell you!"

Gabriel watched Eli's face darken. Darbandi presumably wanted her to kill him. Instead, she leaned closer to Darbandi's ear and murmured a few sentences.

"If you don't tell me, right now, I'll strap a tourniquet on your arm and we'll take you back to Israel with us. We'll put you on TV and tell the world you defected, to work for us against Iran. Then we'll turn you loose. How long do you think it will take them to find you?"

His face contorted, lips drawn back to show his teeth, whether from the pain of his missing hand or the thought of what Iranian security agents would do to a traitor, Gabriel wasn't sure.

It took a few seconds before Darbandi responded in a grating monotone.

"They're in a cave half a mile south of here."

Eli stood. Stepped off Darbandi's supine figure. Took a couple of steps away.

Then she turned and drew her Glock.

"You got this far, Darbandi," she growled. "But no further."

The rounds hit Darbandi in the face. His skull exploded in a welter of blood and tissue.

Without pausing, Gabriel drew his pistol and put two rounds into each of the dead Guards. Headshots. Just to be sure.

"You got him," he said to Eli. "Now let's go. We need to finish the job."

"Wait," she said, sending a text.

Fox dead.

SET TARGET

SECRET MILITARY INSTALLATION, CODENAME "JUDITH,"
NEGEV DESERT, ISRAEL
LOCAL TIME 3.20 P.M. 40 MINUTES TO LAUNCH

Sara Moreno had spent the previous ninety-five minutes monitoring the progress of the launch on a bank of screens on a huge wall in the command centre. Everything she needed to know or interrogate was displayed in green, yellow, red and electric blue. Guidance, navigation and control subsystems; thrust vectoring; arming protocols; targeting software; fuze timers and detonation sequences; motor pressure and temperature. It was a long list.

Every few minutes, she'd look anxiously at the red desk phone, willing it to ring, but so far it had sat mutely on the clear black space. Orders to launch – codeword "spear" – or cancel – codeword "shield" – would also arrive by encrypted messaging systems on a screen, and she also had a mobile phone and a satellite phone, both military issue and encrypted.

It was time to give a new order. She leaned forwards and grasped the stem of the mic with a clammy palm and spoke with a firmness and resolve she didn't feel.

"Targeting Controller, Command, set target, confirm."

"Copy, Targeting Controller confirms. Setting target."

In its dark silo, the Jericho ballistic missile's targeting software received a string of ones and zeroes corresponding to a point on the globe some 810 miles to the east: Vareshabad, Northern Iran.

GOING DOWN

Eli helped Gabriel lift his bike upright then ran for her own, which she'd leaned against the riverbank, making it a hell of a lot easier to pull up. He depressed the starter button. Nothing. Just the whine of the starter motor churning.

"Eli!" he yelled, before she could roar back towards the factory.

She turned.

Not bothering to shout again, Gabriel just ran over to her.

"It won't start. Give me a lift, will you? We need to go back and get the mines."

Space was tight, but Gabriel grabbed her round the waist and held on as she started the bike and rode over to Gabriel's Tiger. He climbed off and unloaded the four magnetic mines from his left-hand pannier and slotted them in wherever he could find gaps in Eli's.

Back aboard, he tapped her on the shoulder. She rode hard

towards the shallower bank they'd come in from and raced up the sloping sand before jumping the bike out onto the flat ground.

She gunned the engine, and they hurtled through the gates before pulling up right outside the building where Gabriel had gone looking for Darbandi. She released the straps holding the Bergen in place on the side rack and ran for the doors, the big rucksack banging against her left hip.

Gabriel thought for a moment of the scientists he'd encountered in the below-ground weapons lab. Were they still there? Or had they run? It didn't matter. They knew what they were engaged in. Now they'd have to take the consequences.

He took Eli's rifle and stood beside her, sweeping left and right. Watching. Hyper-alert. Heart bumping in his chest.

Eli unsnapped the catches on the straps.

"Stand on that," she ordered Gabriel, pointing to a loop of webbing on the base of the Bergen. He did as he was told. She stood and reached inside before lifting out the contents: a black object roughly the same size and shape as an office watercooler bottle.

With bent knees, and arms wrapped tightly around the bomb, she carried it to the lift and used her left elbow to hit the call button. The steel doors slid apart. Crouching between them, she pushed the cylinder inside, tapped a code on an alphanumeric keypad screwed to its curved side and pressed a green button. She looked up at Gabriel.

"It's armed and locked. We've got ten minutes."

Then she pressed the "-2" button and stepped out of the doors' embrace. They closed with a hiss and Gabriel listened as the machinery kicked in, taking the bomb where it would do the most damage. He watched as Eli set a timer on her watch, a chunky, black Casio G-Shock.

They ran back through the doors and climbed astride Eli's Tiger. Gabriel watched as she closed her right fist around the throttle and pushed her thumb down on the starter button. He held his breath. The engine caught on the first turn of the starter and Gabriel breathed out.

He felt the clunk as Eli engaged first, gripped her round the waist with his left arm and held his pistol in his right. As she let the clutch out and roared towards the gate, he pushed his gun hand between her bicep and ribcage, aiming forward.

She wove expertly between the blackened corpses of the Revolutionary Guards before leaving the factory behind and pushing the big bike through all six gears until they were racing south at seventy.

INITIATE ARMING SEQUENCE

ISRAELI NUCLEAR INSTALLATION, CODENAME "JUDITH,"
NEGEV DESERT
LOCAL TIME 3.30 P.M. 30 MINUTES TO LAUNCH

Moreno gave her third major order.

"Strike Controller, Command. Arm missile, confirm."

"Copy, Strike Controller confirms. Arming missile."

A string of LEDs in front of Moreno switched from red to yellow, then, one by one, they turned green.

"Command, Strike Controller. Missile is hot."

"Thank you, Strike Controller. Thirty minutes to launch, confirm."

"Copy. Launch in thirty – three-zero – minutes."

SPELUNKING

The cave was easy to spot. Gabriel supposed the Iranians hadn't really expected any serious infiltration. Alone in the flat landscape, a hundred yards ahead and off to their left, a rocky escarpment poked up out of the sandy soil like a ramp. He pointed over Eli's shoulder. She nodded and leaned the bike over a little to make the turn.

The far side of the escarpment had been hollowed by wind or some ancient sea, long since dried out. Its face was a hundred feet tall or more. The scooped-out roof sloped down to a pitch-black cave mouth forty yards back inside the escarpment. Keeping the throttle almost closed, Eli rode right into the cave, flicking on the headlight. The lamp wasn't really up to the job of illuminating the cathedral-like space inside the rock. But its beam had enough power to pick out the stubby nosecones of a quartet of gigantic, olive-green missiles on their launch vehicles.

She brought the Tiger to a stop, steadied it with both feet flat on the ground and waited for Gabriel to dismount. Then she pushed out the kickstand, settled it onto a flat rock Gabriel had kicked into position, and dismounted. Working silently, they unsnapped the catches on the panniers and began unloading the eight magnetic mines. As they worked, they talked in urgent sentences.

"One on the nose cone and one on the motor?" Gabriel asked.

"Or two amidships?" Eli replied.

"Let's do both. Two and two. OK?"

She nodded.

"OK."

"How long have we got?"

Eli checked her watch.

"Eight minutes, fifteen seconds."

"Set the timers for eight minutes reducing by thirty seconds per mine."

The mines didn't weigh much, just a few kilos each. Each mine was two inches thick and six across. Digital timers occupied the centres of their upper surfaces. Underneath, square steel magnets a quarter-inch thick were let into the polished casings.

They took two each and ran towards the missiles.

Placing one mine on the upper curve of one of the transporter's massive tyres, Gabriel climbed up onto the roof of the transporter before attaching the mine to the nosecone of the nearest missile. The magnet *clunked* as it met the smooth steel surface of the missile. He set the timer for eight minutes, jumped down and grabbed the second mine.

This time, he slammed the mine onto the rear of the missile between two of the fins. Seven minutes thirty.

The third mine pulled itself onto Gabriel's second missile halfway between the rocket motor and the nosecone. Seven minutes dead.

He placed his fourth mine opposite the third. Six minutes thirty.

He turned to see Eli arming her fourth mine.

"Ready?" he shouted.

"Ready!" she shouted back, running for the Tiger.

She mounted the bike, flipped up the kickstand, and he joined her. She pressed the starter. Nothing happened. Gabriel's pulse ticked up. *Keep calm*, he told himself. Eli shook out her right hand then tried again, turning the key to the OFF position, then back on again before pushing the starter button. Dead silence. No starter motor.

Gabriel climbed off.

"Wait! Don't try yet," he said. "It'll probably be either fuel or spark. A fuel line might be blocked, but let's start with spark."

He crouched down on the left side of the bike and pulled the kickstand down. Where it joined the frame, a black plastic cover covered a join between the wires.

"What is it?" she asked.

"It might be the sidestand safety switch. It won't start if it's on. Hold on."

He pulled the male and female halves of the plastic cover apart. Each hid a white plastic connector, one with three pins, the other with three matching holes.

"I need a piece of wire," he said. "Got anything?"

Eli reached up and, as if this was an everyday occurrence, pulled a hairpin from the bun at the back of her head. She handed it to him without a word.

My God, you're a cool one, Gabriel had time to think, before straightening it then adding two right-angled bends to create three sides of a square. He pushed the ends into the outer terminals then yelped as a spark leapt across the wire. Leaving the improvised bypass bridge in place, he resealed the connector and stood.

"Try it now," he said, sounding more relaxed than he felt.

Eli checked the throttle kill switch was off, checked the bike was in neutral, turned the key and thumbed the starter button.

With a roar from its triple-cylinder engine, the big bike started immediately.

"Come on!" she shouted. "We've got two minutes."

Gabriel climbed on, and Eli dumped it into first before spinning the rear tyre in her hurry to get away.

Emerging from the gloom of the cave into blinding sunlight, Eli swerved to the left but kept the bike upright. Maxing out the revs in each gear she powered away from the cave, reaching eighty before Gabriel patted her on the shoulder: *Ease off.*

After a couple of miles, Gabriel saw a rocky bluff towering over a dried-up riverbed to their right. He pointed and yelled in Eli's right ear.

"There. Cover!"

Eli nodded, leaned forwards and added another ten miles an hour to her speed. If they hit anything now, they'd be spilled, if not killed, but Gabriel trusted her. She leaned the bike over to skirt the bluff on the right side, then back the other way. On the lee side, she brought the bike skidding to a stop, nearly dumping them both on the sand, before retrieving the slide and sticking her booted feet out to each side. Gabriel climbed off. Eli followed, this time lugging the bike's weight up and back onto the centre stand. Then they clambered up the rocky slope to watch the results of their handiwork.

Eli looked at her watch.

"Ten seconds."

OPEN HATCH

"Strike Controller, Command. Open hatch, confirm."
  "Copy, Strike Controller confirms. Opening hatch."

The five-foot-diameter steel disc swung open on its lubricated bearings, startling a herd of Dorcas gazelles grazing the red-berried cashew trees nearby. Leaping high into the air, the caramel-and-cream antelopes scattered, looking for a quieter spot for lunch.

PLAYING DIRTY

VARESHABAD
LOCAL TIME 5.10 P.M.

Gabriel shaded his eyes with his hand and kept his gaze fixed on the white buildings of the factory.

"Nine."

Do I hope the scientists got away?

I don't know. They were civilians.

But so was Darbandi.

One of them might have taken his place.

They were working on a fucking nuclear bomb designed to destroy a whole city – a whole country, for God's sake. So they should have—

The explosion interrupted his train of thought. The sound reached them before the flash. Usually, it would be the other way round, but the flash was forty feet or so underground. The boom rolled over them and away into the desert behind them. Then secondary explosions kicked in. Tympani and snare drums to the initial blast's bass drum. Gradually, the whole explosive orchestra tuned up and joined in a crescendo of dull crumps, high-pitched cracks and hammer blows.

Finally, the visuals. A fireball blossomed like an orange rose, directly over the low rectangular block where they'd planted the bomb. A column of smoke rose vertically after it, rolling out into an oily, black cloud. The white sphere to the left of the block suddenly cracked open in a huge explosion, three or four times as bright as the fireball. Flames shot high into the sky above the ruined complex.

Eli turned to Gabriel.

"The missiles should have blown by now."

He shook his head.

"I've used those timers before. They're not one hundred percent acc—"

The rest of his sentence was lost in a staccato barrage of hard-edged bangs, amplified by the trumpet-shape of the cave. Almost immediately, they were drowned out by four deafening explosions as 148 tonnes of highly explosive solid fuel detonated.

When the initial cloud of flames and smoke had roiled upwards – a quarter of a mile was Gabriel's estimate – they could see that the top of the escarpment that had sheltered the Pioneers was cracked apart as if it were made of plaster and not millions-of-years-old rock. Vast sharp-pointed boulders had been thrown into the air and had landed hundreds of yards from the blast site.

Gabriel turned to Eli.

"Come on," he said. "Given what the bomb was wrapped in, we need to get as far from here as possible."

She nodded. Then, in a move that equally surprised and delighted him, especially given their situation, she sandwiched his cheeks in her palms and kissed him.

"I love you, Gabriel Wolfe. You saved my life in Cambodia; now you just helped me save my country."

"I love you, too. Now, like I said, unless you want to start glowing in the dark, let's get the fuck out of here."

"Should I message Uri to tell him we blew the missiles?"

"Wait for a fuel stop. I want to get going."

They slithered down the rocky slope and were back aboard the Tiger and riding hard northwest thirty seconds later. They had to stop to refuel after just ten minutes. Gabriel took the opportunity to send a signal requesting extraction to Polkovnik-leytenant Mammadzi. After refilling the tank and dumping the empty petrol can, Eli called Ziff.

Gabriel listened in on her side of the conversation.

"The fox is dead. We closed the den. Four cubs also dead.

"Yes. One hundred percent. The garden is safe.

"Thank you. I will."

She put her phone away and turned to Gabriel.

"Uri says thank you. Drinks are on him when we get back."

Gabriel smiled.

"Fair enough."

"It's weird, though. He seemed in a real rush to get off the phone."

"Huh, probably had a meeting to get to."

The booted foot lay on its side in the sand, several hundred yards from the epicentre of the explosion at the Vareshabad nuclear weapons facility. The exposed ends of the tibia and fibula were splintered and still leaking blood, despite having been burnt black. Melted brass cartridge cases studded the terrain around the boot like gold nuggets placed to show off some grotesque piece of contemporary jewellery. The wind blowing over the boot from the direction of the former nuclear site was heavy with the stink of carnage. Blood, shit, burnt high-explosives, and the rank smell of naked terror.

A crow hopped closer. It cocked its head on one side, eyeing the foot from a distance of six inches. Detecting no threat, it closed the gap to the length of its beak and stabbed down at the charred flesh of the ankle, jerking its head back until a scrap of meat came free. The Iranian summer didn't usually offer such easy pickings and the crow was happy.

SPEAR OR SHIELD

ISRAELI NUCLEAR INSTALLATION, CODENAME "JUDITH,"
NEGEV DESERT
LOCAL TIME 3.55 P.M. 5 MINUTES TO LAUNCH

Moreno picked up the phone flashing on her desk. She looked at the monitor in front of her. In grainy black and white, it showed the blue-and-white-painted flanks of a Jericho medium-range ballistic missile. Water vapour streamed from a couple of points high on its curved sides. A second monitor showed the view from above-ground. The hatch concealing the missile had swung back revealing a black circle with a white pointed nosecone at its centre. *Like an eye*, she thought. A large red digital counter high on the wall of the control suite flickered through the seconds, minutes and hours until launch. As she answered, it read 4 mins 59 sec. In front of her, the missile controllers turned in their chairs to look at her. Their faces were taut. The *room* was taut. Almost humming with the tension.

The Strike Controller's authority extended to every switch, lever and button involved in the launch. Except one. A red button covered by a flip-up aluminium cover. Two tiny movements of a thumb or finger would be enough to send the 30-tonne, nuclear-armed Jericho skyward. And only the Commander had the authority to make those movements.

Her heart was racing as she spoke.

"This is Moreno."

She held her breath

"This is Chief of Staff Samuel Cohen. Codeword is shield. Repeat, codeword is shield. Cancel the launch."

Moreno looked up at the counter. 4 mins 44 sec. She breathed out.

"Understood. Codeword is shield. Codeword is shield. Cancelling launch."

She replaced the handset and leaned over to the mic mounted on a flexible plastic arm. Pressed the transmit button.

"Strike Controller, Command. Cancel the launch. Cancel the launch. Confirm."

A man answered and even through the scratchy electronics Moreno could hear the relief in her deputy's voice.

"Copy, Strike Controller confirms. Launch cancelled."

And that was that. No panic. No screaming. A set of green lights on the control board flickered amber and then turned red. Everywhere she looked, indicators that gave readings of fuel pressure, ignition sequences and arming protocols switched to NO-FIRE mode, displaying a row of zeroes. She watched on the screen as the hatch permitting the Jericho to launch slid smoothly back into place.

Then, and only then, Moreno sank down into the padded leather chair behind her and closed her eyes. She thanked God for delivering her. Then she shook her head violently, stood, and went to congratulate her team.

TO LIFE!

Back in Jerusalem, Gabriel and Eli were invited by the prime minister's private secretary to meet his boss in person.

Taking tea with prime ministers did not faze Gabriel. He'd met several, and had forced one into premature retirement on an earlier operation. He'd read of Saul Ben Zacchai, Israel's ultra-hawkish prime minister. He knew of his fierce opposition to the United Nations and, in particular, its Human Rights Council. His face, dominated by a heavily stubbled chin like a chunk of rock and those spots of colour high on his cheekbones, was equally familiar.

Yet Ben Zacchai's demeanour, when he welcomed Gabriel and Eli into his office, did take Gabriel by surprise. He'd been ready for gruffness, or cool appreciation, or even a statesmanlike reserve. Instead, as the private secretary withdrew, pulling the door closed behind him, Ben Zacchai enveloped Gabriel in a bear hug that threatened to crush his ribcage. He released Gabriel just enough to plant two kisses on his cheeks, then turned to Eli and repeated his embrace, though Gabriel thought the hug looked slightly less likely to crack her ribs.

When Ben Zacchai let Eli go, Gabriel saw his eyes were glistening. He pulled a white handkerchief from his breast pocket and wiped the tears away then beckoned for Gabriel and Eli to sit on a sofa by a window commanding a view of Jerusalem. He sat opposite them, elbows on knees, leaning forwards with an expression Gabriel read as admiration, mixed with wonder. The grey eyes were wide, the mouth upturned, the head shaking slowly from side to side like a metronome.

"I don't know how you did it, but on behalf of the people of Israel, I want to thank you, Gabriel, and you, Eli, from the bottom of my heart." He looked at Gabriel. "I know you suffered grievously at the hands of the Iranians. I am sorry."

Gabriel shook his head.

"It's over and done with, Prime Minister. Look," he held up his left hand and waggled his fingers as if showing off rings, "good as new."

"Please, call me Saul. After what you did, it's the least I can offer you. Or maybe not. And as for your hand, I served my country in war and was captured for a time. I did not experience the brutality that you did, but I know what interrogation can do to a soldier. Make sure you get the care you need."

Gabriel thought of Fariyah Crace, and her continuing efforts to heal him psychologically. He didn't think he'd need her to get over his rough treatment at the hands of the late General Razi. His own efforts in that quarter had provided all the closure he felt he needed.

"I will, Saul, and thank you."

Ben Zacchai turned to Eli.

"And you, Eliya. You were a credit to the IDF and then to Mossad. I wish we could win you back, but I hear you are doing good work with our friends in Britain. What you did today will live in my memory and, believe me, those of my colleagues in the Security Cabinet."

"Thank you, sir. That means a lot."

Ben Zacchai smiled.

"Sir? You cannot bring yourself to call me Saul like Gabriel here?"

Gabriel saw that Eli was blushing and that she was having trouble meeting Ben Zacchai's eyes.

She shook her head.

"To Gabriel you are a world leader. Another politician."

She glanced at Gabriel before continuing. He nodded his encouragement. Whatever she needed to say, he didn't want her concern for his feelings to get in the way. She continued, speaking more confidently now, not hesitating as she had a moment earlier.

"But, Saul," she smiled as she used his given name, "to me, you are the leader of my country." She placed her right palm over her heart as she said this.

"Right or wrong?" he asked her.

She only nodded.

"Well, I know I have made enemies where my predecessors made friends, but I do what I do because I believe it is the right course of action. If the people of Israel disagree, they can vote me out in two years' time. That is one of the joys of a democracy." He glanced at Gabriel as if expecting a comment but Gabriel held his tongue. "A true democracy, that is. The country of which you were so recently guests lays claim to democracy, but we know where the real power resides, don't we? The modestly titled *Supreme Leader*. I am merely a public servant. But enough. You didn't come here for a lecture on politics."

Ben Zacchai got up from his chair and fetched a silver tray from a polished mahogany cabinet by the window. On it sat a crystal decanter half-full of a clear liquid and three cut-glass tumblers. He added ice to the tumblers from a small fridge placed unobtrusively beside the table, and poured three generous measures and handed a tumbler each to El and Gabriel. He stayed standing, so Gabriel got to his feet, Eli too. Ben Zacchai raised his glass.

"*L'Chaim!* To life! And to friendship."

"*L'Chaim!*" they replied as the rims of the three tumblers *chinked* brightly together, agitating the cubes of ice, which clucked and shuffled in the tumblers.

The ice-cold spirit was smooth and very strong, numbing Gabriel's throat on the way down and filling his nostrils with an aroma that was part figs, part olives, part dates.

"That's very good," he said, his voice raspier by a touch. "What is it?"

Ben Zacchai smiled as he sipped from his own glass.

"Aviv 613. Israeli vodka. Made with water from the Sea of Galilee. It's a special batch I asked them to make for me. Weapons grade."

He put the tumbler down on the desk behind him and hoisted himself up onto its polished surface, so his feet swung a few inches off the thick, deep-red carpet. Gabriel found the move childlike and at odds with the prime minister's aggressive public image.

"Now," Saul said. "I said a minute or two ago that maybe there was something else I could offer you. Because I've done my research, Gabriel. This isn't the first time you've helped us is it?"

Gabriel frowned, searching his memory of other operations. Trouble was, there had been so many. "Forgive me, I'm not sure which one you mean."

Saul waved the apology away with a flat hand as if swatting a fly.

"One of our people in Zurich, Amos Peled, mentioned your actions at a nightclub a year or two back. Ring any bells?"

Now Gabriel did remember. A bunch of obscenely rich Swiss bankers and industrialists getting their rocks off at a Nazi-themed evening of "entertainment" at a private members club. The evening hadn't gone as the club's management had planned. He nodded.

"It does now."

"We don't forget our friends, Gabriel. I promise you, wherever you are, whatever you're doing, if you want help, call me, and I'll make the necessary arrangements. Here's my number. Send me a text and I'll save your number."

He handed across a simple white card with the initials SBZ and a mobile number. Gabriel took a moment to study the card, committing the number to memory, an old habit. Then he took out his wallet and placed it carefully in a credit card slot.

* * *

Later, as Gabriel and Eli sat in the British Airways First Class lounge at Ben Gurion Airport in Jerusalem, Gabriel's phone rang. He looked at the screen and smiled.

"Who is it" Eli asked.

"Britta."

"Well go on, then. Answer it!"

Britta's voice warbled as the cell towers, satellite links and undersea cables connected two people sitting 2,034 miles apart.

"I have a couple of days off next week," she said without preamble. "Can I come to see you?"

He hesitated. But only for a microsecond. If Britta noticed, she said nothing.

"Yes, of course. I'd love that."

"Where are you hanging your hat these days?"

Was that a probing question? Was she sounding him out about Eli? He decided to play it straight. To tell the truth.

"I bought a new place. On the coast. Suffolk. A town called Aldeburgh."

"Old bra? Well, that doesn't sound very nice!"

"No, it's pronounced—"

Britta's laugh was loud, and suddenly the signal cleared so that she might have been sitting right there with him.

"I got you! For once, I got you with a joke about English. You were always picking me up on my English slang. Ha! *Skämtet är på dig*, Wolfe."

"Yeah, yeah, the joke's on me. So, when you've finished demonstrating your command of English idiom, I was about to say it's the last house on the right, but I'll text you my address."

"Cool. Is Monday OK?"

Gabriel thought for a moment. Realised he'd forgotten what day it was.

Thursday, fool!

"Monday would be perfect. Call me when you get to Aldeburgh."

* * *

Their plane touched down at Heathrow on schedule. The following day, they were due at MOD Rothford for a face to face debrief with Don.

"Shoreditch, please." Eli said to the cab driver when they reached the front of the queue.

After paying the fare, Eli slammed the door behind her and fished around in a pocket for her front door keys. She turned to Gabriel and smiled as the key slotted home.

"Beer?"

He nodded.

"Beer."

They sat in Eli's tiny back garden, sipping the cold beers from the bottle. Then Gabriel's phone buzzed. He looked down.

"Text from Don," he said.

The text made interesting reading.

Change of plan. Come day after tomorrow.

Eli's phone vibrated a few seconds later. Gabriel looked across while she read it.

"Don?" he asked.

"Yes. Says I'm stood down until the day after tomorrow. Was it him texting you as well?"

"Mm-hmm. Same message."

"Why the change of plan, do you think?"

"Knowing the Old Man, it'll be some day-long meeting in Whitehall with a bunch of pencil pushers."

Eli smiled.

"Great. So he'll be in a fantastic mood when we see him."

"We should take him a present."

"A punch bag?"

"A stress ball."

"Two stress balls!"

* * *

Several beers and a takeaway Chinese meal later, they fell into bed, too tired to do anything except sleep. The following morning, Gabriel was awake, showered, shaved and dressed by seven fifteen. He brought Eli tea and toast in bed, scarfed a couple of slices down himself, swigged his own tea and left, planting a kiss on her forehead.

"Where are you off to so bright and early?" she mumbled.

"I'm going to start researching my family tree. See you later."

DISGRACE

TEHRAN

After he learns of the disaster that has befallen Vareshabad, Iran's Minister for Defence and Armed Forces Logistics realises what he must do. The Supreme Leader will want to know what went wrong. Why. And who was at fault.

He leaves the office a little earlier than usual and spends the evening walking through Tehran's streets, taking the time to really see his city. He breathes deeply, inhaling the aromas, from roses to grilling lamb. He nods courteously to a few colleagues he recognises.

At 10.00 p.m., he turns for home. His gait is precise, measured, military, as befits a veteran of the Iran-Iraq war.

He greets his wife with a warm and generous kiss, then heads upstairs to see his two sleeping sons. They are old enough to have separate rooms but prefer to share.

He bends and kisses their soft, sleep-smelling heads, one after the other. Then he draws his pistol. Weeping silently, he places the muzzle against the back of his younger son's skull and pulls the trigger.

From downstairs, he hears his wife scream. His older son is stirring. He shoots again. His wife appears in the bedroom doorway. She is silhouetted against the light.

"What have you done?" she whispers, when she sees the pistol.

Then she looks past him, into the gloom. Her eyes widen.

He points the pistol at her and as she screams again, he shoots her through her open mouth.

Finally, he sits beside his older son's body on the narrow bed, places the smoking muzzle of the pistol against his right temple, offers a prayer of apology to Allah, and squeezes the trigger.

BLACKSMITH

WOOLWICH, SOUTHEAST LONDON

The man who'd chosen the codename Blacksmith, and whom the police had named Rabbit, woke once more in a green-painted cell that smelled of disinfectant and beneath that, the sharp tang of urine. The simple cot on which he lay was bolted to the wall. Its corners were all rounded. He was dressed in a Tyvek bodysuit that rustled when he moved. Even if the prisoner were desperate enough to hang himself using a rope twisted from the suit, the room contained nothing to which it might be attached.

His head hurt. He turned it gingerly to the right. The six-by-eight-foot space contained a stainless-steel toilet, bolted to the floor, and that was it. Above him, a recessed light fitting illuminated his surroundings with a depressing off-white light.

He closed his eyes.

* * *

A clang from the door jerked him awake. The door opened. The woman who'd pistol-whipped him in Battersea Park stood there. Behind her, observing him over her shoulder, was a grey-haired, grey-eyed man in a dark suit. He looked trim for his age, which Blacksmith estimated at late sixties or early seventies. The woman spoke.

"Come with us, please, Tim."

A FINAL BLOW OF THE HAMMER

They led Frye along a featureless, windowless corridor painted the same shade of green as his cell, and into a second room. It contained three chairs and a table. A length of chain and a padlock were piled on the table. Stella chained Frye's hands together through a large eyebolt that protruded by three inches from the surface.

"Where's the interview recorder?" Frye asked.

Don looked at Stella and raised his eyebrows. She nodded at him.

"You're not in interview recorder land," he said. "You're in tell-us-everything-and-I-won't-kill-you land."

Frye's eyes widened. His hands jerked upwards, surely an involuntary movement, causing the chain to snap tight with a metallic *chink*.

"What the fuck? What happened to due process? My rights?"

"I'm sorry, I'm not as young as I used to be. And my hearing's not as sharp either. Did I just hear you ask about your rights?"

"Yes. My rights. My *human* rights? Last time I checked, I was still living in England. I assume you're some sort of government lawyer?"

Don leaned across the table. He spoke in a level voice, though his heart was hammering against his ribs.

"Last time you checked, you may *well* have been living in

England. But right now, that's not where you are. As of now, you are living in *my* land. And no, I am not 'some sort of government lawyer.' I am the man whose operation you betrayed. I am the man whose people you attempted to murder. Twice. I am the man who had to arrange plastic surgery for the man you caused to be tortured. And I am the man who holds the keys to your future."

Don could see he had Frye's attention now. The eyes were watchful, alert. The skin was pale and sheened with sweat. He continued.

"You know, a lot of people look at me and they say, 'There goes the old warhorse. Used to be a proper soldier, but now he spends his days in meetings and running a slide rule over budget spreadsheets. Good old Dobbin.' Well, there's more than a grain of truth in that. I *do* spend a lot of time doing admin. And, believe me, it drives me up the wall. But the other part's equally true. Good old Dobbin used to be a proper soldier. And believe me when I say I dealt with a lot of very nasty people. People who liked to dig pits in the jungle and line them with sharpened sticks tipped with shit. People who liked to booby trap dead bodies with grenades. People who liked to rape children then send them into battle armed with Kalashnikovs taller than they were, or shoot innocent civilians through the kneecaps for going to the wrong church." Don paused, struggling to control his breathing, and his temper. "And here's the thing. I'm still alive. And they're all dead."

Frye leaned back in his chair. Then, slowly, his mouth curved upwards. He shifted his weight in the chair, making the chains between his wrists scrape across on the table.

"That was a good speech. You must have enjoyed delivering it. But your silly death threats don't bother me." He looked at Stella then back at Don. "You're not going to shoot me in front of a police officer, so why don't you calm down and get me my lawyer?"

"Death threats? Is that what you think that was? No, no, no. You've got the wrong end of the stick entirely. I just meant that I've broken people far harder and far more wicked than you. And I know what works. So let me make myself perfectly, one hundred percent, *crystal* clear. Either you tell me what I want to know, or I will make sure you never see daylight again. You will never read a book again. You will never have any variety in your diet again. You will spend the rest of your life locked up in a space where even suicide won't be an option. But before that, I will send my colleague out for a break and while she's gone, I will inflict a great deal of pain on you. Tell me, does the word kuznitsa mean anything to you?"

Frye's lips compressed into a thin, bloodless line.

"I think you should answer the question, Tim," Stella said quietly.

"I said I want a lawyer," he shot back.

Don stood up and rounded the table, before squatting by Frye's right side. He waved his hand around the featureless room then resumed talking in a calm voice. Though internally he was fighting back an urge to twist Frye's head sharply clockwise until something snapped inside.

"This isn't a police station. My colleague here is helping me out, but she doesn't want you, or anything to do with you. Whereas I, and the people I work for, do. So, if you don't think you'd cope well with the future I just described to you, tell me everything."

Then he slammed both palms down on the table.

"Now!" he yelled, right into Frye's face.

Frye looked at Stella. When he spoke, it was in the same infuriatingly calm tone of voice he'd been using since they brought him into the interrogation room.

"Please. If you really are a cop, do something. He can't threaten me like that. Fine, I betrayed his operation. But as I said, I want a lawyer. I want my day in court."

"I'm afraid we're not really interested in confessions at this point, Tim," she said, placing her hands on the table a few inches from his own, and interlacing her fingers. "I took a few pictures of you and your friend and emailed them to one of your colleagues. He identified him straight away. Maziah Gul, Head of Security at the Iranian Embassy. No doubt you also know he is effectively the chief intelligence officer there and works directly for the Iranian Ministry of Intelligence and Security. We also have your burner. So, one last time before I go out for a nice latte and a croissant, what do you know about kuznitsa?"

Frye turned to Don. His face was immobile as if every muscle in it had been paralysed. Then his mouth started moving. The words that emerged came out in a monotone as hard and flat as the table under his hands.

"Did you know that back in the days of apartheid, Israel, South Africa and Russia were all in bed together? Each country faced plenty of people who, what shall we say, wished them ill? Each had certain things the others needed. Weapons systems, gold, technology, manufacturing know-how, intelligence. They weren't friends, but they shared enemies. I wrote my PhD on their clandestine collaboration during that period. Then I joined the Russia desk. I spent three years in Moscow, and I met some very interesting people during my time there. One in particular, a veteran of the Soviets' war with Afghanistan. They call them *afgantsy*, by the way. After leaving the Red Army, he found himself at a loose end and, long story short, ended up heading a criminal organisation linked to the Russian *Mafiya*. He did so well for himself, he expanded globally, helped by Putin. He calls himself Max, but it's a name he got in the Gulag. He runs Kuznitsa."

He paused and wiped a palm across his high, smooth forehead.

"There was a text on your burner," Stella said. "Gul called you *Kaveh*. What does that mean?"

Frye lowered his head until his forehead was resting on his chained hands.

"According to Persian myths, Kaveh was a blacksmith. He led a national uprising against an evil foreign tyrant, after the tyrant's serpents killed two of Kaveh's children. It seemed appropriate, somehow."

Something caught at Don's memory like a thorn snagging a sweater. Gabriel had asked one of the mercenaries he'd shot who had sent them. The man had gasped out, "Blacks." He hadn't been talking about black *people*. He was trying to say Frye's codename.

"Why?" Don asked.

Frye stared at him, his brow furrowed, as if curious why he was asking such obvious questions.

"Why what?"

"Why did you do it all? Striking deals with the Russian Mafia, betraying your country to the Iranians. Why did you go to such lengths to have my people killed? To sabotage the operation?"

Frye leaned back and closed his eyes. He was remembering.

* * *

Everyone in the village outside Persepolis had been killed instantly. Blown apart by the Israeli missiles and vaporised in the intense heat. The body count, had there been any bodies left to count, was ten. Two British archaeologists. Two graduate students from University of California at Los Angeles. And six Iranian archaeology students from the University of Tehran's Institute of Archaeology.

Only one person survived the aerial attack. Thirteen at the time, and tanned a dark brown by the unrelenting sun, Tim Frye had accompanied his parents on the dig, which they had arranged to coincide with the long school summer holiday. As the planes were approaching, he had been riding a Kawasaki KX250 dirt bike over the dunes a few miles to the west, on a bird-watching expedition. He'd heard the explosions and for a moment thought there had been an earthquake. Then reality reasserted itself as he realised the bike was still flying along sweetly over the hard sand. Feeling a sense of dread building in his chest, he slowed down, turned and then opened the throttle, racing for the village he'd left thirty minutes earlier.

As he rode into the scene of devastation, he started crying. He wailed and shouted for his parents, for the UCLA students who'd semi-adopted him as their mascot – "Bike Boy" – and the Iranians, who made him the sweet mint tea he loved. But he knew it was pointless. Nothing was left standing above ground level. Blackened masonry and charred pieces of timber were all that remained of the village. The group's two vehicles, an old Land Rover and a Honda pickup truck, had been reduced to twisted tangles of smoking metal.

He dismounted, dropping the bike on its side, and ran distractedly from one end of the road bisecting the village to the other. He retched as he breathed in lungfuls of the acrid smoke drifting through the village. On the way back, a propane tank that had been used to power the simple stove exploded with a sudden bang. He flinched away from the noise then screamed as a flying piece of blue steel from the canister tore open a cut on the back of his hand.

In shock, he pulled the bike upright, kicked it into life, and stamped on the gear selector. Throwing up a rooster tail of sand, he tore out of the village, his grimy face streaked with tears.

* * *

Frye opened his eyes. The intervening nineteen years collapsed into a point. One moment he had been wandering through a blasted village calling for his dead parents, the next he was back in the windowless interrogation room. He realised he wasn't going to live to see his parents' deaths avenged. But at least he could ensure the two people opposite him would never discover why Max had been so eager to help him kill Wolfe.

* * *

Just as Don was beginning to wonder if Frye had taken himself into a trance, he spoke.

"It's really very simple. The Israelis killed my parents. In 1999. A missile strike. They were archaeologists, for God's sake. Fucking archaeologists! They were just digging in the desert looking for old bones with a couple of American graduate students and half a dozen Iranians, and the Israelis killed them all with missiles. Their intelligence was faulty. Ha! That's the understatement of the century, wouldn't you say?"

Frye laughed, but to Don's ears it had the cracked note of a man losing contact with reality. Frye carried on speaking, spit gathering in white blobs at the corners of his mouth.

"You were going to prevent the Iranians from attacking them. I needed to stop you and give Darbandi enough time to finish his work."

He smiled. "You think I'm insane, of course. Who would want to destroy a city or even a whole country to avenge the deaths of his parents?" He paused. "I'll tell you."

His eyes, red-rimmed, were staring, the whites visible all the way round the startlingly blue irises. Then he jumped up into a half-crouch until the chain tightened.

He reared back, yelling at them.

"Me!"

Don watched, helpless, as Frye snapped forwards, jack-knifing at the waist, to slam his head down into the space he'd created between his hands.

With a sickening crunch, his forehead met the tabletop. His torso spasmed twice, then his lifeless body slid back towards his chair. Its progress was arrested by the eyebolt, all three inches of which he'd managed to embed in his own skull.

A lake of blood spread out across the table and began running off the edge. Don and Stella had both jumped back as Frye committed suicide in front of them. Now they took a further step away from the table.

Inhaling the coppery smell of the fresh blood, Don turned to Stella.

"I'll call a clean-up crew."

* * *

Outside the building, an abandoned warehouse down by the Thames, Don exhaled loudly. Then he called Gabriel.

"Yes, Boss?"

"The mole was Tim Frye."

"Wow. OK. He seemed such a nice guy. What happened?"

"Apparently, his parents were killed by an IDF airstrike in '99. This was all about avenging their deaths."

"My God! He was helping them destroy an entire country for two lives lost."

"Well, yes. For his parents' lives. There's obviously a difference."

"What's going to happen to him now? A trial?"

"A funeral. He just killed himself right in front of me. Smashed his skull in on an eyebolt. I think he'd lost his sanity somewhere along the line."

Gabriel paused. Don could almost hear his thoughts. *Good. After what he put me through, I'm glad he's dead.* So his answer surprised him.

"It's hard to stay sane when you lose your loved ones."

DEBRIEF

ESSEX

It took Gabriel and Eli three hours to make the journey from Shoreditch to MOD Rothford. In Don's office, once coffees had been procured, he steepled his fingers under his chin and favoured each of them with a long look.

"I know you both want to hear about what happened with Frye. But I want your reports first. Do you want to start, Old Sport?" he asked – ordered – Gabriel.

Gabriel assumed his boss already knew the bare bones of the operation from Ziff or Mizrahi. No sense in wasting time with the broad brushstrokes.

"As I'm sure you already know, the operation was successful." Don nodded. "We received excellent support from the Azeris. The drone swarm attack was unlike anything I've ever seen. If we're not working on something similar, we should be. We could see RPGs going up, but the drones were too small, too agile. It was like watching someone trying to hit wasps with a handgun. They may have brought down a handful, but they were armed with impact-detonated warheads so when they crashed they exploded anyway."

"Civilian casualties?"

Gabriel thought back to the lab full of frightened-looking Iranian scientists. He shrugged.

"I can't be sure. They may have evacced their lab before the drone strike."

Don wrinkled his nose.

"I'm not sure I care overmuch about the boffins. I know we all need weapons designing, but chaps like that, seems to me they take an unnatural delight in their work. I meant, any *real* civilians? What our political masters are so fond of calling 'collateral damage.'"

Don's lip actually curled as he pronounced these last two words. Gabriel knew how much his boss hated – had always hated – the euphemisms that turned death and mutilation into anodyne phrases that tripped off the tongue in air-conditioned meeting rooms. Civil servants, ministers and generals far removed from the horrors of hand-to-hand combat talked about "friendly fire" or "neutralising assets." While flesh and blood men and women were firing shaped charges at tanks, aiming heat-seeking missiles at helicopters, pumping high-calibre rounds into each other, stabbing and hacking, gouging, slicing – staying alive while trying to kill the enemy. What had Angus Thorne said, back when he was collecting the GLS at Marlborough Lines? The tough Glaswegian's words drifted across Gabriel's mind like battlefield smoke.

Willie jumps down into the trench and he's just going up and down with his bayonet like a fuckin' sewing machine.

"Nobody, Boss."

Nobody? Something, maybe Gabriel's conscience, pricked at him. At his memory. He closed his eyes, willing himself to remember everything clearly.

I'm climbing up into the hills above Vareshabad.

Up the goat track.

It's rocky and sandy.

The heat's intense, but super dry.

Sweat evaporates as fast as it arrives.
I'm watching the facility through the binos.
Nothing doing.
The dry heat.
A whisper of floral perfume on the air.
Roses.
Nobody about.
Not even a goat.
Nobody.
Not even a—

His stomach lurched and he snapped his eyes open, feeling a cold sweat break out on his neck.

"Actually, that's not true. When I was watching for Darbandi out at Vareshabad before I was captured, I was contacted. A goatherd, I think. Going by his rifle, I'd say he was genuine, not an agent. It was an antique. I had to kill him. I dumped the body."

Gabriel stopped talking, aware he was beginning to gabble his words. He looked round. Eli was staring at him. Don took his fingers away from his chin and laid his palms flat on the desk.

"You all right, Old Sport?"

"Yes, of course. I'm fine."

"Only, when you and Eli came to my house, you said you hadn't met anyone up there."

Gabriel tried for an offhand shrug, but it felt mechanical, forced – a puppet being operated by an unskilled apprentice.

"I was probably still in shock from being tortured by Razi."

Don pursed his lips. Then he drew his hand slowly down across his cheeks and chin, before pinching his lower lip between thumb and forefinger. He said nothing for a few seconds. Gabriel counted to five. Wondered what his boss was going to say.

Get yourself a psych eval from The Department's psychologist.
Take some time off.
Give the old brain a chance to relax?
Heat of battle, Old Sport. Happens to the best of us.

"That wouldn't surprise me in the slightest. Any other little glitches in the old grey matter?"

Gabriel shook his head. It was easier than outright lying.

Don turned to Eli.

"And from your perspective? How did it go?"

"The second operation was a total success. We destroyed Vareshabad and put it beyond use. Whatever materials, technology, records and expertise they had, it's all either blown to pieces or hotter than hell. I'd imagine we put their nuclear capability back to square one."

Don smiled.

"Maybe so, maybe so. Although in my experience, rogue states have a way of bouncing back. For every snake, they seem to find a ladder."

"Yes, well, we'll just have to blow up more ladders, then, won't we?" she shot back, eyes flashing. Then Gabriel saw colour rush into her cheeks. "Boss, I mean. Sorry."

Don flapped his hand a few inches off the desk, where it had come to rest, and shook his head.

"Relax. This is The Department, not the bloody Army. I've had enough deference to last me a lifetime, believe me. One last question."

"Yes, Boss?"

"I had your *old* boss on the phone yesterday. Very chatty, asking after Christine, the usual pleasantries. Very pleased with how you two handled yourselves. Staving off nuclear war in the Middle East and so on. And he wondered how you were getting on. So I told him. Said you were an indispensable member of my band of cutthroats – "

Eli smiled.

"Thank you."

" – and then he asked me to release you from your contract. Said that after what you and Gabriel had achieved, he thought they could find a senior position – a *very* senior position was the way he put it – in Mossad. My question to you, therefore, Ms Schochat, is, would you like me to? I meant every word of what I said to Uri. But he and I go back a long way. We both feel the same about our line of work. Individuals matter, but ultimately we're all pawns. What matters is the game itself. If you think you could do more, would enjoy the *work* more, back in Israel, you've only to say the word and I'll make it happen."

Gabriel suddenly became aware just how much he wanted Eli to turn Don down. He felt a hard knot of tension tighten in his stomach as he turned to watch Eli's reaction.

She ran a hand over her hair and pulled on the ponytail into which she'd fastened it before leaving the house that morning. Then she shook her head.

"No, thanks, Boss. I knew Uri was going to pull a stunt like that. He all but got down on his knees and begged me to stay when you recruited me. I like it here, I like working for you. And," she turned to Gabriel and grinned, "I like working with Gabriel. Tell Uri I'm staying with your crew of jolly pirates."

Gabriel exhaled, trying to keep his breathing light. And silent. It mostly worked. Don heard nothing. Eli, however, winked at him.

"What about Frye?" Gabriel asked.

"What about him?"

"How did you track him down?"

"My chap in Frye's department, Faroukh, told me who had access to details of the operation. It was just him, Frye and one other. We were also looking at Gaddesden, Bennett, Julian Furnish and one or two others, just to be sure. Callie's DI, the one we met a few years ago, surveiled Frye for almost a week. We needed to catch him red-handed. She finally arrested Frye in Battersea Park, just after he'd met the chief Iranian spook in their London embassy."

HOUSE GUEST

ALDEBURGH

After the debriefing at MOD Rothford, Gabriel and Eli drove the pool car – another grey metallic Mondeo, sadly; nothing like the spunky little Audi – to Aldeburgh, arriving ninety minutes later. As he drove slowly down the pretty main street, Eli kept up a running and very sarcastic commentary on the *chichi* boutiques and home interiors shops.

"Very nice! A recycled birdcage. Yours for just two hundred pounds. Ooh, look at that *divine* smock, darling! What colour is that? Mud? Driftwood? And those ceramic puffins. We should buy them all. We could have our own flock!"

Gabriel smiled as he neared the end of the road and its cheek-by-jowl Victorian houses in pastel shades of sky-blue, primrose-yellow and rose-pink.

"We're nearly there," he said. "Slaughden Road. I'm the last house on the right."

He pulled onto the gravelled drive of a detached, brick-built house situated next to a boatyard. A white picket fence, peeling in the sun despite its recent paintjob, separated the flower-filled front garden from the road. He climbed out, stretching and rolling his shoulders, and watched Eli do the same. The late afternoon sun was casting long shadows that lengthened ahead of them, across the road.

"It's beautiful," Eli said, looking over her shoulder at the house then turning towards the sea, visible beyond the car park opposite the house. "Even nicer than your old place."

Gabriel opened the boot and took Eli's bag before she could reach for it. He carried their bags inside and dumped them at the foot of the stairs.

"I'll show you around later, but first, let's go and get a drink. The Brudenell Hotel has a terrace facing the sea."

They'd agreed to split a bottle of white wine, so Gabriel ordered a Sancerre. Once the waiter had brought the wine then retreated to the interior of the hotel, Gabriel picked up his glass and tilted it towards Eli.

"Cheers."

"Chin-chin."

He took a sip of the wine. It was perfectly chilled, cool enough to bring out the subtle flavours of flint, vanilla and peach, but not so cold it killed them stone dead.

Eli pointed at the sea, fifty yards distant across an expanse of shingle on which a few families were sitting. The children buried each other under mounds of surf-smoothed stones, or lobbed them into the water. The parents looked on, smiling, or checked their phones, or, rarer still, talked to each other.

"You picked a good spot, Wolfe," she said. "You didn't think of moving to London?"

Gabriel sipped his wine. Then shook his head.

"I did, actually. I gave it a lot of thought. Britta's flat was still up for sale, and for one crazy moment I thought of putting in an offer."

Eli turned to him, eyes wide, chin pulled in.

"Really? You thought that was a good idea? Buying your ex-fiancée's flat?"

He grinned.

"Let's just say I saw the error of my ways. I never even contacted the estate agent. Anyway, I prefer the solitude of the countryside. I brought my boat up from Southampton, too."

"You have a boat?"

"It was my Dad's."

"Oh, OK. Is that, I mean, is it all right, when that's where they died?"

"It was weird at the beginning. I was going to sell her. But in the end, I decided not to. I mean, they were together on it and they loved each other. It makes me feel closer to them, you know?"

Gabriel stared out at the brownish sea, searching for ships in the distance and wondering, as he often did nowadays, whether his mother's drinking was the result of her younger son's death at the hands of her older son. *No!* He heard the inner voice of his psychiatrist, Fariyah Crace, admonishing him. *Not at your hands. You were a nine-year-old boy. A little boy playing a game with his brother. Accidents are nobody's fault, Gabriel. That's why we call them accidents.*

The death of the middle child, then?

* * *

Later, as they lay in bed, Gabriel listened to the sounds outside the window. The master bedroom faced the beach. The windows on the front and side walls were open, and a breeze shifted the floor-length muslin curtains as if someone incapable of standing still were hiding behind them. The metallic pinging of halyards against masts from the boatyard next door formed a counterpoint to the crying of gulls and the distant *shushing* of the waves as the tide came in over the shingle.

"You OK?" Eli asked him.

"Yeah, fine. I think you're right, though. I need to go back to Hong

Kong and try to find out what happened to the baby. I have a lawyer there who might be able to help, and if you did want to come ..."

She snuggled closer to him and squeezed his shoulder.

"Of course I want to come. I want to see where you grew up."

* * *

The following morning – *Sunday*, Gabriel thought with pleasure – they went out for breakfast. Eli ordered "a full English breakfast, please, with poached eggs, white toast and a mug of tea" in an impeccable British upper-class accent that had Gabriel widening his eyes in surprise as the waitress turned away from their table.

"Not bad," he said.

She smiled and shrugged her shoulders.

"I'm a good mimic, what can I say? Half the women in this town sound like the Royal Family."

GIFT HORSES

After breakfast, he and Eli strolled the length of the High Street and back, stopping in every shop that Eli pronounced "quaint," which amounted to half of them. She even bought a pair of the ceramic puffins.

"I looked up the collective noun. It's *circus*," she said with a grin, swinging another shopping bag in her free hand. "Maybe they'll breed, and we can start our own."

They stayed out for lunch, returning to the house mid-afternoon. Eli announced she wanted a shower, and went upstairs. After his fun with the Ferrari salesman back in Swindon, Gabriel realised he still needed a new car. And maybe buying British *was* the answer.

A Jaguar? he wondered.

Bit of an old man's car, Boss, Smudge opined from between his ears.

Something old school, then. A Morgan, or a TVR.

He poured himself a glass of Burgundy from a bottle in the fridge and took it through to the sitting room. There, he plugged his phone into the new amplifier he'd bought when he moved in and flicked through his downloads until he found something to help him think.

With Jimi Hendrix playing the blues on "Red House," and a cold hit of the wine working its magic in his stomach, Gabriel opened his laptop, intending to find a car website and spend a few pleasant hours browsing among the more hairy-arsed vehicles on sale up and down the country. He'd just begun scrolling down a list of car makes when the email program pinged to let him know he had a message.

He swapped from the web browser to email and smiled as he saw the name of the message's sender: Terri-Ann Calder. Not so long ago, they'd been drinking wine and eating steaks in her San Antonio home with a six-foot-four Texas Ranger by the name of JJ Highsmith. They'd been remembering her dead husband. Gabriel had avenged his murder in a series of brutal encounters with CIA operators and a particularly unpleasant and obscenely rich psychopath who'd been planning to test a new bio-weapon on Cambodian orphans.

The subject line was intriguing:

Fancy a "Yank tank" on your drive?

He clicked on the message. His smile widened as he read Terri-Ann's words.

Hey Gabriel,

Guess what? I'm leaving San Antonio. In fact, I'm leaving Texas. In double-fact, I'm leaving the States altogether. I gave notice at school, and I've sold the house.

I'm going to be working, and living, in Cambodia. After I donated Orton's money to Visna Chey's charity, he got in touch. Well, to make a long story short, I mentioned I was feeling lost out here, and he invited me to go and work for him. He said he'd need help managing the charity in light of my donation.

So I said yes. I hardly even hesitated. Daddy told me he was right behind me. He's in great shape and said he'd rather put a bullet in his brain than end up turning me into a caregiver (which is so like him!).

I've got about a month before I leave. Which brings me to the point of my email. I sold Vinnie's truck. But the Camaro was his pride and joy. I can't just put it on Craigslist and let it go to some stranger.

I know you had a blast driving Lucille around when you were over here, so my question is, would you like her? I don't want any money, though maybe you could make a donation of your own to Tom Boh? You'd need to arrange shipping and whatever paperwork the UK authorities want. But if anyone but Vinnie's going to be driving her, I want it to be you.

So, whaddya say, pardner?

Much love,

Terri-Ann xx

P.S. How is work now that you're back in the saddle?

Gabriel took as long to make up his mind as Terri-Ann clearly had before accepting Visna Chey's offer of employment. He took a sip of the wine then typed out a reply.

Hi Terri-Ann,

Great to hear from you. Your plan to work with Visna sounds perfect. And with your teaching skills you could help the kids with their English – they'd love you!

As far as Lucille goes, yes please! That's so kind. I'll look after her. I'll make arrangements to ship her over here. And I'm going to send a donation to Visna as you suggested – brilliant idea. It'll give you even more paperwork to administer when you arrive!

Work is good. Can't say more than that.

All best,

Gabriel x

He pressed Send then closed the laptop. His grin threatened to split his face open as he envisaged thrashing the all-black, '60s muscle car down an English country road.

Eli appeared in the doorway. She'd changed into a pair of white jeans and a nautical-looking blue-and-white striped top, two of her many purchases from their morning shopping expedition.

"What are you looking so happy about? You look like, what is it, a dog with two dicks?"

"Very good. And yes, I am happy. A friend in the States has just solved my car problem for me."

"So who's this friend and how did he solve your car problem?"

"He's a she, actually. A Texan lady. Used to be married to a friend of mine in American Special Forces. Her husband was killed, and she's just given me his car."

"Killed how?"

"It's a long story."

"I'm not going anywhere. Tell me a story."

Gabriel told Eli the story of his mission to fulfil the blood oath he swore with Vinnie. Eli interrupted now and again to ask questions about logistics, or a particular piece of kit. When he reached the part where a superannuated Russian jet fighter had dropped two modified cluster bombs full of a bio-weapon onto a school playground, he felt her tense.

"Shit! I hope you killed the fuckers!"

He shrugged his shoulders.

"I don't know what happened to the pilot. But everyone else got what they deserved."

"Good. People like that don't belong among the living."

* * *

They spent the following morning sailing, and the afternoon on the beach. Eli had changed into a coral-coloured bikini, and stood, legs apart, sending stone after stone plinking off a red metal sign poking out of the water thirty yards from the shore.

Gabriel noticed other people on the beach watching her. *Admiring her*, he thought, with a mixture of pride and pleasure. She'd shaken out her hair and the sun ignited its auburn colour into flares of red. Her olive skin glistened with the suntan lotion she'd had him apply, but the bruises from her encounter with the Iranian security men were still visible. They'd fade, though. In time. *Only to be replaced with others*, he thought ruefully. No scars, though. Not even beneath those two indecently tiny scraps of sand-speckled fabric.

She turned to see him watching her and waved. Her smile sent a flicker of desire through his bloodstream. He waved back.

His phone rang. It was Britta.

"Don't tell me you're here already?"

He looked around, half-expecting the Super-Swede to be walking across the beach towards him, her freckled face cracked with that gap-toothed grin.

"Nope. But I did get an earlier flight. I just got into Heathrow. It's four o'clock now. I reckon if I hire a car and drive fast I can be with you by seven. Is that OK?"

"*Ja! Perfekt! Köra säkert, ja?*"

She laughed.

"Drive carefully? That's *your* advice to *me*, three-time Swedish Army ice rallying champion?"

She had a point. Britta was fast, but never careless. Unlike him. He'd bet she'd never had the urge to floor the throttle and aim the front end at a cliff edge.

"Fine. Drive how you normally do. I'll put something cold on ice for when you get here."

"OK. *Vi ses senare.*"

"Yes. See you later."

Eli plonked herself down beside him on the towel. She leaned closer and kissed him. She smelled of salt, suntan lotion and her usual lemon shampoo. He slipped an arm around her waist and pulled her closer.

"That was Britta. She got an earlier flight. She'll be here at seven. Six-thirty, if I know her."

"Excellent! I get to meet her at last."

* * *

At 6.55 p.m., Gabriel opened a bottle of Puligny-Montrachet from the fridge. Three freshly washed and dried glasses stood on a slatted wooden table in the back garden, glinting in the early evening sun. He pushed the bottle down into an aluminium ice bucket and took it out to the garden. Eli, changed now into a long white linen dress, sat on a folding chair, her feet up on a cushion resting on a second chair. She'd washed and brushed her hair, and tied it back with a white ribbon. The dress and ribbon threw her tanned skin into even sharper contrast than the coral bikini had done earlier that afternoon. He leaned over to kiss her. Smelled perfume. Took in the whisper of shimmering green makeup on her eyelids and the deeper pink of her lips.

"You look nice," he said.

"Thank you. I'm not just an action girl, you know."

She touched her hair and then fiddled with a string of shell beads at her throat, and he had a sudden intuition.

"You're not nervous, are you?"

Her eyes widened, and she touched her hair again.

"Me? Why would I be nervous?"

"About meeting Britta."

"No! Why, should I be?"

Gabriel smiled. Stroked her left cheek.

"I just thought, with her being the ex-fiancée, you might, you know ..."

Eli shook her head then leaned forwards to pour herself a glass of the burgundy. She took a gulp and replaced the glass on the table. She blew out a breath, puffing out her cheeks.

"OK, fine. Maybe I am a little nervous."

"There's really no need. Britta's just—"

"I'm just what?"

Gabriel and Eli turned towards the side gate that led out onto the grassy area abutting his back garden. Britta was standing there, bottle in hand, a wide smile on her freckled face, which was even browner than Eli's. She flipped up the latch and stepped across the threshold and back into Gabriel's life.

He realised as he embraced her that Eli hadn't been the only nervous one. His pulse was rapid and he became aware of the swarm of flittering butterflies in his stomach.

"Hi. You look great!"

"You don't look so bad yourself," she said, though he didn't miss the way her eyes flicked down to his left hand and back.

She kissed him on both cheeks then stepped back and turned to Eli, who had risen from her chair and was waiting to greet Britta. A smile played on her lips, but Gabriel could see it was a nervous one.

"Hi, Britta, I'm Eli."

"Hi," Britta said with a wide smile. "So pleased to meet you."

Gabriel noticed Eli's right hand fluttering at her hip and felt her anxiety – *Are we going to shake or kiss*?

Britta solved the problem, leaning towards Eli and kissing her on both cheeks, just as she had done with Gabriel.

"Wine?" Gabriel asked, when the two women were sitting.

"Yes, please," Britta said. "I left my car across the road in the public car park, though. I didn't know if you had a private space."

"Enough for two. Give me your keys, and I'll move it for you."

Britta handed him a set of keys.

"It's the red Fiat Punto in the front row. It doesn't look much, but if you push it through the gears it's actually quite a lot of fun."

"OK, well I'll see what I can manage in the fifty yards from there to here."

Gabriel left and as he walked across the road he could hear Eli and Britta laughing and talking. And he knew everything was going to be OK between them. Between all three of them.

A TEMPERING

The following day, after a very late breakfast of shakshouka that Eli prepared, Britta suggested a walk out of town along the deserted stretch of beach that led due south towards a Martello tower.

Heading towards the brick-built defensive fort, Eli threaded her right arm through Gabriel's left. She watched as Britta did the same on his other side. Then, companionably, they strolled along the beach, scrunching over a patch of tennis-ball-sized stones.

"These bloody stones are hell to walk on," Eli said after almost rolling her newly healed ankle over. "Have you guys ever thought of having sandy beaches?"

"I'll have you know Britain has some beautiful sandy beaches," Gabriel replied, feigning indignation.

"Yes, that's true," Britta chimed in. "Just not the weather to enjoy them, *hej*?"

Eli enjoyed seeing Gabriel bantering with Britta. After overcoming her initial nervousness at meeting his ex, she'd realised how much she liked her. Most of her friends in Israel had been men, and, since moving to Britain, she'd barely had time to socialise. So finding another woman who could relate to her line of work *and* had a great sense of humour was something she prized.

The wind was whipping spray off the tops of the waves, and the air smelled deliciously of ozone and seaweed. Eli looked out to sea. A few fast-moving white clouds were racing across the sky. Beneath them, she spotted a trio of sailing boats scudding across the water's ruffled surface, a lone fishing boat some way behind them. On the horizon, she saw a long, white ship. *Some kind of tanker*, she thought. Its colour and proportions reminded her of the factory in Vareshabad. And once again, she was struck by the utter contrast between her work for The Department and the way most people spent their waking hours. She tucked a strand of hair back behind her ear, from where it immediately escaped.

"Penny for your thoughts?" Britta asked her, leaning forwards to speak across Gabriel's chest.

She sighed.

"I don't know. I suppose I was just thinking how, just, how normal all this is. And yet, a few days ago, we were up to our ears in an operation. Codewords, infiltration, the works."

Britta disengaged her arm from Gabriel's, stopping the trio, and spoke.

"I know you can't talk about the specifics, but you know you were doing the right thing, yes?"

"Yes. Absolutely."

"Then find a way to let it go. Try some of Gabriel's meditation. Throw some stones into the sea. Get drunk!"

Eli laughed.

"That's not a bad idea. We should celebrate!"

"Actually, it's a very good idea. Because I ..." Britta looked down for a moment, then back at Gabriel. "I have some news."

"Go on then," he said. "Don't keep us in suspense. What is it? Another new job?"

Britta cleared her throat. "Well ..."

Eli sensed the other woman's embarrassment. In a flash of intuition, she knew what Britta was going to say.

You're getting married!

"I'm, uh, I'm engaged to be married."

Gabriel pulled his head back, his forehead rumpling.

"You're, I mean, you said ... Wait. What? I thought ..."

Britta was smiling, but Eli detected the anxiety behind the expression. A tightness around those amazing blue eyes. A nervous pull on that plaited skein of copper-coloured hair. A drawing down of the eyebrows.

"I know, I know. I said before that we shouldn't get married." She shrugged. "But it just happened. Jarryd is a teacher. At a little rural primary school. He's not part of our world. We met at a *Midsommar* party in Uppsala last year. I have a girlfriend there."

Eli nodded, secretly delighted, but scrutinising Gabriel's face for a reaction. Then he smiled, and she relaxed.

Thank God. For a minute I thought you still had feelings for her.

"It's fine," he said. "No. It's more than fine. Listen, I'm pleased for you, OK? Really. Come here."

Eli watched as Gabriel held his arms wide. Britta's smile now looked like the genuine article. She stepped into his embrace, then stumbled on a loose stone and lurched forwards. Gabriel laughed and leaned back as she crashed into him.

Then the crown of Britta's head blew apart.

Blood, brain matter and skull fragments trailing coppery-red hair flew in all directions, and her lifeless body toppled sideways.

The sound of the gunshot crashed into Eli's awareness a split-second later.

Her heart racing, she whirled away from Gabriel, who had been shocked into rigid immobility.

* * *

Time slows down for Eli.

· · ·

The stranger is standing, arms outstretched, twenty yards away. He's tall, over six feet. Rangy. Cropped blond hair. Both his eyes are open. His lips are pursed. He stands, legs apart, one foot slightly ahead of the other. *Classic shooter's stance.*

In slow motion, she sees him preparing to fire again. Gripped in both hands is a semi-automatic pistol, a fat, black suppressor screwed into its muzzle.

Eli's brain is trying to do several things at once.

Shout a warning. Get Gabriel out of the assassin's line of fire. Draw her own weapon. *Thanks, Boss, for telling me to wear one when I'm with him.*

She tries to shout. But her lips feel glued together, as if she's dreaming. From far away, she hears her own voice screaming a warning.

"Gabriel, get down!"

It sounds feeble. Lacking even the force to disturb a dandelion clock, let alone prevent a killing.

She frees her pistol from her shoulder bag, straightens her right arm and pulls the trigger. A ragged, bloody hole appears in the gunman's right shoulder and a spray of red colours the air around him. He staggers back, firing his own weapon.

Eli sees the gun jerk and hears the bang. She feels a splash of something hot against her cheek.

The gunman is transferring his gun to his left hand. She fires again, hitting him in the right cheekbone and blowing half his face away. And she keeps firing until the magazine is empty.

His body falls backwards, fountaining blood over the rounded stones, adding splashes of scarlet to the pinks, golds, greys and whites. Her brain processes the movement as a stuttering series of still images, as if a movie projectionist had braked the spinning reel with his thumb.

Through the haze of sharp-smelling blue smoke, the ringing in her ears, the tang of adrenaline at the back of her mouth, she has one thought. *Gabriel!* She turns. He is kneeling beside Britta, stroking her face. And the woman Eli has only just met lies dead, the top of her head missing altogether, brains showing pinkly inside the cratered bone. Below her oddly unblemished forehead, her eyes are open, staring sightlessly into the blue, blue sky above the stony beach.

* * *

Time sped up.

The gunman's second shot had clipped Gabriel in the triangle of flesh between his neck and his left shoulder. His shirt was soaked in blood, and more was flowing freely out of the wound. Eli ripped open the shredded fabric to reveal an ugly mess of torn muscle and skin. She pulled her T-shirt over her head, wadded it into a thick pad and pushed it down hard against the bullet wound. Gabriel turned to look at her. His eyes were unfocused.

"Come on Gabriel," she said. "Come back to me."

His face was spattered with Britta's blood. She leaned across him and closed Britta's eyelids.

"We have to save Britta," he said.

"We can't. She's gone, darling."

"You're wrong. She's just knocked out. I made this mistake once before."

Eli tried again, though she was close to tears.

"No, Gabriel. Oh, God, I'm so sorry. Can't you see? She's dead."

Gabriel looked at Eli. He was frowning. Then he smiled.

"It's OK. We just need to get her patched up by the MO."

Then he turned away and went back to stroking Britta's cheek.

Pressing the pad down with her left hand, Eli pulled her phone out with her right and called 999. A woman answered.

"This is the operator. Which service do you require, ambulance, fire, police or coastguard?"

"Police and ambulance."

"Hold on, please."

A man came on the line.

"Suffolk emergency services. What's your location?"

"I'm on the beach, about two hundred and fifty metres south of the Brudenell Hotel in Aldeburgh. I have a man with a gunshot wound. He's in shock. And two people dead, also from gunshots. I'm applying emergency first aid to the injured man. My name is Eli Schochat." Then she used the code issued to all Department personnel for emergencies on the British mainland. "This is a seven-oh-seven call."

"Please repeat that number?"

"Seven-oh-seven."

The man's tone sharpened instantly.

"OK, Eli. Listen. I'll get an air ambulance scrambled from Norwich. I can see there's one on the ground. They'll be with you inside twenty minutes. Can you hold on till then?"

"Yes, I think so."

"Good. You know what to do. Keep the pressure on the wound. They're on their way. I'll get a police unit out to you ASAP."

* * *

Eli sat beside Gabriel, holding the improvised field dressing down against his wound. He hadn't moved since she ended the call. A siren broke into her thoughts. She looked up to see a uniformed police officer racing across the beach towards them. A second was ushering the approaching onlookers back towards the hotel.

From the north, she heard the sound of an approaching chopper.

THE END

Read on for the opening chapters of Torpedo, the next Gabriel Wolfe Thriller...

1

ALDEBURGH, SUFFOLK, ENGLAND

My name is Gabriel Wolfe. Death walks in my footsteps. The further I travel in this life, the more Death enjoys himself. Sometimes, if I keep very still, I can hear the soft pad of his stinking, bloody feet as he dogs my trail.

I was a soldier for thirteen years – in the Paras and then the SAS. After a short, peaceful stint in civvy street, I started killing people for a living again. As a government troubleshooter.

My problem is, however much trouble I shoot for the Queen, I always seem to bring down a whole heap more onto my own, uncrowned, head.

I don't begrudge Her Majesty the imbalance in our fortunes. Nobody forced me to accept my former CO Don Webster's offer to join his "jolly band of cutthroats." I re-entered service as an operative for The Department willingly. In fact, I was filled with a sense of excitement. It was good to be back in action. Helping CEOs negotiate takeovers – my former job – was eating away at my soul.

What's consuming me now is my own ability to kill those dearest to me, as surely as a metastasising cancer cell. And I have come to believe that whereas you might dodge the incoming fire from the Big C with a dose of radiation, chemo or plain old luck, contact with me is one hundred percent fatal.

I can sleep. I've always been able to sleep, even when my PTSD was at its worst. But my dreams are populated with people I loved. Love, I mean.

My best friend from Salisbury, Julia Angell. My former comrades in The Regiment: Smudge, Dusty and Daisy. My mentor and the man who raised me after my parents ran out of patience, Master Zhao. All dead. All gone. All because of me.

And now, Britta Falskog. The woman I proposed to just a couple of years ago, who had just told me and Eli that she was engaged again, to a teacher from Uppsala. Britta did a dangerous job, just like I do. Just like Eli does. Counter-terror isn't exactly risk free, even in social democratic Sweden. But she wasn't killed doing her job. She was killed – murdered – because she got between a hitman's bullet and its intended target. Yours truly, once again.

It was a beautiful day. The sun was streaming down onto the beach just south of my home in Aldeburgh on the Suffolk coast. We could smell salt and ozone in the air. One minute she was laughing, the next she was dead. Falling away from me, half of her head missing.

As I sat beside her, I looked down into her sightless eyes. I wondered why my ex-fiancée wouldn't answer me. Shock, obviously. I tried again.

"Britta! Wake up," I said.

Her lips didn't move.

The *whop-whop* of the air ambulance's rotor blades distracted me. I stroked her right cheek with the backs of my fingers. Her head rolled to the left, spilling more brain matter onto the beach pebbles. I shook my head. *That's not good*, is what I thought. I picked up the soft piece of tissue and gently replaced it inside her shattered skull.

From beside me, I heard a voice. A woman's voice. *Eli! That's it*, I thought. I'd gone down to the beach with Eli and Britta. For a walk. They were laughing. Then Britta fell.

Reality was knocking, but I didn't want to meet it. If I opened the door, I'd have to acknowledge the truth. And I wasn't ready for that. I squeezed my eyes shut. I started to hum. That didn't work, so I started singing instead. Louder and louder. The national anthem.

"God save our gracious Queen! Long live our noble Queen! God save the Queen! Send her victorious, happy and glorious, long to reign over us, GOD SAVE THE QUEEN!"

By the end I was shouting. Shouting, and weeping. It didn't work. I knew what had happened. Reality won. It always does.

Eli bent over me and hugged me to her chest. Her scent, of lemon and sandalwood, replaced the smell of the sea.

"The chopper's here," she said.

Her voice so full of compassion I wanted to scream at her.

"No! Leave me here!"

"Come on, get up. We need to let the paramedics take her now," she said. "And you've been shot. You need surgery."

As docile as a newly trained puppy, I stood, hauling myself to my feet on Eli's arm. She drew me back a few paces, and together we watched as the two green-uniformed paramedics, a man and a woman, slid Britta into a black plastic body bag and zipped her in snug. The man brought out a smaller bag and sank to his knees. He began collecting the parts of Britta's skull and brains that the hitman's bullet had splattered over the pebbles.

I remember very little of the helicopter ride to Ipswich Hospital. They gave me some high-octane painkiller – morphine, I assume – and the next thing I recall with any clarity is sitting up in bed the following morning, my shoulder bandaged and hurting like a bastard, with Eli sitting at my bedside, holding my other hand.

"Take me home now, please," I said to Eli.

They discharged me with strict instructions from the trauma surgeon that I should rest the arm for a minimum of six weeks, although it hadn't turned out to be as bad as everyone thought. Then I left with a paper bag full of painkillers and antibiotics.

The next day, we went for a walk. Just down Slaughden Road.

Nowhere near the beach. I saw someone coming, recognised the look. A detective. I pointed at her.

"Tell her to come to the house if she wants to talk to me."

Eli unhooked her arm and went to speak to the cop. She nodded then walked back towards me with Eli. As we neared the house, I found I was struggling to breathe. I closed my eyes. But that didn't help. I saw Britta, my freckled "super-Swede" laughing, revealing her gappy teeth. In happier times.

"Stop!" I hissed to Eli. "I can't breathe."

"Yes, you can. Look at me, Gabriel. Look at me!" she said. Ordered, really.

I complied, focusing on her grey-green eyes, noticing how the very outer rim of each iris was darker. The iron band around my chest released its grip. I gulped down air. The drowning sensation receded like the waves *shushing* in and out over the shingle. I knew what would happen next. I'd been there before. Questions. Statements. More questions. Raised eyebrows when the subject of my profession came up. Trips to a police station. Sour-tasting coffee.

We went inside and the cop began asking questions. Who? What? When? Where? Why? How? Any idea? Can you? Did you? Were you? I gave her the answers I felt able to. Noncommittal, packed full of incontrovertibly true details that would prove utterly useless.

After a while, she left.

And then, from somewhere deep down, way beyond where my conscious mind lives, an ancient, primal emotion gathered itself and forced its way upwards. Like magma racing through a fissure in the earth's crust before erupting and wiping out whole towns.

A desire for vengeance.

* * *

Gabriel Wolfe folded the sheet of paper into three and slid the narrow rectangle inside a thick, ridged envelope. This he placed in the top drawer of the desk in his study overlooking the beach. His teeth were hurting, and it was with a conscious effort that he unclenched his jaws.

He looked at his watch – 7.05 a.m. – then levered himself out of the battered old wood-and-leather swivel chair. He showered and dressed in jeans and a white T-shirt, careful to ease the stretchy fabric over the dressing on his injured shoulder, then padded downstairs in his bare feet.

2

MEDELLÍN, COLOMBIA

Kneeling at the low mahogany table, his python-skin Gucci loafers placed just beyond the edge of the tatami mats, Martin "The Tailor" Ruiz felt his muscular shoulders unlocking. He shook himself like a dog and the day's cares slid all the way off. Running a global business, especially one whose stock in trade was narcotics, really took it out of a man. When that man also had a large and demanding family, the stresses and strains were doubled, tripled even.

Today, he had burnished his reputation. He had slit the throat of a business rival and pulled his entire tongue out through the gash with his fingers, draping it over the man's bloodstained shirtfront. The infamous "Colombian necktie." In a grotesque innovation of his own, which had earned him his nickname, he had proceeded to stitch the thick, twitching length of meat to the writhing man's chest with an industrial staple gun.

Ruiz had discovered Willow Tree Tea House the previous month, and now visited the place at least once a week. Perhaps Colombia was the last place one would expect to find a club dedicated to the Japanese tea ceremony. He didn't care. The girls who served the powdered green tea – matcha – were all slender and beautiful. Or, he supposed, as beautiful as you could be when caked in that oddly erotic white makeup.

His two bodyguards, Yago and Benny, had protested the first time he'd left them on the street. Yes, he'd agreed with Yago, the streets of Medellín *were* dangerous. And for a drug lord, especially so. But within the serene confines of Willow Tree, he was not in danger.

"What?" he'd teased his six-foot-six, two-hundred-fifty-pound minder. "Are you frightened one of the tea girls will stick a chopstick into me?"

Then, laughing at his own wit, he'd entered, enjoyed an hour of tranquillity in the company of a quiet, respectful and utterly subservient young girl who looked like the genuine oriental article, tipped her five hundred dollars, and rejoined Yago and Benny on the street, free of puncture wounds and feeling spiritually cleansed.

Today, Ruiz had something to celebrate. Yes, he had survived another seven days in a murderous, internecine war between his outfit, El Nuevo Medellín, and a gang of Chinese upstarts who called themselves the White Koi. But, recently, one of the drug squad cops on his payroll had informed him that the White Koi were expecting a huge shipment of heroin. The drugs were coming into Colombia from Afghanistan via Kyrgyzstan and then the Balkans. Ruiz had sent a hit team after the traffickers. Now the heroin was his. The traffickers were floating, or hopefully sinking, in small pieces, in the Caribbean Sea. And, he fervently hoped, the local White Koi underboss was shitting bricks, figuring out how to tell his overboss back East that he'd lost ten million dollars' worth of white-powder heroin.

The table in front of him was set in the precise, ordered, calming way he so enjoyed. A narrow-necked, white-glazed vase held a shell-pink orchid. A bonsai tree, cultivated and pruned so that it appeared to have been blown sideways by some mysterious mountain wind, grew in a white porcelain trough. And, facing each other as if about to do battle, two jade figurines. A sword-wielding warrior and a thickly muscled water buffalo, head lowered, needle-pointed horns aimed at the swordsman's midriff.

The serving girl entered his private room, her white-socked feet hissing as she slid across the rush matting. He looked up at her and smiled briefly before bowing. She returned his bow, though her face remained unreadable behind its thick mask of white makeup. Her lips, painted into a scarlet cupid's bow, did, briefly, curve upwards. He noticed the way the girl touched the groove in the centre of her top lip, just beneath her nose.

She leant over and placed the ancient bronze teapot in front of him. A tiny, bone-china cup followed, its walls so thin that the light from the lanterns on the floor shone through the glaze, making it glow.

Her figure was slender, almost boyish, as far as he could tell, though he noted approvingly the swell of her breasts beneath the stiff silk kimono. Kneeling to his right side, she came a little closer as she poured his first cup of tea. He sat straight, resisting the urge, stronger with each visit, to grab her around the waist and kiss her. That would be an instant ban, and his status within the city's criminal fraternity would count for nothing in here.

When the cup was ready, she sat back on her heels and bowed her head. Ruiz raised the delicate cup to his lips and took a sip, inhaling through his nose as he did so, the better to capture the intense, herbal scent that swirled from its steaming surface.

"Arigato," he said, hesitantly. *Thank you.*

He had been practising his Japanese for a month now, mainly using YouTube, and had, he felt, mastered enough to try out a few basic words at Willow Tree. The girl turned to him and raised her finely arched, painted eyebrows with what he hoped was pleasant surprise.

"Sore wa idesu," she said. *That is good.*

He nodded, feeling unaccountably pleased with this kindergarten conversation. He finished the cup and placed it reverently on the table. The girl smiled, more fully this time, and refilled his cup. He raised it to his lips, then coughed and had to pull the cup away from his mouth. He tried again, managing a sip before a second spasm shivered through his chest wall, making him cough again, harder this time so that he sprayed a fine mist of fragrant tea into the air in front of his face.

The girl frowned and said something in Japanese he couldn't understand. *Are you all right, master?* he supposed she'd asked.

"Estoy bien. No es nada," he said. *I'm fine. It's nothing.*

In fact, he was not fine. The coughing intensified. Tears sprang to his eyes and he fished a fine white cotton display handkerchief from his breast pocket and wiped them dry. He coughed into the handkerchief, and when he withdrew it from his lips he noticed with alarm that its pristine white was speckled with red.

His fingertips were tingling and he thought he could hear the faint ringing of bells. Then the coughing stopped as suddenly as it had begun. He reached for the tea. No. In his *mind*, he reached for the tea. In his body, in the real world, his arms remained motionless at his sides.

And in a flash of most unwelcome insight, he realised. Poison. He moved his eyes to his right. And he watched as the girl got to her feet, unfolding her legs and standing in a single, flowing movement, like a cobra emerging from a fakir's rush basket.

Panicking, he tried once again to move. Although he could sense his legs pushing him upright and his right hand moving inside his jacket towards his pistol, in reality they were just dreams. Wishes, maybe.

She moved around into his sightline and pointed at the two jade figurines. Then, in fluent Spanish, she said, "Míralos. El guerrero y el toro. Yo soy el guerrero, y tú eres el toro." *Look at them. The warrior and the bull. I am the warrior. And you are the bull."*

From a gold silk purse tied to the belt at her waist she brought forth a palm-sized scroll of paper and placed it on the table. She walked to a black-and-gold lacquer cabinet out of his line of vision and returned with a small black pot and a bamboo-handled pen. He could hear the *scritch* of nib on paper. When she had finished, she held it up for him to read. In formal Castilian Spanish it said:

A quien le interese,
Robé del Koi Blanco. Ahora he pagado.
Martín Ruiz.

To whom it may concern,
I stole from the White Koi. Now I have paid.
Martin Ruiz.

Still addressing him in Spanish, she clarified.

"I will put this in your mouth, so your friends will find it easily."

Then she left the room.

Ruiz felt a trickle of sweat run into his left eye. It smarted. He thought of his wife and children, and realised he would never see them again. He prayed for his soul to be freed from sin so that he might be redeemed in the eyes of the Lord and admitted to Heaven.

He heard the room panels slide apart and then together again.

The tea girl was back. In her hands she carried a sword. A long, curved blade that glinted in the lantern light. A gold silken tassel swayed to and fro from the hilt. She tapped the jade bull on the back of its thick neck with the point.

Ruiz waited.

The blade whistled back then forwards.

Ruiz saw it coming. Then it bit cleanly through the tissues and bones of his neck, just below his Adam's apple. As the lights dimmed, he had time for one, final thought.

Sayonara.

*   *   *

Wei Mei stepped back smartly as the sword reached the end of its swing. But her ceremonial garb hindered her normally athletic movements, and she caught a jet of bright, arterial blood full in the face. Spitting the hot, salty liquid out, she swore, this time in her native tongue. Cantonese.

"Tā mā de!" *Fuck!*

The blood was issuing from the cleanly sliced arteries in thick, ropy jets, spattering the ceiling. She waited until the heart gave out before stepping closer. Swiping a baggy sleeve across her mouth, she pushed her right big toe against the corpse's chest. Slowly – *gracefully*, she thought – the kneeling torso folded backwards over its heels until its shoulder blades met the matting. Blood flowed out from the severed arteries and veins in the neck, sending a lake of crimson across the matting. When its leading edge reached the sliding wall panels, it soaked in and began climbing up the paper infills, turning them from white to red.

She kneeled at the table and rolled the little piece of paper into a tight cylinder. Then she reached for the head, prised the lower jaw open with her left forefinger, and inserted the message between the tongue and the hard palate.

On the way out, she knocked on the manager's door. Three taps, a pause, one, a pause, three. She stopped at a staff locker to grab a long, black trench coat and a broad-brimmed hat, which she settled low over her forehead.

Leaving the building by a rear door, the head bumping against her thigh in a plastic carrier bag, she waited for a count of sixty. Then she followed the narrow lane between Willow Tree and its neighbour, a travel agency, emerging onto Calle 10, a three-lane, one-way street lined with trees. Another left brought her to Willow Tree's front door, sandwiched between a bodega and a nail bar. The heavies had disappeared, called in by the manager who was delivering a pre-agreed message that an assassin had burst in and murdered their boss.

From the pouch at her waist she withdrew a glossy, garnet-coloured plum she had bought from a street vendor earlier that day. She dropped the perfect, unblemished fruit into the carrier bag. She positioned the bag and its oddly mismatched cargo on the bonnet of the black Porsche Cayenne the three gangsters had arrived in. And then she climbed into the rear seat of a waiting Audi with blacked out windows.

As the driver accelerated away from the curb, she called her employer. They spoke in Cantonese.

"Yes, Mei?"

"It is done, Master Fang. The Colombian is dead."

"Thank you. Fly home now. We will celebrate. There is a new restaurant overlooking Victoria Harbour. The best seafood in Hong Kong."

"Yes, Master."

Back inside her room in the nondescript hotel Fang had booked her into, Mei entered the bathroom and closed the door behind her. Standing before the mirror, she untied the broad gold sash at her waist and let it fall to the ground. Next, the stiff kimono, its white and gold embroidery streaked and spattered with the dead drug lord's blood. Beneath the kimono she wore plain white cotton underwear.

Free of the Japanese garb, she leaned closer to the mirror and inspected her face. In clearing her mouth of Ruiz's blood, she'd smeared her perfect cupid's bow, so that it appeared to be racing to her jawline for safety. From her wash kit, she took a tube of makeup remover and squirted a sizeable puddle into a folded white washcloth. Then, with movements like a cat cleaning its face, she pulled and pawed at the white pan stick, revealing, little by little, the olive skin that was her natural complexion. With the lower half of her face cleansed, revealing, beneath the cupid's bow, fuller, wider lips above a pointed chin, she paused.

From the white bandit's mask remaining, her eyes – large, brown and almost round, despite the epicanthal fold at their inner corners – stared back at her. A direct gaze that she knew strangers found hard to read. She applied more cleanser and went to work on her broad, high forehead.

When her face was restored to its natural state, free of makeup and expressionless, she pulled a dozen pins and clips from her hair. She shook it out so that it fell to her shoulders, a deep-brown curtain through which she peered out at herself.

. . .

Showered, and dressed in tight jeans, a black vest and a denim jacket, her hair braided into a sleek plait, she packed her bag, dropped to her knees and scanned under the bed, took one final look around the room, and left.

As her taxi took her to José María Córdova International Airport, she noted, without humour or alarm, a convoy of police cars driving at top speed into the centre of the city.

3

ALDEBURGH

Eli was sitting at the kitchen table, reading the news on her laptop. She looked up as Gabriel entered the room. Her forehead crimped with concern as she took in his expression. Then she smiled at him and got to her feet. She embraced him, pulling him close, and kissed him, softly, on the cheeks and then, harder, on the lips.

"Hey," she said, softly. "How are you feeling?"

"Mainly what I'm feeling is angry. She's gone and that's that. And I'm sad, too. Not because she was my ex or anything. I mean, not because we were engaged. But she was one of the few friends I had left. And she was so happy, wasn't she?"

Eli nodded, then sighed.

"Yes, she was. She had that look women get when the pieces click into place."

Gabriel reached for her coffee mug and took a small sip.

"Listen. I've been thinking. You should leave."

"What?"

"Get away from here. From me. I'm bad news, Eli. Every second you spend with me you're putting yourself at risk."

Eli put her fists on her hips and jutted her chin out.

"No! Not, going, to, happen. You need someone watching your six. I'm fine."

He shook his head violently, feeling a sudden flash of anger and finding himself unable to stop it.

"Don't you get it? Were you even actually *there* on the beach two days ago? Some fucking hitman shot her dead. He was aiming at me. You need to get some distance. Some perspective."

Eli reared back. Her eyes blazed.

"No! *You* need to get some perspective. You're in shock, OK? I don't believe in death curses and I'm not leaving you on your own while you're grieving, either. So forget it, soldier, and calm down!"

Something in Eli's tone worked on Gabriel in a way that kind words might not have done. He slumped into a chair. Closed his eyes and rested his head on his folded arms.

"We need, well, I do anyway, to go over for the funeral."

"I want to come with you. You shouldn't have to travel alone. Don will give us both time."

Don was Don Webster. Gabriel's commanding officer in the SAS, and now his and Eli's guvnor at a covert ops unit working to eradicate Britain's enemies. The Department.

"When's the Old Man due?"

"Ten, he said. He called me last night. Tell me, do you remember going to the hospital? Or talking to the detective?"

"Sort of. A woman, wasn't it?"

"Yes. I gave her a statement too. The fact that the shooter was there, dead at her feet, kind of made it an open and shut case."

"We need his phone. His passport. His gun. Everything."

Eli shook her head.

"They warned me off. They bagged the pistol and took it away. To the local copshop, I suppose."

"This is them, isn't it? Kuznitsa."

"That would be my guess, yes. They tried to get you, well, us, before. The mercs in the Merc. When that didn't work, they went for a hitman."

Eli was referring to an encounter they'd had with a group of four
tooled-up mercenaries while driving down to the British Army HQ at
Marlborough Lines in Andover. The mercenaries were all dead now,
one by stabbing with a rusty steel prong from a spring-tined harrow,
one from brain injuries caused by his own nasal bones, and two by
shooting.

"We need to find out why."

"I know."

"I'm going to find them, Eli. And I'm going to kill them. All of
them."

Eli frowned.

"We can talk to the boss about what we do next."

"Have you heard any more from the cops?"

"Yeah, the detective called me this morning. What was her name,
Stanwick? No, Strudwick. She's a chief inspector. That's good right?"

"I think so. Pretty senior. Like the woman we had on our side
against the Iranians. Stella, remember?"

"Yeah, she was pretty badass. We could have used a few like her in
Mossad."

"What did she say? Strudwick, I mean."

"They're trying to find out where the shooter was staying in
the UK."

"Don't you think we could do a better job? After all, we're in the
same basic line of work."

Eli finished her coffee. She stood, then reached down for his
hand.

"Come on."

"Come on, where?"

"Out. I think better when I'm walking. Let's head out of town the
other way from the beach, see where we get to."

Gabriel stood, pulling on Eli's hand so that she had to brace
herself to avoid tumbling forward. He opened the door onto a bright,
sunlit day

. . .

They strolled, like any of the other springtime couples, down High Street, heads inclined towards each other, ignoring the shop windows with their expensive trinkets for the well-heeled trippers who flocked to Aldeburgh every year.

"Did Strudwick say whether the shooter had any ID on him?" Gabriel asked.

"No. That's to say, she did say that he didn't."

Gabriel nodded. It could figure. There were basically two ways to go as a contract killer. You kept everything on you, ready for a quick exit, but risked losing it all if you were captured or arrested. Or you put it somewhere so safe you felt comfortable without it. That way, you were a clean skin if caught. You had your legend and you could stick to it. Or you could until your interrogators put the "pleases" and "thank yous" away and reached for the crocodile clips and the car battery. Gabriel had done both. Worked out of a safe house, carrying only a pistol or a knife, and gone in fully armed and equipped for a rapid IKE – infil-kill-exfil.

"He must have been watching us. Otherwise he wouldn't have known to follow us straight from the house and up the beach," Gabriel said.

"So he was probably here for a few days, maybe before we got back."

"Yes. What would you do in a strange town?"

Striding along, Eli looked up, then straight ahead.

"Place like this? Full of tourists? I wouldn't bother with a hide or a bivvy. Unnecessary, and too much chance you'd have a nice middle-class family on a hike tripping over your washing line. So either a hotel or an Airbnb under a false name."

"Did you get a picture of the shooter?"

Eli nodded.

"I tried to get his good side."

Gabriel nodded, his mouth unsmiling. The man's bad side was very bad indeed, having been mostly removed by a 9mm hollow-point round from Eli's pistol.

"We could show it around some of the pubs and hotels. See if anyone let a room to him."

"What if we come across the cops doing the same thing?"

"I don't care! Fuck them! I've been here before, remember? They're fine with smackheads burgling holiday homes or homegrown murderers, but a pro like that guy? No! Never in a million years!"

Eli reared back at his sudden change of mood.

"Hey, hey, calm down, OK?"

She pushed her left arm through his right and pulled him close.

"Sorry. Sorry. I'm not processing this very well."

"You're doing fine. And anyway," she said, with a smile, "there's no law against asking people questions, is there?"

Gabriel managed a small, tight smile back.

"None at all, last time I checked."

They began by calling in at every pub in Aldeburgh that let rooms, plus the hotels, showing the bar staff and receptionists the photo of the dead hitman.

"Are you police, then?" the young woman keeping bar in The Mill Inn asked. "Only we've had them in already."

"No, we're not police," Eli said with a smile. "But the woman who died, you probably heard about her?"

The young woman nodded, biting at her bottom lip.

"She wasn't local was she? Norwegian is what I heard."

"She was Swedish," Gabriel said. "Her name was Britta. She was a dear friend of mine."

"Oh, God, I'm so sorry," the woman said.

"Yeah, so are we," Eli said, picking up the thread as if she'd never dropped it. "We used to work with Britta as well, and we're just asking around to see if we can get an idea of who might have wanted to kill her. I don't suppose you heard about anyone this guy might have made contact with, only we're sure he must have been renting a place here or maybe in one of the villages outside Aldeburgh."

The woman shook her head, setting the gold hoops in her ear lobes swinging.

"Sorry. But I tell you who might know, 'cause he knows everything that happens here."

"Who's that?" Eli asked, leaning forwards.

"His name's Jack McQuarrie. I went out with him for a few months last year. He's a blogger. I mean, that's not his real job. He works over at the boatyard. But he's got this, like, really cool blog where he reports on all the stuff going on in town. If anyone knows, Jack will."

Gabriel felt the familiar tug in his guts. Action beckoning. A sense of a puzzle box yielding the first of its secrets. A sliding drawer or a joint you push with your thumb to spring the next piece free.

"Did you tell the police about Jack?" he asked.

She shook her head, making the earrings swing again.

"Nope. They only asked if that bloke you just showed me the picture of had booked a room here. I said no and they buggered off."

"How do we get hold of Jack?" he asked.

"Easy. He'll be at work now, or I can give you his number."

"Could you give us his number, please?" Eli said, "That way we can call him and fix up a good time to meet."

"And can you tell us your name, too?" Gabriel asked. "So we can tell Jack we met you."

"Oh, sure. I'm Grace."

With Jack's number saved in both their phones, Eli and Gabriel thanked the young woman and left the bar.

"Call first or turn up unannounced?" Eli asked Gabriel once they were back on the pavement again.

He wrinkled his forehead. Courtesy said call first. Action said get over to the boatyard. And while he didn't think they needed the element of surprise, his instincts always led him to find his man as fast as possible.

"Let's go and see if he's at work," he said. "The boatyard's right next door to my place."

Under a sky the colour of cornflowers, Aldeburgh Boatyard was busy, thrumming to the rasp of electric sanders and table saws, and above it all the jocular tones of a DJ on local radio. A half-built wooden boat occupied the centre of the yard, propped securely so that its clinker-built hull could be finished. Gabriel led Eli past the boat and towards a charcoal-grey Portakabin with a single plate-glass window on the side facing his house.

"The office," he said. "I know the owner. He helped refit *Lin*."

Lin was Gabriel's boat. He and Eli had spent Monday morning sailing her. As he looked back to those few, effortlessly pleasurable hours, it seemed that he was being punished, once again, for daring to enjoy himself. He ground his teeth together. This time, he would be the one dishing out the punishment.

Gabriel strode over to the office door and walked in. Eli followed close behind.

Framed pictures of plans, photos of finished boats, and a variety of certificates adorned the walls. Behind the desk, a middle-aged man with a luxuriant white beard sat leafing through paperwork clipped into a scuffed ring binder. He looked up, frowning, then smiled.

"Hello, Gabriel," he said, getting to his feet with a wince, before limping round the desk to shake hands. "What can I do for you?"

He looked at Eli and smiled, then stuck out his hand.

"Brian Salter."

"Eli Schochat."

"Pleased to meet you, Eli." He turned back to Gabriel. "What's up, chief?"

Gabriel sighed and swiped a hand over his forehead. The day was already warm despite its being only mid-morning.

"Did you see all the action over on the beach the other day?"

Salter nodded.

"Bad business. A young lass got shot is what I heard. You caught up in it, were you?"

Gabriel smiled, but it was a humourless expression.

"You could say that. Eli and I were walking on the beach with a friend. She was the one who died. Britta, her name was. Britta Falskog." *And if I keep saying her name I can keep a small part of her alive.*

"Well, I'm sorry for you, lad. Can't have been easy. Did they get the guy who did it? A couple of the lads went to have a look but the cops were keeping everyone well back. Bloody phones. Can't pick your nose these days without some idiot trying to film you."

"He's dead," Eli said, in a tone that suggested Salter would be wise to drop the subject.

"Oh is he? Well, good riddance, then. Bastard," he added.

"Have you got a lad working for you called Jack McQuarrie?" Gabriel asked.

"Yes, I have. Why? Is he in trouble?"

Gabriel shook his head and managed a smile.

"No, nothing like that. Eli and I just wanted a quick chat with him, and I thought maybe you could point him out."

"I'll do better than that. Come on, I'll introduce you. He's working on that open gaffer on the yacht stand."

Eli stood aside so that Salter could lead them out of the office.

"What happened to your leg?" she asked. "Was it a sailing accident?"

He turned to her and smiled, slapping the affected thigh.

"This? No. I was Royal Navy before I bought this place. There's a bit of HMS *Ardent* lodged in there, half an inch from my femoral artery. Argentine Air Force bombed us in the Bay of San Carlos during the Falklands War."

Eli nodded, her face serious.

"Hurt much?"

"Sometimes. Mainly in the cold weather. Now, here he is. Jack!" Salter called out. "Couple of folk to see you. Take a break, OK?"

The young man sanding the boat's coamings nodded, and clambered down to ground level, swinging himself down off the galvanised-steel yacht stand.

He pushed his mop of blond hair out of his eyes with a hand furry with sawdust. Muscular beneath his pale-blue T-shirt, he stood several inches taller than Gabriel.

After the introductions were made, Salter retired to his office with a wave over his shoulder and a demand that they call back in for a coffee soon.

"What do you want?" Jack asked.

Not suspicious, Gabriel felt, just frank.

"We met a friend of yours in The Mill Inn," Gabriel said. "Grace?"

"Oh, yeah? What did you want with Grace, then?"

Gabriel smiled.

"We don't want anything with Grace. It's you that we were looking for."

"Me? Why, what have I done?"

"Look, don't worry, you haven't done anything wrong. She just told us that you're a local blogger and you know what's going on and where in Aldeburgh."

Jack seem to relax. Gabriel noticed the way the tension that had lifted his shoulders towards his ears evaporated and the young man's body language said he was willing to help.

"OK, sorry. I've been a bit on edge recently, and things haven't been going too well at work. What is it you wanted to know about the blog?"

"Would you know whether there've been any strangers staying in Aldeburgh over the last week or two?" Gabriel asked.

Jack wrinkled his nose and frowned, a curiously childlike expression, and then he nodded

"Yeah," he said, "that's exactly the sort of thing I look at. I pop into all the pubs and I know everyone in town – all the shops and the restaurants – they just tell me what's going on and whether they see anything interesting and I report it in the blog. Anyway, about a week ago, I heard that there was a guy in town who someone had mentioned because he didn't really look like he fitted in here."

Gabriel felt another spike of adrenaline in his stomach. This was going better than he had any right to expect. He looked at Jack and spoke again.

"I'd love to read your blog post," he said.

"Sure. You just need to look at AldeBugger.com."

"That's brilliant," Gabriel said. He patted the younger man on his left shoulder. "Thanks so much. We'll let you get back to the boat, which looks really good, by the way."

Jack smiled and ran his fingers through his hair.

"Yeah, she's going to look beautiful when she's on the water. I can't wait to see her launched."

Back at his house Gabriel opened his laptop and typed in the URL for Jack's blog. Eli came and sat beside him.

"Here it is," he said.

He started to scroll back through the entries until he came to the one that set his pulse racing even faster than it had been at the boatyard.

Tall, blonde and handsome. Who is the stranger in town?

A little bird tells us that among the DFLs (Down From London) in their Boden tops and cargo shorts, we have a stranger in our midst who definitely doesn't fit the stereotype. He's holed up in a summer house belonging to a local artist (we can't say which one), and she tells us he doesn't seem to know whether he's here for business or pleasure.

"Tall, blonde and handsome," is how she described him, though we can't say anymore as even mysterious tourists deserve their privacy.

Gabriel closed the browser. He turned to Eli.

"This is him, isn't it? It must be."

She nodded.

"Looks that way. If he stood out enough to make his landlady pass on a titbit like that to Jack, he's our man."

"OK." Gabriel checked his watch. "Don's going to be here soon.

Can you go next door and use your charms to persuade young Jack to divulge the name of the local artist, please?"

Eli got to her feet and flipped an extra button open on her shirt.

"And if my feminine wiles don't work on him?"

"Then try something else," he said.

She pursed her lips. Then spoke.

"Wiles first."

Ten minutes later, while Eli was negotiating with Jack, Gabriel heard the muted rumble of Don Webster's Jensen Interceptor driving past the window of the sitting room. He knew the boss kept the classic car for high days and holidays. Perhaps his being only a handful of miles up the road from MOD Rothford, the army base where The Department had its headquarters, meant Don thought he could risk taking it out. Gabriel went to the front door. Don climbed out from the moss-green coupe, grunting as he straightened after the drive. Gabriel was about to say hello when the passenger door opened. Don had not come alone.

Order Torpedo now

COPYRIGHT

ACKNOWLEDGMENTS

Every time I finish a book, I marvel at the skill, diplomacy and patience of the group of people who help me iron out the glitches and make these stories as good as they can be.

This time around I want to thank the following awesome members of "Team Gabriel":

Jo Maslen and Sandy Wallace, for reading the first draft and helping me knock it into shape.

My editor, Michelle Lowery. Sorry I couldn't help with that one personal request, Michelle!

My proofreader, John Lowery, whose eagle eye keeps me out of trouble with the pedantry.

Simon Alphonso, OJ "Yard Boy" Audet, Ann Finn, Yvonne Henderson, Vanessa Knowles, Nina Rip and Bill Wilson: my "sniper spotters".

My advanced readers for picking up any last-minute typos.

And, as always, my family, whose love means everything.

I must also thank the serving and former soldiers, friends all, whose advice helps me to keep the military details accurate: Giles Bassett, Mark Budden, Mike Dempsey and Dickie Gittins. Any and all mistakes in this area are mine alone.

Andy Maslen
Salisbury, 2018

ALSO BY ANDY MASLEN

THE GABRIEL WOLFE SERIES

Trigger Point

Reversal of Fortune (short story)

Blind Impact

Condor

First Casualty

Fury

Rattlesnake

Minefield (novella)

No Further

Torpedo

Three Kingdoms

Ivory Nation (coming soon)

The DI Stella Cole series

Hit and Run

Hit Back Harder

Hit and Done

Let the Bones be Charred

Other fiction

Blood Loss - a Vampire Story

Non-fiction

Write to Sell

100 Great Copywriting Ideas

The Copywriting Sourcebook

Write Copy, Make Money

Persuasive Copywriting

ABOUT THE AUTHOR

Andy Maslen was born in Nottingham, in the UK, home of legendary bowman Robin Hood. Andy once won a medal for archery, although he has never been locked up by the sheriff.

He has worked in a record shop, as a barman, as a door-to-door DIY products salesman and a cook in an Italian restaurant.

As well as the Stella Cole and Gabriel Wolfe thrillers, Andy has published five works of non-fiction, on copywriting and freelancing, with Marshall Cavendish and Kogan Page. They are all available online and in bookshops.

He lives in Wiltshire with his wife, two sons and a whippet named Merlin.

AFTERWORD

To get a free copy of Andy's first novel, *Trigger Point*, and exclusive news and offers, join his Readers' Group at www.andymaslen.com.

Email Andy at andy@andymaslen.com.

Follow and tweet him at @Andy_Maslen.

Join Andy's Facebook group, The Wolfe Pack.